Northern Rain

A North & South Variation

Nicole Clarkston

Dedication

To all of those who challenge and inspire me,
even when I don't like it very much.

And to my kids, who always keep me guessing.

Contents

~

Acknowledgements

When I sat down to start writing my first book, *No Such Thing as Luck*, I had no idea that it would grow into such a passion. Once I slipped down the slope, there was no return! I tried to keep my Real World and my Writing World separate, but they insisted upon converging- thanks, in part, to a proud but bewildered husband who cannot keep his mouth shut. Thanks, honey.

I would like to extend my sincerest gratitude to Janet Taylor of JT Originals and her blog More Agreeably Engaged. Janet has been a tremendous encouragement through the writing of this book, and has graciously offered comments and proofreading assistance along the way. Without a doubt, her support was instrumental in the completion of this work.

Though this particular story is my own, it is with my most humble appreciation for the characters, the setting, and the background that I bow to Elizabeth Gaskell. Her powerful, yet intimate portrayal of hardship, honour, and tender love continue to inspire generations. I hope I have done her characters no injustice.

Chapter One

George Thornton
Beloved Husband and Father
May 6, 1798 - October 17, 1837

A lone figure stood before the graven stone, head bowed and hat doffed. A few had passed by, but if any remarked on the novelty of the sight, they did so from a distance and at a whisper. It was an annual pilgrimage; one the man before the headstone made with religious precision at half past three of the appointed day, every single October, and always alone.

John Thornton, one of the most powerful men in the prominent industrial city, was not a man to be ruled by emotion. His life- for the past seventeen years and four minutes to be exact- had been one of mechanical drive and unswerving purpose. The work of his life had been allotted him at an exceedingly young age, and he had accepted it as a man.

Ensuring his family's welfare had been his first duty. Restoring its honour had been his second. Everything after that had been another step in the logical progression of his life, as the ambitious young man had risen up the ranks in business. The man who stood today before the cold slab of granite was a man who held his head high among his peers, and at whose command hundreds sought their livelihood. He was a man often applied to for his perceptive advice and infallibly fair judgement; one who by all appearances could have no causes for regret and called the world at his feet.

He squeezed his eyes shut. No causes for regret... except one. It was nothing, really. Not something that should have had any lasting importance. After all, he could not be the first man who had been rejected by a woman. As far as he knew, the consequence was not fatal. There were times, though, when he felt like it ought to be.

Was it the natural state of affairs that he should still, several times a day, fail to remember to breathe? How long had it been? His mind calculated the answer before he was aware it had asked the question. Three months, twelve days, and four hours. Just over a quarter of a year since his heart had found the courage to beat once more, and then had been promptly crushed for its audacity.

He turned his hat awkwardly in his hands, unconsciously brushing the nap smooth as he did so. His eyes blurred. Why was he still standing there? He had paid his tribute, made his annual salute to the man who had sired him and set him upon this course. Nothing else was owed his sense of justice. For the first time in many years, however, he wished he could have asked that man one single question.

The natural question- *Why?*- had long since been canvassed to exhaustion. Nothing remained there but heartache and misery. No, the question he would have asked today was far less profound, but a great deal more practical-and it was one for which he felt sure the man in that cold ground might have once had the answer. *What is a man to do with a broken heart?*

Yes, surely George Thornton would have known, for Hannah Stewart had not been the first woman to catch his father's eye. That first, a London heiress, had been far above the humble reach of George Thornton- even more so than his own remarkable mother.

Perhaps that was the answer. Margaret Hale was not the only woman on earth. His father had found another to admire, and even love, had he not? Though George Thornton's final act had been the ultimate betrayal, he remained convinced that his father's heart had at one time been healed, and at the hands of a woman.

He himself had never paid heed to women, obsessed as he had always been with the all-consuming demands of his life. Never once had he felt the lack- or at least it had not been such a nagging torment that he had not been able to overlook it in favour of his ambition.

Then, something rather extraordinary had occurred. A fire had sparked out of nowhere, a flicker of that aspect of manhood long neglected. Man, after all, was not made only to labour, to produce, and then to expire. He was shaped for life, to search beyond himself and to seek his peace in relationship. He was made to find an answer to his masculine singularity in the form of a complement to himself- an opposite, yet in the greatest paradox known to humanity, a perfect match. Love.

The word flashed through his consciousness, triggering an agonized shudder in his soul. *I admit it!* He gritted his teeth, refusing to allow his emotions to display over his features for the world to see. *Aye, I confess. Yes, I loved her!* No, that would not do; not if he were fully honest. *I love her still.* There was no recourse but to clench his eyes shut again.

The insignificant spark had blazed to a raging inferno in the blink of an eye. He had been wholly unprepared for the awesome ferocity of that emotion. How had he even been capable of it? Rigid control had been the order of his life. One glance from a haughty young woman and all had ruptured. Despite himself, he could not help feeling that the heavens were laughing at him. Fool that he was, he had thought he had the world in his palm, when in truth he barely clung to his pathetic self-discipline.

His father had certainly had the right of it in this one point. There were other women on the planet- women who would receive him. Others would not fling his heart back in his face as though it were the vilest of refuse! There must be yet a woman out there who would not despise him... whose very presence would ignite the long-dead embers of his soul. Surely there was... there had to be another whose every word would inspire him... whose every touch had the power to scorch him to his very marrow. There... there *must* be another woman somewhere the equal of Margaret Hale. And perhaps there was, but never for him.

His eyes were by now blinking rather rapidly. John Thornton never wept. Never. Not even when his father's body had been lowered forever out of sight. Not even when his broken mother had turned to the boy for all that the man had lacked. Never did sorrow dim his eyes. Right now, however, he was grateful for the soft drops of rain just beginning to fall. It would spare any awkward explanations as to why the Master of Marlborough Mills suddenly required a handkerchief for his face.

~

Margaret Hale shifted her pitifully small bundle of letters under the crook of her arm as she manipulated her father's heavy umbrella. He had insisted that she take it today, citing his fears for a coming storm. She had complied more out of a desire to cheer and comfort him than any actual fear of the weather. Of course it would rain. It was Milton! It rained nine months of the year here, though not always heavily enough to justify an umbrella. Most of the town's residents did without one of the ungainly contraptions unless the rain picked up some real vehemence, which it just might do today.

Most of the poorer residents, she corrected herself. The more well-to-do tradesmen's wives and daughters who did not own carriages nearly always kept one near, but Margaret had developed something of a sense of independent competence. She was proud of her newfound ability to cope nearly as well as those who did not possess her resources. The weather was of little concern to her these days.

Of great concern, however, was one particular letter in her clutch. She had been waiting anxiously for many days, calculating and recalculating the length of time it ought to take before it could arrive. Her heart had leapt into her throat when she had claimed that day's mail at the office, and she had promptly trod a direct path out of the city so she might have the privacy she required to read it.

Glancing about, she made her way to a small bench along the path where she could separate out the much-coveted correspondence and break the seal. Her eager gaze flew over the opening script, slowing in sorrowful denial as it continued, and halting in abject mourning at its close. She dropped the missive to her lap.

So, that was it. There would be no reprieve, no pardon which would allow her brother to return to his homeland in safety once more. He was in

Spain to stay. She bit her lip, refusing to cry. Her poor father! How he had counted on that hope, that one chance that his son might return! An unbidden sob pierced her and she felt convicted of her guilt. It was she who had planted that false hope there. Her father had told her it was a futile exercise before she had begun, but naively she had pressed onward, insisting that the world must bend to her wishes.

Her hand stretched out, her fingers curled into a tense little vise to snatch up the letter and crumple it along with her broken dreams. Clenching her fist, she stopped herself. Frederick's letters were now to become all the more precious, as they were apparently the only contact she would ever have with him again. Heartbreaking as this particular specimen was, it would take its place of honour in her mother's old box of memories.

Oh, Mother! She swallowed hard, that shooting pain returning to her heart. At least Maria Hale had seen her son that one last time, and would nevermore mourn his absence. Her father, on the other hand- bruised and jaded from the loss of his wife- still lingered half his days in a dreamy stupor. Once or twice even of late she had heard him speaking as if her mother still sat across the table from him. Perhaps, she mused, it would be best not to share with him the contents of this recent letter right away.

Margaret had, in the last months, grown startlingly adept at burying her own sorrows. She could not afford to show them, not at home. It was only here, far away from all humanity, where she could slowly piece out her troubles; giving them full examination as was their due, and then carefully packing them away again for perusal at a later date.

Her father... no, he should not hear of this just yet. He was not yet strong enough to learn that he would never see his son again. Let him cherish that hope a little longer, if it gave him pleasure.

The other letters in her stack- two of them, to be exact- were meaningless by comparison. One was from Edith and the other was from Mr Bell. Both would be admired and savoured in their proper time, but the dry comfort of her father's study would do for their examination. Tucking the paper stack into a fold of her cloak, she gathered the umbrella once more and began her return home. The few sparse droplets which had begun to sprinkle down as she read Frederick's letter had multiplied in number and in force. Adjusting her umbrella to account for the wind blowing the water back into her face, she set out with long strides for home once more.

There was scarcely a soul about, as she had chosen the rather melancholy route of her walk specifically for the privacy it offered. Thus it was with no little surprise that she made out a tall black figure as she crested a small knoll. The man was standing stock still, only about twenty paces from the path on which she walked. His back was turned, but there was no possible way anyone in Milton- least of all she- could fail to recognize his towering figure. She froze. Mr Thornton. He was the last person whose notice she wished to attract just now.

He gave no indication that he had heard her approach, standing as he was with his bare head lowered. Perhaps if she moved to the sparse grass off the path and stepped very softly, she might hurry out of sight before he could turn from whatever held his interest. What was it?

Curiosity took her, and she craned her neck momentarily to see what had captivated him. He was not the kind of man to waste time in one attitude. It must be something of some marked distinction to command his attention so.

An abrupt chill washed over her when she realized what it had to be. She suddenly did not need or even wish to see the actual object, standing silently just beyond him. There was only one possible explanation for Mr Thornton to pause so reverently in a graveyard, hatless in a pouring rain. Catching her breath, she redoubled her wish to escape as quickly and discreetly as possible. No man would desire a witness to his grief....

That last thought arrested her even as she gathered herself to move away. It had little occurred to her that the enigmatic, powerful man who held sway over half of Milton might yet grieve the father he had lost as a child. For her, the loss of a parent was still raw and fresh. His sorrow could hardly compare, seasoned as it had been with the passing of time.

And yet, if that were the case, what would compel him now to bear such a pitiable sentinel? He stood in only his suit coat, as if the cold rain threatened little further distress for him as he rendered his duty. Intrigued by this notion, she forgot her attempts at escape. Instead she merely stood as silently as he, watching and marveling and wondering what he could be about.

She was still rooted thus when, a moment later, he slowly turned, his eyes down until they encountered her feet on the path. His head jerked up as if he had been shocked. He said not a word, merely stared, dumbfounded, as she gazed quizzically back. Her open, honest expression searched his, and shame filtered into her conscience. The man before her was a man broken and heart sore, and one who no doubt had felt assured of solitude as he explored his pain.

She pressed her mouth firmly, dropping her eyes from his and swallowing. For the first time, she began to feel a trickle of compassion for him. Almost the first time.

Slowly, and not quite knowing what she intended, she took a deep breath and a bold step in his direction. He drew himself back slightly, almost as a frightened animal. She stopped, watching him uncertainly. At her hesitation, he visibly forced himself to an easier posture. Blinking, she took another step, and then another.

There, this was not so bad. Another step, and then a few more. She was within arm's reach now, and with great trepidation, she turned her face up to his. Still, neither had spoken.

Propriety insisted that he ought to greet her by name, and that she should respond in kind, but what would be the point? It was useless to claim they had not acknowledged one another. Indeed, the shock of her sudden appearance and the memory of all that had passed between them reflected in every fiber of his being.

What more could they say to wipe out the misery of their past several encounters? Nothing, Margaret concluded. All she could offer him was basic human civility; what she would offer and what was owed to any other creature.

With that resolve, she deliberately extended the umbrella to him, her manner gently insistent. Surprise flashing in his eyes, he responded in the only way he could. He took it.

He stared rudely, in mute amazement, no doubt appalled at her lack of deference for his privacy. She took another long, trembling breath. It was too late to withdraw gracefully now.

All at once, the carefully ingrained manners of a gentleman reasserted themselves. He replaced his hat, shifted the umbrella and offered his arm, silently inviting her to share in its shelter. With a miniscule nod, she nervously accepted. Her gloved fingers hovered over his drenched coat sleeve until she gingerly touched them down, sealing their uneasy truce.

She found herself standing uncomfortably close to the most bewildering man she had ever encountered. *What on earth have I just done?* She closed her eyes, clenching her teeth. *Given him another reason to doubt my modesty, that is what I have just done!*

She blinked the drops from her briefly exposed lashes and discovered that she was looking directly at his chest, where a very soggy handkerchief dangled uselessly from his breast pocket. Bravely she raised her eyes to meet his face, which was also thoroughly drenched from the rain. He, too, was blinking rather rapidly as more droplets trickled in stubborn rivulets down from his hair.

Still without a word, she held out her own handkerchief to him. It seemed only the right thing to do, she reasoned. No matter how tempestuous their relationship had been, she could not simply walk away from another person whose pain was so obviously raw.

She dropped her gaze again discreetly as he hesitantly accepted the article from her, and so she was unable to witness with what feeling he received it. She was the intruder upon his solitude, and though she found it within her power to offer some simple comfort, she would never betray his vulnerability or seek to encroach more deeply where she was not welcomed.

"Thank you, Miss Hale." At last the first words were uttered. Succinct, but sufficient.

She dipped her head in acknowledgement. "You are welcome, Mr Thornton," she murmured softly.

~

Mr Thornton stared at the top of her head, reaching just to his shoulder. Those glorious eyes would not look up at him again.

They had been the first thing he had noticed about Margaret Hale. She had from the very beginning met his gaze freely, with a refreshing frankness, and idiot that he was, he had looked right back.

Now, even that tenuous connection had been severed. Of course it had. He disgusted her by the gritty realities of his life. The very force of character and willingness to labour which had borne him to his position- placing him at the pinnacle of Milton society- had sullied and defiled him in her scornful eyes, locking him forever out of that coveted place in her company.

Yet, here she was. *Why must she torment me?* He had looked to this day's homage as a temporary escape from the regrets haunting him. To get away from his thoughts of her, and every room of his house where she had once set her foot, and from each street corner where he had ever caught fleeting glances of her; if only for an hour to retreat from those memories, that had been his hope. Despite his efforts, here she had found him out in the most unavoidable of ways.

What could she have been thinking to stop? Would that she had simply walked on, pretending quite properly not to have taken notice of his presence or posture! Not Margret Hale. *Oh, no,* he thought bitterly. *Never she.* She would think to offer some paltry succour to her fellow man, claiming to owe it to her own sense of feminine dignity.

That was, after all, what had once led him on to the agonizing folly which even now he longed to forget. There was a righteousness about her, compelling her to extend her gentle touch in refuge and defence to anyone in need. Yes, anyone- even if that particular one was a man she detested.

He glued an iron gaze to the top of her hat brim, daring her to look up at him again. He could not decide whom he despised more- her for avoiding his eyes, or himself for desiring the fleeting contact. Her head had tipped fractionally, and he intuitively determined the trajectory of her gaze. He tilted his own chin back to the flat stone over his shoulder. She absorbed the cold script in silence, then the corner of his eye caught movement as that hat brim finally lifted.

Her clear eyes studied him, boring into his very thoughts as she held him breathless in her grasp. She needed no snare or noose. He was helpless and utterly at her mercy. Those expressive eyes spoke volumes of her empathy without resorting to words. She, so familiar with grief herself, looked into his brokenness and acknowledged their shared bond.

If that were only the sum total of the pain he carried! *Curse her! I don't want her pity!* She thought she understood. She knew nothing of it! She could not know how this moment, sharing the same space and the same air with her, was equal parts anguish and ecstasy to him.

He stared back unflinchingly, refusing to allow her to know the full measure of the emotions drowning him. After a moment of uncomfortable silence, she dropped her eyes.

"Excuse me, I beg you, sir." Her voice was scarcely audible. "I have been too long from home." Her fingers, still resting lightly on his forearm, lifted and broke their faint connection. She began to withdraw herself.

"This is yours," he stopped her, moving to return the umbrella.

She shook her head slightly, beginning to protest. She would not easily take what she had previously offered to him, though the rules of civility absolutely demanded the item's return. He sighed. "May I see you home then, Miss Hale?"

Her eyes flashed back to his. She clearly wished to deny this as well. Exactly as he would expect. She had made it plain enough before that she never voluntarily sought his company... yet, had she not done just that? He firmed his resolve. She had been more than forthright with him in the past. She ought to bear a little of the same from him.

"Miss Hale, I thank you for sharing the shelter of your umbrella, but if we are to part company you must take it back. I need hardly be reminded that you do not think me a gentleman, but I cannot suffer a lady to leave with me her protection from the elements."

Her eyes flared indignantly. "I meant no insult, sir! I only wished to offer... I at least have a warm coat. You look very cold, sir."

His determined hand, thrust toward her, dipped somewhat at the unexpected concern in her voice. His tone softened. "And much do I appreciate your offer, but one of us must be so. It is my own lack of foresight which brought me out thus." He firmly pushed the contested article back to her.

She glanced disinterestedly at the handle of her father's umbrella, then back to his face. To take it would be to admit that he was in the right, and that, he knew, she was not pleased to confess. She lifted her chin. "Mr Thornton, I would be grateful if you could see me home."

Chapter Two

The rain increased. The only way to comfortably walk together under their small shield was for Margaret to tuck her arm under his, avoiding his steady gaze as she did so. She kept her eyes forward and on the path.

Neither knew of anything appropriate to say. She would not relive the discomfort of that little scene in the cemetery by bringing the subject up again, even in the form of an offered consolation.

He, however, was busily admiring her light and easy movement as she walked beside him. No stranger to exertion was she! Her flushed cheeks glowed with radiant health and her steps were firm and untiring. He repressed a little sigh of aggrieved pleasure as he watched her striding next to him, falling neatly into step at his side. This singular event would live long in his memories, but was destined never to be repeated. More was the pity.

After some moments, he had cause to steer her gently around a large puddle in their path. If it was all the thrill to be afforded him, he would exult in her easy responsiveness to his guiding touch. If only he could think of something to say!

Sighing again, he tried to resign himself to the awkward silence. He would go to his solitary chamber that night having been in her sweet, torturous presence this day, and that, at least, was something in which he could take a small measure of perverse satisfaction.

"May I ask, sir," she ventured, breaking the silence at last, "how does your mother today?" That, she hoped, would be a safe and civil few words they could exchange.

He hesitated before replying. "She never comes with me," was his blunt response.

Her eyes swept up to his in surprise. "Excuse me?"

"To the grave. She never comes."

Her gaze returned to the path. "I see, sir." Her forehead creased. Not such a safe topic after all.

He bit his upper lip. "Forgive me, Miss Hale, I fear you find me somewhat agitated at present."

She considered silently a moment. Though she had been unwilling to return to the melancholy setting in which she had found him, he appeared not to have left it yet. "You come often, then?"

"Only once a year." He studied her reaction, wondering if he were causing her much unease. "I gather you must come more often?"

She flicked a pained expression up to him. "It is a good place to be alone," she answered softly.

He thinned his lips and nodded in wordless commiseration. That was a longing he could understand. In the absence of a true companion of the heart, there were times when the next best thing was complete solitude.

Did she come here for the same reasons as he? Surely her grief over her mother was still fresh, but did she yearn for a shoulder to lean upon in her sorrow? *She found one once*, he remembered bitterly. *Where is that fool now?* Some vengeful spirit hoped viciously that she had been spurned and rejected by the one she had turned to in favour of himself. *Perhaps she does know some measure of what I feel!*

Even as the thoughts were born he angrily shoved them away. He had made his decision, and he made it again every day. He would not despise her for loving another instead of himself. How could he, when the mere sound of her voice took his breath away? He felt like some wandering, homeless knight of old, who devoted his unrequited fealty to a distant and unattainable Lady Fair. That was what she was, was she not? Always holding his undying allegiance, occasionally dropping her errant devotee a token, but otherwise completely beyond his reach.

They had walked on several more paces during his reticent musings. Her musical voice, an even alto, floated to him again, though her face remained turned away. "Why does your mother never come?"

He stared briefly, wondering if she were simply making polite conversation or if she truly wanted to know the answer. He recklessly decided in favour of the latter. After all, what did it matter if he gave offence? It was not as though relations between them could grow any worse. "She does not acknowledge my father. He is never mentioned in our home. She wishes to forget... a good many things, Miss Hale."

His voice had been so soft, so devoid of his recent brittleness, that it caused her to look him full in the face and half draw to a halt. She opened her mouth as if to reply, then, sucking in a deep breath, closed it and looked away again. He wondered at her reaction. The mere death of a parent or spouse would not normally engender such a response as his mother's, but Margaret seemed to take it in stride, as though she knew more than he had once told her.

"Father made some mention of the matter to me," she confessed after a moment, as if she could read his thoughts. She halted her strides and looked up to his face again, those green eyes offering her whole sympathy, and perhaps even a speck of contrition. "I am very sorry, Mr Thornton."

A reluctant smile softened his lined mouth for a moment. "Thank you, Miss Hale." He paused. Did he dare say more? "And if I may, I would also thank you for your company. It has been most welcome to me just now."

Those bright eyes flashed again. She fixed him with a careful expression, tilting her head ever so slightly. "I had thought, Mr Thornton, that we had declared our mutual dissatisfaction with our acquaintance. Was I mistaken? If so," she forged ahead before he could interrupt, her ears turning pink, "I might receive your thanks with complaisance... with goodwill."

"I..." he tried to respond, and broke off, his throat suddenly quite dry. Was she trying to ask forgiveness or extend it? "I do remember words to that effect, Miss Hale, but have since had sufficient time to regret them."

She focused her gaze intently, in the most unmaidenly attitude he could imagine. *Bewitching.* She reminded him of some of the toughest negotiators he had ever encountered as they prepared to unbendingly broker high-stakes transactions.

"I realize, Mr Thornton, that you have reason to despise me, and I accept your censure if I must. Know, however, that in light of more recent events, I consider my own judgement of yourself to have been somewhat in error."

His heart lurched. She did not regret...? Could she? "In error?" he croaked.

"I... I abused your good name when I spoke with Mr Higgins. I spoke prematurely, and I owe you an apology. You are very noble to have taken him on after everything, and I ought to have said as much sooner."

His hopeful breath left him. So, that was all. He began walking again, drawing her reluctantly along. "Think nothing of it, Miss Hale. I was in need of experienced hands, and so far I have no regrets in his employment." He unconsciously quickened his pace, not noticing that she had to lengthen her strides considerably to keep up.

"Also, Mr Thornton..." she tugged his arm, dragging him again to a grudging halt. He faced her unwillingly, waiting as she battled for whatever shocking statement was next to come forth. "As I may not have another opportunity," she took a trembling breath, "I must beg to offer you my gratitude in one other matter."

His eyes narrowed, his tones hardened as he brushed her hand from his arm. "I said before that *no thanks* were necessary!"

Her rosy lips puckered in annoyance. "Then in that, I suppose we are even! We, neither of us, are able to accept the other's gratitude! There can really be no reason for us to go on walking together, Mr Thornton. I will bid you good-day!"

She shrugged her arms further up inside her cape, out of the cold rain, and marched off, squaring her shoulders. His face crumpled in bewilderment. *Aggravating woman!* Contrary, exasperating, obstinate, provoking female! *Magnificent.*

He caught up to her in a few quick strides, his jaw set. He could be just as stubborn! Without speaking, he paced beside her, holding the umbrella awkwardly aloft so that she might still reap the benefits of its shelter without forcing either of them to endure physical contact.

She ignored him, her eyes fixed ahead and her sculpted cheek muscles twitching as she walked on without slowing. She really had quite a ground-covering stride for a young lady. *Idiot. Stop looking!*

It was in this manner that they gained the outskirts of Margaret's neighborhood. Anyone with eyes could detect some spat had taken place between the unlikely pair, and Margaret at last halted. "This is ridiculous, Mr Thornton! I offer you a choice. Allow me to have my say, or let us part company!"

He tightened his grip on the umbrella. Neither seemed a safe option. "I yield to the lady's pleasure," he answered stiffly.

"Very well." Her tone was clipped, irritated, and not at all grateful. "I would thank you, Mr Thornton, for your actions to prevent damage to my reputation. It was most unlooked for, I assure you. Yet my thanks are not primarily concerned with myself. Had an inquest taken place, another would have been compromised, and I speak of the sort of injury which is far more serious than a mere slight to my honour." She narrowed those brilliant eyes, daring him to respond.

Oh, how her words galled his raw feelings! This was why he had not wanted to hear what she had to say. He had somehow done a service for that reprobate, that scoundrel who put her at risk! His very dignity as a man rankled by the association.

"I suppose I am to say now that you are welcome!" he returned icily, his voice threateningly lowered so that she had to strain to make out his words. "You *are* welcome for your own sake, and for your father's. The gentleman, if he can be such, I take no notice of. I wonder at the kind of man who would cower behind a woman!"

He glared right back at her, his tall, powerful figure squaring off in the middle of a public street during a rainstorm with a mere slip of a woman. Had he been able to see himself in that moment, he would have been horrified, but blinded and baffled as he was, all he could see was the livid woman seething before him.

"You know nothing of the matter!" she lashed out hotly.

"Nor do I wish to! Are we finished here, Miss Hale?"

"One thing more, if you please sir!" She clenched her little gloved hands into fists, her eyes blazing with righteous indignation.

He bit back his temper. Awareness of his surroundings was slowly registering, and John Thornton had never in his life raised his voice to a lady. He locked his jaw. "Proceed, Miss Hale," he growled between his teeth.

Her form, rigid and potent with the fury of a moment ago, withdrew somewhat as her face softened. She had not expected him to relent. "Simply this, sir. Had you never considered that my mother may have had those cherished loved ones who would risk the very gravest of consequences, simply that they might see her once more?"

His mouth gaped. What could she be speaking of? "I have not the pleasure of understanding you, Miss Hale."

"Nor, I fancy, will I be able to enlighten you further. I only demand of your justice that you allow the possibility of... of other explanations for what you believed yourself to have witnessed. We both know of my failings regarding that event, and you have been good enough to keep the matter to yourself. I am not afraid of my shame- I quite deserve it- but you have shown yourself to be a man of the very highest honour in this business, Mr Thornton. I feel I owe you what explanation is within my power to offer without compromising another. Things are not as they likely appear to you. I am in your debt, Mr Thornton."

He stared dumbly, not realizing that his hand had begun to slacken and the heavy umbrella tilted rakishly to the side. Both of them stood once more unprotected from the rain. That blinding flash of her ire had spent itself, and she was looking back at him almost beseechingly, begging him to accept her explanations.

He blinked and swallowed, making some effort to command himself. "Come, Miss Hale," he murmured huskily. "I promised to see you to your door." Her petite frame relaxed somewhat, and she meekly accepted his escort once more.

~

"John! How pleased I am to see you!" Mr Hale's gentle voice surprised him through the door as Miss Hale offered her cool parting civilities.

Mr Thornton tore his longing eyes from her downturned face to greet his friend. "Mr Hale," he nodded in acknowledgement.

The father turned his curious gaze on his daughter. "Margaret?"

"Mr Thornton was good enough to walk me home, Father." She removed the drenched cape from her shoulders, hanging it to drip dry. With an uncomfortable little dip of her head, she bid Thornton her farewell and stepped behind her father.

"Oh! Well, that is indeed good of you, John! I thank you."

He offered his friend a tight smile. "Miss Hale is being modest. She happened upon me at a time when I had forgotten my own umbrella, and she spared me the discomfort of a return trip without it. I am most grateful for her thoughtfulness." He searched her face until she raised hesitant eyes to his. Her features flickered, but he could not discern the meaning. Well, if that was to be all he could expect in response... "Excuse me, Mr Hale, Miss Hale. I have appointments to keep."

He removed himself from the top step but Miss Hale's exclamation froze him. "Wait!" she cried. She extended that much-debated object once more, pressing it firmly upon him. "You must not go without. I fear the rain shall become quite fierce, and you have three miles yet to walk."

He shook his head politely. "Thank you, Miss Hale, but doubtlessly you will have need of it."

"Well, as to that, John, Margaret rarely carries it at all, except at my behest," Mr Hale smiled kindly. "You are most welcome to it. I should hate to see you take cold, John. We have not seen you much lately, I do hope you have not been ill! I was hoping you will still be able to read tomorrow- if you are not too busy, that is."

Mr Thornton relented, aware that the pair of them had determined that he should take the blasted thing and there would be no escaping without it. "I did intend to keep our appointment. I am sorry I have not been able to come for the last few weeks." He flicked a meaningful glance at Margaret. "If it is agreeable, then, I shall return this to you on the morrow."

"Of course, John! Do come a little early if you can," Mr Hale peeked hesitantly to his daughter, requesting her endorsement of the invitation. "Well, you know, we are always here, and we would be happy for you to take tea with us later as well, if it suits. I only mean, do not worry on that account. You are always most welcome, John."

He shook his head, both grieved and grateful that he could not accept. "I am afraid I have guests of my own tomorrow evening."

"Oh," Mr Hale's face fell a little. "Well... well, we shall still be most glad for you to come in the afternoon, will we not Margaret? Do get dry as soon as you can, John. Will you give Mrs Thornton our good wishes? She has been very kind to us. We were so honoured when she called on Margaret... well, good day, John." Mr Hale's hopeful smile beamed; his pleasure in anticipating his good friend's call the next day, and his disappointment that it would be cut short, causing him to bumble quite a deal more than was his wont.

Margaret had observed it too. Thornton glanced at her and noted her faintly worried expression. It smoothed almost immediately as her eyes met his once more. She parted from him in complete civility- not offering her hand, as she had done once or twice before, but not shunning him either.

"Good day Mr Hale, and Miss Hale." He tipped his hat, and took his tormented self out of her presence.

Chapter Three

Mr Thornton did not return to his own residence until quite late that evening. He had a score of other matters to attend, not to mention a mind in uproar at the afternoon's encounter. He was not equal to his mother's keen eye, and so he worked well past the evening meal and into the late hours.

When he finally did enter his own door, he found his mother awaiting him in the drawing room. Her sharp senses, finely attuned to every nuance of her son's manner, searched him immediately. There was little he could hide from her, but that did not mean he did not try.

Her gaze frisked over him. She knew where he went on this day each year, but the fact was never spoken between them. She disliked- no, was *infuriated*- that the weak man who had been her husband yet had the power to grieve the noble man who was her son. Her frigid calm gave lie to the anxious turmoil within as she hungrily sought any clues to his thoughts this night.

His greeting was perfunctory- the bare minimum civility from a tired man at the end of a sixteen-hour work day. His exhaustion was understandable, but what remained a mystery to her was the compelling reason behind his excessively long days of late. He was in his office before dawn and home barely in time to crawl into his bed- if, indeed, he went to bed at all. Had she not been so unwilling to believe it, she might have suspected him to be avoiding her.

That, of course, was preposterous. She was her son's only confidante, and he had always come to her with those matters which weighed heavily on his heart. This burden he carried now surely had its roots in that ill-guided strike, and nothing more. The mill was beset on all sides, and John had savagely taken hold with the bite of a determined bulldog, dragging it back to prosperity by sheer force of will.

She took in his appearance as he drew near the evening fire, in anticipation of her mandatory nightly devotionals. The rest of the household would be joining them shortly, though Fanny was always late.

"John, what happened to your collar? It is perfectly limp, and... are those water stains?"

He glanced up at her quickly, and a flash of something crossed his face but he made no answer other than a small tightening of his lips.

"You ought to have changed those wet clothes hours ago," she clucked in admonishment. "You will be down with a fever."

"I never take ill, Mother. My office stays quite warm, next to the stacks as it is." He dropped himself into a chair, listlessly reaching for the paper she had placed there for him. He picked it up and hid behind it. He did not want to encourage the topic further. She would naturally turn to the reason for his long, wet walk and her bitterness would only grow. It would then cause her to wonder at his lack of foresight in taking his own rain gear when the weather threatened so.

He did not want her to know the truth. John Thornton was never caught by surprise from a storm. He watched the weather as keenly as he scrutinized cotton futures and market fluxes, for, as he knew better than anyone, all were in the end tied together. Today's downpour had been fully expected.

His pilgrimage today had been one of self-loathing and penance, and he had intentionally denied himself any comforts. Then *she* had to show up and provide shelter for him! Hours later, he still could not explain her sudden compassion, and he churned in frustration.

He bit his lip behind his newspaper. It would never do to allow his mind to wander back to Margaret with his mother in the room. Mrs Thornton possessed an uncanny knack for sensing his thoughts, particularly when they lingered on the contemptible woman who had rejected him. He would have to wait until he had gained the solitude of his own room before reopening that trove of feelings.

"John, you do remember that the Hamiltons and the Smiths are coming to dinner tomorrow?"

He nodded, only the top of his head visible to her as it bobbed. "Yes, Mother. I shall not be late from the mill."

"I should hope not," she scoffed. It would do John good to sit down to a decent meal with respectable company. He had been obsessively detached of late, shunning all company but hers when he was not working. "Mrs Hamilton tells me," she ventured cautiously, "that her daughter Genevieve has returned from her tour on the Continent."

The black head moved noncommittally over the rim of the paper.

She watched what she could see of him carefully. His fingers gripped the paper until the knuckles were whitened. His heel bounced in agitation, a mannerism he had only recently collected. He was not at all easy. A long breath left her. What John needed was something- no, *someone*- to distract him from the mill, and that pernicious Miss Hale.

~

Margaret saw her father off to his bed, promising him that she was bound for hers. As soon as the door had closed, however, she fled down the stairs and to the rear quarters of their residence. She found Dixon mumbling over a basket of linens to be pressed.

The family servant looked up quickly at her entry. She screwed her mouth into a scowl. "That Martha's taken off again. How many times that mother of hers can be ill, I'm sure I don't know."

"Hush, Dixon," Margaret chided softly, "I was pleased to be with my own mother when her health failed." Margaret reached for the top set of draperies and flicked a droplet of water on the iron to test its temperature. "I cannot think," she continued wistfully, "what it must be like to be stretched so thinly as many are- to have no way of both keeping food on the table and caring for one who is ill."

Dixon made a disapproving face. "That's this uncivilized city talking, that's what! What's become of the kingdom when the scullery maids can up and leave whenever they please?" Margaret reached to pick up the iron after she had spread the drapery out, but Dixon snatched it from her with a demanding glare.

Margaret pursed her lips and deliberately took the iron back. "What makes me any different from Martha? We are both about the same age, are we not, Dixon? Why should I not take a hand in caring for my family and lightening your burden?"

Dixon crossed her arms. "It's not fitting, that's what. Miss Beresford's daughter...." She continued to grumble, but that was no great trouble to Margaret's mind. They had this conversation almost every night of late, when Margaret snuck back to help with the household chores after her father was abed. As always, far more was accomplished than Dixon ever could have wrought on her own.

Margaret found she liked the manual labour. It kept her hands busy but allowed her thoughts to wander, and she was not troubled with much talk. She set her iron aside for a moment to array the fresh linens, then began again. Her deft fingers flattened the cloth and swept the scalding metal plate over it. She watched with satisfaction as the rumpled linen became once more smooth and elegant before her eyes. Indeed, it was gratifying to work something with her hands, to feel and see the fruit of her labour plainly. How very different it was from the nuanced, plodding, invisible work of a scholar!

She set her iron back on the stove to warm and walked her freshly pressed drapery to the drawing room. Dixon followed reluctantly and found her tottering precariously on an antiquated stool as she attempted to hang the article.

"Don't see what all the fuss about them drapes is," she pouted, lifting a corner in half-hearted assistance. "They'll be sooty again by next week, and don't nobody see them. Master hardly never comes down, and you spend all your time in the kitchen these days!"

"It is the dignity of the thing, Dixon," Margaret reasoned, stretching as far as she could manage to reach the last hook. "Mother never wished our house to get into slovenly ways, and no more do I. Besides, we shall have a guest tomorrow. Mr Thornton told Father he would be coming for his lesson."

"Reading in the Master's study, like all the others do," Dixon pointed out. "Not here taking tea, pretending to be a gentleman."

"Dixon!" Margaret pounced down from her stool. "I shall hear no more such talk! Mr Thornton has been very good to us- to poor dear Mother, you remember!"

Dixon frowned. "He don't often come no more for to see the Master. Mark my words, Miss, he'll drop the acquaintance since Master fell out of favour with some of the younger set. All work, that's these Milton folk, just like the Missus always said. How's that for a gentleman, I ask?"

Margaret stretched to her full height, her cheeks flushing. "Dixon! You know very well it was Mr Thornton who helped Father become established in Milton! He is not a changeful man, Dixon, not in the slightest. He has been greatly occupied these past months, and it shall not be for us to judge how he chooses to spend his time. I am most grateful he has found an afternoon to come sit with Father. You know how Father values his visits."

Dixon wrinkled her lips in disdain and gave a reluctant little "Humf." Much as she might have longed to make a saucy retort, she could think of little to say in contradiction to her young Miss. Margaret had taken to checking her tongue of late, for which Dixon could only respect her, but she groused inwardly to hear her young lady defending that tradesman.

The pair retreated to the kitchen once more, where by silent accord they set about separate chores. Margaret returned to the linens, while Dixon washed up. Even had they each desired it, which neither did, it would have been difficult to return to conversation.

Margaret kept her eyes steadily on her work. She felt compelled to do all she could to keep her home to its best standards, so that she might- even in this dreary city and their family's reduced circumstances- always remember what she owed herself as a gentlewoman. All within her influence ought to be nurtured and sustained, from her own personal dignity and the training of her mind, to her relations with her neighbours and the very upkeep of her home. That Mr Thornton intended to visit on the morrow had nothing to do with her desires to present her home at its most gracious. Nothing at all.

~

The clock ticked evenly and ominously in Mr Thornton's office. His eyes drifted to it occasionally as he sorted through his account books. If he sent a note now, it would not be too late to cancel his appointment with Mr Hale... but no! Hooked over his doorknob, so that he might not forget his duty, was that infernal contraption of wood and silk which had occasioned so much distress the day before. Glaring fleetingly at the unfortunate item, Mr Thornton made another mark in his ledger.

Surely it could not be so painful to sit an hour reading with Mr Hale. Where had they left off? Oh, yes, Plutarch. In truth, he would have quite looked forward to the opportunity to hone his mind and speak of deep, philosophical matters for a change, but he dreaded the gauntlet he must face at his arrival. He did not know how he would bear to see her again so soon.

He dropped his pen and rubbed his eyes. Even then, her image danced before him. She was looking up to him with that gentle, vulnerable expression- the one that, for just a moment yesterday, had nearly made him forget that she despised him. With a short gasp, he blinked his eyes open again, fixing them on the papers before him. Perhaps if he stared at his desk long enough, he would see his ledgers before his eyes when he closed them, rather than her cherubic face.

Mr Thornton managed five entire minutes before she again invaded his thoughts. Exasperated, he slammed his pen down and rose to gaze out the windows of his office. Spread before him was a marvel of machinery, a testament to the ingenuity and willpower of man. Willpower. Yes, that was all he needed! Always before it had been sufficient. Surely he could find that inner strength again!

He would not allow himself to wonder at her cryptic statements from the previous day. *What could she have meant?* No! He did not care. Why ought he? Whatever it was she was trying to tell him, it did not matter... *except, perhaps it did.*

What if she truly were innocent of unmaidenly conduct? What if there were some perfectly irreproachable reason for her to have been found alone with... with whomever he was?

Angrily he shut his mind down again. All it could possibly mean was that she may not have involved herself in the sort of disgrace he had imagined. She still disdained him as much as ever, but perhaps he had not truly been deceived in her character... perhaps his devoted admiration had not been as ill-placed as he had feared. But that falsehood! She had admitted to it! Was that wrong not as great- nay, greater- than the other?

He gritted his teeth. Much as he might have wished to be able to respect the woman his heart adored, he no longer could... and he hated himself for it.

~

Margaret intentionally retreated to her room at the time Mr Thornton was expected to make his call on her father. She heard his voice on the stair and tensed. The house was arranged oddly, so that he had to pass by the floor on which her room was located in order to reach her father's study. Her eyes unconsciously followed his unseen movements as he ascended to the third floor, his tread rhythmic and firm.

Once she heard the click of her father's door, she exhaled deeply and went below. She had thought to call on Mary Higgins to see how the Boucher children were getting on. If she stayed long enough, he might be gone when she returned. It would surely be as much of a relief to Mr Thornton as it would be to herself if their paths were not to cross today.

She dressed quickly and set out. Upon reaching the modest dwelling on Francis street, she was promptly met with the sound of sobbing and childish woes. The door flung open and a tear-streaked girl of six dashed out, nearly colliding into Margaret's skirts.

"Jenny!" she cried. "Whatever is the matter?"

The girl turned abashed eyes up to her. "'E's taken me dolly!" she wailed.

"I 'aven't!" Daniel, age seven, followed close on the heels of his sister. "Whadda' I wan' wi' yo'r ould dolly?"

The children paused only a moment at Margaret's feet, then raced down the street. Jenny was crying and trying to escape her disagreeable brother, and Daniel was trying to retrieve his wayward sister. Margaret looked after them in some bewilderment until Mary's voice brought her attention back.

"Don' worry none 'bout them," she sighed tiredly. "The'll be back. 'Appens 'bout ever' day."

Margaret offered her friend an understanding smile. Her firsthand experience with children had been only minimal, but she did enjoy them. The Boucher children were, by and large, sweet youngsters. This display of domestic combat startled her somewhat, but she did remember disagreements with her own... *oh, dear.* Margaret blinked a little as an image of twelve-year-old Frederick, laughing and teasing her from his perch in the apple tree, flashed through her memory.

She shook her head. "How are you today, Mary?"

"Well y'nough, Miss Marg'et," came the shy answer. "Da's been so much 'appier, now 'e's workin'!"

Margaret smiled, an expression of pure joy. "I am so glad! Oh, here, I brought some treats... for the children, of course." She accompanied that comment with a small wink. Nicholas had always vehemently rejected her attempts at charity where his own family was concerned, but she had discovered that gifts specifically intended for the Boucher children were accepted with at least grudging consent, if not genuine grace.

Mary thanked her as she received the basket, uncovering one of Dixon's fresh tarts and several bright apples. The four children remaining in the room admired the shining fruits as Mary placed them on her sideboard, but none dared ask to taste them.

Margaret sighed a little. Children who knew what it was to wonder where their next meal would come from never took such a treat for granted. The apples would be spared, carefully sliced, and shared at the proper time. In all likelihood, they would last the six children far longer than they would have lasted Margaret and her one brother at that age.

Margaret settled herself in a corner chair with a book she had brought, and the children eagerly gathered at her feet. This had become her ritual when she visited. She always tried to bring only the most interesting selections from father's rather musty and cerebral library, but she often found it did not matter what she read to them. They loved the attention she bestowed, the precious time she gave, and they adored the gentle sound of her voice.

Sally, age four, would often place herself under Margaret's hand, simply so she might feel something akin to a motherly touch on her hair. Little Johnny, the youngest, would usually toddle into her lap, while two-year-old Benjamin liked to rest his head on her knee as he sucked his thumb. Five-year-old Joseph typically sat a little aloof, but utterly enraptured.

Margaret's breast swelled in bittersweet contentment. The affections of the children were a soothing balm to her own aching heart, and it was likely that they did her as much good as she could hope to do them. Mary, too, benefitted from the respite for that half hour when Margaret paid her visits. She laboured over her stove, but her curious gaze often found Margaret from across the room as she listened to the story.

All too quickly, her time came to an end. She did not like to be long from home these days, as her father seemed to depend upon her more and more. She bid each child an affectionate farewell, promising to come again soon.

~

Back in her own neighborhood, she scampered lightly up the stone steps to her door. Just before she touched the handle, it swung open to her. Her head came up in surprise, and she found herself again staring at Mr Thornton's chest. She took an awkward step back. "Excuse me, sir!" she fumbled, nervous at nearly crashing into him.

Thornton stood uncomfortably in the doorway, unsure whether he ought to back into the house once more or hold the door for her from the outside step. Either solution would bring her into close physical proximity, but if he stepped back into the house, he could shield himself behind the door. Moving quickly, he did just that, realizing only after he was inside again that he would be forced to say something to her.

As an afterthought, he swept his hat off his head once more, then offered her a perfunctory nod in greeting. The unattended door rocked on its hinges and creaked nearly closed. They stood face to face in the darkened entry, each trying to work up the courage to meet the other's eyes. He drew a deep breath. "Good afternoon, Miss Hale."

Margaret swallowed, taking a small step to angle herself a little more out of his path of escape. "Good afternoon, Mr Thornton." She forced herself to meet his gaze, but could not hold it long.

He glanced down to his hat. "Well... if you will pardon me, Miss Hale...." He reached for the doorknob to let himself back out of the house, replacing his hat as he neared the threshold.

Margaret's breath was catching. Her conscience scolded her viciously, demanding that she speak some words of welcome, or gratitude... something! Her father set such store by Mr Thornton's visits, and it was because of her that he had been lately denied that pleasure. If she could only say something to smooth the way, to encourage Mr Thornton to continue as before... before everything had happened!

"Sir!" she cried, then her voice halted.

He turned curiously, finding her face awash in shock at her own audacity. He paused, allowing her a chance to collect herself. "Miss Hale?" he prompted.

She drew a deep breath, her lashes fluttering. "I- I wanted to... to thank you, sir. For finding time to visit, I mean. I... I know you are very busy."

He narrowed his eyes, studying her in silence.

"I only mean," she defended herself, "that Father was most pleased you could come today. I hope that you can find it possible... what I mean, sir, is that if it would be easier if I am not here...." She stopped, her hands gesturing vaguely as she looked helplessly to him, wishing she could articulate what she wanted to say.

Mr Thornton was gazing at her in what could only be described as a mixture of gratification and distress. His breath had quickened and his eyes dwelt on her face for what seemed an age before he responded. "I have no objections to your presence," he answered softly. "It is your own home, after all."

"Then..." she raised her eyes timidly to his, "... you will come again? That is, if you are not otherwise occupied? It is not my wish," she hurriedly explained, "to impose upon your time. I only thought... if you would be more comfortable if I should be out... I do not wish to be the cause of my father losing his friend." She dropped her eyes to his feet, swallowing hard. What an awkward muddle she was making of it! Why could she not simply speak her mind?

"Miss Hale," he bit his upper lip, "may I?" He indicated the door with a tip of his head, and she nodded, stepping out of his way again so he could enter the house once more. He closed the door, removed his hat, and held it as a barrier before himself. He stared down at it for a moment to gather his thoughts, then summoning his courage, he faced her.

"I do not pretend to understand what you spoke of yesterday. I am willing to accept the explanation that you are protecting someone, and it is clearly no business of mine. Your affairs are a matter for your own conscience. I believe we have already settled between ourselves that we are common acquaintances, nothing more. I do esteem your father, and I very much value my lessons with him. Do you think, Miss Hale, that we may proceed from such an understanding?"

She nodded wordlessly, her brow furrowed.

"If that be the case, it matters not to me whether we should meet in passing. I hope my occasional presence does not trouble you overmuch."

"No!" she shook her head, holding up a hand. "I shall not be troubled, sir. I would be most pleased... that is, you are most welcome," she stammered, her cheeks flaming.

He looked down to his hat again, fingering it briefly, then abruptly dipped his head in farewell. "I shall bid you a good day, then, Miss Hale."

Margaret released a long breath, watching him turn out of her door and proceed down the street without a backward glance. "Good day," she murmured after him.

Chapter Four

Thornton gave himself a cursory final glance in the mirror, smoothing the front of his dinner jacket and checking his tie. He would much rather not be entertaining this evening, but the invitation had been a strategic one. Gerald Smith was the new president of the primary bank in Milton, and Stuart Hamilton one of his best customers. These were contacts he would do well to cultivate.

He found his mother in the drawing room. The swift uplift of her brow requested his approval of her arrangements. With a quick glance about and a satisfied nod, he gave her a thin smile. Hannah Thornton took great pride in her position as mistress over his home, and her hospitality was always utter perfection. He released a tight breath. What need had he of a wife? In his mother he had a devoted companion who required so little of him! She presided over everything of his with a fierce dedication. Surely none could surpass her faithfulness.

Fanny arrived presently, fussing over her gown and stealing glimpses of her hair in any reflective surface she passed. She had looked forward to this night with the greatest anticipation, eager to renew her acquaintance with Genevieve Hamilton... and possibly with her brother Rupert.

Mr and Mrs Smith arrived first. They were well into their sixties, but Gerald Smith showed no signs of retiring. His professional ambition rivaled Thornton's own, and he had ascended to his position through strategic connections, sound business policies, and relentless toil. Thornton still knew little of the man, but he respected what he did know. Mrs Smith was a prim woman, preferring to observe rather than speak.

The Hamiltons, all four of them, were shown in only a few moments later. They were an old Milton family, and Stuart had increased greatly in consequence after a few lucky investments in his youth. Thornton generally frowned on desperate speculations, but that was not the way of Stuart Hamilton. He was a cautious and strategic investor, and it was known that Hamilton never gambled anything which was not wholly his own. He had resources to spare, and found amusement in backing struggling enterprises, then reaping the benefits later. He had a keen eye for business and a long string of success stories to his name.

Thornton greeted Mr and Mrs Hamilton, then turned his attention to Rupert. The son was several years his junior, and only just returned from three years in London rubbing elbows with some of England's new money.

"Thornton!" Rupert shook his hand firmly. "Good to see you again, old chap. I say, very handsome of you to invite us!"

"The pleasure is mine, I assure you." He smiled broadly at the younger man. He remembered Rupert to be... entertaining. Certainly their tastes did not perfectly coincide. Perhaps some maturity had settled the young man a little.

At last, he moved on to Genevieve Hamilton. She was about Fanny's age, and she had been touring the Continent with her former governess some while. He had not seen young Miss Hamilton in two or three years, at least, and had hardly given her a second thought.

Time, it seemed, had been exceedingly kind to the young lady. She was slightly taller than Fanny, with a most womanly figure. Her hair was the exact shade of honey- a rich blonde with traces of auburn, all coiled and arranged tastefully to accent high cheekbones and a perfect brow. Something about her face was immediately striking, though he could not at the moment put his finger on it.

He did not dare allow himself the luxury of openly satisfying his curiosity. He had learnt years ago that unless he wished to be forcefully ushered to the altar, it would not do to pay extra civility to any female, and never yet had he been in any serious danger. *Except in that one case... much good my caution did me there!*

Drinks were served and Thornton moved smoothly among his guests until the bell was rung for the dining room. He found himself near Miss Hamilton at that point, so it was the natural thing for him to escort her to dinner. She had a light, pleasing voice, and with some mortification he was forced to concede that her manners were far more refined than those of his own sister. She took her seat with a demure smile to him. Fanny, he noticed, had contrived for Rupert to escort her, and she occupied the younger man's attention.

"Well, Thornton, what do you think of this mess over in the Crimea?" the elder Hamilton asked from the other end of the table once they had settled.

Thornton pressed his lips thoughtfully. "I think little good can come of it."

"Little good!" Rupert Hamilton cried, affronted. "Did you not hear? We won at Alma!"

"Aye," Smith put in, "but to what end? Menshikov has hordes behind him. We can drive him back, perhaps, but what then? No one lasts long against the Slav's winter, eh Thornton?"

"I believe our dear neighbors to the south discovered that regrettable fact," Thornton nodded, flashing his eyes over the silent ladies seated at the table. It was really in rather poor taste for Hamilton to have brought up the subject in their presence, but he dared not offend his guest so bluntly by pointing it out. "I agree that our commercial interests, and thereby our sovereign security are best served if we control the region, but the cost in English blood may be rather a steep price to pay."

Rupert Hamilton lifted his glass in acknowledgement. "Aye, Thornton, but what's to be done? Too strategic to lose that ground, I say. Mark my words, Thornton, if we lose the Baltic, the Tsar will be at our doorstep by spring."

Thornton's mouth curved faintly. "I tend to doubt that. He has enough troubles at home to occupy him."

"Bah," Hamilton waved his glass. "He needn't invade England- indeed, he cannot move so many so far across land. All he need do is dominate Constantinople and he will shut down our trade with the Orient. He is after the Mediterranean, and his motive is not faith but commerce- I don't care what those young friends of yours in London theorize, Rupert. Once he has that... well, I only hope we do not see it."

"You just may," Smith gloomily persisted. "Our ranks are riddled with incompetence. Wait and see, there will be some grievous blow! The entire country will cry out against the war. Aberdeen will take a black eye, and Her Majesty will be forced to withdraw."

"I disagree." Thornton crossed his arms, his accustomed air of authority settling a matter which none present could influence by words alone. "Though I believe you are correct that it will come at great cost. The Tsar is far too unstable to make any occupation last. He will extend his hand too far, and it will at length be cut off."

"I think you are quite right," a gentle voice to his left concurred. His eyebrows rose. Genevieve Hamilton smiled warmly, and directly at him, before she continued. "I am to understand that our own troops have the superior weapons, is that not true?"

Thornton felt the corner of his mouth tug upward for the first time in some while. "It is, Miss Hamilton. Recent advancements in technology certainly carried the day at Alma."

He allowed himself one more glance at her face. *Brown eyes. That was it.* They were unusual and striking in one of her complexion, and he found the combination rather less than unpleasant. He turned away to speak again, almost feeling himself a cad for even noticing the other woman's beauty. He still bore that one uncomfortable thorn in his heart, and could not hope to dislodge it so readily. It had been worked in with much care, and would not easily be shifted.

"And in truth," he continued, so smoothly that none might have noticed his hesitation, "you have hit upon my pet topic. Technology is allowing us to lead the world to a better future. To cite only one example, the precision of modern industry, such as produced the new age of rifles for our troops," he gave a nod in Miss Hamilton's direction, "can supply the free markets of the world with consistent quality, larger quantities, more affordable prices, and superior products to what has ever been seen."

Smith gave a short laugh. "I had heard that was your particular fixation, Thornton. I myself am something of an industrial sceptic, but I cannot deny what it has done for our army- to say nothing for the economy."

"And well do I know your concerns," Thornton smiled at the older man. "Our industry here is yet young and there are many difficulties we have still to work through, but we have made much progress."

"Hear, hear!" Rupert cried, banging his glass rather raucously with his spoon. "I heartily agree with you, Thornton. Fellows in London wring their hands over strikes, but it's all rot. What you have achieved here in such a short time is nothing short of miraculous! Our Milton has quite become the industrial capital of the empire."

"Well," Thornton smiled modestly, catching a proud gleam in his mother's eye. "I am not ready to make that claim, but I believe our industry here has done much toward the progress of the nation. We have much yet before us, but I believe it possible to improve the quality of life for every individual in the kingdom."

"That is a bold claim!" Smith cried, lowering his glass. "What of the complaints of the workers? I hear all manner of grumbling, and not all of it is limited to their opinions of the masters' looks and character," he chuckled.

"Of course there is much to be done," Thornton leaned in his chair with a little smile, settling into the oft-canvassed debate. "I do not argue that point, but I believe industry supplies the platform from which the next phase of progress must spring. Without such progress, gentlemen, we are back in the dark ages."

"What you say makes sense," Genevieve Hamilton arched a graceful neck about to look him in the eye once more. "Is it not true that the factories supply a needed product at a fraction of the cost, freeing up a greater portion of a working family's income for such necessities as food and housing?"

"Indeed, Miss Hamilton," he narrowed his eyes thoughtfully. Genevieve Hamilton appeared to be a woman of more substance than he had at first given credit for. She might be worth... *but her voice is all wrong.* He sighed. He was a fool. As he glanced away, he caught his mother's arched brow.

He looked Miss Hamilton in the eyes again and forced himself to make more of an effort. "In addition to the benefits provided by the mechanized fabrication of goods, the greater profits realized by the mills allows a decent wage for my hands. I grant you, few of them would agree that it is such, but I challenge anyone to find many more opportunities for a better."

"Thornton," Hamilton cocked his head thoughtfully, "what do you see as the chief impediment to progress at this point?"

Ah, at last they had come to it. He steeled himself. "Progress comes at a cost, gentlemen. We are all gamblers in business, are we not? To maximize a mill's potential, to gain the absolute highest efficiency... and safety standards," he glanced quickly to Miss Hamilton, thinking of another young lady's humanitarian concerns, "one must invest.

"We must think of the future of our industry, with an eye on where we would envision ourselves in ten, twenty, even fifty years. That is an eternity in this business, but we must plan far in advance if we intend to progress toward our goals. Capital is currently our limiting factor, and the only thing I see which stands between Marlborough Mills and a most promising future- one in which we do, in fact, become known as the industrial capital of the world, and the standard to which others strive."

Hamilton's eyes twinkled shrewdly. "Your notions are intriguing, Thornton. Tell me, might you find time to show me about your operation at some near date?"

He dipped his head politely, but his mind shouted in triumph. "I should be delighted, sir," he answered with all graciousness.

~

After the meal, the entire party adjourned to the drawing room for drinks. Thornton had initially drawn aside with the Hamilton gentlemen, both senior and junior, while his Mother's attention had been dominated by the Smiths.

The younger Hamilton spoke mostly of his escapades in London at the track and the gentleman's club. Had he been any less the masterful industrialist, ever searching the words of potential partners and rivals, Thornton's eyes would likely have glazed over. Men, however, had their caprices, and one never knew where an avenue of opportunity might present itself. A casual social connection could easily flourish into a prosperous venture, if only a man kept his eyes and ears about him.

Presently, however, it seemed the only benefit to entertaining Rupert Hamilton's tales was to oblige the rather indulgent father. The fellow quite possibly had the most disengaged, fruitless mind Thornton had ever encountered. Apparently Rupert had not, after all, matured any since they had last spoken.

His rescue at last came from an unusual quarter; the two young ladies approached. "Rupert, dear," Genevieve Hamilton joined in cheerfully, "I am certain that Mr Thornton does not care to hear how many pounds you lost at the track last week!"

"What shall I talk of then, Gen?" laughed her brother. "Those are all of my most entertaining tales!"

The lady was shaking her head, smiling broadly. "Do forgive my brother, sir. I have always been terribly fond of him, but he *does* prattle on so!"

"All the better to entertain the ladies," Rupert grinned. "Miss Thornton, may I assist you to a fresh drink?" Fanny accepted at once, batting her lashes and causing her brother to stifle a chagrinned roll of his eyes.

"I say, Thornton, they are a fine looking pair," Hamilton gestured with his glass toward the couple as they moved across the room. "Do you know; I am still in awe that I have never become intimately acquainted with your family. How long is it that you have been Master at Marlborough Mills? Five years?"

"Eight, sir, last August."

"Eight! By thunder, I've no idea how that could be."

"I took over after Simmons' retirement, as you recall. I believe you and he were on less than friendly terms."

"Ah, yes." Hamilton quirked his lips to the side in a regretful frown. "I tried more than once to purchase the mill property from Bell, but Simmons talked him out of the sale every time. I am afraid I thought him a meddling old fool!"

"I had not heard that. It was shortly before his retirement, I believe, that you developed interests in London, and were required for a few years to spend much of your time there."

"True. You are something of a newcomer to the game here, Thornton," Hamilton winked.

"We are all relative newcomers to this novel world of industry, sir."

Hamilton saluted with his drink. "In that, I cannot argue. Still, eight years and I can hardly believe we have not known one another better!"

"Fanny and I have always been good friends, Father." Genevieve, who had been standing quietly by, patted her father's forearm. "You remember; we went to school together. I called here with my governess so many times! It seems only yesterday," she sighed, casting her eyes dreamily about the room.

"Fanny and I would take our tea in the dining room, and then we would play the piano in here until shockingly late in the day- and so loudly, too! I remember once or twice, sir, you had even returned from the mill for the day before we had done. I am afraid I must beg your forgiveness for my terrible manners back then." She tipped him an arch smile which looked anything but apologetic.

"No harm done, I assure you, Miss Hamilton. I regret to say, I do not even remember the events of which you speak, but I am sure we were glad to welcome you in our home."

The young lady's smile dipped slightly in disappointment at the failings of his memory, but shone anew at his reassurances of her welcome. "Your family was always very kind to me," she affirmed. "I have many happy memories in this house."

Hamilton had been observing his daughter with something akin to surprised pleasure flickering in his eyes. At last he spoke again. "This *is* a most elegant home, Thornton. One does not expect to find such a fine dwelling so close to the mill. Does not the noise trouble you?"

"One grows accustomed to it," he smiled. "Just as the fisherman does not complain of the smell of the sea, so the noise of the steam engine has taught me to look to the source of my livelihood and be thankful."

"Of course. You are obviously very proud of your mill, Thornton. I must say, it has been many years since I have seen it, and it must be quite different now. You are making me look forward to my tour very much," Hamilton raised his glass.

Thornton grinned. "That is my hope, sir."

Chapter Five

The remainder of Margaret's week was largely spent trying to keep her father as contented and as comfortable as a daughter could. She spent many an hour reading with him; though they were seldom engaged in discourse, it brought him pleasure to have her in the same room and a kindred occupation with him. His eyes would wander occasionally, lingering upon her until some sixth sense pricked her attention. When she met his gaze, he frequently only offered a vague smile and returned to his own book.

Richard Hale's days trudged forward in a steady rhythm, as his regular pupils made their customary visits. He rallied for these times, as they were his only diversions these days, but often seemed the lower and more fatigued after they had gone. The only true interruption to the plodding week was on Sundays, when Margaret accompanied her father to church. It was not the familiar Anglican service which her father sought these days, which discomposed Margaret for more than one reason, but it gave him pleasure and assuaged the nagging doubts which had driven them from Helstone.

Mr Hale was far from alone in his thinking, for a great many of the Milton families attended the Unitarian church... *all of the ones of note*, she thought with discomfort, as she glanced across the aisle at a dark figure already seated. They found their customary pew as the minister expounded upon the virtues of patience and long-suffering through trial. Margaret listened devoutly- so devoutly, in fact, that she entirely missed the pair of hooded eyes in the pew across the way struggling not to stray to her.

After the sermon ended, she and her father silently rose to go. There were few enough persons here who would wish to detain them after church for conversation, and it was their habit of late to visit with the Higgins family on a Sunday afternoon. It was a comfort to poor Mr Hale as well as Nicholas Higgins to sit for a time, pretending to banish the sorrow which bound them as brothers.

"Miss Hale!" Margaret turned at Fanny Thornton's cry. Her eyebrows rose faintly in genuine surprise. Attention from that quarter was somewhat remarkable, particularly of late. She unconsciously held her breath when she realized that Fanny was hurrying toward her with another young woman in tow. She fought a desire to bolt. That Fanny might have genuinely friendly intentions in this overture did not occur to her.

"Miss Thornton," Margaret smiled with a timid kind of warmth. "How do you do today?"

"Right as rain, to be sure," Fanny chirped. "Do you know Miss Hamilton?"

The other young woman offered Margaret a courteous dip of her head, and Margaret responded in kind.

"Miss Hamilton is just returned from touring the continent," Fanny informed her blithely. Turning to the other, she added, "Miss Hale is lately moved to Milton from... where was it, Miss Hale?"

"Helstone, in Hampshire," Margaret replied, wishing to move away. She was in no mood to be made an amusement for Fanny Thornton and her new friend. Some spirit rose within her and she added, as an afterthought, "I did spend much of my youth in London." A flash of jealousy, quickly tamped, rose in Fanny's eyes.

"I am pleased to meet you, Miss Hale," Miss Hamilton finally answered for herself. "I have heard that Hampshire is lovely. Can you tell me much of it?"

"Indeed, it is beautiful, at least the parts of it that I know," Margaret smiled. "I am afraid I am not the traveler that you are, Miss Hamilton, but I should be pleased to tell you of Hampshire someday, should you care to hear."

"Indeed, I shall look forward to it!" Miss Hamilton enthused. "Perhaps I may call on you this week? I have been away from Milton so long, you see, that I am eager to renew my old acquaintances and to make new."

"Oh... why, of course, Miss Hamilton, I should like that very much. It is rare that I... that is, I am out so little. I seldom leave my father," Margaret stammered, a little flustered at the other's unexpected interest in herself.

"To be sure," Fanny smiled woodenly, plucking at the fingertip of her glove. "I am certain, Miss Hamilton, that you will find the *Crampton* neighborhood greatly changed since you were in Milton last."

Margaret's slowly warming smile fell, but Miss Hamilton's quick dismissal of Fanny's slight restored her confidence. "It is settled, then! Mama and I shall call on you Tuesday morning. Will that suit, Miss Hale?"

"It would be my pleasure," Margaret assured her.

Fanny lifted her shoulders in a silent huff, signaling her desire to move on. "Well, Miss Hale, I am afraid I cannot likewise call. Mama has me at the dressmaker's all next week!"

Margaret offered a wan tilt of her head. "That must be very trying, Miss Thornton. I know how you would dearly have loved to come."

Fanny flicked her a withering glance. "Indeed, Miss Hale. It has been too long since I have had the pleasure. Good day!" Fanny dipped a little curtsey and turned, drawing Miss Hamilton somewhat reluctantly behind.

Margaret turned back toward her father, who had wandered a few steps away. He smiled cheerily, patting her hand as he took it. "Well, my dear! It seems you have made a new friend. She appears a genteel young lady, I've no doubt the two of you shall get on."

Margaret smiled bravely. "I do hope so, Father."

~

"John?" Mrs Thornton pulled down her reading glasses as her son wandered into her favourite room in the middle of the afternoon. She tilted her head. "My eyes must be deceiving me! I would not have expected to see you in so early."

"Aye, Mother, but it is true. I shall sit with you this Sabbath, rather than returning to my office as I have done lately." He offered her a bashful smile, the sheepish grin of a wayward boy lately scolded.

"A wise choice," she affirmed, restoring her glasses and cocking an eyebrow over them. He had found his paper, but his eyes were not focused upon it. "Do you think," she recalled his attention, "that your tour with Mr Hamilton yesterday will bear fruit?"

John lowered his paper with a long sigh, staring into the fire. "I have cause to hope. He likes speculating, and I have given him every reason to think optimistically of Marlborough Mills' future. I should think that if he is looking for a place to deposit some of his money, he could do far worse."

Her sharp ears did not miss a single nuance of his inflection. "And you?"

He shifted his gaze to her. "Me? What do you mean?"

She narrowed her eyes. "You said you had given *him* every reason for hope here. What of you? Have you not that same impression?"

He draped a tired hand over his eyes. Of course she could perceive his doubt- he had been a fool to think she would not. "I do not know, Mother. It has so long been my habit to believe that if I considered myself unstoppable, I would be. A man's destiny is shaped by his beliefs, and well do I know it. I have, however, learnt more practical lessons of late; regardless of my wishes or intentions, there are some matters beyond my control. I can command and will and work until I have not an ounce of strength left in my body, but if it is not ordained, there seems little I can do to come against it."

She shook her head, returning to her sacred reading. "You are weary, John. That is all. I think your long hours are beginning to be a detriment rather than a benefit."

His hand had dropped to his chin, and he stroked it thoughtfully before he replied. "No, that is not all, Mother. Certainly I have not the youthful energy I had when I first began, but I think I know my physical limits. It is of other matters I speak." His voice dropped softly. "Much was not foreseen- and that which was, was misunderstood. I was wrong before. I could easily be wrong still."

Mrs. Thornton lowered her spectacles once more to pierce him with her gaze. He acted as though unaware of her scrutiny, lapsing into thoughtful silence as the hearth fire flickered over his face. She studied him some while, reflecting that never had he seemed to her so resigned.

"John," she ventured at length, mostly to change the subject, "I want your advice in something."

"Hmm?" he turned his gentle face toward her once more.

"It is Fanny," his mother admitted. "I think she is trying to put herself in the way of this Rupert Hamilton."

John's brow furrowed. "Has she done anything untoward? Is she cultivating gossip?"

"Not as yet, but as you so recently informed me, Fanny is a girl of whom others must be a guardian." She watched him visibly flinch, and knew she had indeed hit her mark. It had not been so very long since John had heatedly defended Margaret Hale's abominable notions of discretion, while in the same breath pointing out the glaring flaws in his own sister. Mrs. Thornton knew what Fanny was, to be sure, but still suffered some in annoyance over that slight.

He considered for a moment. "I do not think she can be in any danger, Mother," he shook his head dismissively. "Rupert may be the frivolous sort, but he is a respectable young man. Surely his father will not allow him to lead a young lady on if his intentions are less than honourable."

"It is not that young man's intentions which concern me. If he be so inclined, he may come ask you for Fanny's hand as soon as he pleases, but it should not disappoint me if he does not. I only object to you permitting your sister to conduct herself in an unmaidenly manner."

John stiffened. "*I* permit? Mother, do be careful! You have made my role concerning Fanny very clear. I pay for her lessons and her wardrobe and keep her handsomely. Her conduct and upbringing were to be entirely your concern!"

"She is entering the world of men, now, John," his mother protested. "As head of the family and her only male relation, it is your place to govern her flirtations and courtships!"

"Then you would do best to inform me where my attention ought to be directed before she involves herself in some scandal!"

"John," Mrs. Thornton's voice was flinty and cold. "That is what I have just done."

He closed his eyes and sagged back in his chair. He was silent a long moment. "Forgive me, Mother."

She nodded curtly. "As I said, you are tired, John. You can scarcely attend to a serious conversation."

He took a cleansing breath, shaking his head to refresh his thoughts. "What, specifically, concerns you about Fanny?"

All business once more, Mrs Thornton flicked over a page as she spoke. "She has been spending a deal of time with Miss Hamilton. They have been in company every day since last Wednesday, and they intended to walk together this afternoon."

"Walk? Fanny never walks, particularly not in cool weather. She must indeed fancy Miss Hamilton!"

"She may. Or she may be trying to press an intimacy with the family. In any case, I think it likely they are only walking in the most populous areas, where one can be seen in fashionable company."

John laced his fingers, tapping his thumbs together in thought. "I cannot yet see cause for alarm, although it is rather unseemly for her to spend so much time... did you say they had been together every day? At whose initiation?"

"Miss Hamilton's at first, but Fanny's since then, as far as I can tell. I may question Fanny's motives, but at present I cannot disapprove of that friendship. Miss Hamilton seems a modest, respectable girl..." She darted quick eyes to her son's face to discern his reaction.

"Indeed," was his only response.

"...yet, a truly respectable girl would sense the impropriety of such sudden intimacy," Mrs Thornton tested.

John only offered a soft hum in affirmation, his eyes back on the fire. He seemed lost in his thoughts.

"John!" she cried after some minutes of silence.

"What? I am sorry, Mother. What is it you wish me to do?"

"Find out what you can about this Rupert, I suppose. I have arranged Fanny's schedule so that she will be unable to wait upon Miss Hamilton for a few days, but without good cause I hesitated to say more to her."

"Why, Mother, if your concern at present is nothing more than Fanny's seeming impropriety in being constantly in Miss Hamilton's company, surely you can say as much to her. She must again learn civility, if she has forgotten it."

"I surely can, but I do not wish her to sense that I suspect her true ambitions. Fanny is not like you, John. She is of such a nature that she may become devious and deceitful if she thinks she cannot have what she wants. I have no fear of her willful nature, but I do not wish to arouse it if my concerns are unfounded. I shall choose my battles wisely, if I may."

He sighed again. "I shall do what I can, Mother. Remember that my own situation with the Hamiltons is rather delicate as well. I do not wish to appear over-eager to Mr Hamilton, but neither do I wish for an immodest sister to tarnish our family's reputation. Perhaps for now you ought to encourage Fanny to invite her guest to wait upon her here rather more often than not."

Mrs. Thornton's eyes twinkled. "I shall do so. I do not think Miss Hamilton will object." She allowed her warm gaze to linger upon him.

"Hmm?" he caught the uncustomary expression upon her face in some puzzlement.

"She is, after all, a very proper young woman. What can be more proper than calling upon the sister of Milton's most respected Mill Master?"

His eyes thinned to sceptical slits. "I do not need you to play matchmaker just now, Mother. She is a handsome enough woman, I grant you, but I have other matters which require my attention at present."

She scoffed. "When has it ever been my desire to bring another woman into this house? You must realize, John, that you have caught that young woman's eye."

"I have never caught any woman's eye, Mother. I beg you would leave off trying to excite my hopes toward any such notions."

Mrs Thornton's dark eyebrows quirked over her sewing glasses as she tried once again to concentrate on her paragraph. She lapsed into silence, with an occasional sly glance at her son's face as her words settled into his thoughts. Was it possible she detected a flicker of pleasure there? *Well.* She had no particular wish to secure a wife for her son, but if thoughts of Miss Hamilton might banish his melancholy, she would continue to plant them there.

~

Margaret and her father found Nicholas and Mary Higgins, as usual, doing their best to wade about with six high-spirited children milling round their meagre abode. "There yo' be, Lass!" Nicholas greeted her warmly as he waved them inside. "'Adn't seen yo' a' the week, 'as we Mary?"

"Aye, Da', Miss Marg'et was 'ere Wen'sd'y last. Mind, the tart."

"Aye, so 't'was!" Nicholas patted his belly, a little less thin now than it had been some weeks ago. "A right toothy treat, Lass. Mary set 'side a bite for me," he winked. "'Tis 'ard, tho', yo' mos'ly ca' when I'm workin' these days, Lass!"

"You are looking well, Mr Higgins," Mr Hale offered in his soft, gentle way.

Nicholas may have been a man of modest means, but his pride was as fierce as any man's. It made his strong heart faint to observe Mr Hale's steadily weakening manner. "'Ere, sir, set," he insisted, carefully leading Mr Hale to a pair of chairs. The old man gratefully took his seat, panting slightly despite the gentle walk. Nicholas promptly drew his own chair near and trained worried eyes upon his guest.

Margaret and Mary had lingered near the stove, granting their fathers some modicum of privacy, but the children quickly garnered Margaret's attention.

"Miss Marg'et," begged Jenny, "Coul' we play the slipper game?"

Margaret laughed and consented. This had become another favourite of theirs, a parlour game Margaret had taught them for the afternoons when they were too restless to listen to a story. Mary procured a small stocking which was not currently in use, and all but little Johnny gathered round her in a circle.

Margaret picked up the youngest herself and plopped him in her lap. The stocking was passed and the guessing game began, eventually ending in squeals of childish laughter when Daniel came up with the elusive item.

By this time, Mary was ready to present a humble tea for their guests, and their fathers drew their chairs near. Margaret seated herself next to Mr Higgins, with a few of the youngest children casting longing glances toward her lap. At a sharp look from Mary, they withdrew with their little meals to the other side of the room, to be seen and not heard through the duration of the repast.

Margaret spared them one last warm smile, then turned to her friend. "How are things at the Mill, Nicholas?" she asked.

"Oh, well y'nough, Miss. That friend o' yo'rs is a 'ard master, but 'e's treated me fair y'nough."

She dropped her eyes. "Mr Thornton is hardly my friend," she replied, her tones hushed.

"Aye, may'ap," Nicholas rubbed his jaw, eyeing her sceptically, "but 'e's right decent when it comes to it. Folks's sayin' 'e's gone soft since the riots, talkin' gentle-like to the children an' such, but Thornton was allus a fair one. Jes' see if there's another strike, 'e's as much bulldog as e'er."

"Surely, you cannot expect him to give way to every demand made of him?" Margaret questioned gently. "Were he to do so, where would it end? I expect he must make certain the mill remains profitable, for if it does not, where would everyone find work?"

"True, Lass, 'tis true." Nicholas stroked his bristling chin for a moment, then opened his arms as little Jenny boldly climbed into his lap in defiance of Mary's edict.

"Why Margaret, I believe that is the second time I have heard you defend Mr Thornton," her father commented, tilting his head. "I am glad to hear you speak so justly. Surely, Mr Higgins, Margaret is quite right. I do hope some better understanding has been reached between the union and the masters."

"Oh, things's settled some," Nicholas assured them. "Win'ner's come on, and mouths've gots to be fed. Now'but i's a 'ard pinch, all ways 'round. Wages 'an't gone up an' the masters say they can't 'ford more pay."

"I am sure it is true," Margaret interjected, then reddened when both men looked quickly to her in surprise. She took a deep breath and rushed to explain herself. "Have you not both agreed that Mr Thornton, for example, may be many things but he is certainly honest- a master with integrity?"

"Aye, tha's true," Higgins pulled his mouth to the side in a resigned grin. "There's talk," he continued, "tha' Master's lookin' for deeper pockets. 'Ad a pair o' dandies with 'im yesterday. Spent hours, they did, lookin' o'er e'r'thing. 'Amilton, the older fellow's name was. Ca'ed th' other 'is son."

"Margaret, was that not a Miss Hamilton you met with Miss Thornton today at church?" Mr Hale queried.

"Yes, Father, it was."

"Ah," he smiled in pleasure, "I think her father must be the same gentleman John introduced me to at one of his Master's dinners, some while back. He did not seem to know the man well, though, and I spoke with him but little. They must be well-to-do, indeed, if Mr Hamilton is such an investor! I do hope he decides to offer his support. It is a distinction, is it not, my dear, to be brought to her notice? I shall be most grateful to the Thorntons for welcoming you into their circle of friends. Very kind of them, I daresay."

"Yes, Father, I am sure it is." Her eyes drifted to Higgins, whose own opinion of John Thornton was somewhat less warm than her father's. Higgins, however would never dare slight his employer in the presence of his guest.

Nicholas offered her a friendly wink. "Well, Lass," he spoke to his daughter, "'Ow's 'bout that mess o' your'n in the oven?"

Mary scolded her father with a look of affronted dignity, but swept to her little cooking alcove, returning to her guests with a bubbling pot of stewed and spiced apples. The children's careful training broke, and they crowded round the adults, their mouths clearly watering.

Margaret recognized the apples at once, and along with them, her friend's mischievous smirk. Try that she might to continue in the charitable ways in which she had been brought up, the Higgins family somehow always found a way to return to her what had been given.

Chapter Six

Margaret spent all of the next day preparing for Miss Hamilton's expected call on the following morning. She was a flurry of activity, though her father barely noticed, as she was careful to do her dusting and polishing in whichever rooms he did not occupy. By midday, her shoulders ached and her back was sore from stooping. She stretched her stiff muscles, reaching to massage her own tired shoulders.

Dixon, passing by with a tray for Mr Hale, shook her head and clucked in annoyance. "Plain wear yourself out..." she predicted balefully over her shoulder as she left the room.

Margaret grimaced, rolling her neck. Perhaps it was dignity, perhaps it was pride, but when she received her guests on the morrow, there ought to be nothing about her home to cause undue shame. Their family's current reduced circumstances would be obvious enough. It certainly would not do to present their home as anything less than perfectly ordered and welcoming.

With a last glance about herself, she let out a sigh of satisfaction. The little drawing room, her main focus this morning, fairly gleamed. Tilting her head, she tried to see it through the eyes of a more privileged young lady- one who was not accustomed to the surroundings. *How would Edith see this room?* she wondered. Edith's tastes, at least, she knew. Miss Hamilton was still an unknown quantity, but perhaps the two were alike.

Casting her eyes about, she forced them to look on the worn furnishings, the aging carpet, the tattered bookcase and the cheaply framed portraits on the wall. She cringed a little.

At least, she reflected, *the new papers on the walls brighten the room somewhat.* She was grateful to their landlord for relenting on this one point, although she wondered what had changed his mind after their first negotiations. Surely her father had been able to offer little to persuade him. Occasionally, she fancied that Mr Thornton had had a hand in... but no, she must not allow her thoughts to wander more in that direction. That door was closed, rather firmly.

Gathering her dusting rags and polish, she decided she ought to look in on the entryway. It would, after all, be her guests' first impression of the home. The most prominent item to catch her notice, of course, was her father's umbrella where it dangled from its place on the hook. She groaned softly. Could she not even move about her own home without being reminded of Mr Thornton?

Her opinion of him had undergone a substantial revision in the months since she had first met him. Where at first she had seen only a man of business, set upon bending the world to his will, she now saw quite a different person. There was a kindness there that she had missed before, one which humbled her in her prideful former notions. More recently, however, she had recognized in him the same mask she herself wore. His armour was more difficult to chink, but she had glimpsed through it, nonetheless.

Was it her natural feminine compassion or something else which bent her thoughts more frequently toward him? Was it her kinship with the sorrows in his life which made her think kindly of him? Why else would she so often find herself wondering what he was doing each day, and if he had thought back on that rainy walk at all?

Her brow furrowed as she gently swept her oiled rag over the little table in the entryway. Had he others to whom he could turn when his troubles weighed upon him? Somehow she doubted it. His position in Milton society forbade any display of vulnerability. From what he had spoken of his mother, Margaret expected that Mrs Thornton would not be inclined to give ear to grief over her former husband. A tug of compassion softened her heart. His position was much like her own.

There was truly no one in whom she could confide. None could bear her burdens with her, for all had enough cares. Of those whom she could trust, her father was too weak, Mary Higgins too overwhelmed with her own worries, and Dixon too bitter for her to open the depths of her heart to. *If only Frederick or Edith were near....* She clenched her eyes shut, squeezing out a stray tear.

She was effectively isolated.

Another tear joined the first and dripped on her freshly dusted surface. Margaret blinked, chiding herself. What if Dixon, or worse, her father were to happen upon her! She sniffed, cleared her throat, and completed her task with less sentiment and more efficiency than a moment ago. What was she about, drowning in self-pity when her very purpose was preparing to welcome a possible new friend?

Schooling her posture back into that of a sophisticated and dignified lady, she collected her cleaning items and paced by the little rack of hats and scarves in the hall. Reaching to straighten them, her notice shifted instead to her hand. She paused, and drew it close again for inspection.

Turning her palm over, she brushed her fingers together with a new cognizance. Her hands were growing strong and hard, exhibiting a roughness which had never before been present. Her nails were very practically blunted. There were new work lines crossing over her palms, and even a few callouses. They were scarcely the hands of a proper young lady! She sighed. Perhaps Miss Hamilton and her mother would not notice.

~

"Ah, Thornton, I did not expect to see you so soon!" Stuart Hamilton rose from his desk and extended his hand.

"You asked to see our forecasts," Thornton replied frankly, taking the other man's grip.

"So I did, but I typically must wait a week or longer for such figures." Hamilton waved his guest to a chair, and sat again behind his own desk.

"I make it a point to know exactly where I am at all times," Thornton replied. "It required very little additional preparation."

"I had heard, Thornton, that you were particular with the numbers. It explains your reputation rather well, I think. A man must know where he is if he is to move beyond that place."

Thornton tipped his head graciously as Hamilton took the thick folder he offered. Hamilton flipped to a summary sheet on the top of the stack and grazed his eyes over it quickly. "Interesting," he nodded. "I will spend some time looking this over.

"In the meantime, my wife was hoping to repay the compliment of the other evening. Would your family be available for a small dinner party next week? It was my wife's desire to host a party of sorts, celebrating Rupert's and Genevieve's return home. Knowing my wife," he smirked wryly, "what she calls 'small' shall be anything but."

"Of course, I shall be delighted, sir. I am certain my mother and sister would look forward to it." He rose and shook the other man's hand again.

"You will hear from me soon, Thornton," Hamilton promised.

~

Mrs and Miss Hamilton came promptly at their expected time on Tuesday to the little house in Crampton. Mrs Hamilton's eyes swept the dingy parlour at her first entry, but she politely schooled them forward. Still, Margaret felt more than saw a faint sneer in the woman's manner.

Genevieve Hamilton displayed no such hesitation. She warmly opened conversation, inquiring about Margaret's life in Hampshire and London before her removal to Milton. Margaret, a not a chatty personality herself, felt somewhat disconcerted at first, but slowly became at ease in the other's company.

"Oh!" Genevieve exclaimed at one point in Margaret's narrative, "I did not know you had family in Marylebone! Why, my brother Rupert has friends in that neighborhood. I am quite sure that is right, is it not, Mother?"

Mrs Hamilton dipped her head. "I think you are right, my love. My son," she turned to Margaret, "has lived there some while, until just recently. He has been affiliated with the Exchange, you see," she explained with a slight sniff. Margaret arched a brow, reflecting that there was certainly no shortage of filial pride among the matrons of Milton.

"I am monstrous fond of Rupert," the younger woman interjected, losing some of her formality. "Miss Hale, have you not much family of your own? You have no brothers or sisters, I understand."

"I... no, I suppose my family is rather small. Beside my father, of course, I have only my aunt and cousin I told you of, and my godfather Mr Bell who lives in Oxford." Margaret swallowed. How it pained her to share anything but the plain truth! Perhaps someday she might trust Genevieve Hamilton enough to share Frederick's story, but a family which moved in such circles as the Hamiltons were guaranteed to talk. She would have to be very sure of her new friend first.

"Bell!" Mrs Hamilton scoffed. "He is a Milton man bred and born, whatever airs he puts on. There are some," she paused significantly, "who would say he is wasting his life away as a useless academic. Most in this town say that he ought to be doing his part here, working like a man, rather than simply reaping the profits from afar."

Margaret smiled gently. "I believe Mrs Thornton might share that opinion."

Mrs Hamilton straightened somewhat, fixing Margaret with an evaluating gaze. "No doubt. I take it you do not?"

"I think Mr Bell has been blessed with the opportunity to study, which suits him rather well. He is not of the right temperament for industry, I suppose, but he has been of great material good to many in Oxford. I think, too, that even from afar he has been instrumental in many affairs here in Milton. Has not Mr Hamilton himself partnered with Mr Bell in some matters?"

Mrs Hamilton's lips twitched in amusement. "He has. You seem to be quite well-informed, Miss Hale, as well as rather outspoken for a young lady." Margaret caught an unconscious flick of Mrs Hamilton's eyes as they glanced once more over the room's shabby furnishings. "I take it, Miss Hale, that you must have received much of your education elsewhere?"

"I was brought up largely with my cousin," Margaret admitted softly. Inwardly her hopes began to die just a little. Mrs Hamilton was clearly less than impressed with what she had to offer as a companion to her daughter.

Margaret may have indeed been gently bred and brought up in the very best circles, but the truth of the matter was that she was but a poor relation- the grateful recipient of her aunt's goodwill. The dignity of her station as a clergyman's daughter was no longer even afforded her. Here in Milton she was simply Margaret Hale; a penniless young gentlewoman likely destined for permanent spinsterhood, with hardly a claim or connection to recommend her. Her mouth tugged to the side as her eyes dropped to her hands.

"I think that is most charming," insisted Genevieve, causing Margaret to look back to her in mild amazement. Genevieve glanced back and forth between Margaret and her mother. "Do you not see? You always had a friend, like a sister to grow up with. I had only my brother, and he was *such* a bore when we were younger. Rupert was forever pulling my hair and calling me dreadful names! Oh! I do not mean to say he is not a very fine man now, Miss Hale. It is only a girl wants something other than a rowdy boy sometimes. I say, Mother, shall we not introduce Miss Hale to Rupert? It would be so helpful, Miss Hale, if you should know what he really is like before I run him down so very much!"

Mrs Hamilton inclined her head, conceding to her daughter's whims. Margaret began to suspect that was the normal state of affairs in this family- though her mother at first appeared severe, Genevieve Hamilton exhibited every symptom of a young lady who often got her way.

"Of course, my love," the older woman answered, with only a touch of stiffness. "Miss Hale, we are hosting a small dinner party next Monday evening. A celebration, if you will, in honour of Genevieve's return to Milton. We would be most obliged if you- and your father, of course- could attend."

Margaret's brow rose sharply. "I am most grateful for your invitation, Mrs Hamilton, but my father has not been well, you see..." she darted her eyes back to Miss Hamilton. Oh, how she had longed for this chance! Only now, when the possibility of continued friendship with a cultured and educated woman near her own age seemed within her grasp did she fully admit how greatly she had desired it. She blinked a little, trying to decide how she could be both honest and receptive to the other's invitation.

"Oh, do come, Miss Hale," Miss Hamilton pleaded. "There is so much I would like to talk to you about! I heard from Fanny Thornton that you have a great many concerns for the working class, and I had hoped to introduce you to the founder of one of the local charities!"

That was more than sufficient inducement for Margaret. "I shall speak with my father," she decided firmly. "I know he would very much appreciate your hospitality, if he is well enough."

Mrs Hamilton answered with a prim nod of her head, but Genevieve gushed her delight effusively. "We shall have so much more time to talk! I am afraid we really must be going now, for Mama is expecting callers later. Miss Hale, you will call on us soon, I hope?"

Margaret assured the other young woman that she would, and her company departed. As the front door closed, she collapsed against the wall in the entryway- exhausted but at the same time brimming with hope. For the first time in a very long time, she had found a young lady she might call a friend.

~

The next afternoon brought Mr Thornton for his regular visit. Margaret had braced herself all day to face the cold blue of his eyes, steeled against any flicker of emotion. It was somehow worse now- now that she knew a real heart dwelt within him, and that he hardened his features for her benefit.

Dixon happened to have gone to the market, and Margaret was obliged to answer to his knock herself. His face reflected a flash of surprise, but he quickly composed himself. "Good afternoon, Miss Hale," he greeted her with perfect equanimity.

She managed a shy half-smile, hoping she would seem welcoming. "Good afternoon, Mr Thornton. Father is in his study. He asked if you could come up directly."

He nodded. "Of course, thank you." He began to move off when she stopped him.

"May I bring you any refreshments?" she called hopefully.

He turned, his eyebrows quirked curiously. Margaret was a mesmerizing hostess, but always in the drawing room. It had never been the norm for her to bring anything to Mr Hale's study herself. Mr Hale always offered him something, and on the rare occasions when he accepted, it had been Dixon summoned to serve the tea.

He felt a soft tug playing about the corners of his mouth. Fool he likely was, but any overture from Margaret could not help but lift his spirits. "I thank you, Miss Hale, that would be most welcome."

His heart flipped involuntarily when a gentle smile warmed her face in reply. Even when cool and distant, she was the loveliest woman he had ever laid eyes upon. When she smiled- at him! - he was utterly bewitched.

He must have remained there, smiling back at her, for a little too long, because her eyes began to shift uncomfortably to the side. She had trapped one taper finger nervously in her other hand, and stood as if she were longing to step away as soon as he turned his back. Blinking, he recalled himself. "Excuse me then, will you, Miss Hale?"

With a sigh to himself, he turned and mounted the stairs. What was it about her that instantly brought him to his knees when she was around? Why was he, a man of maturity and wisdom, constantly humiliating himself before her? She was only a penniless daughter of a reduced gentleman, just one among dozens of others in Milton! Ah, but none other possessed her gentleness, her intelligence, her frankness... or her sweet, soothing voice.

He closed his eyes, relying on his hand on the rail to guide him up the steps. *She refused you, do not forget that! Her heart belongs to some other!* Margaret Hale was not the kind of woman to change her mind on a whim. What she had determined, she would bring about, and what she had rejected, she would not return to. *Exactly the sort of character I should admire....*

His fingers found the end of the stair railing and he opened his eyes. He drew a long breath. *She is not for you,* he reminded himself harshly. He paused another moment before knocking on the door, cleansing his thoughts and preparing himself once again to become the student rather than the master.

It was a service to his friend, if not to himself. This afternoon, Mr Hale's spirits were only marginally improved. As their lesson unfolded, it was obvious to Thornton that Hale still possessed much of the air of despondency which had lingered since his wife's death.

Thornton sat quietly as he waited for Mr Hale to answer his question about the bonds of brotherly affection. The older man had canted his chair so that he could as easily gaze out the window as look directly at his pupil. Mr Hale's style of conversation tended to involve many spaces of silent contemplation, and he was uncomfortable with eye-to-eye discussion. He stroked his smooth chin now, his gaze soft and unfocused.

"Do you think," Hale answered at last, "that Plutarch allows for cases in which there is no brother or sister to be had?"

Thornton glanced down, smiling faintly. It was like his friend to answer a question with a question. "I do not think he disallows it, certainly, but it is not the context of this essay. I believe the emphasis here is on the preservation of sibling affection in preference to others, as a means of honouring one's parent and blood family."

"Indeed," Hale nodded slowly. "But he does not go into detail about how one is to manage after the loss of this relationship- or in the complete absence of such."

Thornton narrowed his eyes thoughtfully. "He does speak about the loss of a brother as irretrievable, but when he speaks against other relationships- a friend, for example- it is never in the absence of a brother, but in preference to."

"Yes, irretrievable, that is precisely it. I wonder, then, what affinities Plutarch would endorse had the mortal severing of that bond in fact taken place." Hale rocked back slightly in his chair, his gaze on the steady downpour of rain against his window.

"I would suppose," Thornton answered after a moment, "that one who is *like* a brother, in spirit and comradeship, would be the best possible replacement, although in this case Plutarch is silent."

"Or a sister...." Hale made no further answer but the slight narrowing of his eyes. Thornton puzzled over his words. Hale's manner this day was even more introspective than usual, and he wondered what personal quandary his friend was sorting out.

At that moment, a soft knock at the door sent Thornton's heart into his throat. His breath quickening, he stood to answer the door and moved to allow Margaret to enter the little room with her tea tray. He rapidly cleared a space among the stacks of books on Mr Hale's desk for her to set it down.

Her eyes flashed quickly to his, with such an expression of gratitude and... was it warmth he saw there? Perhaps that was only the product of his active imagination, but most certainly the cold hostility he had previously known was gone. He answered her gaze with a boyish little grin, the one he wore for his mother when she did him some small gesture of kindness.

Margaret's own smile deepened, and with a flutter of lashes she looked quickly away to serve the tea. Thornton felt his face warm. He was blushing like an adolescent! Mercifully, her back was to him, her eyes trained steadily on her tray.

He indulged his craving, hungrily watching her graceful form as she moved about the tea tray. To his regret, she had not worn that troublesome bracelet today and he had not the pleasure of musing over the way it dimpled her delicate flesh. Her long-sleeved dress was a disappointment as well, but he consoled himself by admiring the loosened tendrils of hair curling above her prim collar as she bent her neck. Seldom had he been afforded such a view.

"Thank you my dear," Mr Hale was smiling at his daughter. "That was very thoughtful of you, though I had not expected you to trouble yourself. Is Dixon still out?"

"Yes, Father, she is," Margaret dipped her head, too embarrassed to look Thornton in the eye again. She was well used to facing down his challenging stares. She had even had opportunities to grow uncomfortable under a gaze which could only be called one of manly desire. Today's warm, friendly expression was entirely new- and eminently preferable.

Shyly she dared herself to raise her head... and found his eyes shining tenderly at her. Her stomach fluttered.

"Thank you for the tea, Miss Hale," he bowed slightly, flashing a most distracting smile.

Flustered anew, Margaret inclined her head sharply and made a dash for the hall, where she could be safe from the confusing swell of feeling. Her fingers white on the tray she carried, she scolded herself. Why, she had practically flirted with him! It would serve her right if he thought her more shameless now than ever. Yet... his look had been far from disapproving.

She shook her head. What did it matter what he thought? He was much too complicated for her to sort out at the moment. For now, she had a dinner gown to make over and a visit to the Higgins family to prepare for.

Chapter Seven

Thornton's mind was difficult to manage through the rest of his time with Mr Hale. They digested the Greek essay slowly, painstakingly, but sibling affection could not hold his interest. His feelings were far from fraternal. His imagination instead filled with a vision of plum satin and ivory lace, peeking through a curtain of dark curls, all tumbling down....

"John?"

He started. "Forgive me, I think I did not hear your question."

Mr Hale gazed carefully back for a heartbeat before replying. "I asked whether you thought a man's loyalty could be given to a sister as easily as to a brother."

His eye twitched involuntarily. His friend seemed obsessed with the concept of a sister today! "I suppose it must be, but I have no experience in that case, as I have no brother to compete for my loyalty," he almost grumbled. He then clenched his jaw in remorse at the surprised lift of Mr Hale's brows.

"Forgive me for sounding so terse," he sighed. "To be quite frank, I have a difficult time applying Plutarch's wisdom in this essay to any of my own affairs. I found the Moralia essays on virtue far more valuable."

"But, John, you do have a sister," Mr Hale protested. "Do you not find his insights meaningful?"

"Not particularly," he frowned. "Fanny is nearly thirteen years my junior. I have felt more of a father than a brother these many years."

"Ah, yes, I can see that." Mr Hale tipped back toward the window, his fingers gently stroking his chin once more. "So we must return to my earlier question- what of cases where there is no sibling?"

Thornton was, by this time, growing more than a little tired of the subject. "I do not suppose it is a necessity of life," he answered shortly.

Hale glanced back in surprise. "I speak of enriching one's life, John. It is the comradeship of one like in heart that is so valuable. The lifelong bond, not severed by time or distance..." his voice grew soft, "... it is encouraging, to know there is another such as oneself in this world."

Thornton's eyes narrowed slightly. "You never spoke of a sibling before."

Hale turned back to him. "I? No, not I. Bell, I suppose, would be the brother of my spirit... and Maria was..." He covered his mouth with his hand, and his younger counterpart looked respectfully away as he composed himself. He drew a ragged breath, blinking and making use of his handkerchief. "It is for the next generation that I am concerned, John," he murmured at length.

A glimmer of insight finally came upon him. "In that case, it is regrettable," he answered gently, "that Miss Hale has not the comfort of a brother... or a sister, as you say."

If he had meant to commiserate with his friend's concerns, he failed utterly. Mr Hale's head dropped to his hands and his shoulders began to shake uncontrollably.

Sensing himself at a loss, Thornton glanced at the clock on the mantelpiece. His time was at an end, but his friend was in no state to be left alone. Soft noises emanated from him and his face remained hidden. There seemed little Thornton could offer in the way of comfort.

Swiftly he rose and exited the room, careful to keep the door from thumping loudly as it closed. He took the stairs down in a quick staccato rhythm, but drew up abruptly on the first landing. Margaret had just exited the room there, and turned just as he reached her. The landing was small- barely large enough for them to stand without touching, and certainly not large enough for him to pass by her full skirts without some contact.

"Excuse me, sir!" she backed away, reaching behind herself for the knob of the door she had just closed.

"No, I was looking for you," he put out a hand to stop her from retreating. She hesitated and he continued. "Your father... I think you should go to him."

Worry crossed her features. "Is he unwell?"

"I do not know. He seems greatly troubled. I think it was something I said," he admitted.

Though he expected and possibly deserved an accusing glare, instead she graced him with an expression softened by sympathy. "I see," she answered quietly. With a gesture of her head, she indicated her willingness to follow him. He led her back up to Mr Hale's room, where the older man had lain his head and arms in despair across his desk.

She stepped quickly to her father, resting gentle hands upon his shoulders and stooping to murmur soft reassurances. Thornton gazed upon the sight for speechless moments, wondering if it were right for him to remain, yet unable to command himself to go. His concern for his friend was too real; moreover, it was far too beautiful a scene to tear his eyes from.

His friend's words played again through his mind. His view grew hazy over the young woman before him and he saw her with new eyes. She was alone. He still could not erase his reservations about her character, but she did not deserve the solitude she had inherited.

Was it that which had so troubled his friend? Margaret had no one but an aging, frail father and a sour, battered old maid. Surely Hale must fear for her. She needed someone able, one she could depend upon- someone who would not take advantage of her... She needed him.

Not as a lover... No, that she would not accept. Could he become as a brother, a friend? Was it even possible to rein in his own feelings for her good? Would she reciprocate, or would she reject any sort of fellowship as she had before?

There was yet another concern- if he were known to be too close to her, her reputation truly could be damaged beyond repair. He blinked, his breath tight. The risks were great, but the need greater. He owed it to his friend- and to his love, unrequited though it was- to try.

At length she looked back to him with a curious tilt of her head, surprised at still finding him there. He nodded in response to the silent question, recalling the cold realities of the rest of his day. "I will see myself out."

She offered him one last fleeting smile before the door clicked between them.

~

Two hours later, the last thing Thornton had time to think of was making friends with Margaret. He leaned over the high scaffolding, affording him an unobstructed view of the cavernous room where dozens of looms filled the air with a deafening cacophony. His sharp eyes were on every worker, every machine by turn. If he could identify some little inefficiency, some small thing which, multiplied, could save him tens of pounds....

Williams, his overseer, found him there toward the end of the shift. Words were pointless above the clatter of the looms,. but he extended his tally sheet for the day. Thornton took it with a quick nod and scanned it, his brow creased. With a questioning glance, he pointed to a particular line. Williams' only answer was a shrug.

Thornton set his teeth. The older combing machines had been breaking down a great deal of late. If only he could have afforded some of the newer Heilmann combers last year! He frowned. These were what he had to work with. There simply had to be a way to better maintain them. He passed the paper back to Williams and wordlessly descended the scaffolding just as the whistle blew. Machines almost instantly began to fall silent.

All about him, men and women began to flood into the rows between the machines, all eager to leave their day's work behind. For just a moment, he envied them. When they went to their beds this night, their concerns would be only for their homes and families. It would not be the additional burden of orders, supplies, machinery difficulties and labor distribution which kept them from sleep.

A harried mother, tugging her recently hired daughter behind her, ducked out of his way. She glanced over her shoulder, apparently fearful that the girl's awkwardness had offended the master.

He shook his head. *I am being unfair*, he chided himself. All had cares enough. Glancing about at the people filing out before him, he reflected that it had been many a year since any of the Thorntons had wanted for a meal or a new set of clothing.

"Master Thornton! Sir!"

Thornton turned at the voice of one of the local union leaders. "What is it, Miles?"

The shorter man huffed up to him. "There's been a complaint to th' Union, sir. Jonas Sacks says yo' d'smissed 'im 'bou' cause!"

"I had cause enough. He cannot perform his duties." Thornton began to walk away.

"But sir!" Miles caught up and followed at Thornton's heels as he walked. "T'was only on account of 'is injury, 'tis nobbu' temp'rary. Union Rules, sir! Another place mu'n be found for now, one what 'e can do. 'E's a wife and four childer!"

"Then he would have done better to spend his wages on food and not drink. A man who brawls publically, then breaks his arm in a misguided prank such as drayage theft is a menace to his family and a danger to other workers. He ought instead to be grateful he is not locked up."

"Master Thornton, Jonas's willin' to work, and 'e's ne'er drunk on the job!" Miles protested.

"That last bit is not true. I ought to have dismissed him long ago. Tell him that for a few weeks, he can practice some personal restraint, then reapply for the position once both his character and his arm have mended. You and I both know, Miles, that he has been at the Dragon nearly every day of late. Where, I ask you, has he found the funds?"

Miles sputtered. "Master, yo've said yo'r own self that a man's private 'ffairs's none of yo'r bus'ness!"

"Certainly not, but the safety of every worker at Marlborough Mills is. The man is a liability. My decision stands."

Miles stopped trying to keep up with the master, crossing his arms in affected fury. Thornton strode off, then abruptly turned back. "Is not Sacks' eldest nearly fourteen, and a well-grown lad?"

Miles thought for a moment. "B'lieve 'e is. 'E's been workin' in the cardin' rooms."

"A position has opened up in the loading docks. Five and ten a week. Tell the lad to be there tomorrow morning. The next younger child can take his old place. Remind them not to be late!"

Miles gave in, knowing that the master's mind was made up about the man he defended. "Aye, sir."

By now the mill was almost entirely emptied. Thornton turned and continued about his errand, unmolested by any more requests. At last he reached the older wing, where two or three dinosaurs of machinery daily cast fear into the hearts of the mechanics. He glared at them for a moment, thrusting his hands to his hips and chewing thoughtfully at his lip.

Without warning, an old cap appeared from under the furthest machine. It was followed by the rest of the man's head, and a face which turned into view as the man wormed his way through the downy drape of combed cotton. "Oh, g'd'evnin' sir!" Higgins greeted him cheerfully.

Thornton arched a brow. "Trying to get paid past your time, Mr Higgins?"

Higgins gave a wry laugh. "Much good it'd do me, eh Master? Naw, this ould girl 'ere," he banged a tool in his hand against the machine, "she jes' needed a lovin' touch."

"What was wrong with it this time?"

"Eh," Higgins finished clambering out and stood to his feet, pushing his cap back on his head. "Drive gear's plumb worn, sir. She just sets there, bidin' 'er time when the belt's a-spinnin'." He drew a rag from his pocket and wiped his brow, then his greasy hands as he spoke.

Thornton gave him a sharp look. "Thompson spoke to me last week about that. I ordered it repaired. Why has it not been?"

"'E fixed it, sir, but tha' was that'un o'er there," Higgins jerked his head to another rack of combed cotton. "Ran out o' parts, 'e did. Went to the smithy to build more."

"So what brings you over here? If I recall correctly, you are assigned to the looms." Thornton cocked a challenging expression at his employee.

Higgins' face blossomed into a slow grin, a twinkle in his eye. "Aye, sir, bu' when the whistle blows, I do as I please. T'morrow'll be better for the lads. I got th'ould girl wired back t'gether for 'nother day."

Thornton stared thoughtfully back for another moment, then abruptly changed the subject. "What of the Union, Mr Higgins?"

The other's eyebrows arched innocently. "Sir?"

Thornton crossed his arms. "Are you not still one of the leaders? What will your friends say, Mr Higgins, when they learn you were working after hours without pay, while another member of your order was doing his duty by challenging me over Sacks' dismissal?"

Higgins pointed his tool, smiling. "What 'ud they say if the combs was still down?" He bent to gather a few other odds and ends into a little satchel. "And Sacks 'ad no business workin' in 'is state."

"It would be said that the machine was my fault, and that Sacks ought to have been given lighter work for now."

"I don' mean 'is arm." Higgins straightened. "'E's a troublemaker, that'un. Most ev'r'one's glad to 'ave 'im out from our 'air. 'Tis a shame, though, that poor wife o'his. My Mary's been 'elpin' 'er where she can."

Thornton's eyes drifted over the room as he lapsed into silence. Higgins watched him carefully, shrugged his shoulders, and began to saunter away. The master seemed to have done with him.

"What has been done?" Thornton's voice stopped him.

"Sir?" Higgins turned.

Thornton narrowed his eyes. "Contrary to what you may believe, Mr Higgins, I do have some concept of what it is for a family to suffer for their father's mistakes."

"Aye." Higgins studied his employer. "May'ap yo' do. Well, sir, 'tis a pinch. Sacks drinks most what 'e brings 'ome. 'Is Missus takes in sewin', but the childers- they're most a' clemmin'."

Thornton nodded vaguely, his thoughts churning. "And what of your family, Mr Higgins? Are the older children in school?"

Higgins grinned sheepishly. "I've saved 'most 'nough for Daniel to start. 'E'll make a scholar, I'll lay to it. Lad's read most ev'rthing I 'ad."

"I see," murmured his employer, still gazing at the thick swaths of pearly cotton covering most of the combing machine. He squinted briefly, then turned fully toward the other man. "And what of the boy's spirits?"

Higgins cocked his head. "Sir?"

"I have seen many a good young lad ruined by shame and anger. His circumstances put him at risk, if he is not properly guided."

A twinkle of understanding flashed in Higgins' smile. "Aye, sir. 'E's a good lad, 'e is. Got's much 'eart as any boy, and p'raps more'n most."

Thornton shook his head, muttering under his breath. "What a pity he had such a worthless father to look up to."

Higgins shrugged. "When a man's lost a' 'ope, an' sees only despair, 'e's past condemnin'... if you'll 'scuse me, sir."

Thornton snorted a little, eyeing the man curiously. "You had little enough liking for Boucher! His cowardice brought both of us nothing but trouble for weeks, and left you with a lifetime obligation. How is it you can speak so civilly?"

Higgins drew a deep breath, pursing his lips and daring to stare down his employer. "I've gots to look tha' lad in th' eye when 'e grows to a man, sir- 'im and 'is brothers. It'll be for me to show 'em they don' 'ave to worry their 'earts over their da'. Boucher... 'e 'ad 'nough cares for one lifetime, and that's the end o' it. There be no sense in ca'in' 'im a coward, not anymore."

Higgins looked down to the rag he still clutched, stroking it gently between his fingers as if it were a lock of a child's hair. When he spoke again, his voice was softer than Thornton had ever heard it. "I can' fathom wha'd lead a man to do it, but 'e musta thought 'is childer'd be better off 'bout 'im." He sighed and shook his head, then looked back up with a friendly smirk. "'Sides, they won' be the first childer to be made a' the stronger for it. Others's done it."

Thornton raised a brow. His past was certainly no secret in Milton, but no one ever dared bring it up- particularly not one of his hands, and a probational hire at that! Margaret's friend was proving a fascinating specimen, and one he would not mind coming to know further.

Higgins smiled once more at his baffled employer, tipped his cap, and began to move off.

"I have books," Thornton interrupted him.

Higgins stopped, turning back curiously. "Sir?"

"How many of the children are old enough for school?"

"Oh. Jes' Danny and Jenny, but the lass'll 'ave to wait till next year, I'm 'fraid." Higgins suppressed a little sigh of frustration.

"Has she any aptitude?"

Higgins stared at him in silence.

"What I mean is, does she have an interest? Has she had any schooling at all?"

A sly twinkle came to the old weaver's eye. "Jest a bit, at 'ome. She likes it well 'nough, and a good worker she is."

"What would you say, Mr Higgins, if I were to stop over some evening to see how they get on? I have no children of my own, nor am I ever likely to. It would do me good to take an interest in the orphans."

Higgins broke into a wide, toothy grin. "I say come as yo' like, sir. Yo' know where to find us."

Chapter Eight

Dixon looked up from the kettle she was scrubbing as Margaret entered the kitchen. "Is the master sleeping already, Miss?"

Margaret heaved a long-suffering breath and tied on an apron. "I believe so. He had a very trying afternoon."

Dixon's only reply was a pursing of her lips as she clattered around with her kettle. She polished and ground mercilessly at a stain in the bright metal, setting her teeth and wrinkling her nose. Her hands flew ever faster, but the stain refused to be done away with.

Margaret tipped her head, watching carefully. "Dixon, is something wrong?"

Dixon's face scrunched, her entire body now fighting the spot on the copper, until her temper broke. She flung the stubborn bit of cookware across the kitchen with an angry sob. Quickly she wrapped her hands in her apron and covered her face.

Margaret was there immediately, draping an arm about her shoulder and drawing her to a stool. "Dixon! Dearest Dixon, do tell me what the trouble is!"

Dixon shook her head and gave a pained little sob. She wiped an eye with the corner of her apron. "There ye go again, Miss! Just like Miss Beresford, you are. You don't have to be so gentle-like. Go on, scold me for denting the kettle!"

"Dixon, you know I would do no such thing! I demand, however, that you tell me what the matter is."

At this, Dixon actually managed a little smile. "And there's Master Frederick. How I do see him when you pluck up that backbone of yours!"

Margaret's tense shoulders relaxed. "I miss him too, Dixon."

Dixon's lips started quivering again and she made another pass at her face with her apron. Margaret reached for her hand and gave it a solid squeeze. Dixon was shaking her head and blinking. "If only the master hadn't 'llowed little Freddy to join up with the Navy! Your mother were dead set against it. If he'd stayed, he'd have never let the master leave Helstone! And the mistress...." Dixon searched in her pocket for a well-used handkerchief and blew loudly.

Margaret closed her eyes, fighting for calm. Dixon was right, in her way, but it could never have been so simple. "Dixon, you know that Frederick would never have stayed in Helstone. Father agreed to let him join the Navy because he was so restless, and Father feared he would leave to seek his fortune in America. At least in the Navy, there was hope he would someday return. Mother's health... did not Dr Donaldson say that she had been ill for some time before we came to Milton? You tended her yourself, Dixon, you must know the truth."

Dixon heaved, still locked in stubborn denial. "She'd ne'er have had to leave her home," she pouted. "That were what done her over, Miss. Broke her heart, it did."

Margaret smiled sadly. "I know, Dixon. It was hard on all of us, but certainly the worst for Mother." She was silent a moment. "Even after everything though, I do think that coming here has not been all bad. I have learned so much, about the world... about myself. We have met so many interesting people, have we not?"

Dixon tried to hide a reluctant smile at the touch of irony in Margaret's voice. "Do you mean like that weaver fellow with the muddy boots? Oh, he's an interesting one, and that's a fact. He asked me last week for four tarts- one for each meal of the day, and another for a midnight treat!"

Margaret chuckled. "He was teasing you, Dixon. It was a compliment!"

"Hmmf. He'll get no more of *my* cooking, I'll promise you!"

"Yes, he will. I will sneak my own desserts to Mary when you turn your back."

Dixon gave a warning glare. "Not in my kitchen, Miss. I'll not let you waste away to nothing, you're skin and bones as it is!"

"I am quite strong, and you know it," Margaret asserted.

"Strong as a scullery maid," Dixon frowned. "I just don't think it's fittin', Miss. You oughtn't be carryin' coal buckets and water kettles about. You're a lady! If you were in London...."

"But I am not in London, nor do I wish to be," Margaret cut in.

"... you could catch as fine a husband as any, and be treated proper like a lady," Dixon finished stoutly.

"'I spent time enough in London, and never saw anything there that I could not live without," Margaret answered with a saucy lilt, then her face softened. "I do miss Edith, though. They are set to return from Corfu within the month, did you hear? And they have a little boy now. Oh, I do wish I could see him!"

"You ought to go, Miss."

Margaret shook her head. "I cannot leave Father." She sighed nostalgically, her eyes on the fading light outside the window. "I wish... but Edith would not come here, and Father will not go."

"No reason she can't come here, she travels everywhere else," Dixon muttered, the bitterness returning to her tones. "She's got a fine husband to see her here, and she could come lay flowers on her aunt's stone. She ought to bring that mother of hers- high time she paid a visit."

"Dixon," Margaret warned, "I must not have you speak so of my Aunt Shaw."

Dixon simply stared, her plump lips drawn into a sulky pout.

Margaret sighed. "You are right in a way, I suppose. But we must not judge her too harshly, you know. It is all so foreign to her. Milton would terrify her, with the factory noise and the workers flooding the streets at odd hours. And where would we put her? She would not know what to do with herself when Father receives his pupils. No, I am not certain I wish my aunt to come."

A slow smile spread over Dixon's face as she silently imagined Mrs Shaw having her toes tread upon by a clumsy pair of muddy boots in the Hales' drawing room. With a shrug, she gave up the fantasy. Higgins would not come near the house if he knew such a woman were in residence.

More likely was the possibility of the London matron clashing cultures with the likes of Mr Thornton. How she might like to be a fly on the wall for such a meeting! He would not back down from Mrs Shaw, that was certain. That fellow had a mysterious way of swaying others to his manner of thinking- after a fashion. He took some getting used to, and as Dixon still had not quite achieved that feat, surely Mrs Shaw would take even longer. Oh, how she wished she could see that man set down the proud sister of her beloved Miss Beresford!

Margaret could not quite interpret Dixon's strange little smile, but she was glad to see it nonetheless. She patted her mother's maid on her beefy forearm. "Come, let us see what we can do about that stained and dented old kettle, shall we?

~

Thornton was deep in thought when he made his way to the dining room that evening. A myriad of ideas swirled through his mind- some mortifying, some inspiring. He had made so many mistakes, but there seemed yet reason to continue on. So engrossed was he that he was taken utterly by surprise when he discovered the guest in his dining room.

"Oh, John, there you are!" Fanny cried, bounding from her seat. "Genevieve came to see my new gown. Just look, is it not simply *exquisite*?" Fanny tugged at the voluminous blue skirt of a gown draped over the dining room table. Genevieve Hamilton rose to stand beside her.

Thornton gazed blankly at the satin frills. His mother, still seated just to his left, was rolling her eyes and drumming her fingers.

"Oh, see, Gen, I told you he would not even notice!" Fanny complained. She struck a petulant expression and began stuffing the lavish gown rather carelessly back into its box.

Thornton shook his head and cleared his throat. "Forgive me, Miss Hamilton," he bent slightly forward in greeting. "It is good of you to call."

Genevieve smiled boldly. "I was only too happy to receive Fanny's note. I know she was very much hoping this gown could be completed in time."

He narrowed his eyes in some puzzlement.

"Mr Thornton, you *are* coming to dinner next Monday, are you not?"

"Oh! Of course, Miss Hamilton. I am afraid you had me at a disadvantage just now- my mind was elsewhere. I beg you would overlook my poor manners."

"Think nothing of it, sir," she assured him smoothly. "You are a man of many cares, I am certain. Surely, one such as yourself could not be expected to have such matters at the fore of his thoughts. What interest can feminine adornments and frivolous parties hold for a man of business?"

He gave her a lopsided smile. "A great deal of interest, if he be a man of any wits, Miss Hamilton. I assure you, I am looking forward to the evening with the greatest anticipation."

Genevieve looked well pleased with his sideways compliment. "As am I, Mr Thornton. Good evening, sir." She dipped him a full, deliberate curtsey as she took her leave.

Thornton arched a brow, not quite reciprocating. "Good evening, Miss Hamilton. Please give your family my compliments."

Genevieve bade her farewells to Mrs Thornton and Fanny, promising to walk again with Fanny after services on Sunday.

After her departure, Fanny sent the box with its haphazardly packed contents up to her room. Suddenly the much coveted item had lost all appeal for her, as her audience had vanished. Thornton took the seat the box had occupied, grateful to finally be off his feet.

"I declare, John, you could have been nicer to her!" Fanny pouted.

"Fanny!" Mrs Thornton scolded.

"No, let me hear this," he leaned forward over the table, an opportunistic half smile on his face. "How is it, Fanny, that you think my manners must be improved? I could do with a little entertainment."

"You never even moved to take her hand! She was quite ready to offer it, you know. You have the manners of a boor!"

"If you mean that I did not make her a formal greeting, perhaps I could have done better, but it is far past the normal hours for calling and I was quite off my guard."

"Well, it's certain *she* was not. Did you see the elegant way she bade us farewell, Mother? *That*, Brother, is how it is done by all of the fine ladies of London."

Thornton cast his eyes up and to the right for a second in thought. "No... no, it is not. Surely I would have noticed before."

"Well!" Fanny at last took a chair, plucking restlessly at her sleeves. "*I* think her quite sophisticated, and I shall endeavour to learn the trick myself."

"It is ostentatious; moreover, it is immodest with such a low neckline as she wore. Does the lady not prefer a wrap at this time of the year?"

Next to him, his mother stifled a chuckle, turning her face away rapidly.

"Oh, what can you know?" Fanny huffed. "You are impossible, John! Emmeline was right about you; you will never find a wife!"

"Emmeline..." he shifted his eyes to his mother, who had not yet recovered from her mirth.

"Sullivan- or rather Draper now!" Fanny cried. "My dearest old friend from school- aside from Gen. You remember, we were at her wedding last month! I declare, John, you forget everything but the mill!"

"Oh, that one," he rolled his eyes. "I am glad to hear she had such a high opinion of my prospects."

"She was right, John. Why, you did not speak a dozen words to Miss Hamilton!"

"Surely I spoke at least that. Am I right, Mother?" He made a show of ticking off the number with his fingers, causing his mother's dark eyes to sparkle with merriment. It was worth goading Fanny once in a while just to see his mother smile so.

"And you really could have taken more notice of my gown." Fanny whined, her arms crossed like a child.

"My pocketbook took quite enough notice of it, I imagine," he answered drily. "Tell me, how much extra did you offer to have it finished so quickly?" he asked, rubbing his tired eyes and beginning to think it time to put an end to the discussion.

"You did not even remember the dinner party until poor Genevieve had to remind you! I cannot say how embarrassed...."

"Fanny," Mrs Thornton warned. "That is quite enough."

"Hmmf," she pointedly looked away from him. "It really is no wonder," she mumbled, just loudly enough to be heard clearly.

Thornton could not help himself. It was both aggravating and amusing to let her go on. "What is, Fanny?"

She turned her head back, staring frostily. "You are no gentleman, John! How can you ever hope to get some woman to look twice at you? The only one I ever saw was that Margaret Hale-"

"Fanny!" Mrs Thornton interrupted. "Go to your room this minute!"

"No!" John held up a hand to his mother, his face ashen. "Let me handle this, Mother." He turned back to his sister, eyes narrowed. "What do you mean, Fanny?"

"Oh! She would have given her right eye if you would have married her John, but you were right not to offer for her. So brown and coarse, and poor in the bargain! To be sure, I never saw any great beauty in her, though she does put on *such* airs. You could do so much better- like Emmeline! You could have had her if you had only pulled your head out of the factory long enough to court her, John. She liked you well enough, you know, though I cannot fathom why. Gen seems to find you tolerable, though. You really oughtn't to let her slip away."

He was shaking. He put a white hand to his face and swallowed hard, trying to compose himself. His pulse thudded in his ears. Fanny was entirely wrong- she had to be! - but she had hit very near his heart.

"Fanny," his mother's sternest voice echoed from far away, "leave him be. Go to your room."

"No!" he rose abruptly. "No, stay. Forgive me Mother, I will not be taking supper. I... have much work to do."

"John!" His mother came quickly to him, worry inscribed in her features.

He sighed heavily. "It is nothing, Mother. Truly, I am well."

She raised a brow, unconvinced.

He looked away, catching his sister's eye. "Fanny, we will address your outburst at a later date."

Fanny twitched her mouth, crossing her arms in defiance. John had never yet taken her to task, and she did not believe he was about to start now.

"I will bring a tray up, John," his mother promised.

"No, nothing, I beg you, Mother. Thank you." He tried to smile, failed, and made his escape.

Chapter Nine

Thornton had finally collapsed into his bed in the small hours of the morning, but even then he had been tormented by wild, incomprehensible dreams. Fanny's words, Mr Hale's inexplicable melancholy, and Margaret's hesitant welcome captured even his unconscious thoughts.

Was it possible... No! Of course it was not. Margaret could never care for him. She had told him so! She simply needed a friend, and he was the only one at hand.

His common sense warned him to leave well enough alone- that there were young ladies enough in the city to fill that void without risking her respectability. Heavens, she did not even like him! Then the more valiant part of his soul would whisper again his fears for her.

What would become of her if Mr Hale's health were to fail? Had she anyone to turn to who could provide the assistance she would need? Certainly she would not trust in him unless he had first taken the time to befriend her. He could only hope that some part of her would not reject his olive branch.

That was his greatest fear. His heart was in agony that she would reject him again, even in so simple a thing. He tossed in his bed, tangling himself in the blankets until it was late enough to rise without disturbing the household. How would she respond? He could not wait even a single day to find out.

Unfortunately, it was midafternoon before he was able to escape from the mill. He had, he thought, a plausible excuse for his call, and he walked the three miles to Crampton with a light but nervous heart. It beat to a crescendo as he knocked upon her door, and nearly burst in relief and joy when Margaret herself answered.

"Mr Thornton!" she offered him a bashful smile. "We did not expect the pleasure today. Do, please come in."

This was better than he had hoped! His errand could have been accomplished from the doorstep, but he gratefully doffed his hat and followed her into the house.

Margaret was surreptitiously glancing at the hat rack and the little side table near the door, perhaps expecting him to say he had left some article and had come to retrieve it. "It is a pleasure to see you again so soon, sir. I am afraid my father is with a pupil at present, but I am certain he would not mind...."

"No, thank you, Miss, Hale, I do not wish to interrupt. I only came to bring him this." He extended a small brown box, which she took hesitantly.

"Tobacco?" she asked, her forehead dimpled.

"Uh... yes, it was given me. It is a very fine aromatic blend... if I am not mistaken it is of the kind your father prefers, but I do not smoke."

Those clear, bright eyes searched him curiously. "I think you are the first gentleman of my acquaintance who does not! I thought all gentlemen did so, at least occasionally."

Her use of the word 'gentleman' brought an immediate light to his face. Here was something of note! Perhaps his was not a hopeless effort. So great was his pleasure that he was a little slow to respond. "I... I never cared for either the odour or the expense, Miss Hale."

A genuine smile warmed her features, drawing his eye to a delicate little dimple below her cheekbone- just the right size to be kissed. "I suppose," her words stole his attention back where it belonged, "that is the reason my father so seldom indulges. He does not often purchase luxuries for himself."

She waited for some response, but Thornton merely gazed back in hypnotized silence.

"I... I do not mind this sweet pipe tobacco," she continued uncomfortably, "but I find cigar smoke most objectionable."

Thornton blinked back to reality. "Indeed, Miss Hale, I quite agree. Unfortunately, most of the gentlemen in Milton do not share your opinion. My jacket, when I come home from our monthly masters' dinners, can testify to that fact. My mother forbids me to sit in her furniture until I have removed it."

Margaret's taper fingers flew to her mouth and the most glorious laugh he had ever heard bubbled forth. Her eyes sparkled and she looked more at ease in his company than he had ever seen. He could not help a pleased chuckle of his own. He had made her laugh! By Jove, this was going to work!

Margaret quieted, still smiling. "Mrs Thornton is not a woman I would like to annoy. I imagine you do not often dare to do so!"

He shook his head. "Not if I wish for anything but porridge for dinner, Miss Hale."

Margaret laughed lightly again- not as freely as before, but neither did she hide that beautiful smile behind her fingers. He gazed on in rapt adoration. Mission of mercy though this might be, it would surely be the most rewarding labour of his life.

Margaret glanced down and cleared her throat gently, composing herself. "I am sure my father thanks you, Mr Thornton."

He drew a long, satisfied breath. "Certainly he is most welcome, Miss Hale. I am afraid I must get back to the mill."

"Oh, yes, of course. It was good of you to call." They exchanged real smiles once more- smiles of camaraderie which warmed the cheeks and touched the eyes. Perhaps the spell of awkwardness between them had at last been broken.

Thornton started for the door, but Margaret's hesitant voice stopped him just before he reached it. "Sir... if I may...." He turned back, blue eyes twinkling, and watched her open a small drawer in the little entry table. She drew out a pair of thick leather gloves which struck him at once as agonizingly familiar.

Biting her lip, she came forward, her fingers smoothing over the gloves. "You left these here once," she murmured softly, extending them within his reach. "I am afraid I... forgot to return them."

He blinked several times, his euphoria crashing down. He took them from her hand and dropped his gaze. "Thank you, Miss Hale. I would not have had you go out of your way..." his mouth tugged into a vulnerable, sorrowful expression. "I believe you had cares enough at the time. I ought not to have troubled you."

His eyes still down, he stroked the rich leather, then looked curiously back up to her. "Have these been oiled? As I recall, I had been out in a rainstorm only the evening before... the... the riots, you remember." His voice was low and miserable.

Margaret was nodding, her eyes too still on the gloves. "They were stiff... it was no trouble, my father's gloves required the same treatment."

He took a significant step closer to her, forcing her to tip her head up. He gazed long into those brilliant eyes, softened now with humility. "Thank you, Miss Hale. I have missed these gloves." How he longed to say more! The only expressions he possessed were those of the heart and not the tongue. He could only hope she could read his contrition, his gratitude, and his joy at reconciliation.

Margaret's lashes fluttered and her lips quivered once more into a tender smile. "You are welcome, Mr Thornton." There was a shift in her posture, and then her hand was extended to him- not palm down, in the fashion of fine ladies, but forward and strong, as he was accustomed to greeting his equals.

He took it with a crooked grin, marveling at the strength in her slim fingers. He grasped her hand as long as he dared, still holding her steady gaze. "Good day then, Miss Hale," he spoke huskily. She dipped her head graciously in reply as he released her hand.

Fearing what he might say or do if he stayed longer, he reached immediately for the door and closed it behind himself. He did not see the door crack open again as he descended the steps, nor did he sense the watchful eyes which followed him as he strode briskly up the street.

~

On Friday, Margaret returned Miss Hamilton's call. She stood before the ornate front door, reflecting that this was the first Milton house she had seen which truly aspired to aesthetics as well as function. Her father believed the family to be quite well-to-do, and it appeared he was correct.

Tilting her head, she surveyed the elaborate stonework at the entry. She could not help comparing it to the stark utilitarian façade of the first fine Milton home she had visited. *Now why,* she asked herself, *can I not go even to a new place without thinking of Mr Thornton?* She put the thoughts roughly out of her mind as she lifted the knocker.

A liveried butler led her to the parlour, where Genevieve and her mother sat with their needlework. "Miss Hale, I am so glad you could come!" Genevieve rose to greet her, then offered her a seat. Mrs Hamilton inclined her head in greeting, but a note brought by the butler only a moment later called her away.

Genevieve seemed relieved to have her guest all to herself. She seated herself a little closer. "I was just saying to Mama how I hoped you would be able to come to dinner next week. Will your father be well enough, do you think?"

Margaret accepted a cup of tea from the maid with a smile, then turned to her hostess. "Yes, that was part of the reason for my call. I hope it is not too late to accept your invitation?"

"Not at all, to be sure! Oh, I do hope you will enjoy it. Mama has brought in a famous violinist from London to entertain us after dinner. I do so love music, and Rupert had heard this one play before, so it was his idea. Of course we shall open the piano afterward. Do you play, Miss Hale?"

"I am afraid not well. It has been some while since I have even sat at an instrument."

"Oh, you must not let that stop you! Surely you had a master in London, did you not?"

"Yes, of course," Margaret admitted. "I was a marginal student, though at least I took more pleasure in playing than in dancing. However, I am quite out of practice. The last time I played was well over a year ago at my cousin's wedding. I should hate to disappoint your guests with my very uninspiring performance!"

"Oh, pish posh, Miss Hale. I am sure nothing you could do would disappoint! But there, you promised you would tell me something of Hampshire. Is it much warmer there in the winter, Miss Hale?"

"Warmer, yes, but the country has its own unique challenges," Margaret smiled, reminiscing. "The roads are often impassable when it has rained much, but the spring roses are quite enough reward for putting up with the soggy terrain."

"It is decided, then! In the spring, you and I shall take a tour. Would you be my guide, Miss Hale?"

Margaret winced, wishing to accept with alacrity but knowing that her reality might make it impossible. "I shall try, Miss Hamilton," she promised.

"Oh, do not let us go on so. May we not simply call one another Margaret and Genevieve?"

They continued on amicably for a quarter of an hour before Margaret began to feel it the proper time to take her leave. As she was beginning to rise, another caller was announced. Genevieve seemed greatly pleased at the new arrival, and Margaret stepped back slightly.

A stunning blonde beauty was ushered into the room. She extended her arms jubilantly. "Gen, darling! I heard you had come back, and I had to see for myself. How did you find Paris?" The pair exchanged school girl greetings and Margaret felt herself edged out.

"Emmeline! I heard of your wedding. You beast, you ought to have waited for me to come back! I did so have my heart set on being a bridesmaid, you know."

"Yes, well, Randall simply *would* not wait, and Italy was completely marvelous, darling." Emmeline extended a hand to pull at her gloves and began to search for a seat when she finally noticed Margaret. "Oh! I did not know you already had company. I do not believe I have had the pleasure, Miss...?"

"Do you not know one another? Oh, how dreadful of me! Emmeline-Draper, fancy that, darling! This is my new friend Margaret Hale." Genevieve gestured for Margaret to come forward, and the two exchanged courtesies.

"Margaret Hale..." Emmeline tilted her head slightly. "Are you the same Miss Hale who is acquainted with Fanny Thornton? I believe she has mentioned you once or twice."

"Why, it was she who introduced us, is that not right, Margaret?" Genevieve put in.

"Yes, indeed," Margaret agreed. "I am very honoured to meet you, Mrs Draper. May I congratulate you on your marriage?"

Emmeline smiled slowly. "Thank you. It is a pleasure to make your acquaintance, Miss Hale."

Genevieve put her hand to Margaret's arm. "Margaret, dear, do you remember the charity I spoke to you of? The founder I wished to introduce you to is none other than Randall Draper, Emmeline's new husband! Is that not a happy coincidence?"

Margaret turned back to the blonde woman, eyes wide with appreciation. "It is! Tell me, Mrs Draper, is there any capacity in which my services might be useful? I have few enough skills to offer, but they are at your disposal. I should like to do what I can for those less fortunate."

Emmeline's brows rose in interest. "I shall speak to my husband, Miss Hale. Certainly something can be found for one of your talents."

"I would be most grateful, Mrs Draper." She shifted her gaze again to Genevieve. "Thank you for your hospitality. Until Monday evening, then?" She bade her farewells and left the others to their reunion.

Margaret departed the house with as much, if not more hope than she had brought to it. Perhaps she had made another new friend! Most assuredly, the other woman's connection to such a worthy cause raised Margaret's esteem for her. A spring in her step and a song in her heart, she made her merry way home, completely ignoring the rain.

~

Behind the closed doors Margaret had left, the pair of old school friends were comparing notes about their recent travels on the continent. "Italy," insisted the new Mrs Draper, "is the only place worth visiting again."

"Oh, but France was lovely," maintained the other. "We went for a pleasure cruise to Italy last August, but it was so hot, darling!"

"Not at all! Perhaps you were there at the wrong time of the year. I have already informed Randall that I shall insist upon him taking me there for a tour each winter. He can afford it, you know," she leaned forward confidentially.

"Oh, is he really so well-to-do?" Genevieve gushed in a whisper. "I did not know!"

Emmeline lifted her ivory shoulders. "Well enough, though not as well as others. I hear," she leveled a teasing gaze at her companion, "that you have one such in the palm of your hand."

"I cannot possibly know what you mean," Genevieve tossed her head airily, but with a sly smile.

"Oh, come, darling, you cannot suddenly have developed such a fond intimacy with Fanny Thornton! She was always such a silly thing. Why, do you remember how we used to call her?"

"'Fanny the Fidget!'" Genevieve laughed. "I had forgotten about that! She is just the same as ever, you know. Her brother, however, is quite a different story. I have always thought so, you know, but until now I was far too young to take his notice."

"Buona fortuna, darling. He never leaves the mill. I tried, I confess, but I believe the man is both blind and deaf."

"John Thornton blind! Far from it. You only have to give him something worth looking at." Genevieve pursed her lips and cocked a saucy eyebrow at her friend, pulling her shoulders back suggestively.

"Oh!" laughed Emmeline. "That old trick! Well, my very best wishes to you darling. Now, tell me about this Margaret Hale. How well do you know her?"

"Not well. She is a modest little thing, and is slow to open up. Nevertheless, she is a pleasing companion after spending so much time with Fanny Thornton! At least she has better things to talk about than asking after silly old Rupert all of the time."

Emmeline lifted a brow. "Fanny has little enough liking for her. Did you hear what happened during those dreadful riots a few months back?"

"No," Genevieve shook her head innocently. "Oh, do tell me, I can see you know something juicy!"

"Well! It seems your little Miss Hale is not *always* modest. Why, she absolutely flung herself at John Thornton! Right on the front steps of the house! Fanny said that her maid saw the whole thing, and they cannot believe she is not ruined. He refused to marry her, of course, and she has been withdrawn from society ever since."

Genevieve's nose wrinkled in thought. "That does not sound right. Margaret is far too quiet and refined to do such a thing, and what is more, she is from old gentility. You know how they look down on our Milton men! I am sure she never looked at him twice. No, you must be quite wrong!"

"Well, if I am, you ought to ask about that head wound she received. They had to have the doctor! Perhaps she fancied she was saving that big, strong man from the rioters. The very idea!"

"Head wound? That cannot be. Why, she is perfectly in her right mind. Fanny must be imagining things- she always did, you know. Besides, Margaret lost her mother nearly three months ago, so at that moment Mrs Hale must have been quite the invalid. I cannot believe she would publically run after a man with her mother sick at home."

"Think what you may, but Fanny says that Margaret Hale has had her cap set for John Thornton for well over a year. And who can blame, her, eh, darling? Oh, do not worry, for you will have far better luck. You have a much prettier face and a far more attractive bank account," she winked.

"Oh, that is not enough to turn the head of a man like John Thornton, else another would have succeeded already! No, Emmeline, I believe he might fancy a woman of some cleverness. A man wants for interesting company, after all. He is rather the quiet sort, I think, preferring his own hearth fire to the gentlemen's club- or so Rupert says."

"Well, darling, in that case, you must do what you can to inspire the man's imagination. I can think of many worse fates than a quiet evening at home with John Thornton!"

Genevieve laughed loudly. "I nearly forgot that you are a married woman now! Oh, you are too wicked, Emmeline. Why, I could not possibly have thought such things!" she fluttered her lashes.

"Spare me, darling. Now, then, let me give you some advice...."

Chapter Ten

The afternoon of Sunday that week found Thornton again loitering restlessly in his own drawing room. He had gotten out of the habit of late, and had resolved once again to spend these few hours each week keeping his mother company. Much as he tried to enjoy the time of rest, it chafed.

Mrs Thornton set strict rules for herself on Sundays. The house was quiet, dinners were served cold, and if she sewed at all, it was only from her charity basket. She was glad of John's company, but it was hardly restful this day. She arched a brow over her squared glasses as she finished off another plain stocking. "John, you are going to wear a path in my carpet."

Thornton paused, realizing that he had, in fact, been pacing before the fire. With an abashed little smile, he took the seat nearest her. "Pardon me, Mother."

She silently picked up another stocking, watching him out of the corner of her eye. He shifted constantly, as though it gave him physical pain to remain so long at rest. Taking a wild guess at what might be troubling him, she murmured, "Fanny ought to be back within the half hour. I expect she will invite Mr and Miss Hamilton to take some refreshment before they leave us."

Thornton stilled, but only momentarily.

"You spoke rather harshly of her the other day, John," his mother chastised.

"Did I? I do not remember doing so."

"I find nothing immodest in her manner."

"Hmm? Oh, yes, that." He made no other response, still gazing at the fire.

Mrs Thornton frowned. "Perhaps she was a little forward in her attentions to you, but when you are so oblivious...."

"It is never attractive when a woman tries too hard, Mother. However, it was nothing very serious." He propped his chin on his fingers and resumed staring at the fire.

Mrs Thornton sighed and set down her sewing. "She was only trying to pay you her highest compliments, John. Perhaps that is the fashion on the Continent now." She shook her head in faint annoyance over the frivolities of youth.

When her son made no reply, she went on. "Come now, John, if you are not going to pursue the young lady, you must make your intentions known. She is quite willing to impress you, but you will cause her to disgrace herself if you do not put some stop to it."

He turned to face her, eyes narrowed. "I was not aware that I had offered her any encouragement."

"Not encouraged her! She hangs upon your every word, John, and you assured her only the other day that you were eager to attend her party and see her in all of her finery."

"I meant only to be polite! Surely she could have read no more into my words."

"I assure you she did. Your words were quite encouraging enough, for she seemed already taken with you from the beginning. I think the young lady shows remarkably good taste," she sniffed proudly.

"Mother," he pinched the bridge of his nose, "aside from Miss Hamilton's own brother, I am the only single man of means in Milton who still has both his own hair and his own teeth."

His mother snorted dismissively. "You do yourself too little credit, John. And you are not quite the only man! What of Watson? He is only five years your senior."

"You have never seen him without his hat on, perhaps."

"And that Draper fellow, the one recently settled here from Scarborough!"

"Forty-five if he is a day, and, lest we forget again, recently married- for the second time, if I remember correctly."

Her face froze, then she broke into a reluctant chuckle. "Perhaps you are right, but my point was, Miss Hamilton is not without her options. Why, her father could send her anywhere to find a husband, but she seems to have settled on you, John. Tell me, what do you think of her?"

"I have not had time to think of her, Mother. I am a great deal more concerned with what her father thinks of me- or rather, of the mill."

"He has given you no indication of his intentions?"

"Not as yet. I respect that; it means he is a cautious fellow and not inclined to rash investments. However, I must know something soon, for it will determine the orders I bid, the machinery I choose to repair or replace, and whether I ought to hire on more hands in preparation for next summer's orders."

"Perhaps," murmured the sage Mrs Thornton, "Mr Hamilton would be more inclined to invest with a son-in-law."

"That is the furthest thing from my mind, Mother. I could never dishonour any woman, to say nothing of shaming myself, by marrying only for business advantage."

"I do not attack your nobility, John," his mother stopped her sewing again to smile kindly at him. "I know you are not so vulgar, though others may be. However, if the lady is suitable and willing to be courted, you could do far worse."

"And what of love, Mother?"

She raised a brow. "I imagine it would come, if given the chance."

He leaned forward in his chair, his voice low and intense. "I have tasted it once, Mother- you know I have! I cannot pretend otherwise, and I cannot manufacture it where it does not exist."

This brought an immediate scowl to his mother's face. "I do not call it love to suffer as you have, John. But there, to spare you, I shall say no more on that subject."

He closed his eyes and rested his head back against his chair. His thoughts he kept to himself, but his mother could easily guess them. Silence reigned for several minutes. To the relief of one and the chagrin of the other, two merry feminine voices and one cheerful male voice at last sounded in the entryway.

Thornton groaned and rose. "Excuse me, Mother, I am rather behind in my Greek. I will be in my study." He strode quickly to a side door and escaped the room before their company could find him.

~

"Mrs Thornton," Rupert Hamilton saluted the lady of the house upon his entry. "It is a pleasure!"

The matron inclined her head with all dignity. "Good afternoon, Mr Hamilton. I trust your mother is well?"

"Quite, Madam. She is all aflutter planning tomorrow night's dinner- although I suppose it is impolite for me to say as much. She is very much looking forward to having your family. I say," he looked round the room curiously, "Is Mr Thornton about?"

"He had other matters to attend," supplied the lady cautiously.

"Even on a Sunday! That's the good Milton spirit for you, my dear Gen. We were hoping to see the old chap!"

Fanny, who had drawn aside with Genevieve, sighed rather too loudly. "John is always working. Never a thought for anything important!"

"Surely, Fanny, his work must take precedence," Genevieve soothed. "Mr Thornton would not be the man he is if he shirked his duties."

"You speak very sensibly, Miss Hamilton," Mrs Thornton dipped her head in respect.

"Work is well and good," Rupert insisted, "but a man has to rest once in a while. Life has its pleasures to be sought out as well."

"My son finds great satisfaction in his work," Mrs Thornton returned proudly, and perhaps a little stiffly. "A man does not achieve what he has by 'seeking his pleasures,' as you say."

"You are correct, of course," Rupert acknowledged. "I only meant that surely, in his stage of life, he has earned the right to at least a little leisure. Rest, you know, can restore a man's constitution just as hard work serves to build it."

Mrs Thornton opened her mouth to reply that a noble man of good character could not find it within himself to rest when there was still much to set right, but she was interrupted by a gentle laugh from Genevieve Hamilton.

"You will have to forgive my brother, Mrs Thornton. His thinking has perhaps been a little too shaped by his years in London. We have had many good, long debates since returning home to Milton! I am sure Mrs Thornton could not be interested in our family discussions, Rupert."

Shortly after this, Jane arrived with some refreshments for the guests. Rupert and Fanny retired to one end of the drawing room, while Genevieve chose a seat near Mrs Thornton. "I have been very glad," the young lady offered, "to renew our acquaintance, Mrs Thornton. I had little opportunity to know you well before I left for the Continent."

"You and Fanny were still in school at that time," Mrs Thornton replied. "I remember only brief encounters, Miss Hamilton."

Genevieve smiled. "That is something I should like to change in the future, Mrs Thornton. I think very highly of your entire family."

Hannah pursed her lips. "My son is a remarkable man," she suggested, watching the young lady carefully.

"Indeed," Genevieve agreed. "He is a force to be reckoned with, as my father would say!"

"I wonder what you can mean by that. He is no monster, Miss Hamilton."

"Of course not! Mr Thornton is a perfect gentleman, but surely, Mrs Thornton, you must have noted that he commands the attention and respect of his peers. He enters a room and all eyes turn his way."

"A position he has earned, Miss Hamilton, through diligence and careful management of his own affairs."

"Precisely," the younger lady agreed. "I do not mean to imply that Mr Thornton craves honour, only that it is given him whether he wishes it or not."

Mrs Thornton's eyes narrowed slightly. "You have spent much time observing my son, I see."

"One does not live in Milton very long without doing so," Genevieve replied modestly. "Perhaps I might say that even as a schoolgirl, I was fascinated by my dear friend's older brother. His rise to the ranks of Milton's elite businessmen is truly inspiring, Mrs Thornton. You must be very proud."

"Indeed, I am." Mrs Thornton signaled an end to the conversation by lifting her cup. Once before, another young lady had sat in that exact seat and laughed at the very notion of putting herself in the way of the mother so that she might attract the notice of the son. As offended as she had been by the slight, Mrs Thornton could not quite find satisfaction in this reversal of that circumstance.

At least, thought she in mild annoyance, *Margaret Hale dealt with me openly.* Miss Hamilton's flattery was gratifying, but she could have preferred a more artless admission of the young lady's designs. Manipulation cloaked as modesty wore rather quickly.

~

That same afternoon, Margaret and Mr Hale were sitting with the Higgins family. Higgins had procured a sheet of paper and a pencil, and was trying to describe to his very interested guest the principles of the loom.

On the other side of the house, Margaret had nestled comfortably into a chair, surrounded by the children. She had just finished reading them the story of Daniel, and was greatly amused at the open mouths and rounded eyes reflecting all round her. Breathless, childish questions followed, and Margaret could not help laughing at their sweet innocence. What delight they brought her!

After a while, Jenny shyly approached, holding out another book and smothering a bashful grin. "What have you there, Jenny?" she asked.

The little girl wordlessly twirled her hands in her threadbare skirt, smiling at the floor.

Margaret lifted the book and read the title with interest. "A primer? Is this yours, Jenny?"

The girl bobbed her head with a pleased blush. "The gen'lman brough' it," she whispered for Margaret's ears alone. "'Tis all me own, I dinna 'ave to share wi' Danny."

"Oh, I see! Does this mean that you will be starting school soon, Miss Boucher?" Margaret spoke with a highly dignified inflection, causing the girl to puff in pride.

"Mr Nich'las says I can start t'morrow, Miss Marg'et!" The girl clasped her hands before her and rocked in pleasure. "I can already read the first two pages!"

"That is wonderful news! Why, our lessons must have paid off," Margaret laughed. "I am certain you will make an exceptional student. You will work very hard, will you not? Perhaps soon you will be reading all of the stories to us," she winked. She handed the book back and the girl giggled, then scampered back to her little sleeping pallet with it.

Margaret turned and found Nicholas, across the room, watching them with a grin. "That friend o' yo'rn, Miss Marg'et, 'e's a great 'un wi' the childer."

"Friend of mine? Which do you mean?"

"Th'ould bulldog 'imself. 'E's taken an int'rest in seein' to their schoolin'. Came yest'rd'y to 'ear Danny read. The lass," he jerked his head in Jenny's direction, "she's sore taken with'im."

Margaret felt a broad smile spreading over her face. Mr Thornton paying visits to the Boucher children? She would have to thank him. "I am so pleased to hear it! I wonder what could have brought that about?"

Nicholas shrugged. "Says 'e likes the childer, and isn'a often 'e can sit with'em. 'E's not a' bad, Miss Marg'et. Even 'ad some idea 'bout a kitchen a' the mill. T'would never work, but me and the lads, we talked it o'er some, 'ad some ideas."

"In other words," Margaret smiled knowingly, "you like his idea, but you do not want him to be the one to see it carried out."

Higgins' bristling cheeks plumped into a grin. "Mr 'Ale, sir, you 'ave a right clever lass 'ere."

Chapter Eleven

The evening of the dinner party came at last. On his arrival, Thornton had quickly found Watson and Hamper, and it had seemed safe to cloister himself with them. Their conversation would demand very little of his actual attention and at the same time deter any unwanted feminine company.

He tugged uncomfortably at the wider cravat he had worn this evening and surveyed the room. Fanny had instantly taken up with a foursome of other young ladies at the far end of the house. One was the very Miss Hamilton who had him so flustered.

He watched discreetly and from a safe distance. Genevieve Hamilton had a fine figure- slim in all of the right places, generous in others. She carried herself with an easy grace, and the rich wine-coloured gown she had chosen lent warmth to her lively features. There could be no argument that she was a very beautiful woman. Clever enough, too, he remembered. He had determined to spend much time this evening observing her, to decide if his mother were correct and if his own traitorous feelings were truly leading him astray.

It was possible- no, probable- that a marriage into the Hamilton family would secure not only the immediate survival of the mill, but its long-term future. Indeed, that was only the beginning! Stuart Hamilton would one day pass the reins of his little empire to his pampered son and coddled daughter, neither of whom had a steady enough hand for such an undertaking. No doubt, whomever Genevieve chose as her husband would truly end up as the power behind the accounts.

He tried to imagine marriage to her. His face pinched in revulsion. It felt unfaithful, somehow, to even consider the notion when his heart was already sworn to another- the one who would not have him. He closed his eyes and swallowed. His mother was right. He had to make some effort. Perhaps his stubborn heart was truly doing him a disservice.

He made up his mind to talk to her, and had only just excused himself to make his way across the room when he saw her break off from her companions. Another guest had arrived. As she went to greet the newcomer, Thornton followed her movement and froze, his face alight.

Suddenly, there was only one woman in the room, and she was not Genevieve Hamilton.

~

Margaret forced herself not to clutch her father's arm nervously as they entered the large antechamber. *Silly,* she chided herself, *this house is no grander than any I have known in London, and the family of considerably less standing than some of Aunt Shaw's friends!* She was taught better than to cower before finery. She glanced worriedly at her father, but his expression so far was open and cheerful, with no symptom of distress or fatigue.

At the entrance, she once again met Mrs Hamilton and was introduced to her husband. Margaret spared him little attention, though her father remained some minutes getting reacquainted with his host. Margaret arched up to her full height, searching the room for any familiar faces. She found Genevieve and caught her eye.

"Margaret, darling, I am so pleased you could come!" Genevieve wove through the swirl of guests and made her way to Margaret's side.

"No more than I," she took her friend's hand. "I am honoured by your invitation."

"Oh, Margaret, you will not believe- why we are all talking about it! Only look at old Mrs Smith's headpiece. It looks like a peacock landed in a nest!"

Margaret's gaze followed Genevieve's indication and saw, indeed, a truly memorable work of art adorning the woman's hair. Her eyebrows rose. "I am sure it took a great deal of trouble to arrange."

"Ah, I knew you would find some tactful comment! You are too good, Margaret. Oh, but come, let me introduce you around. Let me see- oh! Mr Thornton, good evening!" Genevieve quickly lifted her hand for him to take, and this time she was not disappointed.

Margaret's wide eyes flew to his face. How foolish of her not to have expected him to be in attendance! It was easier now to speak with him in private, or if she were prepared, but an unexpected meeting in public was a great deal more than she had anticipated. She took a deep breath, calming herself. Who was she to be so rattled?

"Good evening, Miss Hamilton," he returned the greeting smoothly, but his attention moved to Margaret even as he withdrew his hand from Genevieve.

Extending it in his customary handshake to Margaret, his voice carefully measured, he smiled. "Good evening, Miss Hale." Before he could stop it, his gaze swept from her strong, delicate arms to her bare, sculptured shoulders, held square and proud, and brushed lightly over her exposed décolletage before returning to her face. It was a treat to again see her so attired.

Margaret caught her breath at his warm touch. The way he was looking at her... it was like his own dinner party all over again. She forced herself to speak, but her voice trembled slightly. "Good evening, Mr Thornton. How does your mother this evening?"

"Very well, Miss Hale. I believe she is just through the next room." He stopped short of the quip he had been about to make regarding his mother's intentions to keep a close eye on Fanny. Margaret might, perhaps, have found it amusing. He would admit to a nearly insatiable desire to see her laugh again, but he had to remind himself that he was not alone with her.

Genevieve, watchful now, observed the shy smiles and tense greetings the pair exchanged with a twinge of displeasure. Goodness, they were both nearly blushing! She had looked for such a reaction from Margaret, but not from Mr Thornton himself. Clearly Emmeline was right, that there was, or had been, something between them. A diversion was certainly in order.

"Oh, look, Margaret, just over there!" She placed a hand on her friend's arm. "That is Mr Draper, the gentleman you wished to meet. You will excuse us, will you not, Mr Thornton? Come, let me- oh! Mother, what is it?"

Mrs Hamilton, looking greatly disturbed, approached and leaned near to her daughter with low words. The others watched her face change to a look of annoyance.

Genevieve at length turned back to them, after a brief struggle to compose her features. "I beg you would excuse me, there is a matter my mother in which my mother begs my assistance." She smiled at Margaret and dipped gracefully to Thornton as she took her leave.

Thornton was elated to have Margaret all to himself for the moment. Never before had it required his concerted efforts not to stare at a woman, but when Margaret Hale was at his side, he could not drink in her presence enough. Everything from her rich, heavy coils of shining dark hair, framing delicately around her angelic face, to the form-fitting white gown he remembered so well... ah, here was the Creator's masterpiece. Except... yes, except that she was not *quite* perfect. He must remember that, and not make a fool of himself again!

He led her to the sideboard. "May I help you to a drink before dinner, Miss Hale?"

Margaret glanced hesitantly over her shoulder before answering.

"Your father is still talking to Mr Hamilton," he supplied. "I believe he has already seen us and will find us again shortly."

She looked back in mild surprise. "Of course. Thank you," she said as she accepted the drink he offered. She took a hurried sip, for no other reason than to break his intense eye contact.

"I was pleased to discover that you and your father were in attendance this evening," he continued lightly. "It is always agreeable to find good friends in such a gathering, is it not?"

Her eyes darted back to his strangely. She swallowed hard and lowered her glass. "It is, indeed, Mr Thornton."

"I did not realize that you were such intimates with Miss Hamilton."

"I have only just become acquainted with her. I believe we shall come to be very good friends."

"Do you? I would not have imagined her to your taste," he mused thoughtlessly.

"I beg your pardon!" she set her glass down a little more roughly than she had intended. "What business is it of yours?"

"None at all, Miss Hale," he backpedaled quickly. "Perhaps I am mistaken in the sort of company you prefer."

"What can possibly make you think I would not be pleased to know an educated, well-traveled, and intelligent lady of nearly my own age?"

"It is not the peripherals, but the particulars I think of. Her disposition strikes me as quite different from your own."

Margaret was truly becoming irritated now. "If you know her so well, then, do enlighten me! I am curious about the nature of your relationship with the lady, Mr Thornton." She tipped her chin up and stared him down.

His eyes widened and he wished he could tug at his collar again. "I can claim no such intimacy as you presume, Miss Hale. My opinion is merely based on observing you both. I make it my business to learn characters quickly."

She cocked a brow. "And have you never been mistaken, Mr Thornton?"

He gulped and set his drink down to purchase him a second. "I have, Miss Hale," he murmured quietly. He raised his eyes again to hers. "I hope I have in some measure made amends for my wrong assumptions."

Her expression softened. She inclined her head gently, allowing him the point without a verbal concession. Thornton reclaimed his drink and began swirling it as a distraction, and soon Margaret did likewise. They stood uncomfortably for a moment, looking anywhere but at each other.

Margaret was about to make her excuse when he spoke again. "Did Miss Hamilton intend to introduce you to Mr Draper?"

She looked up in surprise. "Yes, he apparently operates some sort of a charity. I asked to learn more of it."

He pressed his lips tightly together, looking back at his drink.

Margaret lifted that delicate brow again. "You do not approve of Mr Draper," she observed.

"I think he could do better with his time," he answered in a neutral tone.

"Better than helping his fellow man?" she challenged.

He looked down without speaking for a moment. At length, he replied, "There are charitable organizations which are useful, and those which are not, Miss Hale. I would not like to think of you wasting all of your worthy intentions."

"Something is better than nothing," she insisted. She glared blankly across the room, seeking to control her tongue. "You may take books to one family, Mr Thornton, but what of the others?"

He turned sharply in mute surprise.

"It was good of you," she continued more gently, "but there is so much more to be done. I must applaud Mr Draper's efforts, even if they yet bear little fruit."

His face darkened. "An organization such as that is no better than the man at the head. You gain little by condescension and compromise."

Margaret felt a swell of fury. "You speak so of another gentleman! You, who have done so little yourself! How do you dare, sir?"

Little! He bristled. "I only try to warn you, Miss Hale! Do you presume to have never been deceived or misled?" He leveled a significant gaze.

She narrowed her eyes and stepped nearer. "*Never*, sir. I will thank you to allow me to depend upon my own judgement!"

He rolled his eyes and turned away in disgust. She, who had so many times proven herself wise and mature beyond her years, could be so naive! She seemed to have a terrible knack for trusting the wrong people.

A laugh from another corner of the room brought him the sudden realization that they had once again been standing toe to toe in a heated debate. Their voices might be low, but all of the room could see if they cared to. "Let us speak of this another time, Miss Hale. I do not wish to argue with you at such a gathering as this."

She glared at him. "You are correct, sir. It is so much more pleasant to argue in privacy." She handed him her drink, reclaimed her elegant bearing, and swept away.

His shoulders sagged and he chewed his lower lip in frustration. There, he had gone and done it again! He had only intended to help, but Margaret was furious with him. Blasted was any hope of asking to accompany her at dinner. He watched in helpless vexation as Genevieve Hamilton and Margaret once again found each other. A moment later, he saw Genevieve introduce her to Rupert Hamilton, who was making his first appearance of the evening. This did little to improve his mood.

"Oh, there you are, John!"

He tore his attention from the white gown across the room. "Good evening, Mr Hale," he greeted with as much enthusiasm as he could summon.

"I thought I saw Margaret with you. I expect she must be mingling." The old man glanced about, searching for his daughter.

Thornton indicated in the direction which still held his interest. "She is with Miss Hamilton."

"Ah, of course. Margaret seems very taken with her. It was very thoughtful of her to have invited us this evening." He searched the mass of young people until he found his daughter.

"What a lovely group of young ladies! I declare, John, it does give a man pleasure to see it," Mr Hale beamed in satisfaction.

Thornton sighed and looked away for good. "Indeed, it does."

~

Rupert Hamilton instantly attached himself to Margaret. He made it his sworn purpose to make the sophisticated and thoughtful Miss Hale laugh as many times as he could that evening. So far, he was up to four.

"...And so Williams bet the sorrel, though his jockey swore the horse was lame, but wouldn't you know it, Miss Hale, the nag lagged in the backstretch but caught them just at the wire and won! Jackson- you remember, my friend who lost his shirt- he says old Williams paid them off, but I said he could not possibly have afforded to, after allowing his wife to redecorate!" Rupert's little audience burst into gales of laughter, many of them well acquainted with tales of Rupert's extravagant friends from London.

Margaret chuckled softly, more at Rupert Hamilton's expressive storytelling than his actual tale. It troubled her that he would be so coarse as to laugh at the expense of his friend's marital harmony, but that was

the way with some of Edith's friends too. She had convinced herself that
while it might be in poor taste, it did little enough harm.

"Miss Hale, you are very quiet," Rupert boldly claimed her hand and
linked it through his arm, leading her a little away from his audience. "I
realize I must not be very interesting after all of the dreadful matters you
people in Milton have had to suffer of late."

She smiled. "No, I find your tales amusing, sir."

"Ah," he guessed, "you do not think I can be serious. I see it! Come,
Miss Hale, try me. What shall we speak of next?"

"What can you tell me of Mr Draper over there?" She flicked her gaze
across the room to a middle-aged man who appeared engrossed in
conversation with Mr Smith.

"Draper! Oh, he's a brick. Solid chap, Miss Hale. Oh, of course, Gen
told me you met his wife Emma! She's a doll, is she not, Miss Hale? Did
you want to meet him?"

"Very much."

"Easily done." He walked her across the room.

As they passed by, Fanny Thornton could hardly keep from glaring
daggers in Margaret's direction. While Rupert Hamilton's attention had
been distracted, that oaf James Watson had caught her alone. She'd had
no choice but to agree to be his dinner companion. She pouted into her
drink. This was not how she had imagined the evening turning out.

"Such a shame, darling," Genevieve Hamilton murmured as she sidled
close.

"I simply *do not* understand what he could see in her," Fanny
grumbled.

"Oh, you know Rupert! He is only playing the gallant because she is a
new acquaintance. You've nothing to worry about, for I declare he will be
back in your drawing room within the week."

Fanny, somewhat encouraged, tilted her head with a little "Hmmf." She
glanced about as though she were about to share a great secret, but her
voice could be clearly heard. "Do you know, that is the very same gown she
wore at our house months ago! She has done something at the neckline
and I think that is new lace about the bodice, but I declare it is the very
one. Can you believe it?"

Genevieve tipped her shoulders and smiled. "I expect she must have to
make do. What a mercy that we do not have such a difficulty! I always feel I
look my best in something fresh and new, do not you?"

Fanny frowned in Margaret's direction. "Your brother finds the old one
interesting enough."

"As does yours," Genevieve mused.

"John! Not at all! Why, anyone could see earlier that they can hardly
stand to talk to one another."

"Is that what it was?" Genevieve wondered.

"Believe me, he is quite taken with you. I know him well, you know. He
would never marry Margaret Hale! She is always so grave. I always feel as if
she is looking down on me. Me! I do not care for a lady who puts on airs,"
she sniffed.

"And what are you two talking about?" Emmeline Draper sashayed
over to them, looking terribly sultry in her new green gown. Neither had to
answer before she picked upon the cold looks Fanny was sending across

the room. "Ah, I see my husband has met your friend. I am sure he will find some pamphlets for her to distribute or something."

Fanny snickered. "Did you see her shaking hands with all of the men like a tradesman? I think she tries a little too hard to fit in in the North."

Emmeline pursed her lips. "Your brother was the one who moved first, I saw. There you have it, Gen. The gentlemen treat her like one of their mates from the club, not a lady."

"Absolutely," Fanny agreed with a definitive jerk of her head. "They will find her tiresome soon enough."

Emmeline tipped her chin up. "Mrs Hamper was just telling me that your Margaret Hale makes a habit of taking baskets to the strikers, and that she is even intimate with some of the Union leaders! I say, Fanny, what *does* Mr Thornton think of that?"

"Oh, he thinks her quite the fool, I assure you! There, did you see the looks they gave one another as he passed by her again just now? It is just as I said, they can scarcely stand in the same room without some quarrel."

"Well, darlings, I wish I could stay and chat," Genevieve grinned smugly. "However, the dinner bell will be rung soon, and I see a very lonely man over there who will need a companion."

Chapter Twelve

Margaret almost enjoyed the meal immensely. The young Mr Hamilton was excessively attentive, giving her a good many reasons to smile. Unfortunately, every time she looked up from her plate, the glowering presence across the table distracted her.

He looked for all purposes to be intently engaged in conversations with everyone else, including Genevieve. The dark cloud he cast, however, was for her alone. Margaret sighed and looked instead to her father, who sat at her left. Mrs Thornton was just beyond him, and the cold gaze that woman flicked her way made it a less than desirable direction to turn her attention.

That left Rupert Hamilton as the only pleasant outlet for conversation. He had a penchant for turning from the heavier topics favoured by the man across the table, which suited Margaret well. The less John Thornton spoke, the less she was obliged to look in his direction. The more irritated he became at being cut off, however, the more regret she felt.

"London!" Rupert announced with a laugh. "That is where all of the future is, Miss Hale. These fellows," he raised a glass in the general direction of Thornton and Hamper, "they may be the gears, but the crank is in the hands of the fine ladies of Grosvenor Square. It is a wise gentleman, is it not, Miss Hale, who looks well to his business affairs so that his lady might be kept in comforts?"

"That is hardly a man's only worthy aspiration," put in Thornton's low voice.

Margaret's eyes shifted quickly in his direction, and he coldly met her gaze before she could look away.

"But it is the most important!" insisted Rupert. "Did not Socrates once write that it was better to live in the corner of a roof than with a, er, dissatisfied wife?"

"I believe that was Solomon," Margaret smiled. From the edge of her field of view, she saw Thornton scowl, his jaw set, as he turned back to Miss Hamilton.

"Someone wise, then." Rupert lifted his glass in a small salute. "I jest, of course, Miss Hale, but there is truth to it, you know. London drives the economy of the free world, and none have more power over the purse than the ladies. It is to their superior sensibilities that the purveyors of fine textiles must cater."

"Not entirely," Margaret corrected him. "Milton has made its name in the manufacture of steel as well as textiles. Many of my acquaintances in London do not find cotton a fashionable enough fabric for their tastes. It is a highly serviceable, as well as economical material, and I doubt not that its ready supply has done much to lower the price on my cousin's favorite linens." This was met with a small chuckle from her companion. "Cotton is a consequential product indeed," she continued, "but I do not think that market is driven exactly as you claim." She did not miss the quick glance her direction from across the table, but she ignored it.

"You do have a point, of course," he admitted, somewhat surprised at finding himself bested by a young lady with a logical turn of mind. "But let us talk of other things, Miss Hale. I tire of talk of business during dinner parties. Time enough during the day for that, I say. Now, Miss Hale, my sister tells me you spent much time in London. May I ask where?"

"My Aunt Shaw resides in Harley Street. I lived with her a great deal, and my cousin and I took lessons together as children."

His brows rose. "Shaw? Why, then, your cousin must be... let me see, what was the lady's name? Oh, that is it, Edith Lennox! Her brother-in-law, Henry and I were at University together."

Margaret felt her cheeks warm. "You know Henry Lennox?"

"Oh, quite well! He introduced me to his brother the Captain at the club. They invited me to dinner, just before his marriage- to your cousin, correct?"

"Y-yes," she admitted. Her forehead creased. She risked a quick glance across the table, but Thornton's attention was on Mr Smith. She spoke lowly, "Have you seen him lately? Henry Lennox, I mean- is he well?"

"Last month, I think it was. Yes, it must have been. I was having a party before I came back to Milton for good. Saw him in passing and tried to get him to join, but he claimed he was too busy. The fellow is all work, Miss Hale. A lot like some others I know," he jerked his head with a grin toward the others at the table. He looked to Margaret, expecting a sympathetic smile, but her face had turned thoughtful.

~

Thornton tried remembering half of what was said at dinner, but within minutes of the ladies parting from their company, he found all that he could remember was what he had overheard between Margaret and Rupert Hamilton. As a matter of fact, he realized, he was staring hard at the younger man this very minute.

He grimaced and turned to Mr Smith again, seated at his right. He would never make any headway toward building the business relationships he desired if he could not get his mind off Margaret Hale. Smith was busy shaking his head with the elder Hamilton over the dreadful reports of the battle at Balaclava.

"I told you," Smith repeated, "did I not? It was a disaster! Aberdeen is finished, that is what I am hearing. Are we now simply to stand by as the Tsar marches right through our lines?"

"They've stopped him up at Sevastopol," Hamilton objected. "They'll be set up for the winter there. More time, that's what our boys need. A good English soldier is worth four Slavs, eh, Thornton?"

"You would keep sending our boys up against that, with such incompetent leadership?" Smith interrupted before Thornton could respond.

"How else is Her Majesty supposed to keep the best Navy in the world?" Hamper laughed, looping his thumbs into the pockets of his waistcoat.

"Aye, now that's what it's all about!" agreed Watson, lighting a cigar. "The way I see it...."

Thornton sighed and rose from the table. The war dominated every conversation of late. He was, in truth, vitally interested in developments in the Baltic- not only as a businessman, but also as a fellow man. He could never imagine the brutality that young boys on both sides were living in every day. However, his nerves were already frayed this evening. He could little bear more of such useless talk between men wholly unconnected with the business.

He began to help himself to a drink from the sideboard, but thought better of it and took coffee instead. He had only just turned round again when Rupert Hamilton appeared at his side.

"Bleeding awful, that," the younger man nodded toward the others.

Thornton agreed with an inarticulate noise as he swallowed his hot coffee.

"I hear," Rupert added, pouring his own drink, "that shipping costs are up because of all that mess."

"Naturally," Thornton replied.

"Does that not cut rather substantially into your profits? I shouldn't wonder that everyone is worried."

"I think of those who suffer for the war, I have possibly the least to complain about."

Rupert lifted his glass. "Ever the gentleman, Thornton. I applaud you; it is refreshing to talk to a businessman who is not crying loudly about his losses."

Thornton merely gazed back with a raised brow.

Rupert cleared his throat and tried another subject. "I say, how well do you know Miss Hale?"

"Her father is a dear friend of mine," Thornton answered slowly. "He was sitting just opposite you."

"To be sure, I met the gentleman. It was the lady I inquired about. Surely you have become acquainted with her, if you know her father so well."

Thornton lifted his cup and drank long before responding. "Rather well," he said at last, "although we are not good friends."

"You don't say!" Rupert laughed. "I could see that. I was wondering if you could tell me any particulars about the lady."

"Perhaps you would do better to let Miss Hale speak for herself," Thornton started to turn away. "I doubt not that I would be mistaken about a great many points."

"You are very little help, my friend," Rupert stopped him. "Ah, I see, you are annoyed that I paid so little attention to your sister this evening!"

"Not at all. I do not make it my business to arrange suitors for my sister."

"For good reason," Rupert answered smoothly. "Miss Thornton is a fine young woman, and worthy of any man's regard."

"But not yours?" Thornton tested.

"Well, Thornton... you know, a man likes to look about himself before settling. If he sees a pretty face, why should he not please himself by taking a second look?"

Thornton narrowed his eyes dangerously. "I will warn you only once, Rupert. My sister does not exist for your amusement, and neither does Miss Hale!"

Rupert drew back slightly, hands held before him. "Now, see here, Thornton! I have done nothing out of line, and have given neither any reason for disappointment. I ought to be saying as much to you in defence of my own sister, but I let Gen handle her own affairs! If she has her mind set on you when she could do better elsewhere, why, that is her concern, but...."

Thornton set his empty cup down with a bang. "The conversation is over, Hamilton."

He turned sharply and moved again toward the table. Mr Hale smiled at his approach, and he took an empty seat between his friend and the elder Hamilton. Here, at least, he would be certain of more constructive discourse.

~

Margaret found the half hour immediately after dinner excessively uncomfortable. She felt herself completely shunned by Mrs Thornton and Fanny. The former occupied herself in conversation with Mrs Smith and Mrs Hamilton. Fanny, however, flitted about the same circle of young ladies which also sought to include Margaret.

She was flattered that her company seemed to be so coveted, but found the banalities of their chatter bored her rather quickly. With a wistful glance over her shoulder, she longed to feel welcomed in the motherly group behind her. It looked to her as though the older women, particularly Mrs Thornton, had better things to talk of than lace and sleeve fashions.

She was infinitely relieved when the door to the drawing room opened and the gentlemen began to pour in. Her father came first to her, offering a pale smile.

"Father, are you well?" she murmured in concern.

"Oh, do not worry my dear," he assured her, patting her hand. "I am only a little weary."

She glanced about the room. "We may leave early if you wish, Father. I do not think...."

"No, my dear!" he objected. "It is nothing a nice long rest on the morrow will not mend. I am sure it will do me good to hear the music this evening." He smiled and turned his attention to Mrs Hamilton's violinist as he was introduced.

The musician played exquisitely. It had been a very long time since Margaret had been able to enjoy such a performance, and she thoroughly relished it. Closing her eyes, she allowed the sweet melodies to soak into her soul. This was one of the few things she still missed about London. Her breath slowed and deepened as her entire being relaxed.

Thornton, standing in an opposite corner, was able to observe her delight without attracting anyone's notice. Merciful heavens, but she was lovely! Her thick lashes fluttered over dusty cheeks, and whether she realized it or not, her shoulders swayed almost imperceptibly to the music. He felt as though he had been offered a glimpse into her private feelings, and he did not know whether he ought to think himself privileged or ashamed at gazing on without her leave.

A faint jostle at his shoulder returned his attention to the lady nearest him. Genevieve had just turned about to smile at him, but he could not return her goodwill without a sinking feeling. His enjoyment chilled. There seemed to be nothing terribly offensive about the beautiful woman at his side, but she was not Margaret Hale. No amount of cajoling would ever be able to convince his heart that she could take the other's place. Whatever ideas he might have ever had to the contrary were dismissed in that moment.

The soloist played for well over half an hour. Thornton continued to steal glances at Margaret, but only very briefly. It would not do for his distraction to be noticed again by the highly attentive young woman at his side, and he really did need to learn to live without gazing raptly at Margaret at every turn.

After the London musician had finished his last selection and buttoned his instrument away, Mr and Mrs Hamilton stepped to the front of the room. A pair of young men passed quietly through the room with champagne for all.

"Ladies and gentlemen," Hamilton began, "my wife and I wish to thank you for helping us celebrate the return of both our son and daughter to Milton. You all know, of course, that Rupert had been busy making his mark in London- and doing his best to upstage his dear old Papa- since he finished his studies. At the same time, Genevieve has been touring all over Europe, living in high style at my expense." Mild titters broke out in the room.

Hamilton held up a hand, smiling. "A man ought rightly to be pleased to have his children once again under his own roof. They return only briefly, however; I've no doubt that in time they shall both fly again. I hope you will join me in wishing them both well. To my son and daughter- may fortune smile upon them as they seek their futures."

Hamilton lifted his drink in the direction of his daughter, and Thornton suddenly felt the eyes of the room turned his way. Miss Hamilton beamed and smiled up at him as her father toasted her, causing more than a little speculation by the onlookers. The curious gazes were awkward enough, but when he saw Margaret looking at him with that raised brow, he began to sweat. He quickly gulped his champagne.

It was Mrs Hamilton's turn to speak now. "I hope that everyone has enjoyed the music this evening. I pray you will indulge a proud mother and listen to a little more." General murmurs of approval rose from those assembled. "To that end, I have asked some of our own Milton ladies to open the piano. Genevieve, darling, will you play first?"

Thornton began to sigh in relief that the young woman would at last be leaving his side, putting an end to their social association for the evening, when she turned to him with an arch smile. "Mr Thornton, might I trouble you to turn the pages for me?"

He paled and it was three full seconds before he could utter his excuses. "I... I beg your pardon, Miss Hamilton, but I fear my own lack of musical knowledge prohibits me. I would be very much distressed if I were the one to mar your lovely performance."

Her face betrayed her disappointment, but Rupert stepped up quickly. "I can sit with you Gen," he grinned, casting a long glance at Thornton as he led his sister away. "It will be just like old times, will it not?"

Thornton closed his eyes and bit his upper lip. That had been too close. His mother was right. He needed to put a stop to all of this idle conjecturing regarding himself and Genevieve Hamilton, or he might find himself an unwilling sacrifice at the altar.

He opened his eyes just in time to catch Margaret's sombre glance in his direction. It pained him that others were whispering and suggesting such things in her presence. Blast it all, she did not think... she could not think him inconstant!

He blew out a silent breath as the piano began its first notes. What would it matter if she did think that of him? She had refused him! It would make her think less of his honour, however, if he were so rapidly to appear to switch his loyalties after once threatening to continue in his love for her. A man who could pursue another after so passionately proclaiming his undying devotion to her alone would be unworthy, in every sense of the word. Margaret would surely be thinking the same thing.

Growling inwardly, he crossed his arms and forced himself to appear to attend the music. His mind turned furiously. There had to be some way of tactfully avoiding the daughter without alienating the father.

Genevieve was in time succeeded at the piano stool by the new Mrs Draper, who currently held the reputation as Milton's finest pianist. She chose an evoking, intricate piece which displayed her talents well, but Thornton scarcely noticed. He was staring at Margaret again. Her intense enjoyment of music was truly captivating to behold. Just as Genevieve had done, Mrs Draper happily performed an encore for her admiring audience. She was in time followed by Mrs Hamper, who played creditably well.

Fanny eagerly took her turn at the keys, causing her brother to grimace. His sister's skill was somewhat lacking after the sterling performances of the others. He had hired the finest master available and she practiced diligently, but Fanny was simply not a natural musician. His mother, sitting near, was pressing her lips tightly, but gave no other sign of her opinion.

Rupert Hamilton, he noticed, listened to Fanny's performance with a thoroughly nonplussed expression. Mr Hale went so far as to quit the room, though with one glance at the older man's pale face, Thornton felt sure that his friend's rudeness had little to do with Fanny's performance. The one party who truly did seem to enjoy Fanny's playing was Watson, who had leapt at the chance to turn the pages for her. Thornton's forehead puckered. He had never noticed any connection there, but any sensible man wishing to indulge his sister would be worth remembering.

Fanny finished her piece and paused, expecting the gathering to plead for another, but Genevieve Hamilton stepped quickly forward. "Margaret, dear, would you play for us next?"

Thornton straightened in interest, but Margaret was turning white and shaking her head. "Oh, no, Genevieve, please!" she begged. "Surely no one here can wish to hear...."

"Nonsense, darling!" Genevieve caught Margaret's hand and forced her unwilling friend to rise. "We so wish to hear you! Margaret studied in London," she informed her guests, with a sly look in Thornton's direction.

"Oh, but it was so long ago, and I did not play well even-"

"It is all right, Margaret," Genevieve assured her. "You have played in public before, you said- at your cousin's wedding, is that not right?"

"But I have not played since," Margaret objected softly. She looked about to her father for assistance, but he had not yet returned. "Oh, please, Genevieve. Surely, you are so very much more talented than I!"

"Do come, Miss Hale," Rupert joined his sister. "After all, one of your taste cannot possibly disappoint. Do play something for us!"

Margaret was maneuvered artfully to the front of the room, still hanging back and now turning a succession of pinks and crimsons. "Please," she begged once more, "I have quite forgotten...."

"Miss Hale," Thornton at last stepped forward, hoping to save her. He came close and bent near in a low murmur, just loud enough for Genevieve and Rupert to overhear. "Your father passed by me a moment ago, and I noticed that he is looking rather unwell. I think perhaps he is quite fatigued. Would you like me to call for a cab so that you might not have to walk home?"

Margaret at last took a breath. She looked up to him with such profound gratitude that he almost felt he had succeeded in washing away their earlier argument. "That would be most appreciated, Mr Thornton," she sighed. "I thought he looked ill myself, but he assured-"

"I will call for one straightaway." He turned about briskly, not wishing to allow her to elaborate on her father's prior dismissal of her concerns. Had she, in her outright honesty, continued so, her excuse for not playing would evaporate.

Later that night, alone in his bed, he would reflect back on that thought. Margaret was frank and artless to a fault in all situations he had ever seen- save the one involving another man. That one circumstance was such an anomaly in contrast to the character he knew that it still baffled and tormented him.

At this moment, however those ideas had yet to emerge. With only a word to Hamilton's staff, the carriage was called for. Margaret had reclaimed her seat at her father's return and was peering into his face with concern. She looked up at Thornton's arrival.

"The carriage will be but five minutes. There was a driver standing by," he whispered.

"Thank you," she mouthed back. "And..." she flicked her eyes to the piano, which had been reoccupied by Mrs Draper, "... thank you."

He gave a quick nod. "Mr Hale, sir, may I help you with your coat?"

Mr Hale, who had been listening to the music, gave a start. "My coat? Why, yes, I am rather weary, but Margaret, did you not wish to listen...?"

"I am quite tired, Father," she smiled and lovingly caressed her father's arm. "I think it best that we take our leave."

Mr Hale looked both disappointed and relieved. "If you think so, but will we not offend our host? I never like to leave too early, it seems quite unsociable."

"It is rather late, sir," Thornton assured him. "I intended to depart soon, myself."

"Oh. In that case, John, I would welcome your help." Mr Hale rose unsteadily, supported by his daughter, and bade a good evening to his host. Margaret turned about her, doing what she could to properly bid each person a good night without disrupting the room's enjoyment of Mrs Draper's playing.

The carriage arrived exactly as Thornton had promised- thanks, in part, to a generous tip supplied beforehand. He went down the walk with them and helped his friend to settle inside the carriage. He then turned to offer his hand to Margaret. She took it and turned her face up to his, her eyes reflecting a soft new shade in the pale moonlight.

"Thank you again," she spoke earnestly.

He daringly squeezed the gloved fingers curving over his hand. "Think nothing of it, Miss Hale. I hope your father rests well tonight."

Her mouth quivered into a conflicted smile. "I expect he shall. Good evening, sir."

"Good evening, Miss Hale." He supported her as she stepped inside, then closed the door behind her. The carriage rattled away, with shades drawn so that he could no longer see its occupants.

He slowly mounted the steps again to the house. With the most interesting guest of the evening departed, the party held no further appeal. He resolved to collect his mother and sister to make their excuses as soon as he could gracefully do so.

~

Mr Hale leaned wearily against the squabs of the carriage. "I know you are concerned, my dear," he patted her hand, his eyes closed. "Fear not, I am quite well. I only slept so little these last nights. I am afraid it has caught up with me."

"Father, you look so pale! It is not like you. Are you sure we may not call the doctor?"

"What did you learn of that charity, my pet?" he asked, by way of distracting her.

"Oh, I had nearly forgotten. Mr Draper is trying to raise funds for a hospital in Milton. He is in need of someone with a fine hand to pen and mail letters to sponsors. I thought it might be something I could do from home, so that I would not be away much, but still something helpful."

Hale opened his eyes and gazed lovingly at his daughter. "So much like your mother... Maria... you always wished to do a good turn, did you not, my darling?" His eyes clouded and dropped closed again. "You were always so good to me, Maria," he murmured.

"Father," Margaret's voice raised a little in alarm, "it is me- it is Margaret!"

"Yes, my girl," Hale gently agreed, his eyes still closed. "So much like her. Always doing good to others."

"If that is so, my first good deed tomorrow shall be to call the doctor!" she asserted firmly.

"For what need, my love? No, I am certain it is only the excitement of the evening. I did so enjoy everything, but I am weary now. I think I shall have to cancel tomorrow's lecture at the Hall. Oh, I am glad it is not John's lesson I shall miss! It was very good of him to arrange the carriage, was it not? It would be such a shame to miss John."

Margaret sighed. "Yes, Father, that would be a shame."

Chapter Thirteen

T he next morning found Margaret bent over her writing desk. She had only just finished a reply to Edith's most recent letter, announcing their travel plans and imminent return to London. Margaret held up the envelope she had addressed with satisfaction. This was the first letter in some while which bore the familiar old Harley Street address. Perhaps when spring came she might be able to pay a visit- if her father were stronger by then. Her face clouded in worry.

With a sigh of resignation, she turned her attention next to the musty old tome which lay at her elbow. It had been far too long since she had devoted any time to her own studies. She set to work, transcribing the ancient tongue in her own elegant hand.

"Miss," Dixon's voice interrupted some while later. "There's a gentleman to see you."

"Gentleman?" She set down her pen. "Show him in, please, Dixon."

Rupert Hamilton strode into the room, his smile radiant. "Miss Hale! How do you do today?"

"Mr Hamilton," she dipped her head. "I am well, thank you. To what do I owe the pleasure?"

"I came to inquire after your father, naturally. I did not have an opportunity to bid you both a good night, as you had to leave so quickly. We were all rather concerned for Mr Hale. Is he well today?"

"That is very kind of you, sir. He is not taking visitors today, but I expect he only needs rest. Will you be seated?"

"Thank you, Miss Hale. I am not disturbing you, I hope?"

"Not at all, sir. I am glad you have come, for I wished to call on Genevieve with my thanks for last evening, but I have been unable to leave my father today. May I offer you any refreshment?"

"No, thank you, I shall not impose on you long, Miss Hale." He glanced appraisingly about as he took a seat. "What a very comfortable room you have here! Ah, you have been busy writing, I see." His eyes lit upon the writing desk, littered still with her labours of the morning.

"Oh," she glanced over her shoulder. "Yes, I was reacquainting myself with Cicero today."

"Cicero? I never had any head for Greek and all of that."

Margaret's mouth twitched. "Latin," she corrected gently.

"There, you see! My classics teacher would be appalled, I am sure. The greatest day of his life was the day I left his tutelage. May I ask, Miss Hale, why you return to such a dreary task? Surely there are much better things to hold your interest."

"I enjoy the challenge. It is a puzzle of sorts. My father taught me that a mind must be disciplined, and such an exercise requires deep concentration. I also find that once I am satisfied with my translation, I have then the pleasure of ruminating over the wisdom of the great sages."

"But the world is moving forward, not backward, Miss Hale! What bearing can such ancient thought have on this modern age?"

"A great deal, though I believe it fruitless to argue the point. I am sorry you found it so tedious, so perhaps we ought to speak of other things. My earlier task this morning was a letter to my cousin in London- I wrote that I had the pleasure of meeting you. I am sure she will mention it to her husband the captain, and his brother."

"Excellent! This world of ours is shrinking, Miss Hale- what a coincidence that we know some of the same people. I wonder how old Henry Lennox is doing."

"Edith tells me he is well," she supplied hesitantly. "She has not seen him lately either, but he writes them."

"Well, Miss Hale, as I said before, the fellow spends most of his days in his office. He ought to marry- perhaps that would divert him from his work."

"Yes," Margaret's voice was scarcely above a whisper. "I suppose it would."

Rupert shrugged nonchalantly. "For all his disdain over my low-class roots, he is, in the end, little different from these Milton captains of industry. It must have been quite a shock to you, Miss Hale- coming here from the genteel south. How have you acclimated?"

"Well enough," she smiled. "I have come to appreciate the ingenuity and motivation which characterizes many of the people I have met here."

"Truly? I imagine such an appreciation was slow to develop! I would be curious to hear your initial impressions. How did the city- no, let me be more specific. How did the manufacturing crowd, say a man like Thornton, strike you at first?" He knit his fingers together and leaned back in his seat, his searching gaze resting upon her.

"I... I think perhaps it would be ungenerous for me to repeat my first impressions. I have since had time to reconsider them."

Rupert laughed heartily. "You disliked him that much! I might have expected that, Miss Hale. He is quite different from what you would have known previously."

"That is to his credit," she replied, a hint of loyalty rising in her tones. "Those attributes which make him unique among my previous acquaintance have served him well in his endeavours."

"Forgive me, Miss Hale, I had not meant to attack the man's character. I have known Thornton, at least by reputation, since I was a boy, and he is a regular brick. I only wished to learn more of your own sentiments. Tell me, have you truly found satisfaction in our dirty old Milton?"

"As much as anywhere, I think. I miss many things about my old home, but I am content to remain with my father. I have met a good number of interesting people here- aside from Mr Thornton," she clarified, "and I find it a fascinating city."

"I heard," he smiled, raising a brow, "that you had friends among the strikers. That is a very strange choice in friends, Miss Hale."

"They are not so very different than I," she returned quietly.

"I beg to differ, Miss Hale, but I should think they are!" he chortled in amusement. "They are largely a rough, uneducated lot. You, Miss Hale, are clearly a young lady of taste and sophistication. I wonder that you have anything at all in common with the working class!"

"We are all the Lord's children, are we not?" she inquired softly.

He sobered at the dangerous flicker in her eyes. Margaret Hale might appear gentle and refined, but there was a regal iron in her which he had missed before. "Indeed, Miss Hale," he replied after a pensive interlude. "Well... I am afraid I have lost track of the hour. You will give your father my respects?"

"Of course, Mr Hamilton." She rose, her bearing stately and poised. If he had had to guess, he would have assumed her to be greatly irritated with him, but, of course, that would have been mere conjecture. She tipped her chin up, icy formality returning to her tones. "Would you take my compliments to Miss Hamilton? Please tell her I shall call once my father has improved."

"I will," Hamilton found his hat and began to make his escape. "Good day, Miss Hale."

~

"I wish I could help, Thornton," Smith pulled the wire-framed spectacles from his face and dropped them unceremoniously on his desk. "We have already extended the loan and reduced your interest payment as much as possible. You have always been a good customer, but this," he waved his hand over the papers arrayed on his desk, "is attracting the notice of my shareholders."

Thornton shifted in his seat, frowning. "The mill's prospects are far from bleak, sir. Much has been invested in the future. To abandon all hope now would be a tremendous waste, and a sizeable loss to your institution."

"There are those among the board who feel that in economic times such as these, it is sometimes wisest to withdraw while we yet can."

"Mr Smith," Thornton leaned forward, steepling his fingers, "Marlborough Mills is a proven profit generator. I challenge you to find another manufacturing plant in the region which is not still suffering ill effects from the strikes. Downturns in the market, particularly in winter, are not unknown either. It is but a season, sir, and will pass like every other has before it."

"Thornton, I respect your position, but you must also understand that the bank is a business as well. We must look to our own if we are to honour all of our other clients. Your mill has promise, I know, but you are also completely leveraged. Other mills with fewer financial obligations are quite simply a more attractive option for financing right now."

"Your board must realize, then, that we do not speak of equivalent operations. The collateral I have put against my obligations is far more valuable by comparison. Your institution is not the loser in this circumstance, Mr Smith."

Smith shrugged helplessly. "I am not the board, Mr Thornton. I was expressly forbidden to offer any further extensions on the loan. May I suggest that your better option is to search out an independent source of funds? Find a man of vision and deep pockets, like Hamilton. I am just coming to know the man, but I understand him to be the sort who might be interested in a share of your enterprise. I wish I could offer you something else, Thornton, but there is little more I can do."

Thornton pinched his lips into a tight line. "I understand. Thank you for your time, Mr Smith."

He collected his hat and began the long walk back to the mill. The disappointment burned at the pit of his stomach. He had most zealously hoped that the bank might see his point of view in the matter. He had never yet fallen behind on his loan, but it had been a near thing for the past few months. Twice now, he had been forced to pay partial instalments to make up each month's crushing obligation.

His mouth pressed into a frown. Things could not continue so. His buyers were falling ever farther behind with their own payments, and cotton prices had not dropped in goodness knew how long. There was always a dip in the winter as the great American warehouses sold off their less desirable stock, but such had not been the case this year. He feared what that could mean for next year's fresh cotton prices.

To add to his present misery, a steady rain drizzled from his hat. Ducking his face somewhat, he thrust his hands within his caped coat and continued on his sullen way. If he had to walk in the rain, he could at least put himself in mind of the last time he had done so with any measure of enjoyment. The corner of his mouth twitched. How he might have wished for the comfort of Margaret and her umbrella today!

Perhaps it was true that she could not have understood his immediate financial concerns as well as his mother, but her bright mind could have at least diverted him from his troubles for a time. She could have offered him some challenge to his thinking, as she so often did, and perhaps after turning her logic over in his mind he might have seen his own troubles more clearly. He sighed regretfully. It was a shame- a travesty, really- that the one woman so well suited for him bore him only Christian goodwill and nothing more. Still, it was a fair sight better than it had once been.

"Thornton! I say, Thornton, you are cutting me rather sharply!"

He halted abruptly and raised his head to identify the man who had addressed him. "Good afternoon, Rupert," he answered civilly.

"It looks as though I am going your way!" the younger man replied cheerfully. "Do allow me to join you, my good fellow."

Thornton tipped his dripping hat obligingly. "By all means. How does your family today?"

"Oh! Mother has taken to her couch. She always does after a party, you know, but do not let on that I have told you as much. I expect it is the delicate constitution of her sex telling upon her, for surely it is an experience common to all fine ladies who entertain."

"Such has not been my observation," Thornton commented mildly.

Rupert laughed. "Mrs Thornton is the exception, of course! I believe none have quite her air of majesty," he intoned gallantly.

Thornton kept his head down as he walked, but he could not resist the point. "My mother is far from the only strong woman of my acquaintance," he replied lowly.

"Quite so! Why, I do believe you are correct, as I come to think of it. I have just left the Hale's residence- to inquire after Mr Hale, you understand."

Thornton's head came up suddenly and he pierced the other with a narrow gaze. He hesitated only a second before speaking. "How did you find my friend today?"

"Oh, I was not able to speak with him at all. I did see Miss Hale, though. I think perhaps she may be one you would number among these ladies of fortitude. Am I right?"

Thornton walked on several strides without answering.

"I do apologize, Thornton, if you find me to have spoken indelicately!" Rupert protested. "I only meant to pay the lady a compliment."

"Miss Hale has borne much," Thornton confessed at length. "and she has done so with grace. I believe she is a great comfort to her father." He clamped his lips shut, resolving not to betray his feelings any further.

"Aye, but she does a good deal more than that!" Rupert enthused, and Thornton had the distinct impression that the other was attempting to lure some confession from him. "She takes a great interest in matters which seem to me rather a waste of her energies. Why, I wonder where she can find the time!"

"Her interests and pursuits are her own," Thornton replied in irritation. "It is not my business to judge her affairs."

"Nor mine!" Rupert exclaimed. "I believe the lady was rather clear about that."

Thornton cocked him an interested frown. "Oh?"

Rupert smiled, and for a second Thornton feared that he had, indeed, betrayed himself. "She was rather short with me just at the end of my visit," Rupert shrugged. "I cannot fathom why a sophisticated young lady would take such an exhausting interest in the working class. And those enormous books! Have you seen how she occupies herself? How very odious!"

Thornton turned his eyes back to the paving stones before him, a small smile quirking his mouth on the opposite side from his companion. Though she may never be his, neither did he have to fear that she would be deceived by Rupert Hamilton's frivolities. It seemed she had already pierced the veil of his charm. If only his sister could be so discerning!

Aloud, he simply answered in a neutral tone, "Miss Hale is the daughter of a parson and a scholar. You must allow her credit for her upbringing."

"Indeed." Rupert studied his companion thoughtfully. "For myself, I prefer a young lady of more spirit."

"You find Miss Hale lacking in that respect?"

"Oh... why, of course not. Perhaps I mean that a more sociable young lady suits my fancy better. What of you, Thornton? Surely you have had time enough to consider your preferences."

"I do not foresee myself ever marrying, so the matter is of little import."

"Never! Do not let the matrons of this good city overhear such talk, Thornton! You will find yourself matched and at the altar before you know it!" laughed the young Hamilton. "Surely there are a number of beautiful ladies about who would be inclined to oblige. I say, Thornton-" he slanted a bold gaze at the taller man, "what is your impression of my sister? I believe she might look upon you favourably."

Thornton stared in mortification. "You speak rather plainly!"

"Well, I ask, you know, because as her older brother I must look out for her, do you see. I would not see her disappointed by a cad."

Thornton narrowed his eyes threateningly. "You may be at ease, Rupert. Miss Hamilton is in no danger from me. If you will excuse me, this is where I turn." He tipped his hat coldly and spun on his heel up Marlborough Street.

Internally, he was raging. Perhaps Rupert Hamilton had grown coarse in the London clubs, but to openly speak so of any young woman- particularly his own sister! He would have been righteously furious, had it not been for the surety the other had given that at least there was no mutual interest between Margaret and the dashing young rake- for Thornton had no doubt that he was such. At least the woman he admired was clever enough to conduct herself with wisdom in that case.

Thornton chewed his lip as he approached the yard of the mill. Fanny was unfortunately rather taken with Rupert, but he did not relish the idea of his sister united to such a worthless, vulgar young man. Fanny must be diverted somehow, but he would have to leave her management to his mother. He had his hands full enough with the mill.

Chapter Fourteen

Mr Hale had not stirred from his room for the better part of that Tuesday. At last, when Margaret threatened again to send for the doctor, he emerged. He bundled himself near the fire, but was rather quiet through the late afternoon and retired early.

After he left, Margaret and Dixon held a hushed conference in the kitchen. "Dixon, he is growing worse! He has called me by Mother's name a dozen times this week, and earlier by the fire I heard him rehearsing a sermon for Sunday! He was nearly breathless just now after climbing the stairs. He is very ill, but he refuses to see a doctor!"

"What he needs," Dixon declared, "is some of this good bone broth. Cure anything what can be cured, I always say." She ladled a steaming portion of the liquid into a mug for herself and dabbed her sweating forehead.

"I cannot get him to drink it. You know he insists that all he needs is a good cup of strong tea. But Dixon, you look rather ill yourself! Are you certain you oughtn't to be in bed as well?"

Dixon waved her apron, fanning her face. "It's only that hot fire, Miss, and I was out at the market when it started raining."

"Go to bed and rest, Dixon, or I shall have two patients in this house."

Dixon groaned and rolled to her feet. "You don't have to tell me twice, Miss, long as you promise to get there yourself."

The next morning found Dixon still feverish and aching. "Enough," Margaret insisted, "back to your room at once! You are staying in your bed today."

Dixon grumbled. "Nay, Miss, I gots to get the breakfast on."

Margaret crossed her arms. "I can manage, and you know Martha said in her note that she would be back today."

"She said that yesterday and the day before. Don't know why you don't dismiss her."

"We had enough trouble securing Martha. Here, you must take some hot bricks for your bed."

"Don't you go in my kitchen, Lass, or I'll... I'll write your aunt!"

"You would have to get yourself to the office to mail the letter, and by the time you were well enough to do so, I would have made the dinner. Now, go back to bed! I would rather not share your fever."

Dixon allowed herself to be bustled off, and with a reluctant huff, she thanked her young Miss. It was really no wonder the master sometimes confused his daughter for the dearly departed mistress. Margaret was just as determinedly good to her.

~

To no one's surprise, Martha did not return that day. Margaret had her hands full learning to prepare humble meals on her own, as well as seeing to all of the needs of the house. The wash needed wrung out and hung, the coal bucket must be replenished, the stew kettle filled and set to simmer, the books re-shelved... never had she tackled so many different tasks simultaneously.

At midday she managed to patch together a respectable cold luncheon for her father and carried it up to him. She was pleased to find him puttering about his library as he usually did, rather than in bed as he had been the day before. He soon assured her that he was quite well enough for Mr Thornton's visit, and asked if she would please have Dixon bring tea up when his guest came.

Margaret flew downstairs in a panic. There was still so much to be done, and she had quite forgotten in her busyness that *he* was coming today! How could she let him see her with her apron filthy and her hair all disheveled? She whirled about the house, tidying everything as best she could, and then got herself to her room just in time to tend to her own appearance. The easiest garment to dress herself without assistance was her nice walking skirt with the lace blouse, though it did seem a little too fine for merely staying about the house. She felt a little foolish, but it was preferable to letting *him* see her looking like a scullery maid!

She had not been downstairs five minutes before his knock came. She hurriedly tugged the last of the drying laundry out of sight and hid it in the kitchen on her way by, noting that her stew kettle was bubbling energetically. It also would require tending soon if she did not wish it to boil over! She scrambled to the door, hoping she looked less frantic than she felt.

Mr Thornton greeted her with a hesitant smile. "Good afternoon, Miss Hale."

For half a moment, perhaps in response to his ever more frequent smiles, her eyes kindled warmly. "Good afternoon, Mr Thornton. Please, do come in."

She waited patiently by as he hung his hat and overcoat, chuckling softly at his bashful little grin when he made an exaggerated point of stuffing his gloves into the pockets of his coat.

"How does your father today?" he asked. "I hope he has recovered from the other evening."

"He assures me he is well, sir."

He looked down in some dismay at the briskness in her tones. Before he could reply, she was starting to spin away in a swish of skirts.

"I will be up shortly with the tea, sir!" she promised, and disappeared into the kitchen.

He grimaced in mild confusion at her abrupt departure. Perhaps he had not yet been forgiven for their argument the other evening. Yet, she had seemed welcoming for a moment- he might even venture to claim she had seemed glad to see him! He shook his head as he started up the stairs. He never would understand the feminine mind.

~

Mr Hale had quite forgotten about Plutarch, which was just as well, because Thornton never had caught up in his readings this week. In some puzzlement, he responded to his friend's questions about Plato. It had been months since he had read the essay on justice, but it had made such an impression upon him that he still remembered all clearly.

"An implied contract," Hale unfolded his glasses and set them upon the bridge of his nose, "an obligation placed upon all citizens simply by existing under the laws of the land. You and I, John, are of such an age that should we *not* make the decision to remove ourselves from our home country, we are justly bound by all her laws and statutes. Does this rightly include those which are unfair? Socrates felt it his duty to the state to remain in prison and meet his death, eschewing his opportunity to escape. He did this in spite of the fact that you and I would have considered the state's judgement in that case to have been in the wrong."

"All men are called to fulfill their duty," Thornton agreed, "but I disagree with Plato in one point. Where a man does not have the choice and where his government is insensible to correction from within, I do not consider the man bound. We, as free Englishmen, have a voice- though sometimes I fear it is a silent one. It is plausible that the laws of our own land might be changed from within."

"'Obey, or he must change their view of what is just,'" Hale quoted.

"Precisely. I wish rather that Plato had elaborated some on that point. The state can be wrong or unjust, and in some cases there is nothing a man can do within the law."

"I think, John, that that is the case as frequently as not. Certainly Plato had seen his share of corrupt or poorly organized government. Even our Lord spoke of honouring whatever government had been placed in authority over us."

"Not if those human laws conflicted with the overriding natural law," Thornton reminded him.

"Of course. However, if we are to have a civil society and any respect at all for a state, we must have these laws, just or not, and they must be obeyed... else we descend into anarchy." Hale leaned back in his chair as his voice grew strangely soft.

Thornton narrowed his eyes, watching his friend carefully. At first Hale had seemed full of vigour, if confused, but now he could almost watch the man's strength ebbing.

"I think of this," he reasoned slowly, "from the opposite side. Perhaps the Americans said it best when they claimed that the government existed for the people, not the reverse. An authority which must be obeyed without question becomes tyranny if that authority is not also itself a subject. If the citizens have a duty to their country, which is right and fair, then those placed in a position of trust and authority have at least an equal responsibility."

"And what do you say that is, John?"

"Naturally to serve without prejudice, to see that justice is done, and to look to the longevity and stability of the state so that its citizens may long enjoy its benefits. Perhaps I could use Marlborough Mills as a very small example. My men work for me, under my authority and my rules. They have the freedom to go elsewhere, and they have a means- through the union, though it is not perfect- to redress wrongs. Their duty is to perform their work to ensure the prosperity of the mill, and observe to the rules, which all exist for good reasons.

"Likewise, I have an obligation to each of my workers. If I fail in governing the finances or cultivating more orders, or if I treat my workers unfairly or refuse to maintain the equipment and it fails, I betray my duty to my hands. I would be worse than a blackguard, injuring hundreds for reasons of selfishness or incompetence. I would not be deserving of the trust which has been placed in my keeping."

Hale had grown very still as he listened, his hand over his mouth. "Socrates does not make his obedience conditional upon the existence of such wise authority, my boy. If such an authority does not exist- in the presence of tyranny, with no means of redressing wrongs, as you say- ought we to be mute in the face of injustice, knowing that acting to right a wrong is against the laws placed over us? And so, my son, should a man remain silent, or is it better to act according to conscience and to accept death or banishment?"

"Perhaps," Thornton mused quietly, more than a little warmed by his mentor's endearments, "that is the same kind of courage and honour which kept Socrates in prison. Socrates had faith in the justice of the law, though it was flawed, because it served society. A man who does what is right in the service of others, knowing the costs, is performing the same kind of duty, is he not?"

"Yes, duty. And honour." Hale dropped his head into his hands and a sigh, nearly a sob, escaped him. "You always did believe in duty and honour, Frederick."

Thornton could not help glancing over his shoulder, but they were alone in the room, with the ticking of the mantel clock the only sound. "Mr Hale?"

"I told you, did I not?" Hale went on softly, shaking his head in his hands. "There would come a day when your notions of justice would be tested. Why did you do it, Fred? Why did you have to leave your mother so? It nearly killed her when you could not return!"

"Mr Hale?" Thornton leaned near in growing concern. "Shall I bring your daughter- shall I call for Margaret?"

"Margaret- yes. Little Margaret has been asking for you, Fred. What do I tell her- that her brother is a traitor, or that he saved dozens of lives? My son...." Mr Hale's voice dissolved at last into choking breaths, and where Thornton could see his face, it was wet with tears.

Thornton felt the room hollow and echo around him. His pulse hammered and his throat went dry. Mr Hale had a son! Margaret's words about one dear to her mother drummed again in his ears. She... she had a brother! It had to be he! He ached to race down to her, to cast himself at her feet and beg her forgiveness for ever doubting her, but he could not leave Mr Hale so.

The older man was still sobbing quietly. He touched Mr Hale's shoulder. "Sir, let me help you rest."

Hale looked up blearily. "John? Is that you? Oh dear, is our time over?"

"I am afraid so. Come, you are weary. Let me help you to the sofa." Tenderly, as only a man in the full vigour of his strength can do, he helped the frail gentleman to his feet and guided him across the room. He settled his friend to rest and carefully tucked a coverlet over him.

Once certain the man would not stir, he charged down the stairs. He had to speak to her, to tell her that it was all right, that he understood everything and would never again lose faith in her!

He took the steps at a sprint, amazed that he did not stumble in his haste. Just at the bottom, Margaret was starting up with a laden tea tray. He accosted her as she made the first step.

"Frederick! You have a brother named Frederick!" he panted in triumph.

Margaret's face drained of all colour. Her gasp of horror could not be heard over the shattering of the tea tray as it crashed to the floor.

~

"Take another moment," he urged her gently, pressing a fresh cup of tea into her hand. He found a mop to soak up the pool of cooling tea, then a broom for the larger shards of the destroyed china. All the while, he watched her from the corner of his eye as she calmed herself. At last he took a seat beside her and spoke softly. "I am sorry that I surprised you earlier. I had no right."

Margaret took a deep breath. "No, I suppose it is right that you should know. We have not told anyone, not even Martha, the house maid... oh, please, I can trust you, can I not? You will keep it to yourself? If anyone were to find out...."

He quieted her. "Of course I will, but what is the matter? Why must it be such a secret?"

She swallowed a sip of tea, blinked two or three times, and confessed, "Frederick was in the navy and accused of treason."

An assortment of expressions washed over his face in succession as he digested the import of her words. His recent discussions with Mr Hale suddenly took on new clarity and magnitude. A brother who could nevermore return, a mother succumbed to her grief and infirmities, and a father who might soon follow- he began to truly comprehend the oppressive weight placed upon Margaret's fine shoulders.

Margaret watched him with apprehension, uncertain of his thoughts. Thornton was a magistrate, after all! Fearfully she sought to defend her dear brother. "Fred is innocent! You must believe me, he tried to save the crew when the captain went mad! It is not Frederick's fault. He only did what he thought was right!"

Thornton found his voice at last. "I... I believe you." She raised a dubious brow. "I *do* believe you," he repeated more firmly. "I think that any son raised by your father could not be otherwise than purely noble."

Margaret stared at her tea cup, biting her lip. "Thank you," she whispered.

"I think," he touched her shoulder, causing her to look him in the eye, "that your father ought to be seen by Dr Donaldson."

"I have been saying that as well, but he refuses," she shrugged helplessly.

"He will not refuse me," he assured her. "Come, I would see you rest yourself while I go for the doctor. Your woman Dixon can...."

"Dixon is ill!" she interrupted. "She has not roused for hours, which for Dixon is grave indeed."

He leveled a careful expression at her for a moment. "I see. I suggest, then, that you take..."

She was shaking her head determinedly. He sighed, knowing he had no power to insist that she lie down. "At least do not attempt the last of the broken china. I would not have you cut yourself. That is my fault and I will attend to it when I return."

Margaret's thoughts were far from the shards on the floor. "Can we trust Dr Donaldson? If Father is really as bad off as you say- why, he has been delusional so often of late! What if he speaks of Frederick again? It would kill him if he were to learn what he has said!"

"I have known Donaldson since I was a boy. I have only to explain that your father lost a son long years ago and occasionally thinks him still present. Donaldson is a discreet fellow. He was very wise and gentle when...." He stopped, thinning his lips.

"When you lost your own father?" she guessed.

He drew a long breath. "Donaldson shielded my mother. There is much that she will never know, and I prefer it that way. Yes, Miss Hale, we can have confidence in Donaldson."

She nodded. "Please bring him if you can."

~

"Well, Miss Hale," Donaldson tugged the spectacles from his face and began to put them away. "It is a good thing you sent for me."

Margaret's eyes darted to Thornton, just behind the doctor, hoping his more familiar face might yield some clues about the doctor's findings. "My father will recover, will he not?"

"In a manner of speaking, Miss Hale. He has been growing steadily more frail of late, has he not? Short of breath and confused, I shouldn't wonder."

"Yes, that is true," she admitted.

"I thought as much. I believe his heart is weak. The blood is not traveling well to his head or his lungs, Miss Hale. I suspect that, combined with his recent emotional distress, could account for the delusions you say he experiences from time to time. I do not have a cure, I am sorry to say, but I have left a compound which should help. I have seen it prolong lives some years. Without it," he admonished, "he would not be with us by the summer, so take care that he receives the correct dosage every day."

She nodded vigourously. "I will see to it myself, Doctor!"

"There's a good lass, I knew you would." The doctor smiled kindly.

"Is there anything else I can do for him?" she asked anxiously.

"Oh, yes, keep him well rested. Light walks once or twice a week should not trouble him, but no more, Miss Hale. He should wait a couple of weeks, at least, before resuming his public lectures. Also, some of that excellent bone broth your woman Dixon makes might do wonders for his blood."

Margaret smiled. "Dixon will be pleased to hear it. Thank you, Doctor." She bent her head to peer into a purse she had already collected. "How much...."

"Oh, no, please! It is nothing, Miss Hale," Donaldson waved his hands as he slid into his coat.

Margaret shot a suspicious gaze to Thornton, but he shook his head innocently.

"Think of it," Donaldson insisted, "as my way of honouring your late mother. I could do so little for her, and it pleases me that I can do something for your father. Take care of him, Miss Hale. I will return next week to check in on him." Donaldson collected his hat and saw himself out.

"Well!" she huffed in surprise at his departure.

Thornton grinned. "That was always the way with Donaldson. Don't worry, Miss Hale, we will see to it that he is adequately recompensed for his trouble."

She shook her head in wonder. "I do not like being indebted to anyone." She then turned her eyes up to him. "I find myself once again in your debt as well."

"Not at all, Miss Hale. My motives were purely selfish. Your father is very dear to me."

"Of course." A sceptical smile played at her mouth. "Thank you, Mr Thornton, I could not have persuaded him to- what are you doing?"

"Taking off my coat," he answered reasonably, draping that article over a chair back. He began to unbutton the cuffs of his shirt sleeves to roll them up.

She narrowed her eyes, mystified. "I can see that, but for what purpose?"

"Well, you do not expect me to wash up dressed like that, do you? Come, I see that you have already cleaned up the mess that I was responsible for, so it is only right that I should return the favour."

"Wash up? What are you- you cannot go into the kitchen!" she cried in dismay, following his determined strides.

"You think I do not know my way around a kitchen?" he teased over his shoulder. "I am a very good cook, Miss Hale, as long as you only care for porridge."

"Yes, but this is not your-"

Thornton pushed the swinging door aside, cutting off her objection. "Now, let me see- ah, yes, the kettle, I remember," he muttered to himself, rather ignoring Margaret's affronted pleas. He lifted the heavy kettle and poured the hot water into a basin. "You must dry, Miss Hale, for I do not know where everything goes once it is clean."

"Mr Thornton, this is quite out of line!" Margaret cried.

He made a face into his basin as he reached for the cake of soap. "'Mr Thornton' sounds so formal for a kitchen. I have taken off my coat! You must call me John."

"*Mr Thornton*," she repeated in baffled annoyance, "let us be done with this foolishness! I cannot allow you to work in my house like-"

"Like you do?" he shot over his shoulder with a probing gaze.

The words died in her throat. Her face went ashen. "How did you know?" she whispered in abject mortification.

He turned and crossed the room in one long stride. He took her hand in both of his own and spread her palm before her face. "Here," he murmured gently, touching his fingers over the hardened ridges of her hand. "And here," he turned her hand over, brushing across the firm muscle above her thumb.

Margaret snatched her hand back and stared at the offending appendage in betrayal and angst. She swallowed her hurt and snapped, "I might say it is most ungentlemanly of you to mention it!"

He sighed, smiling, and took her hand back. "I do not think the less of you, you must understand. On the contrary, it shows your true character. It proves you are not afraid to do what must be done. This," he squeezed her hand gently, testing her strength, "is a badge of honour. It is evidence of your courage and your fortitude. You have learned resourcefulness and your own ability, and the value of honest labour. Not one in a hundred ladies will ever discover what you already know, Miss Hale."

"I..." the word came out garbled. His fingers, tracing so intimately over the lines of her palm, wrought havoc with her ability to speak. Gamely she tried again. "I only help. It is nothing so very remarkable," she mumbled. For a second she thought of reclaiming her hand, but his touch was... distractingly pleasant.

"That is your natural modesty speaking. I think I know exactly how much you do. You are the glue which holds this household together." He gazed long into her eyes, searching to discover if she believed his words.

Margaret gazed back in stunned silence. She tugged softly and he allowed her hand to slip from his grasp. She brushed it self-consciously over her skirts, recollecting that she had earlier donned one of her nicer dresses. She ought not to ruin this one. Her brow furrowed in thought, she turned from him to pluck an apron down from its hook.

Looping it over her head, she reached behind herself to tie it, but her nervous fingers fumbled. Without a word, Thornton stepped behind her and, taking the ties from her hands, knotted them himself. Her breath came quick and ragged as a pit of awareness tingled through her core. She turned again to look curiously up at him for a moment.

"The china is not going to wash itself," he winked with a sly smile.

She let out a small laugh, relenting. "Very well, Mr Thornton. I would welcome your help."

"*John*, or I will not help you," he grinned recklessly.
Margaret blushed deeply, fighting a smile. "John, then."

Chapter Fifteen

"D o you not need to return to the mill?" Margaret wondered aloud. The soiled cooking implements and the last of the china which had remained unbroken were already dried and put away. The labour had been undertaken with such efficiency that she scarcely remembered the task. Thornton- or rather John, as she had agreed to call him- was now turning over Dixon's stained old water kettle in his hands.

"It is a little late now." He drew a pocket watch from his slightly damp waistcoat and flicked it open before her eyes.

Her brows rose. "I had no idea! I am sorry to have taken so much of your time today."

"It was time well spent, I assure you," he smiled. Gingerly he closed the face of the watch.

"It is very fine," Margaret nodded toward the timepiece. "Is it quite old?"

"Over sixty years, I believe. The latch here is very fragile." He held it up for her to indicate the place. "It was my father's. Mother would not hear of selling it, even when times were at their worst. She wanted me to have just this one thing of his."

Margaret's eyes lingered on the watch as he returned it to his pocket. "Your mother is very noble," she replied softly.

He nodded, resuming his inspection of the kettle. "She is, Miss... please, may I call you Margaret? We are friends now, are we not?"

A shy smile broke forth on Margaret's face. Blushing again, she dipped her head in acceptance.

Beaming his pleasure, he looked back to the bit of cookery in his hands. "Yes, Margaret," he savoured the name as it rolled off his tongue, "my mother is a remarkable woman. She had much to bear, and she weathered all with dignity. I only regret that she has yet to truly find joy once more. I have tried all I know. Perhaps it is too late for that," he sighed. "I think, Margaret, I can pound the dent out of this edge here without compromising the copper. How ever did that get there?"

"You are changing the subject," she observed with a lifted brow.

"What more is there to say? My mother is a proud woman. One does not always know what is on her heart."

"Surely she must have been merrier when you were young, from the way you speak of her. What did she find delight in then?"

He smiled, reminiscing, and looked up to her with a boyish expression. "Me, mostly. I am sure there were other things; I am not quite vain enough to think I was the centre of her universe, but all I remember is a devoted mother. Whatever was to my benefit or enjoyment, that is what she pursued."

He set the kettle down and looked thoughtfully up to the ceiling. "I know she cared for my father in the same way. Everything was done to secure his happiness- but we cannot depend on another to create our happiness, can we, Margaret? We have to seek it ourselves."

"Do you think," Margaret probed gently, "that she felt... betrayed? That he had flung away her love- that all of her care and worry were for naught?"

He pursed his lips and looked quizzically to her. "I had never thought of it quite so. Why, you may be right! I suppose that is my weakness as a man, that I do not see matters in the same way a woman might."

Margaret laughed lightly. "I might say I suffer from the same weakness! Frederick, for instance- I never understood that wanderlust which drove him from home. It did not make sense to me that he was so restless and could not wait to join the navy to seek adventure. Mother could never fathom it either."

John shrugged. "Every man feels driven to make his mark upon the world. It makes perfect sense. I do not see what you do not understand." His words were spoken distractedly as he poked about the kitchen in search of the right implements to repair the kettle.

Margaret shook her head and spread her hands. "There, do you see? Perhaps the sexes are fated to never come to a right understanding."

"I do not think that must of necessity be true. Half a moment-" He disappeared behind an old shelf dividing the kitchen from a utility nook which they had virtually ignored during their residence in the house. Margaret heard him clattering and rummaging among the various items he found there.

A moment later he returned to where she stood with a rusted hand iron and a small, nearly worthless hammer from the previous tenant's cache of forsaken tools. "Pardon me. I was just thinking that where there are intelligent individuals committed to open communication, there cannot help but be an improvement in understanding. Do you not think so, Margaret?"

Something in his tone caused her to flush. He locked eyes with her, a curve tipping just the corner of his mouth. Heavens, but he looked so temptingly alluring standing there, smiling at her in his shirtsleeves! Margaret's pulse was skittering. If he continued in this friendly, easy way, she felt certain that her heart was in very great danger- if it were not already wholly compromised.

"I..." she shook her head slightly to clear it. Where had all of her reason gone? "I think it possible, sir- John. I think, however, it is rather difficult to manage such free and open discourse between unrelated people without some breach of propriety." She gulped. Whatever had made her say that?

"Why?" he tipped his head in genuine confusion.

"Well, it is hardly the thing for a gentleman to go about behind closed doors with a lady in the kitchen! People would talk, you know."

He dismissed it with a shake of his head, seating himself on Dixon's stool with the kettle. "In my experience, people will talk even if there is nothing to talk about. Not that one ought to behave with deliberate impropriety, but I do not intend to live my life in fear of the gossips."

"Nor do I!" she rejoined eagerly, "but a reputation can be a delicate thing, particularly for a lady."

He squinted and looked up at her seriously. "Margaret, would you prefer that I had not stayed? I do not wish to cause you any difficulties. I only thought to be a friend."

She pressed her lips together, her forehead creased in thought. "No... no, I am grateful that you remained, whatever anyone says. You have been a very kind friend, and... and I am glad of your company."

His teeth flashed brilliantly in the dingy little kitchen as he shone back the most stunning smile she had ever seen on his face. "Good," he answered simply. He bent his head over the kettle again to hide the triumphant gleam in his eye.

They were quiet some minutes as he manipulated the hammer and iron, banging and tapping expertly on the kettle. Margaret watched his able hands in fascination. She never would have expected him to know of such things, but the dent gradually vanished beneath his practiced fingers. At one point he stopped to rub his fingertips over the finished edge. Margaret would have thought the task complete, but he was not yet satisfied. With a few more taps, the edge of the kettle looked almost new to her eyes.

"There," he grinned, passing it to her for her inspection. "It is not perfect, but somewhat improved. It would be far better had I a forge here, but it should at least rest evenly on the stove once more."

"It is- why this is remarkable!" she enthused. "How did you learn to do this?"

"When I first started at the mill it was under old Simmons, a former associate of my father's. He took me under his wing, taught me all he knew. He insisted that I learn every single moving part in the entire building, and how to repair it. I am no master mechanic or smith by any means, but his teaching has proven useful once or twice," he smiled modestly.

She set the kettle back in its place, still admiring its newly clean and stable edge. "I do not know how to thank you for all that you have done today," she spoke earnestly as she turned back to him.

"Do you not?" He cocked a sly eyebrow as he set the tools aside.

Margaret's being quivered. She had not meant... he could not be suggesting...! Her eyes grew wide. "What did you have in mind?" she asked nervously as he drew close, his face only inches from hers. Did he mean to kiss her? Did she even want to refuse, as she knew she must? Her stomach fluttered wildly.

He lowered his mouth near her ear, his tone dropped to a whisper. "I want to hear you play the piano one day. I would lay good money that you are better than you claim."

She broke into a relieved laugh as he drew back. "Is that all! You had me terrified! How fortunate for me that I no longer own an instrument."

"I do," he crossed his arms smugly and leaned against the countertop. "Someday, Margaret. You must sing as well, for a strong, clear voice such as yours would be a treat to listen to. And do not forget either, for I may be patient, but I always collect on a debt."

"You will have to be *very* patient, I expect."

"Naturally. At the moment, however, what I am is very hungry. That stew you have had simmering has been driving me mad this past hour."

"Oh! I am sorry!" Her face reddening, she flew to get him a bowl, then ladled it full of the hot food. She filled one for herself as well, and as one, they found seats at the rude kitchen table. As an afterthought, she leapt up and returned again with a basket full of rolls.

"Do you mind?" he asked quietly, and she glanced up at him in confusion. When she understood, she nodded enthusiastically, then bowed her head and listened as he asked a humble blessing over their simple meal. Smiling and blushing her pleasure at his unexpected and unassuming piety, she offered him one of the rolls after he had done.

He took and broke it as she passed him a small crock of butter. "Thank you." He took a bite and his eyes widened in surprise. "These are excellent! Did you make them?"

"Yesterday," she felt her cheeks warming still more. "What I mean by that is that I had Dixon's help. You may not find the stew quite so appealing, as I made that on my own."

"You make me all the more determined to like it," he grinned disarmingly. He took an eager bite as she cast her eyes to the side, blushing furiously at his deep interest. When he was silent for a long moment, she looked back to him in concern. He coughed. "Salt, Margaret. It only wants a pinch, not a bucketful."

"Oh! I am afraid I must have salted it... let me think... before I shelved the books, and then again after, and then... oh dear. Is it very dreadful?"

"I have surely had worse," he winked, bravely taking another large mouthful. He swallowed with a gulp, then reached gratefully for the glass of water she set before him.

Margaret felt terrible. Here he was hungry and oh, so kind, and the best she had to offer him was a ruined dinner! "I am so sorry!" she apologized miserably.

"Do not be. That is an excellent carrot just there. See? Perfectly tender but not overcooked." He managed to choke down another spoonful. Her expression remained morose, so he reached across the table to take her hand in his. "Take heart, Margaret. I am sure there is some chef's secret to mending such a malady, but tonight let us simply savour our feast- for savoury it most certainly is."

Margaret sputtered, trying to conceal her most unladylike outburst but not succeeding. She bowed her head in peals of laughter, resting her forehead on her free hand. John was laughing as well, his eyes sparkling dazzlingly at her. Gracious, where *did* the man get those mesmerizing eyes, and why had she never had so much trouble before in looking away?

~

They laughed their way through the pungent meal, trading stories from their childhoods. He was eager to hear all he could of Helstone and her early years there, particularly anything she could tell him about her youthful exploits tagging at her older brother's heels. He cherished a vision of a dark-haired little maid with freckled cheeks doing her level best to climb an apple tree in her Sunday dress. He nearly forgot his hunger for laughter as he dragged tale after tale out of her about Frederick, the greatest prankster of the New Forest, and his deceptively innocent-looking young accomplice.

"I do not believe it!" he stopped her at one point to wipe his eyes. "*You* dressed the neighbor's dog in stolen laundry? And then it truly ran through the churchyard on Sunday?"

"It was not precisely stolen..." she cringed uncomfortably. "It was from the charity basket, the one where the parishioners would donate unwanted items for the poor. That horrid green dress, though- everyone recognized it as Mrs Jenner's old one. No one else would have it! Oh, how angry she was!"

"May I ask what your father said to you?"

"Not a thing." She blinked wistfully. "Frederick immediately stepped up and took my punishment. It had truly been his suggestion in the first place, but I do not think he imagined I would actually do it." She gazed at her hands with a sad little laugh. "No one thought twice about punishing Frederick. He never did anything *truly* wicked, you know. He only loved a good laugh. However, Fred was always the first one to step forward when there had been some injustice. A good many of the rougher boys hated him, but never dared anger him. I was never troubled by anyone, for his sake."

"Then he did right. A brother ought to look out for his sister."

Eager to leave behind the melancholy subject of her absent brother, she turned his words about. "Has it been difficult? You have almost raised your own sister, have you not?"

"Different, perhaps, than you might expect. I had little to do with most of her upbringing. I went to work."

Something in his tone caught her attention. "You gave up your own education to do so," she stated.

He sighed. "Yes, but you must understand, that was not thought to be such a hardship as it sounds to you. Many lads here in the North leave the schoolroom by that age and never turn back. It is considered a waste to leave a promising youth languishing behind dusty classics when he ought to be earning a living and learning the ways of business."

"You had no regrets, then?" she probed softly.

His mouth tugged in that easy, boyish way she had grown fond of. "You sound as if you do not believe it."

Margaret tipped back in her chair and gazed carefully at him. "Perhaps regret is the wrong word. You are not the sort of man to pine for what might have been, I think."

He met her assumption with silence and a raised brow. She reddened for a moment, wondering if there were some significance behind his expression. She winced and forged on, wishing to smooth over her apparent blunder.

"I- I think you are not sorry," she conjectured, "but you were glad enough to meet with my father, to revisit what you had left behind. He is very proud of your progress, you must know. He says he is quite certain you must have been an outstanding student as a boy."

"I would hardly call myself outstanding. I was quick enough, you might say, but always my mind was on my ambitions. Father once counseled me to patience, saying that I would have time enough to forge my way in the world, and that I ought to take my opportunity to study and refine myself whilst I could. I did not listen as I ought." His gaze grew misty and his voice trembled slightly. "That was only a week before he died."

Margaret closed her eyes. "I am sorry I brought it up," she whispered bitterly.

"Do not be," he assured her, his voice once again firm. "It is past time for such regrets. I have learnt to remember the joy instead. Up until that point, my youth was not so very different from yours, I imagine. My father was a hard businessman, but he appreciated the finer things. He was determined that I, as his son, would have the opportunities denied him as a boy. During the best times he sent me to London for two years, though my mother strenuously objected. I lived with one of his business partners and learned the classics, fencing, riding, and music alongside wealthier boys."

She cocked her head, "You studied music? I never would have expected that."

"And dancing! I will be frank, though, I am a terrible dancer. I had not then the proper motivation, perhaps, but I would be willing to again take lessons from someone more accomplished." He graced her with a suggestive smile.

"You will have to look elsewhere, for I gave up dancing at age nine. I did enjoy the piano while I played it, though."

"So did I," he agreed.

She narrowed her eyes. "Why, Mr Thornton! You told Miss Hamilton that you did not know enough music to turn the pages for her! I thought you were always a paragon of honesty, sir!"

"I may have exaggerated a little," he grinned. "I was not the only one, surely. And the name is *John*... Margaret. Please do not let us return to yesterday. I like today better."

She drew a contented breath. "So do I, John."

He smiled back at her, then down at his empty bowl. "Well... it looks as though it is time to wash up again. May I?"

Margaret nodded, her cheeks pleasantly warm. They worked even more efficiently together this time than the last, and they finished quickly. Margaret dried her hands and he caught her wistfully turning her palms over as she hung up her towel. His lovely, strong Margaret... he felt a sympathetic pang as she tried to hide her hands once more in her skirts.

"Look, Margaret, this is what Mother used to do." She turned curiously as he found a small crock of cooking lard. "Come here," he beckoned hopefully.

She came cautiously. He dipped his fingers in the crock and held out his other hand to take hers. She gave it willingly and shivered as he began to stroke the rich emollient into her skin. She could not tear her eyes from his delicious fingers as they caressed her tender flesh.

She gave him her second hand when he reached for it, and he resumed his gentle ministrations upon both hands at the same time. He took rather longer about the task than strictly necessary, as he instinctively found and massaged the tired places within her palms. Margaret felt the release of tension traveling through her shoulders and down her spine as her skin prickled delectably over her arms and neck.

When he had done, both took half a step back and simply stood in breathless silence. Margaret could not even swallow, and it is likely that John suffered even more agonizingly from the sweet, sensuous contact. He gazed long down into her eyes, contemplating far more than only her hands.

Margaret stared down at her palms, brushing her greased fingers together. "I smell like a side of pork," she managed at last, with a whimsical little smile.

John cleared his throat uncertainly. "One of the most irresistible perfumes known to man, I assure you."

Margaret laughed merrily, holding her hands before herself with awkward care. "Whatever am I to do now? I shall stain everything I touch!"

"You are meant to wipe off the excess," he frowned defensively, holding his own hands aloft.

Still laughing, Margaret found an old rag which could not be harmed by a little excess oil. "Allow me," she chuckled, reaching to swipe his hands off after she had cleaned her own.

"Thank you," he grinned when she had finished. "I think my hand will not slip from the door latch now."

She sighed a little sadly, recognizing that the most pleasant evening she had passed in a long while was drawing to a close. "I suppose not. I expect my father will be looking for some supper by now, and possibly Dixon as well."

John blew out a long regretful breath. "Of course." He turned his forearm over and began to roll his long sleeves down once more. As he finished, he noticed that Margaret's smile had vanished. She was gazing vacantly at the floor.

"Is something wrong?" he asked in concern.

She started. "No! It is only..." she shook her head in exasperation. "Sometimes I do not understand you. You seem at times so harsh and unyielding, yet when I see you like this...." She gestured vaguely with her hands, not certain what she dared to say.

"You think I am duplicitous?"

"Oh, no! I am only confused. I understand that at the mill you must be in unquestioned authority, and in Milton society you must appear confident among your business rivals, but... well, what of that hospital charity? I know now that you are not so churlish as I once thought, but I do not understand your position against such a worthy enterprise."

He bit his upper lip thoughtfully. "Were you any other woman, Margaret, I would simply tell you what I believe to be the truth and that would be the end of it. You, however, are of a character which must know the whole of the matter. I would encourage you to investigate for yourself- find out if my own concerns are justified, as I fear they are. If I thought harm could befall you, I would not encourage you so. I think only that your time might be wasted, and perhaps you may feel yourself badly used. On the other hand, it is quite possible that I may be wrong, and that you will find it to be a useful endeavour. In either case, I have faith that you will in time discern the truth of the matter."

"I see," she responded slowly, considering the utter confidence he appeared to place in her judgement. It was truly a high compliment. "Thank you for your frankness."

He gave her a thin smile and looked to the floor. "Well, I must be going."

They slowly wandered together to the door, collecting his jacket and overcoat along the way. Once he was attired for his walk, with the exception of his gloves, he drew near once more. "You will look well to your father?"

"Of course. And... would you give your mother my compliments?"

His eyes lit. "I most certainly will. Thank you for a pleasant evening, Margaret."

"You are quite welcome, John." She smiled and extended her hand to shake his, as she had often done of late.

He took it, and with a calculating glance, he turned her hand over in his so that he could swiftly bring her knuckles to his mouth, drawing a surprised gasp from her. He risked a single, gallant kiss- chaste and not too terribly improper, but oh! so delicious! "Good night, Margaret," he murmured huskily.

Before she could cry in offense or slap him, he dropped her hand and placed himself at a safe distance in the doorway. A last parting look at her face as he opened the door revealed not an affronted glare, as he had feared, but a bewildered, flattered warmth.

"Good night, John," she called softly to him as the door closed.

Chapter Sixteen

"Iohn, there you are at last! Where have you been so late?"

John shook the rain droplets from his overcoat as he entered his own door. His mother had heard his arrival and met him in the entry. Had it not been for the worry in her tones, he might have taken offence to her demanding question. After all, he was a grown man who often worked late!

"I was out, Mother," he smiled privately to himself.

"I could see that," she retorted drily. "You were not in your office, and Williams said he had not seen you since midday."

"True," he replied cryptically, then dropped a cheery kiss on his mother's forehead. He strode jauntily down the corridor, a merry whistle on his lips.

"John!" his mother followed him in exasperation. "What has got into you? Come, I doubt you ate any luncheon and you have not had supper. You are going to starve yourself. Why, you have lost your head already!"

"I am perfectly in my right mind, Mother, and I have already eaten, thank you."

He curled into his favourite chair by the fire, but he needed no paper to divert his thoughts on this night. A pair of green eyes would do nicely....

"John!" Mrs Thornton huffed to catch up, then placed herself squarely between him and his fire. "What is happening? I have never seen you so flighty!"

"All is well, Mother." He leaned back in his chair, and if he had been a smoking man, he would have tapped his pipe in satisfaction. "In fact, things could not be better!"

She knelt before him, her eyes shining. "Mr Hamilton has agreed to invest in the mill?"

"What? Oh, no. Well, I suppose things could be marginally better."

A shadow crossed her face. "What has you so preoccupied, then? Has someone asked for Fanny's hand?"

"Good heavens, no! I should imagine that would distress me rather than please me. Have you any idea what her wedding will end up costing me?"

"John!" she thundered firmly, in her best maternal tone. "Tell me what the matter is!"

He grinned hugely, leaned forward, and pecked another kiss on her cheek. "Mother, do you remember that diamond betrothal ring that you said I might have one day? The one that your aunt left you a few years back?"

Her gaze darkened suspiciously. "Ye-es," she replied slowly.

"Do you know where to find it? I might have need of it soon."

Her hand fluttered to her breast. "Miss Hamilton? I am glad to see you have come to your sens-"

"What? Do not be silly! Miss Hamilton? I could not afford to keep her, even if I did fancy her, which I most certainly do not."

Mrs Thornton was by now thoroughly confused. "Tell me at once, John David Thornton, who on earth has caught your eye? For I see this is no mild infatuation you have!"

He cupped her face lovingly in his hands. "Margaret. Margaret Hale is the lady, and my heart is more firmly hers now than ever before."

"John!" she cried in dismay. "I thought you had already learnt-"

"Hush, Mother. I learned much more today." He drew her to the sofa, and with his arm around her shoulders, gently unfolded the events of his afternoon.

"And so!" Hannah Thornton stared blankly at the wall in utter astonishment. "That other man was not her lover after all!"

"No, but I beg you, Mother, you must keep this in complete confidence. I swear you to it, by all you hold dear! Even should she never become mine, I would not see her injured by betraying this secret. Do you promise, Mother?"

"Oh, you needn't be so dramatic, John. Of course I promise. I am certainly glad to hear the young lady did nothing so unmaidenly as I once thought, but what does this change? She thinks herself a great deal too good for you, John. I hardly think she has changed her mind," Mrs Thornton snorted expressively.

"She is not prideful, Mother. I believe she was frightened of me."

"Frightened! She had no cause to be."

He brushed his chin thoughtfully with his fingers. "We talked a great deal tonight. I think I understand her better than I ever did. The move to Milton was more traumatic to her senses than I had realized. To her, I represented everything which mortified and offended her about life in an industrial city."

Mrs Thornton rolled her eyes. "Fine sensibilities. I've no use for such a skittish maid. You would spend all of your time trying to appease her, John, to no avail, for she will never be made content. Mind the 'low spirits' her mother claimed!"

"That is uncharitable, Mother, and you know it. Mrs Hale was suffering a mortal illness and was too dignified to speak candidly. Margaret possesses her mother's gentility to a great degree, but she is more frank."

"Aye, she is a salty lass, and no mistake," Mrs Thornton scowled. "Oh, now I said nothing very funny, John, why are you laughing?"

John was chortling softly, but sobered. "It was nothing, Mother, only you have just reminded me that I am very thirsty."

She stared quizzically. "I believe that girl has bewitched you, John. You are not at all yourself! I can see that you are plain set and determined to offer for her again."

"Absolutely, but not yet. I will not ask again unless I can be certain of her answer."

She clucked, shaking her head. "If you think she will make you happy, John... she is quite penniless, you know. She has nothing to offer-certainly Miss Hamilton would be the far more practical choice. She may be a spendthrift, as you say, but your pockets would be much deeper if allied with her father. Is there no thought for that?"

"None whatsoever. Besides, Mother, if you look beyond her purse, Margaret is infinitely more practical. If I am to choose a woman to stand by me, I would choose a woman with some backbone and a will of her own. I would wish for a wife who had the heart and the spirit to inspire me and who would desire my love, not my position. She must be a woman with your kind of strength, Mother; one who can stare down adversity and yet hold herself with grace."

"Pretty words, my boy." She raised a cynical eyebrow.

He gave her one of his lopsided smiles. "If I am considering matrimony, I had best practice the art of paying my compliments well, do you not agree?"

"And you think Margaret is such a woman?"

His eyes shifted from her face to the fire, then back again with firm resolve. "I know she is, Mother. I have seen it for myself."

Mrs Thornton blew out a long breath of resignation and screwed her mouth into a tight little frown.

"You are not convinced, I know," her son pulled her more closely under his arm. "Please do try to give her a chance, for my sake."

She scowled. "A mother does not soon forgive or forget, John. You ask me to look kindly upon the young woman who has ruined your happiness, who-"

"The woman," he interrupted, "who holds the key to my happiness! By the by, she sends you her regards."

Ever the sceptical mother, Mrs Thornton frowned more deeply. "I'd wager she does. She will give you no end of trouble, John. You know how she carries on with the Union folk. She will manipulate you and undermine your authority, taking baskets to the very rabble who would try your resolve. You remember how she spoke during the strike!"

"I do. Mother, you cannot expect her to understand all of the necessities of business in such a short time; it is not native to her. It is a hard thing if a young gentlewoman can possess the cold-heartedness that a man of business must assume. It was her compassion which impressed me. Not one other young lady in all of Milton found the heart to act as she did."

"For good reason," Mrs Thornton grumbled. "And that is not quite true either, John. You are unfair to the charities which took in the ailing children during that time. Why, my sewing circle alone donated twenty blankets!"

"Did any of your friends take time to know the families, Mother? An organization is a fine thing and can accomplish much, if managed properly, but there is something irreplaceable about personal relations.

She knows them, Mother, and does not shrink from them. She does not patronize but cares deeply for the families, and they adore her for it."

"John! I see it already; she has corrupted your thinking. You have gone soft!"

"Not at all, Mother. I have only come to see that a means for communication with my hands has lain open before me all of these years. I mean to explore it. Have I told you about that kitchen I am allowing the men to set up in that old outbuilding at the south corner?"

"Twice, and I told you both times that I thought it foolish. They will take advantage of you."

"It is they who are paying for it, after a fashion," he returned defensively. His brow furrowed. "Was it really twice?"

She rolled her eyes again. "John, I thought that you suffered from lack of sleep, but I think now that your head is addled."

A slow smile crept to his lips. "Perhaps I have been a bit distracted of late. The mill has kept me rather preoccupied."

Mrs Thornton's mouth twitched. "Only the mill?"

He laughed softly. "I will confess to no more tonight, Mother! You have quite bled me of all of my secrets. Ah, and I see I am saved, for here come the household for your evening devotions."

She did not release him from her gaze just yet. "Just do nothing rash, John. You cannot be certain of her, and I would not see you compromise your dignity again!"

He sighed. "Of course, Mother."

~

Dixon had recovered tolerably well by the next morning. Though still weak and feverish, she refused to be sent off again. Her strength had returned enough so that she scolded her young mistress rather roundly for invading the kitchen and creating an abominably over-seasoned disaster of a meal. "Waste of good broth," she was heard to grumble- until, that is, she saw her repaired water kettle.

She huffed into the front parlour, where Margaret was shelving her father's books. "Miss! You didn't dare touch my kettle, did you? This is a man's work! If you-"

Margaret hushed her, her cheeks a beautiful shade of rose. "Mr Thornton repaired it, Dixon."

Dixon's arms lowered, the freshly scrubbed kettle catching the light as it dropped. "Mr Thornton! What was that man doing in my kitchen? I suppose that's why half my good china is missing!"

"Oh, I am afraid you have me to blame for the china, Dixon. I dropped the tea tray yesterday."

Dixon's eyes widened anew. "If that don't beat all... you just see if I ever stay abed again!"

Margaret laughed shyly behind the book she was holding. "It was an accident, Dixon. Mr Thornton surprised me coming down the stairs, but he was kind enough to help me clean up."

Dixon's brows knit suspiciously. "Is that all that man did?"

"Well, and the kettle... yes. Why do you ask? Oh, I suppose I did forget to tell you that he finally convinced Father to be seen by Dr Donaldson. I am very grateful for that. The doctor prescribed a medicine which should help improve him."

Dixon took a step closer, lifting her large kettle as she would a scolding finger. "I mean in the kitchen. Were you alone with that man?"

Margaret's face changed hues again, but after a few seconds of guilty silence she squared her shoulders. "I do not see what business it is of yours! It is not your place to chastise me, Dixon!"

Dixon's mouth twisted into a sulky pout. "If your mother was here, Lass...."

"She is not," Margaret interjected softly. "Much as we both would wish it. Dixon, I should hope you have better faith in me than you imply!"

Dixon drooped somewhat. "Aye, Lass," she mumbled. "Beg your pardon."

"I give it freely. There is nothing to fear, Dixon, Mr Thornton was a perfect gentleman last evening. I was grateful to have his help, most especially with Father."

"Beggin' your pardon again, but it's not your father that man's interested in." Dixon stared hard at her young mistress.

Margaret reddened again. She turned from Dixon to shelve the book she still held. "I know, Dixon," she returned in a low voice. She remained there, her fingers resting on the spine of the old tome as she took several deep breaths. "Dixon, there is something I never told you about Mr Thornton."

She turned again to her expectant maid, who was glowering with white knuckles on her kettle. "The night that I walked Frederick to the station, he was seen. Leonards, he happened upon us, and attacked Frederick."

Dixon's face drained to an ashen shade. "Master Fred?" she asked tremulously.

"He got away safely, Dixon, but he had to fight the man off. Later, however, I heard that Leonards had fallen and died of some injury. You remember the inspector who came here after Mother's death? He had a witness who identified me at the station that night, and he desired a statement. I refused to give it... I lied, Dixon."

Dixon blinked. Such a thing was unheard of. "I don't understand, Miss."

Margaret's face pinched and she sighed. "I thought Fred was still in London, and I could not risk them searching for him after they had heard my statement, so I... I told the inspector that I was not there at all."

Some of the colour had begun to return to Dixon's face. "You were protecting Master Fred, Miss. I'd've done the same. He didn't hurt that Leonards fellow no more than he deserved, I'm sure."

Margaret shook her head. "No, you do not understand. It is shameful enough to have lied- and twice! It is worse yet because Mr Thornton also saw us at the station, and he was the magistrate presented with the case. He knew that I was not telling the truth from the beginning."

Dixon narrowed her eyes. "It ain't my place, Miss, but what do you care what that tradesman thinks? Hmf! Only think, Miss Beresford's daughter, fearing for offending some rough-edged-"

"He blocked the inquest, Dixon," Margaret interrupted. "He thought the very worst, I am sure; nevertheless, he protected me, and by extension Frederick."

"Well, I'll be jiggered...." Dixon muttered, staring aghast at her young mistress. "And has he- well, what I mean, Miss, is... well, has that man threatened you? Is he trying to force you to... begging your pardon, again Miss."

Margaret almost laughed, and likely would have done so if Dixon had not appeared so frightened. "No, Dixon, as I have said, he has been a perfect gentleman, though I most assuredly did not deserve such kind treatment. You may as well know the whole of it. Father was rambling again during Mr Thornton's lesson yesterday, and he knows everything now. He has proven a friend, Dixon, and I will hear nothing further against him."

Dixon scowled a moment in thoughtful silence. "Has he declared himself, then? Beggin' your pardon, Miss."

Margaret closed her eyes and bit her lip. "A little too soon, unfortunately. Had matters then been as they are now, I may have answered him very differently. I am afraid I was very harsh with him. I can scarcely believe he will still speak to me!"

Dixon's frown softened somewhat. "I know it's not my place, Miss, but if you ever need... the Mistress, you know, she was an angel to me. I'd be right pleased, Miss, if...." she sighed, flustered. She wished to offer her girl motherly counsel, but as she was only an irreverent serving woman and had neither man nor child of her own, such counsel would carry little weight.

Margaret stepped near and rested a hand on her shoulder. "Thank you, Dixon. That means a great deal to me."

Dixon blinked quickly against eyes which had suddenly gone quite misty. She cleared her throat. "Well, now, Miss, no harm done. If Mr Thornton protected our lad Fred, he can break all the china he pleases. We can always have tea out of this old kettle. And just look at it, good as new!"

Margaret laughed. "Perhaps he is a rather agreeable guest after all!"

"As long as he doesn't bring that mother of his," Dixon harrumphed.

~

"How do you do today, Mrs Hamilton?" Hannah Thornton set aside her needlework and rose grandly to meet her callers.

"Quite well, thank you Mrs Thornton," the lady inclined her head.

"And Miss Hamilton, it is a pleasure to see you again so soon. Jane," she turned to her favourite housemaid, "ring for my daughter, please."

The maid bobbed a smart curtsey and Mrs Thornton returned to her guests. "Will you be seated?" Fanny arrived promptly and the four decorous ladies set upon the refreshments which came soon after.

Fanny was all enthusiasm, as she had not had the pleasure of her dearest friend's company since the evening of the dinner party. "I declare, Gen, it has been an *age* since I saw you! I called yesterday *and* the day before, you know, but I was told you were out," Fanny pouted.

Genevieve looked stiffly to her friend. "Yes, I received your card." She lifted her tea cup, indicating that she intended no further comment.

Mrs Thornton watched the pair in silence. Perhaps Fanny's ulterior motives had at last soured Miss Hamilton's opinion of her. She gave an inward sigh. She could not have the entire family put out with them, for John's sake.

"Mrs Hamilton," she graciously ventured, "I must again compliment you on the success of your dinner party. It was a most elegant affair."

Mrs Hamilton nodded primly. "Indeed, it was rather well spoken of. I was very pleased- until just the end, that is."

Hannah's jaw set. There was a challenge in the other woman's voice, one she could not leave alone. "Were any of your guests displeased? They had no cause to be, I assure you."

"Well! I hardly know. That former parson and his daughter left so very abruptly, and after her refusing to oblige on the piano! I told dear Genevieve that the girl would be sure to cause a scene, and I am proven right."

Hannah tensed cautiously. "I understood that Mr Hale had taken ill."

"Ill! He was no more ill when he left than when he arrived. I thought it a rather artificial excuse, if you ask me, Mrs Thornton." She raised her cup and leveled a significant stare over the rim at her hostess.

"I would not have described it quite so," Hannah returned mildly. "I thought Mr Hale looked unwell after dinner myself. They appeared to be thoroughly enjoying the evening until that point."

"Yes, right up until Miss Hale found herself unable to compete with my Genevieve," Mrs Hamilton sniffed. "Abominable rudeness!"

"Surely," Mrs Thornton soothed, "many young ladies would feel rather intimidated to perform in such accomplished company. Miss Hamilton and Mrs Draper both play exceedingly well, but Miss Hale informed me upon our first acquaintance that she did not."

"She *does* play, though. She said she studied in London and performed for a wedding party! If you ask me, she feared to be found wanting in the eyes of my guests- or rather, *one* of my guests in particular."

Fanny chose this moment to make a petulant face. "It was so very rude of her to monopolize your brother!" she whispered loudly to Genevieve.

Hannah glared icily at her daughter, silencing her. To her guest she turned next. "Forgive me, Mrs Hamilton, but I did not see her exerting any particular effort to garner your son's attention."

Mrs Hamilton frowned pointedly. "It is not *my* son's interest which took my notice, Mrs Thornton. After all, it was not *he* who arranged for Miss Hale's untimely departure when she declined to play."

Hannah bristled. "If you mean to imply that my son's manners were anything but irreproachable-"

"Of course not!" Mrs Hamilton waved her cup airily. "We have nothing but the very highest regard for Mr Thornton, do we not, my love?"

Genevieve smiled charmingly at that gentleman's mother.

"There, do you see?" Mrs Hamilton gestured sweetly to her daughter. "The man can hardly be blamed for allowing himself to be distracted. Oh! Surely you must have noticed, Mrs Thornton, for we all did, how frequently he looked her way the other night. Never fear, I think her a rather artful young thing, and Mr Thornton is but a mortal man, after all. We only felt some concern that this young lady, of whom my dear Gen has taken such obliging notice, might be forming designs upon a gentleman who is not her own."

Mrs Thornton hesitated. "My son has given his name and honour to *no* young lady as yet, Mrs Hamilton."

"Quite so," the other agreed. "I must applaud your son for not settling too quickly, as young men are apt to do. He has many more advantages open to him at his stage of life." She paused, allowing her words a moment to have their proper effect. "He must be a man of remarkable resolve to have so long been immune to the allure of so many pretty faces."

"My son is a man of high standards," Hannah straightened and her face tightened ever so slightly.

"Oh, to be sure! We were just saying as much the other day, were we not my love?"

"Indeed," Genevieve answered smoothly. "Mr Thornton seems to appreciate an outspoken and disciplined intellect, which I find refreshing in a modern gentleman."

"As well as modesty and ladylike deportment," Mrs Thornton added drily.

"Precisely," Mrs Hamilton affirmed. "I am glad to hear you speak so, Mrs Thornton. I am rather concerned for our young Miss Hale- I fear she knows not what she is about, attempting to work her arts upon such a man as your son. Why, she leaves herself open for scandal! I understand it was a near thing once before. I wonder, ought she to be cautioned? She has no mother to offer such counsel, you know."

"Miss Hale has very much a mind of her own. I think if you were to speak to her on such a matter, she would be deeply affronted- and rightly so, if you ask me. I assure you, she has not sought my son's attentions. I can answer to that quite positively."

"Well, I do beg your pardon! I only heard some rumours about Miss Hale's actions during the riots, and, well, I wished to spare her any further embarrassing incidents. It was clear to me the other evening that the girl wants for guidance, Mrs Thornton. I thought it might come best from you, as your family are such intimates with hers."

"My son thinks very highly of Mr Hale," she supplied carefully. "I am not close to either father or daughter. I think she would not appreciate my interference."

"It is to her own detriment, then. I should hate to see the young lady publically disappointed." Mrs Hamilton put aside her cup and saucer in preparation for her departure.

"Excuse me, Mrs Hamilton, but I fail to understand your concerns," Mrs Thornton huffed defensively. "I saw nothing at all alarming the other evening in Miss Hale's conduct, and even less in my son's. I noted, in fact, that they seemed rather annoyed with one another through most of the evening."

"Oh, come, now, Mrs Thornton!" the other matron smiled sweetly. "I never saw two utterly *disinterested* people as troubled as they by a mere quarrel! Mr Thornton is a man of insight, however. I trust that he would not act rashly."

"I do not presume to speak for my son, Mrs Hamilton. I am certain that he will do as he feels is right, as he has always done."

"Well said. We shall bid you a very good day then, Mrs Thornton. My love?" Mrs Hamilton rose and was helped into her wrap at the door. When they had gone, Hannah returned to her settee and slid exhaustedly into it, her hand kneading her eyes.

Now she knew why Fanny's calls had suddenly met with such a cold reception. The family was trying them, and it seemed that young Miss Hamilton was determined to have John for herself. She wondered briefly whether they had already attempted to test the hapless Miss Hale and been left dissatisfied with her response. She could be a rather contrary young woman. Mrs Thornton almost chuckled aloud imagining the fireworks from such a confrontation.

"Well, I declare!" shrilled Fanny. "I wish you had allowed me to speak more, Mother. I should have given them the right of it!"

"You do not even know what that is, Fanny," Mrs Thornton muttered from behind her hand.

"Of course I do! Margaret Hale has had eyes for John since she first came to Milton, and she sees now that she has missed her chance to ensnare him. She has befriended Miss Hamilton to put herself in his way again, but I think it's ridiculous!"

"Fanny," her mother growled in annoyance, "your understanding of matters could not be further from the truth. Do not meddle where you have no knowledge."

"Mother! You know what happened at the riots, how she flung herself at John! She is quite desperate for him to make her an offer. I shouldn't wonder, as she is grown so poor, but-"

"Enough!" Mrs Thornton thundered. "If Miss Hale is not wed to your brother, it is by her own choice, not his."

Fanny paled. "Impossible! No, he would never!"

"Many things are more impossible. As the matter does not concern you, I expect you to say nothing further about it- under *any* circumstances, am I quite understood?"

"Not concern me! I hope to call Genevieve my sister! You tell me now that that dreary Margaret Hale could take her place? Do you know what this might do to my chances with...." she gulped, cutting herself short.

"Aye, my girl, go on!" her mother challenged. When the young lady remained in blushing silence for a change, she continued. "Fanny, it is time you learnt some discretion in your own affairs. I will no longer see you running after this Rupert Hamilton as you have done. You will leave John to his business affairs with the Hamiltons, and keep your own counsel regarding his personal matters. If this young Mr Hamilton should pursue you on his own, we shall be glad to entertain him, but Fanny, you are set to bring disgrace upon yourself, and I will not have it!"

Fanny hung her head sulkily. "Yes, Mother," she mumbled with the greatest reluctance.

Chapter Seventeen

Blissfully unaware of the call paid to his mother, Mr Thornton had buried himself in his office behind a solid wall of ledgers and orders. He dipped his pen again as he scanned down the latest sheet, making marks where needed.

It was a perfect task for this day, as his current state of seclusion allowed him time to bask in the sweet afterglow of his glorious evening with Margaret. Merciful also were the demands of his work, which kept his mind well enough occupied that he did not fully descend into a fantasy world of his own making. The fantasy, he promised himself, alluring as it was, would some day soon be far less appealing than the reality! If Margaret would have him... he tingled with impatience.

How long before he could go to her without the pretense of calling on her father? He daren't frighten her, but certainly after last evening, his intentions must be obvious to her. If he courted her properly, as he ought to have before, would she accept his suit?

If she only would! Perhaps one day his lonely heart would know the pleasures and the communion of marriage. If they were truly blessed, he might even experience the joys of fatherhood! He vowed to himself that should he ever have that honour, his sons and daughters would grow up in a real family, the kind which were bound in love such as he had so often longed for. His heart swelled briefly in rapturous anticipation.

His pleasant visions dissolved with a quick rap at his office door. "Come," he called over the towering stack on his desk.

Williams entered, craning his head about to meet the master's eye through the mountain of ledgers. "Good morning, sir."

Thornton nodded quickly in greeting. "Did Thompson get that last combing machine repaired?"

"Aye. I had that Higgins chap lend a hand. He's a respectable mechanic, sir. I've been having him roving about the mill looking for maintenance issues before machines break, and it's been a help. He's a quick eye, and the hands don't slack off when he's around either."

"I had noticed. Excellent idea, we have had fewer breakdowns this week. Higgins seems to know every machine better than we. Tell me, how is that new lad in the yard working out?"

"Sacks' boy? Sharp enough, but he's too small for most of the work. I don't know if that was the best place to put him."

"Placing him there was my idea," Thornton squinted up at his overseer.

"Pardon me sir, I didn't know. Well, I'm sure he'll work out in the end."

Thornton sighed. "No, you're right. I saw him yesterday and realized I had made a mistake in assigning him there. I had thought he was a larger chap. You said he was rather clever, though?"

"Aye, sir. Ciphers the load sheets better than most, and I saw that Higgins fellow teaching him to read during the break. A great thick book they had."

"Hmm. What if you were to have him shadow Higgins? It seems that timely maintenance is saving us a deal, and if the lad shows promise, I would train him up under another in whose judgement I am confident."

Williams stretched his face into a thoughtful frown, pushing his cap back as he stroked his forehead. "He won't be earning his pay, sir. It will be a long while before he's any good."

"But," Thornton raised his pen at the overseer, "he will become invaluable soon enough, and has many promising years before him. Thompson is not the man I would choose to train another- he is a sour old curmudgeon. Higgins, however, is nearly as skilled, and might do the lad much good."

Williams shook his head and shrugged. "As you say, sir, but why Sacks? Any number of lads could do, if that's your purpose."

Thornton crossed his arms and leaned back smugly in his chair. "You said yourself that he is good with figures, and he is learning to read at an age when many an uneducated youth has long since given up. Combine that with what I know of the boy's past, and I believe he will prove an uncommonly motivated fellow. Aye, I would invest in a man like that."

Williams caught the twinkle in the master's eye and relented. It was rare, but always intriguing when Thornton took a particular interest in one of the hands. He was nearly always right. "Yes, sir. I'll talk to them both."

Another knock sounded on the door, and with a motion of his head, Thornton indicated for Williams to open it. He stood in surprise when he recognized his visitor. "Mr Hamilton, sir. Do come in." He dismissed Williams and offered Hamilton a seat. Taking his own again, he cleared a path for conversation through the ledgers on his desk.

"Thornton, thank you for seeing me." Hamilton eased himself into a chair and blew out a long breath. "Bleeding cold out today!"

Thornton smiled. "One of the advantages of the mill, sir. It is always warm in here, even when we would not wish it. What can I do for you?"

Hamilton pulled a sheaf of papers from a leather bag at his feet, and Thornton recognized his own writing. A thrill of hope shot through him.

"I've been over your forecasts- a number of times, you might imagine."

"I would have expected no less. May I ask your impression?"

Hamilton leafed through the pages until he reached one of particular interest. "Intriguing. You have much potential for growth, Thornton- more so than any of your competition by a fair shot."

"I think so. We are still replacing some of our outdated equipment, but Marlborough Mills is easily the most modern cotton plant in the region."

"Indeed. All of this modernization has, however, placed you under a significant financial burden." He fingered the page which had caught his eye. "Three hundred eighty-five pounds still owed to the bank, and another two hundred from private monies."

"Expenses which," Thornton observed confidently, "will easily be recouped within a couple of years, thanks to our increased yield."

"If you have the orders," Hamilton pointed out. He shifted in his chair, crossing his knees. "I see there has been a shortage of late. If you were not still behind from the riots this summer, you would have scarcely enough work to keep all of your machines running."

"All part of the normal ebb and flow of the market," Thornton shrugged. "We have found over the past years that the cotton market is steadily growing stronger as a whole, and such periods are always short-lived."

"They are not, however, short enough at present." Hamilton's face pinched cynically. "Let me be frank, Thornton. By my calculations, you will be bankrupt by next fall- or possibly sooner- without either an immediate turn in the market or a fresh supply of capital. With enough such capital, you could easily ride out this lean time and be poised as the premier cotton manufacturer in the entire region. Without it- well, it is not likely that the bank will extend your loan."

Thornton pressed his lips and fixed his visitor with a firm expression. "You of all men must be familiar with the hazards involved with investments such as this. The risks to yourself are lower than in most circumstances, for in this case we are speaking of an established and historically profitable enterprise- it only wants growth and a little time at present."

"How much time?" Hamilton questioned. "I've four other ventures of interest on my desk, all of which are also poised to return me a sizeable profit rather quickly if I should so choose."

"I have heard, and I know what your options are. However, a man with only a very little patience would stand to gain far more by investing in Marlborough Mills."

Hamilton laughed. "Or a man with less patience could quickly reap his profits and reinvest them, thus doubling his return in that same time."

"With respect, sir, Marlborough Mills is no gamble. These other schemes... speculations," he almost spat the word, "may yield high returns in a short time, but only *if* they pay out. You know as well as I do, sir, that many times they do not."

Hamilton laughed again. "I know your opinions in that regard. You do not mince your words! I have won and I have lost in such strategies, but always I diversify enough that I come out ahead. Come, Thornton, let us understand one another. I like you, and I know your reputation. You have a sterling record with your creditors, thus I feel rather secure in that regard. I am simply not persuaded that I would do best by investing with you. I have a great interest in your enterprise, so perhaps if I were more personally invested- if, say, there were some hope of a greater share in your future profits- it would sweeten the pot for me."

Thornton stared quizzically at his guest. "You are seeking a long-term partnership? That is rather more than I might bargain for."

"Perhaps a partnership is too rigid of an arrangement. My son, Thornton, wants direction. He understands finance, but has little head for the grittier realities of business. I should like him to spend some time under a man such as yourself. In light of his and my daughter's relations with your family, perhaps a more permanent arrangement could be found."

Thornton felt his blood chill. He spoke in a low voice, choosing his words carefully. "I was not aware that such relations were on the verge of being formalized. Has your son made my sister an offer? They barely know one another."

Hamilton pursed his lips and crossed his knees in the other direction. "I am not expecting that, no. I would not imagine that Rupert will be intending to settle anytime soon. You, however, are of the perfect age and stage of life for marriage."

Thornton swallowed, his stomach lurching. "Forgive me, Mr Hamilton," he murmured distantly. "I have given Miss Hamilton no cause for expectations. You cannot believe...." He took a deep breath and steadied himself. "Sir, I would prefer not to mingle whatever plans I might have for matrimony with our business dealings."

Hamilton's eyebrows lifted innocently. "Business matters often overlap with the personal, Thornton. My daughter is a lovely young woman; do you not agree?"

"Very," his voice cracked. "However, what cause have you to think it would be a... a suitable arrangement for her? Surely Miss Hamilton might prefer a younger man, perhaps a London man- a man of the financial business, such as yourself. A manufacturer's life is perhaps not what she would wish for."

"My daughter appreciates a man of some maturity whom she can respect, I think." Hamilton allowed himself a sly smile. "As a father, I should wish to see her settled well with a man she likes, but as a businessman, I am looking for a son-in-law with wisdom and experience, whose assets bring material consequence and the prospect of a growing fortune to my family. In you, I think perhaps I have found both men."

"Mr Hamilton," Thornton took another trembling breath and leaned forward on his desk, steepling his fingers. "I appreciate your candour. Few men would deal with me so forthrightly. I must say that marriage... to Miss Hamilton... has never been a factor in my aspirations toward a business relationship with you."

Hamilton's forehead creased. "Surely it is worth consideration, Thornton. As I have made clear, you are far from the only man soliciting my interest in his venture, but if certain matters settle in our favour, we might both look forward to a very long and profitable relationship. My daughter has exhibited a marked interest in you, and I believe you might do much for my son. He could use a steady brother, Thornton, one with a firm hand." He frowned unhappily. "I am afraid my own influence upon him has reached its zenith."

Thornton clenched his teeth. He would not give up Margaret at the pleasure of any man, not even one as wealthy as Hamilton! "I am very sorry, Mr Hamilton, but I cannot oblige you. Perhaps we could arrange for your son to work with me, if that is your wish, but I cannot commit to Miss Hamilton."

The older man cocked his head. "You have not obligated yourself elsewhere, have you Thornton? I never heard any talk of the like."

"I... I am not at liberty to discuss such matters at present, sir."

Hamilton's bushy brows jumped in a sharp gesture of resignation. "I see. Well, then I shall bid you a good day, sir."

Thornton rose with his guest, his mouth now quite dry. "I do hope you can overlook this inconvenience to your plans, sir."

Hamilton turned slightly. "Quite, Thornton. Do excuse me, I have taken more than enough of your time." He took the offered hand in a perfunctory farewell, and saw himself out.

John Thornton sank back into his chair in a daze. He had just lost his most promising investor and all hope of future support from that quarter. He swiped a hand over his suddenly throbbing forehead. There simply had to be another way, and he would find it. He always did.

~

Margaret had once again found a few moments to spend on her embroidery. It was not her favourite activity, but it felt somehow familiar and proper to resume such a genteel, feminine pursuit. A small- very small- part of her wished that Mr Thornton might find some excuse to call unexpectedly this afternoon, as he had the prior week. She might feel justified if he were to interrupt her in the midst of this utterly sedate and ladylike activity, rather than the flurry of the day before.

Her heart tripped lightly when she heard Dixon answer to a caller, but neither of the voices which soon echoed in the hallway were his. She rose to receive her callers just as the door to the drawing room swung open to admit a tall blonde woman and her only slightly taller husband.

"Mr and Mrs Draper!" she smiled and came forward, her hand extended. "It is very good of you to call."

"Miss Hale," Emmeline Draper inclined her head. "We were in the neighborhood, and as we had been meaning to call upon you, I do hope we are not troubling you overmuch just now."

"Of course not, I am very pleased you came." She glanced at Dixon and, with eyes which implored rather than instructed, silently requested some refreshments for her guests. "Please, do be seated."

Draper was glancing quietly about the room before his wife nudged his elbow gently. He came to himself. "Forgive me, Miss Hale, I am not normally so rude. I have bought and sold two houses on this block, you see, and it seems the builders used nearly the same style for all of them. Oh, my, that is a rather unique way to position the staircase."

Emmeline Draper gave a small cough, and her husband snapped his attention back again. "Oh, dear. I must beg your forgiveness once more, Miss Hale."

Margaret smiled hesitantly. "Think nothing of it, sir. I find it charming to learn what interests different people. You must have a fascination with architecture? You might enjoy speaking with my father."

Draper shook his head. "Not architecture per se, Miss Hale. I like to see cities improved, beginning with the most modest dwellings. A house such as this, for example, while not precisely an eyesore, does little to enhance the attractiveness of our neighborhood. The floorplan also is terribly inefficient."

Margaret stared for half a second, appalled that the man did not even seem to recognize his own rudeness. His wife seemed annoyed, glancing at him from the corner of her eye with a look of distaste. Margaret resolved to give him the benefit of the doubt. Perhaps the man was merely blunt, and truly had no idea how his words might be perceived. She had known others who suffered from the same sort of social awkwardness.

"We are comfortable here," she ventured after a moment. "There are many dwellings in the city which certainly boast fewer luxuries than we enjoy. Not all are so fortunate, I think."

Draper turned his eyes back to her. "Ah, and that was the reason for our call, Miss Hale. We spoke the other night of my little pet project, and you mentioned an interest in supporting our endeavours. Is that still something you would entertain, Miss Hale?"

"I think I should like to know more of the specifics of your charity, Mr Draper," she answered carefully.

"Well, I had already told you that we are attempting to fund a hospital of sorts. To do so, we must garner the support of the upper class for sponsorships. It is the fine ladies who are of the greatest help in this instance, thus it is far more preferable that a lady should pen the letters of solicitation. I trust, Miss Hale, that you write a fine hand, and are able to commit a portion of your time each week to some correspondence?"

"Why, yes. However, I had hoped for more details of the hospital itself. Is it truly a worthy foundation?"

He looked mildly surprised. "I think you are the first lady to ask such a question, Miss Hale. What could possibly be objectionable about a hospital? We have need of one, do we not?"

"Of course, I heartily agree with you. I only wonder what you meant just now when you called it 'a hospital of sorts.' Is it not to be a traditional medical facility? Have you an able administrator?"

Draper laughed. "I love the educated ladies of this modern age! Ten years ago, Miss Hale, never a feminine soul would have dared evoke such questions. As you have asked, I shall answer. I have already attracted a notable physician from London who has drawn up an operating strategy. His focus is on isolation of the sick, and prevention of the spread of disease. He has been working amidst the cholera outbreak and has much to contribute to our growing city, Miss Hale."

Margaret paused in thoughtful silence. There was something about this plan that John Thornton did not trust, and if a man of his experience and judgement felt so strongly about the matter, it was certainly good enough reason for her to hesitate. What she heard, however, sounded exactly as it should. Thornton- John- had admitted, had he not, that he could possibly be in the wrong?

She drew a tight breath and gave a quick nod. "I would be honoured to be of service, Mr Draper."

"Excellent, Miss Hale! I have here a list of names and a sample letter for you to transcribe."

Margaret took the portfolio he handed her, noting that the list of names was so long that it would take her nearly two entire days to work through.

"My dear wife," Draper was saying, "has the most elegant hand you have ever seen, has she not, Miss Hale?"

Emmeline Draper observed her husband coolly, then offered Margaret a long shrug of her delicate shoulders. "I simply have not the time to pen so many letters. I trust you will have no trouble emulating the original copy, Miss Hale?"

"You write beautifully indeed, Mrs Draper. I shall certainly give it my best efforts."

"Excellent Miss Hale!" Draper stood and helped his wife to her feet.

At that very moment, Dixon arrived with a hastily assembled tray of refreshments, her face pink with the combined effects of her haste and her lingering fever. The fashionable couple looked somewhat askance at the humble offering and made their excuses. For a moment, Margaret feared that Dixon would pick up one of the little finger sandwiches and force feed their guests herself in her vexation. To Margaret's infinite relief, she merely returned to the kitchen in silence.

"I shall send someone by to collect the letters in a few days, Miss Hale," Draper promised. They departed, and Margaret stepped back to the kitchen with the very greatest of trepidation.

"I am sorry to have troubled you, Dixon!" she apologized. "I know you are still ill! Had I known they did not intend to stay long, I... what did you do with the sandwiches?"

Dixon looked up from her kitchen chair, her cheeks rounded and full. It was a moment before she could respond. She swallowed hastily and with a painful gulp. "Well, Miss it was those little sandwiches or that stew you made yesterday. Beggin' your pardon, Miss, but one bowl of that was enough."

Margaret chuckled. "Have you any more sandwiches?"

Chapter Eighteen

Thornton had spent the larger part of that Thursday exactly where Hamilton had found him earlier in the day- at his desk trying to conjure numbers which simply refused to materialize. He ached to call again upon Margaret after everything which had passed, but his reason told him it was too soon- both for propriety's sake and for his own duty. He had no business pressing matters with her when he did not know where he stood financially! A wife had a right to expect to be supported, naturally. That last thought lent new vigour to his efforts.

He churned through stacks of documents until the numbers swam before his eyes. He dragged himself to bed late that night and spent the next day in a similar pursuit. There simply must be something he was overlooking!

During the dinner hour he had stirred, only to refresh his mind and stretch his legs. He had been gratified during that short tour to note Higgins keeping vigil over the looms with the young Sacks boy. The older man shot him an irreverent wink as he passed, warming him somewhat. At least there was one man who thought well of his efforts.

The return to his office, however, was a cold reminder of his circumstances. Hamilton had been generous in his estimate. If cotton prices spiked again or his buyers continued to delay their payments, he would not last long enough to see the expected uptick in summer orders.

He drafted reminder letters to the most delinquent of his buyers, and at last determined there was little else he could accomplish at his desk. Late in the day, he emerged once more. There was nearly an hour left in the work day, and all of the machines and workers hummed along with utmost efficiency. He was not needed for the moment.

He frowned and took a determined breath. One obligation had weighed upon him for two days, and fulfilling it would be a pleasure he was going to allow himself- now, while he could still afford to do so.

He walked briskly into the market square until he reached the shop he had destined for himself. The door jingled as he entered.

"Why, Mr Thornton, good afternoon!" the proprietress came from behind her counter to offer a warm, motherly greeting. "What can I do for you today?"

"Good afternoon, Mrs Andrews. I am looking for a new tea service."

"Oh! We have several new designs to choose from, Mr Thornton. I never thought you would persuade Mrs Thornton to a new set!"

"Er... it is a surprise. I was rather hoping you had something with a... with roses? I think... I think she might like that."

"We have this rosebud spray, sir, but I might urge you more toward the ivy leaf. Mrs Thornton tends to prefer these colours, I believe."

Thornton leaned carefully over the counter as the matronly shopkeeper drew out some of her samples. He made his mind up quickly. "*This* one," he declared, turning over a delicate cup in his large hands. Dusty roses trailed along the edge, and the shape was very fine while not appearing overly ornate. Yes, it was perfect! It looked something like the set he had caused her to drop. More importantly, it reminded him of *her*. "Do you have the entire set here in the store?" he asked hopefully.

"One moment, sir, let me check." Mrs Andrews waddled to her storeroom, and he could hear the woman chattering breathlessly for her husband's attention as he moved about the crates in the back room.

He could quite imagine her excitement. She had been trying to persuade him to expand his mother's already generous porcelain selections for years, but Mrs Thornton was far too practical to permit it. His mouth curled in secret delight. If only the woman knew the true recipient of his purchase! She would embark upon the wildest speculations if she imagined her modest little shop to be the purveyor of such a gift.

He sighed happily as he imagined giving the set to Margaret. She would thank him, say he was thoughtful... but she would try to refuse it, of course. Her modesty alone would require her to... he frowned. Perhaps he would need to have it delivered by someone else.

It would be a shame to miss the light in her face when she first beheld the set, but she might be more comfortable if he were not present. He tamped down his disappointment. This was for her benefit, after all, and not his own. Though he had been responsible for the previous set's destruction and rightly owed her a replacement, it *was* a most suggestive gift. He would have to see things done as properly as could be.

"Here we are, Mr Thornton! The entire set." Mr Andrews followed his beaming wife, carting the fully loaded crate of china. The top had been left off so that the sample cup and saucer from the display could be included. Thornton reached inside and lifted another piece of the set from the crate with satisfaction. Yes, it suited her wonderfully!

The door jingled behind him to admit Mrs Slickson and Mrs Hamper. He drew to the side, keeping his face turned, but his presence in such a shop was rather notable.

"Mr Thornton, what a pleasure to see you today!" Mrs Hamper sidled close, peering indiscreetly into the crate. "A gift for Mrs Thornton?"

He clenched his teeth. "A surprise. Good day, Mrs Hamper, Mrs Slickson." He paid for his purchase and arranged for the crate to be delivered to his own door, then fled the shop. He would have to work out delivery to the crate's final destination later.

~

He was walking back into the yard gate just as the last string of workers were making their way home for the day. Higgins, of course, was among the stragglers. "G'd'evenin' Master!" he tipped his cap.

"Good evening, Higgins. How are you finding your new assignment?"

Higgins chuckled. "Wondrin' what yo're abou', Master. Did I do some'at amiss?"

"We'll find out, I'm sure," Thornton half-smiled. "I have been meaning to ask you- how are the children getting on in school? They began already, did they not?"

Higgins smothered a proud grin. "Come wi' me now, Master, see for yo'r own self. The'll be ri' pleased. The lass, sir, she's been workin' 'ard, 'opin' t'impress yo'." There was a crafty twinkle in the old weaver's eye, almost as if he were daring his employer to accept the invitation.

Thornton looked beyond Higgins to his own residence. If he returned home now, he would feel compelled to spend more fruitless hours behind his study desk. There was the additional misery of a recent war waged among the female denizens of his household- he had not been quite late enough last evening to avoid an entire recounting of their day. He did not look forward to another such uncomfortable evening! He drew a long breath. "Do you know, I believe I will."

They walked together, Master and Union leader. It would have been an entertaining experiment to be able to observe the onlookers as they passed, but they kept to themselves as they walked and talked.

Higgins expounded upon his recent ideas about the kitchen. He had already spoken to a meat wholesaler and seen to the relocation of an unused cook stove. His daughter, he thought, might make the perfect cook. He hoped they would have all of the necessary arrangements complete by the end of the following week.

"What do the men say? Is the idea well received?" Thornton wondered.

"Ever'one's clamin' 'e thought of it first," Higgins grinned.

"It ought to be a benefit," Thornton mused. "I cannot help but think full bellies would do much for everyone."

"Aye, Master. Yo' should'a seen young Willy Sacks when 'e 'eard o' it. I think it's been a long while since the lad 'ad a square meal."

Thornton scowled. "His father is still spending his days at the Dragon?"

Higgins shook his head. "'Is wife tossed 'im out. She said she won' 'ave 'im takin' the childers' wages and drinkin' 'em. Trouble is, now 'e's workin' o'er the Union folk, tryin' to start trouble again. 'Tis just noise, sir, don' bother with it."

"The last time I had a particularly discontented worker, he stirred enough trouble to incite a riot."

Higgins winked. "I'd almos' say yo' deserved that, sir, but it still wasn'a right. Broke up a perfectly good strike, it did."

"Yes, what a pity," Thornton turned a sardonic expression upon his employee.

Higgins grinned, facing forward again as he walked. "Don' worry 'bout Sacks, Master, no one pays 'im any mind."

~

Margaret's week had altered rather drastically from the prior one. Her father was improving already, which gave her great reason for hope. He seemed stronger and better aware of his own vulnerability, and she had already begun to fear much less for him.

She looked forward to longer and more frequent walks now, but her charity work had kept her constrained to her writing desk for many hours together. She had intended to visit Mary Higgins on the previous afternoon, but she had felt it only right to complete her task before venturing on any pleasure outings.

At last she had finished, and she was pleased to settle into the old chair in Mary's kitchen. The children filed dutifully around her, the older two eager to display their new learning. She admired their neat scrawls and encouraged their blossoming phonetic skills with enthusiasm. The glow of scholarly achievement was still fresh upon them, and they humbled her with the great pride they took in their education.

Margaret had just shifted Jenny onto her lap to listen to her new words when the door opened. She looked up, smiling. "Nicholas! You see, for once I have come when you are... oh!" Her cheeks burned as a tall man stepped inside the little house behind Higgins.

"Aye Lass, I won'red if yo' mighn' be 'ere," Higgins slanted a sly grin over his shoulder. "We 'adn' seen yo' a' week. Mary, we've 'nother guest!"

Margaret's eyes were still on the figure in black, who now approached her with an enchanted warmth upon his face. She could not rise with the child on her lap, but she smiled shyly. "Good evening, Mr Thornton."

His pleasure wilted into disappointment. "'Mr Thornton' again, is it? I shall have to remove my coat once more." He turned to his host with a bemused expression. "At least one of us is on first-name terms with the lady!"

Margaret felt the heat crawling up her neck. She coaxed Jenny off her lap and rose to draw near. "I am a guest here as well, sir," she blushed, keeping her voice low. "I had assumed such informality extended only to my own home."

"And I had hoped otherwise," he whispered, bending close. In a more conversational tone, he looked to little Jenny, who had leaned bashfully into Margaret's skirts. "I understand your studies are coming along very well, Miss Boucher. Mr Higgins invited me to come see for myself."

Jenny nodded, giggling and looking up to Margaret with a beaming smile. Margaret felt her breast swell beyond explanation. This man who had slowly captivated her interest appeared to have thoroughly won over the heart of the small girl at her side. Was there any surer way for a man to secure a woman's affections than by seeing to the pleasure of a child? She met his eyes once more and found them silently waiting for her approval.

Higgins was tactful enough to make a great show of greeting Mary while his two guests shared their private exchange. After a proper pause, he raised his voice. "Miss Marg'et, I see yo' brou' a wee tart!" He chuckled loudly. "yo'r Miss Dixon vowed I'd na' get another!"

Margaret turned. "I pleaded your case, Nicholas. I threatened to make it myself if she did not. She has a reputation to uphold, after all."

Higgins guffawed. "Thank yo', Lass! Tho' I'd be righ' pleased to try yo'r own cookin', if it came to it!"

Margaret reddened again as the tall man by her side shot her a knowing wink and a secret smile. "*I* have had that honour, Mr Higgins, and the pleasure was most certainly mine."

"Ho! I thou' as much." Higgins chortled.

Margaret's eyes were wide with disbelief. "What- a pleasure! Why, we could hardly stand to eat it!"

"Miss Hale is too modest, Mr Higgins. It was the most delightful meal of my life." He offered a kindly little bow in her direction before submitting to Jenny's pleading tugs on his hand. Danny by now had found him as well, and eagerly pressed his primer into Thornton's other hand. He followed the children to a chair, his warm gaze lingering on Margaret as he went.

Margaret could scarcely meet his eyes. A strange, new feeling welled up within her. Her stomach tingled when he looked at her, and her old maidenly independence warred with the pleasant allure she felt whenever *he* was in the room. He drew all of her attention, and it mortified her to consider what others watching her might think. The temptation, however, was too great. Her cheeks stained crimson, she dared to raise unwavering eyes to where he sat across the room.

He was looking steadily back at her.

Margaret's limbs quivered with a thrilling little flutter. She caught her breath and forced herself to look away, but not before he treated her to another of his crooked smiles. *Oh, dear! Silly little fool that I am, but that smile of his!* Clenching her fingers tightly to still the tremble in her hands, she rushed to help Mary as the girl made ready to serve Dixon's fresh tart.

Though her eyes were down before her, her thoughts were trained only on the rich, deep voice across the room as he spoke with the children. His tones were utterly unique to her ears; a voice which could belong to him alone. At once cultured with the sophistication native to his bearing and roguish with the autonomous spirit of his northern heritage, the now familiar cadence of his speech lilted comfortingly to her as she listened. *What would it be like,* she wondered fleetingly, *to lay my head upon his chest and listen to that deep rumble of his voice, as Jenny does?*

Shocked at her own unbidden thoughts, she lingered with Mary far longer than was necessary. *You are supposed to be a lady!* she scolded herself. What immodest ideas would occur to her next? She bit her lip in vicious self-chastisement and drew near to Nicholas at last with a serving tray.

He looked up from his seat, a suspicious twinkle in his eye. "Nay, Lass, yo' dursn' serve me. Set, Miss Marg'et, yo're a guest!"

"It pleases me, Nicholas," she smiled and pressed a little saucer of tart and cream upon him.

She came to Thornton next, who had just shuffled both children off his lap in anticipation of her offering. She lifted the tray slightly, and softly-very softly- spoke. "John?"

His clear blue eyes, shining in delight, met hers. He held her gaze for a second before he accepted, assuring himself that she sensed his pleasure and gratitude. "Thank you, Margaret," he murmured quietly.

A giddy tickle raced through Margaret's core and she turned quickly to the children before she could embarrass herself further. What had come over her? She could only hope that Nicholas Higgins was either less astute or more prudent than she had previously given him credit for. Had they been in any other company, her moonstruck behaviour would have fueled the local gossip for weeks.

The visitors did not stay long after. The family offered to share their entire meal, of course, but neither party would dream of imposing further. Margaret found herself tangled among the four smaller children as she made her farewells to Mary, while Nicholas and John lingered near the door with the two older children in anxious attendance.

"Master," Higgins stroked Daniel's fair head fondly, "'t'were righ' decent o' yo' to come see the childer. They were 'opin' yo'd be back for a visit."

"I shall come as often as I can," Thornton promised. "It is a pleasure, I assure you. Higgins," he hesitated, then looked the other firmly in the eye, extending his hand, "you have done right. My respects."

A slow smile tugged the old weaver's bristling cheeks as he took his employer's hand. "Thank yo', Master." With a sly peek across the room to where Margaret was still trying to disengage herself, he leaned close in a whisper. "Tha's a fair lady, Master, and no mistake. Yo're a lucky man, sir."

Thornton's eyes narrowed ever so slightly, and the ghost of a smile touched his lips. He held up a single finger in a mute plea for silence as Margaret at last made her way to them.

"Miss Hale?" he extended his elbow as she came near. "May I see you home?"

Margaret smiled bashfully and took his arm. She then looked beyond him, through the door, and her smile faded. "Oh, dear. It is raining terribly!"

"Which is why, Miss Hale, I offered to see you home. I see that once again you thought to bring an umbrella, while I did not." He winked toward Higgins.

Margaret surveyed him with mock indignation. "I was under the impression, Mr Thornton, that it was for the gentleman to make such provisions!"

"How fortunate for me, then, that I am not a proper gentleman. My lack of foresight seems to have served me well thus far. Shall we?" He drew out Mr Hale's old umbrella and popped it open outside the door for emphasis.

Higgins was laughing heartily as he bid Margaret his farewell. "'Least 'tis a short walk, Lass!" he chuckled as the pair set out. He closed the door and looked to his daughter. "Well, my girl, tha's a man wha's a fair sight 'appier than I've e'er known."

Mary frowned at her father. "I don' understand, Da'."

Higgins groaned in relief as he sank into his chair and began to pull off his boots. "A man's 'eart wants the touch of a woman, that's a', Lass."

Mary tilted her head quizzically. "Yo' think Master's soft for Miss Marg'et?"

He sighed contentedly. "Girl, a' I know is th'ould bulldog's been gen'led."

Chapter Nineteen

John and Margaret had huddled under their shared umbrella, he offering his broad shoulder as additional shelter against the weather. The lingering noise of the street and the falling rain made conversation difficult, but neither felt discontented. Their recent encounters had bred a familiarity between them which dispelled nearly all of their former discomfort.

Margaret's confidence in him had tottered, wavered and then begun to flourish after he had learned the truth behind her actions concerning Frederick. He could have shamed her, as she had herself, but instead he had extended grace and gentle understanding. Within his unpolished exterior dwelt a man in whom she could trust. She smiled down at the ground as she walked, and unconsciously tightened her arm through his.

John's mouth pulled into a satisfied expression. Heaven help him, but his vaunted patience was unraveling. She cared for him, he was certain of it! If only he felt right about falling on his knees the very moment they had gained the shelter of her door! Alas, he owed her a future, and he could not ask her to share in his fears and trials just yet. He wished to give her joy, not trouble.

And speaking of trouble... he glanced about, wondering if their closeness had attracted anyone's attention. Eyes turned their direction through a few street side windows, but perhaps fortunately for them, it was dark and all of the shops along their way had already closed. Any onlookers, he assured himself, would only notice a gentleman assisting a lady in hurrying to escape the rain. It is likely that he underestimated the novelty of himself, the famed bachelor of Marlborough Mills, giving his arm to a pretty young woman in that part of town.

Only a few moments later they blew with a strong gust of wind through the Hales' door. Mr Hale, who happened to have just been descending the stairs, peered at them in surprise. "John? Margaret?" He made his slow, careful way to the front door where the two stood breathless and dripping.

Margaret was laughing as she tried- with John's help- to shed her wet cloak without soaking her dress beneath. "Good evening, Father!" she greeted him with unusual cheer.

Thornton extended his hand. "Good evening, Mr Hale. I had the very great pleasure this evening of encountering Miss Hale at the Higgins' home."

"Oh! Are they well, Margaret?" Mr Hale looked curiously to his daughter.

"Yes, Father, very well. I was about to ask Mr Thornton to stay for tea- or at least to dry off a little." She came to him, smiling, and clearly asking with her eyes that he might second the invitation.

Mr Hale turned in mild bewilderment to his favourite pupil. "Why, of course, John, you must stay a while."

"Sir, I would quite understand if you are feeling poorly. I do not wish to impose," Thornton offered, but the hope in his eyes was evident.

"No! No, you must stay. I am feeling much better. I think I must thank you, John, for encouraging me to see Dr Donaldson. Come, I was about to enjoy the drawing room fire."

The two men adjourned to the fire, but Margaret separated herself to summon Dixon. Thornton looked back questioningly as she left them, but she glanced over her shoulder with sweet assurance in her eyes.

"John," Mr Hale eased himself into a cushioned chair before his fire. "I must thank you for seeing Margaret safely home once more. I worry for her when it has grown dark, or when the weather is so trying."

Thornton chose a seat opposite him. "It was my pleasure, Mr Hale, but Miss Hale is a very capable young lady. You need not worry for her."

Hale smiled softly. "She is. She is very much like..." he sighed, his voice trailing off, then suddenly fixed his eyes more firmly upon his guest. "Margaret tells me that she spoke to you of my son. I wish you could have known him, John."

"As do I. I believe I would hold him in the very highest regard."

An inarticulate noise escaped the old man. He nodded, his eyes faraway and misty. "You are of a kind, John. Frederick is a man of duty and responsibility, much like you."

Thornton leaned forward, lacing his hands together and resting them upon his knees. "So I gather. I must respect a man who can make such a hard choice, weighing the welfare of others against his own good."

The weathered flesh around Hale's eyes softened sadly and he began to blink. For a moment, Thornton feared that his friend would crumble into grief once more, but Hale only gave a trembling sigh. After a moment, he changed the subject. "How are things at the mill, John?"

The happiness which had been his for the past couple of hours withered away. It had been a pleasant dream to push aside his worries for a time, but now the black cloud descended once more. His face fell visibly. "They could be better," he confessed.

"Oh?" Hale's brow puckered. "I had a letter from Mr Bell today. He spoke of you."

"Of me? I have not heard from him in some weeks. Is he concerned for the stability of the mill?"

"Not specifically. It seems that Mr Hamilton had written him as part of his investigation into the mill's financial prospects, wishing to discover if it were a sound investment. They are old associates, you understand. Bell did not give him very much information to that regard, I do not believe," he hurried to say. "He would not have spoken a word against you, John."

"I doubt he could have said anything which Hamilton did not already know." Thornton's jaw set in frustration. There was nothing he could do about Hamilton now.

Mr Hale covered his mouth uncomfortably with his hand. "No doubt," he mumbled beneath his fingers. "I hope you have been able to work something out with Mr Hamilton. He could offer you much assistance, could he not?"

Thornton sighed. "If he desired it, but I do not think we will be able to reach an understanding."

Hale was silent a moment, his gaze for once penetrating rather than vague. Truly, he was one of only a handful of individuals who could question Thornton so boldly, and he did not take that regard lightly. At last, he suggested, "Will not the mill suffer- and by extension, the workers- if you do not attract new investors?"

"Yes," was the simple admission.

Hale lapsed into commiserating quiet. "I trust," he murmured after a few moments, "that you will do what is right, John."

Thornton's eyes rose from the floor back to his mentor. "I would not see others suffer for my decisions, if I can at all help it. It is," he smiled, recalling a conversation at a long-ago Master's dinner, "the Christian thing to do, my friend."

Hale's face split into a broad smile at the memory. Such a long road they two had walked in just over a year! "As well as a sound business practice, John," Hale returned.

They were still chuckling lightly from this exchange when Margaret reappeared with Dixon in tow and a tray of hot coffee. She came to John first, pouring him a cup and offering it. "I thought this might warm you better for your walk."

"Thank you, Margaret. This is very much appreciated." He smiled up at her with his eyes as he blew the steam from his cup.

Margaret darted a quick glance to her father, whose face reflected speechless surprise. She looked back to Thornton in some concern, but his reassuring little wink, shielded from her father's view by the coffee pot she still held, lent her courage. She took a deep breath. "You are welcome, John. Father?"

She turned and poured a hot cup for him as well, then gave the pot to Dixon to serve the sugar and cream. So stunned was Mr Hale that he only gaped in awe when his daughter drew near. Margaret waited for him to reach for her own fingers to serve himself the sugar, as he often did, but she was obliged at last to simply drop two lumps into his cup herself.

She returned the coffee things to the tray, then took a cup for herself before Dixon returned it all to the kitchen. She chose a seat strategically placed at equal distances between the two men and stirred her coffee in nervous silence. Her father was glancing back and forth between them, his coffee largely ignored.

John certainly noticed Mr Hale's sudden reticence, but chose to let it pass without comment. Mr Hale was not a man to be set at his ease by bluntly approaching matters. He opted for small-talk instead, which was wholly out of character for him, but might settle his friend. "This is a very fine blend," he noted to Margaret, lifting his cup fractionally. "I should find out where you acquired it."

"Oh, yes," she roused in relief. "Dixon was dissatisfied with the shop she used to purchase from. I believe she obtained this from a place called Willards, though I cannot think where it might be."

"I know the place. It is just next to the tobacconist's," he replied carelessly. "I was there only last week."

Margaret replaced her cup with the barest clink upon the saucer. Narrowing her eyes, she pinned the oblivious Thornton with a searching gaze. "I thought it was a gift to you, and you did not smoke, sir."

She had arrested him in the midst of enjoying another sip of his coffee. His dark brows lifted above his cup and he caught himself just before he spilled the hot liquid in surprise. Lowering it again, he cleared his throat. "So I do not. I am afraid you have found me out, Margaret."

Margaret quickly hid her guilty smile behind her own cup. So, he had fabricated an excuse to see her! Her eyes sparkled in pleasure and amusement as she peered at him over the rim. If he were embarrassed at her discovery of his ruse, he gave no indication. Rather, he seemed delighted with their private joke.

Mr Hale's brow clouded with the deepening mystery played out before him. "Tobacco?" he wondered aloud. "Oh, you must be speaking of last week! John, do forgive me, I believe I forgot to thank you for the gift you brought by. It was very thoughtful of you, and I do apologize for not sending a note."

"Think nothing of it, sir. I am only glad to see you recovering your strength once more, and so quickly, too! It is nothing short of remarkable."

"Margaret takes excellent care of me," the father smiled fondly at his daughter.

"Indeed, she does," Thornton agreed. "You are most blessed, Mr Hale."

Margaret glanced self-consciously between the affectionate gazes leveled in her direction. It would have been warming, even exhilarating if *he* were to look at her so tenderly with no one else about. Her imagination flourished suddenly with visions of the intimate encounter which might soon follow such a look... but with her father present! She cast her eyes to the floor, lashes lowered over her rosy cheeks.

John was the first to sense her discomfort. He set his cup aside, catching her eye with the movement and tipping his head in quiet contrition. "You must forgive me; I am afraid I have stayed too long. My mother will be wondering what has become of me."

"But John, you must wait yet a little while," Mr Hale objected. "It is still raining rather hard, but it cannot last much longer, I think."

"It is only a good stout Milton storm," John laughed lightly, rising from his seat. "I have been out in many such, Mr Hale. Fear not, I shall be home before the downpour has even thought about lightening." His host and hostess rose with him, and both followed him toward the door.

He donned his coat, which was still far from dried, and shook hands with Mr Hale. "Good evening, sir. I expect I will see you at service on Sunday."

"Good night, John, and do take care. I should hate to see you fall ill!" Mr Hale admonished.

"I shall, sir." He turned to Margaret, who came softly near with their family umbrella in one hand and his gloves in the other. "You must not forget these," she smiled playfully.

He laughed outright. "Would that I could! They seem to follow me." He clapped the borrowed umbrella beneath his arm. With one hand he accepted the gloves, and with the other he took hers. "Good evening, Margaret."

After he had gone, Mr Hale stared in mute amazement at his daughter. She tensed. The light-hearted, flirtatious friendship she had so recently struck up with John Thornton gave her every cause for pleasure, but she knew not how to explain it to her father. She, who had once so roundly abused the virtues of this industrial titan of a man, now could think of nothing more pleasant than many more hours in his company.

She winced inwardly, knowing the conversation which had to follow. It would do her little good to hide in the kitchen with Dixon this evening- it would only cost them both a restful night's sleep. "Come, Father," she offered. "We should enjoy that lovely fire while it lasts."

~

"I am pleased that you and John seem to be on better terms these days." Mr Hale drew his chair nearer to the fire, turning a little away from Margaret as he did so. Margaret knew this gesture well- it was a sure sign of an impending serious discussion.

She took a seat nearby, nibbling her lip. "I think him a fine man, Father. I am sorry that it took me so long to appreciate his qualities."

"I am glad you have done so now; he is a good man. I think very highly of him. I was surprised, though, that you are so suddenly on first-name terms with him!"

She arched her neck, perhaps a little too proudly. "But I speak familiarly with Nicholas, and some of Edith's friends- Henry, for example."

Her father tilted his head to look directly at her. "We speak so with Nicholas because he is uncomfortable with formality. As for that Henry Lennox fellow... I have wondered once or twice if his intentions were only friendly."

Margaret lapsed into convicted silence, confirming her father's suspicions. Mr Hale's forehead knit thoughtfully as he returned his gaze to the fire.

"Margaret, did I tell you that I received a letter from Mr Bell today?"

She looked up, relieved at the change in subject. "No! Oh, how is he? I think of him so often!"

"He has suffered from some sort of complaint. I had hoped he would come to us this winter, but he does not desire to travel in the cold weather. I was just telling John," he touched his fingers nervously to his lips as though he wished he could toy with a pipe, "Bell said that Mr Hamilton had inquired of him regarding Marlborough Mills."

Margaret tilted her head. "Why would he have done so?"

"Well, it seems that John had hoped that Mr Hamilton might become a financial backer at the mill. It has fallen on rather hard times since the strike, you know, and John told me recently that the market is bad in general at present."

"Oh," she nodded. "That would indeed be a godsend for the mill. Was Mr Bell able to offer much information? I am certain," she went on confidently, "that Mr Hamilton will find Mr Thornton an honest and clever business associate."

"Margaret," Mr Hale's voice lowered seriously, "Mr Bell believes that Mr Hamilton desired more than a business associate."

She shook her head vaguely. "I do not understand."

Mr Hale draped his head back upon his chair, his fingers digging into his eyes as he worked up the courage to speak. "Mr Hamilton was searching out information on John's personal life and character. It was this of which he wrote to Bell, not the financial particulars of the mill. Hamilton seems to be interested in joining his family to Mr Thornton's."

Margaret's breathing slowed. Her hands went suddenly clammy and she fought a tremor through her heart. "In what manner?" She did not like the way her voice shook.

Mr Hale raised pained eyes to his daughter.

She blinked, clenching her fingers into her skirts. "I... I see." Her vision blurred inexplicably. If she had yet suffered in any doubt regarding the nature of her feelings for John Thornton, it vanished in that moment.

"My dear," Hale reached between their chairs for his daughter's hand. "When Bell was last here he said something which shocked me very greatly, and I disbelieved it at the time, but I think..." he sighed and forced himself to continue. "I think I must now ask you. Have you any reason to believe that Mr Thornton cares for you?"

Margaret's head bowed, her lower lip quivering faintly. She could not find her voice, so she simply nodded.

"Are your feelings also so engaged?" her father asked quietly.

She drew a long breath, then another. At last, in a whisper, she choked out, "Yes, Father."

Mr Hale squeezed her hand, but his own grip was unsteady. "I can think of nothing," he murmured, "which could please me more, my dear."

Margaret tried to swallow the tight knot which had formed in her throat. "Father, if... if Mr Thornton requires a dowry... or if Mr Hamilton's support is contingent upon...." Her voice broke and she huffed a quick breath for composure. "I would not see him injured, Father."

"If I am correct in my guess, my dear, it would injure him very greatly if you were to refuse him."

"It did, Father." She trapped her upper lip in her teeth as she met her father's eyes once more.

"You... you refused him? But I do not understand!"

"It was some while ago, Father. Matters are different now, but he has not made any further mention of... but I suppose no man would wish to be refused twice. Perhaps," she tried to sound cheerful, though every instinct objected to the insincerity of her words, "he truly has only acted as a friend of late. It would be more prudent, of course, for him to be considering Miss Hamilton. She is a- a respectable...." Her voice began to break, and she was not able to finish her words.

"He may not be," Hale offered hopefully. "He did not sound as though he were moving toward any such arrangement."

Margaret tightened her fingers through her father's hand. "Father," she whispered, "I have nothing to offer him. So many depend upon the mill! It would be selfish to consider such a possibility."

Hale rose stiffly from his favourite chair and came to sit next to his daughter on the sofa. Her eyes were closed and she was trembling. He placed an arm about her, drawing her head to his shoulder as he had when she was a little girl. "Would that I could feel right in encouraging your feelings for him! I do not desire for you to be made unhappy, my child."

Margaret's only answer was a shuddering sigh.

"I wish," he mused softly, "that Bell had not already invested most of his available capital."

"Oh, I had not considered Mr Bell!" she looked up quickly. "But he cannot help?"

Hale shrugged. "Bell is a businessman, Margaret. Not the typical businessman, you understand, but he must look to his own affairs. When he was here this summer, I believe he was consulting a Mr Watson regarding some scheme- you must forgive me, my dear, but I had no head for such matters. I do not remember the particulars."

"I remember Mr Watson," Margaret squinted in thought. "He was at the Hamiltons' dinner party. I heard someone make mention of his financial strategies." Her typically serene face crumpled in disappointment. "I am certain that Mr Bell knows what he is doing, but oh, Father! Such a pity that he could not have purchased a share in John's business instead!"

Mr Hale stroked his dear child's hair. "It seems to me that he put himself at great risk, chancing so much in one place as he has, but I am sure I do not rightly understand such matters.

"Come, my dear, it is possible that it all may come to nothing. John is a clever fellow, after all. I am certain he will find a way. He has built from nothing to where he is now, you know."

Margaret sighed a deep, quivering breath. "But what if he cannot, Father? After everything, how would such a loss affect him? The mill has been his life's work; it is who he is! If he were to lose everything now, after so many years of work and so much devotion, I fear for his spirits."

"'Take therefore no thought for the morrow: for the morrow shall take thought for the things of itself. Sufficient unto the day is the evil thereof,'[ii]" Hale quoted. "But I am weary now, my dear. I think I shall retire upstairs." He kissed her temple and rose unsteadily.

Margaret blinked away her cares for the moment and took a cleansing draught of air. "Let me see you upstairs, Father."

He turned, smiling gently, and rather leaned on her arm than offered his. "I do not know that I would wish any man to take you from me, my child. If it had to be any, I would be delighted if it were John, but I do not know how I would do without you."

"And now it is you who are borrowing trouble, Father!" she teased half-heartedly. "That path is not presently before us, and we shall only rob ourselves of sleep tonight with such worries."

Chapter Twenty

"Rupert! Rupert Hamilton, open this door at once! Where have you been?" Genevieve's muffled voice drifted under the oaken door to her brother's chambers as her flattened palm pattered upon the outside. "I know you are in there!"

There was an exasperated grumble, the rustling of blankets and the tapping of light feet. Finally, her brother's heavy tread sounded and the door cracked open. "What now, Gen?" Rupert's hair was tousled and he was still in his bed clothes, but that was all she could see, as he pressed his body firmly into the gap of the open door.

"Where have you been?" she hissed, her little hands fisted upon her hips.

"Right here. Why?"

She scoffed. "Not until late in the night! Where have you been the last two days? You crawl into your room after everyone is abed and then you disappear before breakfast!"

A rakish grin formed upon his lips. "You wouldn't want to know."

"Oh, bother! Let me in, the servants are going to hear us!"

He glanced over his shoulder. "Not now, Sis."

She slapped his face as it turned back into her view. "Swine!" she spat. "Is it that same little kitchen tart you were 'detained' with during the dinner party?"

His cheek flickered, wincing just a little- she did not hit that hard, after all- and he looked over his shoulder again. "I don't remember. Was she blonde?"

"I still cannot believe you! Mother was so cross! Of all the foul, vulgar...." She pinched his nose, a remnant of their long-ago days of youthful skirmishes. "You are a disgusting rodent, Rupert!"

"Ow!" he pulled back, rubbing his abused face. "I'm closing the door now."

"No!" she whispered fiercely, sticking her foot in the door. With a frantic gesture, she pointed his attention down the hall, where two or three of the household staff could be heard from around the corner. "Let me in!"

"Oh, suit yourself!" He threw his hands up and backed away from the door, allowing her entry.

She marched indignantly into the room, her resentful gaze sweeping the corners and window ledges for a third occupant. She even went so far as to peer under the bed. "You cad, there is no one here!" she cried at last.

"Not anymore," he grinned smugly.

"Oh, spare me. Rupert, I am serious, I needed to talk to you! Why have you been avoiding me?"

"I haven't been avoiding you, so much as finding better things to entertain myself."

"It's Father you're avoiding, isn't it!" she stalked toward him, shaking a finger.

He spread his hands helplessly. "The old man? Bleeding right. Why would I let him chain me to a desk? He's been on that again, Gen, making threats to indenture me out as some," he shuddered, "*manufacturing* clerk! Me! I could write a few letters to my mates at the Club, and men like Hamper or Thornton would topple!"

"Father doesn't seem to believe that. Why *was* it, Rupert, that you had to return to Milton?" She crossed her arms and tapped her toes. "Well, go on, I'm waiting! It wasn't *really* just to come welcome me home, was it?"

"Father cut off my funds," he grumbled. "He doesn't understand that for a fellow to get his foot in the door in places like the Exchange, he has to live in style! And you don't make much to begin with. Oh, I have money of my own, Gen, but it has yet to come through! You'll see, I'll be out from under Father's thumb soon enough."

"You are not out from mine, Rupert. You promised! Did you ever go talk to Margaret Hale like I asked?"

"Sort of." He rubbed the back of his neck and took a seat on his rumpled bed. She glared at him. "What?" he cried. "Look, if your delicate sensibilities cannot handle seeing a man's bed, maybe you shouldn't force your way into his room!"

"I'm waiting, Rupert! What did you find out?"

"She's smarter than I am," he groused. "And she thinks I am a fool."

"She said all of that? You're making that up! Margaret is at least polite, if you are not."

"Oh, polite, yes. And has no sense of humour. What on earth do you see in her, Gen?"

"It annoyed Fanny Thornton that I was friends with her, that's what. After that, I started liking her for her own sake. She is the one person I know who speaks only the truth, without ulterior motives. I thought I could at least count on her as one trustworthy friend, until I saw the way John Thornton was looking at her. What did she say about him when you asked?"

"She despised him, or rather she *used* to. She doesn't anymore. Why have you always been so stuck on Thornton? I've a dozen friends in London I could introduce you to!"

"Oh, you wouldn't understand!" she waved a hand in angry dismissal.

"Well, then you'll get no further help from me." He crossed his arms obstinately.

She blew out an irritated huff. "Oh, very well. I told you how I used to call on Fanny when we were in school? My governess insisted that I learn to make proper calls on all of the other girls, and Mother was not often around in those days; you remember, she and Father couldn't stand one another for years!"

"I remember. Father finally made Mother come back under the same roof because people were starting to talk."

"And I had to make do with old Mrs Mitchell instead of my own mother!" Genevieve pouted. "She took me to the homes of all the girls my age- I suppose she thought she was doing right. I barely knew Fanny, and I was terrified of her mother, but one day when we were there, I saw *him*. He only passed by the hall, then spoke a few words to his mother, but I saw how his mother and sister respected him. It was so strange! He was so young, but they looked up to him far more than we ever did to Father."

Rupert shrugged. "Mrs Thornton is a queer one. You heard what her husband did, did you not?"

"Yes, but Rupert, you don't understand! It fascinated me to watch them. He was so strict, even in a way with his mother, but so protective at the same time. I started wishing that Father had been more like that. He always let us do whatever we wished."

"Precisely!" Rupert cried. "It was marvelous!"

"You don't remember when old Mitchell would use the switch on me for just about anything? Father never did a thing about it!"

His face sobered. "I do remember a little. One time was because you made a mistake during your piano practice. That was harsh, Gen. I hated her for you."

"Well, I started thinking that a man like Mr Thornton would do more than hate her for me. He would have put a stop to it. I said as much to Father- without naming any names, of course- and that was when he started making plans to send me away to the Continent. It was easier, I suppose."

"Father was always one to throw money at us," Rupert frowned. "I never had any objections until he stopped doing so. Besides, I thought you liked shopping well enough!"

"Never mind, Rupert," she sighed in resignation. "I said before that you wouldn't understand. Just tell me what Margaret said!"

"Why do you care?" he wondered intractably. "She's no competition for you! I'd imagine Thornton is rather desperate for Father's support, after all."

"Mother got Father to tell her what Mr Thornton said the other day. Rupert, he doesn't want me!" She buried her face in her hands and began to sob dramatically.

He stood and began to pat his sister's shoulder awkwardly. "What do you mean, Gen? I hadn't heard anything about this."

"He- he refused Father's offer!" she blubbered through her fingers.

"Bah," Rupert scoffed. "Thornton is too fond of his own way. He'll come round, Gen, he just didn't want Father to dictate terms to him."

She raised her face, sniffling. "Do you really think? You think I've a chance?"

He sneered distastefully. "Women!" he muttered under his breath. "Gen, you can have any man you please. *Trust* me," he emphasized his remarks with a leering smile.

She snatched the pillow from his bed and slashed at his head with it. "You are revolting!"

He actually laughed. "No doubt." He stretched in self-satisfied pleasure and resumed his comfortable seat on the bed, draping his arm over the rail of the footboard.

"Rupert," she turned seriously to him, "I think he has been thinking of Margaret Hale! I don't believe half of what Fanny Thornton says, so you must tell me. What did she say about him? You don't think she would accept him, do you?"

"She might. She seemed rather uncomfortable when I brought his name up, and she refused to be baited into abusing him."

Genevieve growled and at last fell to a seat beside her brother. "If only Father had not sent me away for so very long! I feared surely he would be married by the time I returned, and it is nearly as bad as that. He has found another while I was away!"

"Don't be ridiculous. Thornton and Miss Hale fought all evening last Monday! Didn't you see them?"

"I'm not blind, Rupert, but you must be. If Margaret Hale cast him a bone, he would be hers in a heartbeat. I don't understand it!"

He merely shook his head and rolled his eyes, bracing his weight back behind him with his hands.

"Rupert," she turned, grasping him by the shoulders. "Do you think you might be able to interest her in yourself instead?"

"That would be disastrous," he predicted with a little laugh. "She's frightening."

"Margaret, frightening? Why, she is the least intimidating person I know!"

"You do not know her as well as you think. Believe me, Gen, I know women. She is the sort who would find some way of proving me the fool before everyone. No, thank you."

"There must be *some* way of diverting her! Surely, if she were to lose interest, John Thornton would as well!"

"Well..." Rupert scratched his cheek thoughtfully. "She has mentioned Henry Lennox a couple of times now. She seemed a little embarrassed when I first said his name. I wonder if I could get him up here."

"Oh, do!" his sister pleaded, grasping his upper arm in desperate entreaty.

"Get off of me!" he scowled. "And get out of my room. It's high time I dressed and got out of Father's way for the day."

Chapter Twenty-One

John trotted down the stairs of his home, still smoothing his suit coat and only a few minutes later than his usual precise time. His dreams this morning had been far too pleasant to interrupt in favour of the reality of his work day. "Good morning, Mother," he greeted cheerfully as he entered the dining room for the morning repast.

Hannah wordlessly raised her coffee cup, her dark brow curved suspiciously.

Her son took a seat near her, rather than his proper seat at the head of the table. "I am sorry I was out so late again last night. How are you this morning, Mother?" he inquired gently.

Rather than replying, she raised her own embossed cup again, pointedly inspecting the design work on it. Her son's eyes narrowed in confusion.

"I had not realized," she answered at last, "that you were so weary of my ivy leaf, John."

"Ah!" He flushed with mortification. He had assured himself that his own motives and actions were above reproach, but he did not relish explaining yesterday's delivery to his mother.

"I thought the pattern," she went on, eying her own cup, "looked a little garish- like some country squire from the South. If you wish to purchase me a gift in the future, you ought to solicit my opinion on the matter."

"Now you are teasing me," he smiled in embarrassment.

Her eyes sparkled, but she made no admission of the kind. "I thought it was customary," she probed, "to have obtained a lady's acceptance before one began purchasing household wares for her."

"Perhaps, when one is not responsible for breaking what was doubtless a precious family heirloom."

"John! What on earth have you been doing during these calls to the Hale residence?"

"A great deal, it would seem," he chuckled, then sighed, leaning back in his chair. "I think I must soon have a conversation with Mr Hale. I believe he suspects my intentions. I did not wish to make Margaret uncomfortable, but I will not dishonour her father."

"How do you intend to explain the tea service? Responsible or not, John, you are apt to compromise the young lady."

"I have thought of that. No one would think it terribly extraordinary if Higgins were to deliver an unmarked crate to their house, and I believe he would be pleased to do me- or rather, her- this service. I will make it well worth his time. You are correct that I cannot deliver it myself."

"Mr Hale would not sense the impropriety of such a gift? Think, John, if Fanny were to receive such an extravagant gift from a gentleman!"

"I know," he fingered his own cup distractedly, imagining it to be another piece of china in another house. "Margaret is prudent, Mother. I believe I can count on her forbearance and my own good relationship with Mr Hale."

"Do you intend to offer for her again soon, then?" his mother asked quietly.

He was silent a moment. Blinking, he finally met her eyes. "I do, Mother. I think... no, I *know* she would receive me more favourably. My only cause for delay at present is the mill. I would not ask her to share in my own uncertainties. She deserves better."

"If she is the kind of woman you claim she is," Mrs Thornton observed slyly, "she would be glad to share your burdens, John. A girl whose heart is truly given to a man would wish to stand by him. What she deserves, John, is a chance to prove herself."

He rested his chin in his hand, stroking his upper lip thoughtfully. If he sensed the challenge in his mother's tones, he chose to ignore it. At last he sighed. "I believe she also would feel that way, Mother, but I think it too soon to ask it of her. We have come to understand one another so much better in such a short time! It cannot be very much longer, I think. I only need to be certain of her feelings, and to know that she is as well."

"And she will not think this... gift of yours presumptive? Any young lady of sense will be forming certain expectations, John."

A smile tugged at his mouth. "Possibly. In any case, it ought to be an interesting conversation the next time I see her."

~

"Is Miss Marg'et 'bout?"

Dixon stood, cross-armed, in the doorway of the Hale's residence looking out into the evening quiet of the street. Her ample form blocked out the view of the house behind her as she frowned down upon their visitor. "She is, Mr Higgins, but she is occupied at present."

"I am not, Dixon," came the light voice from behind her. A moment later, the lady in question peeped over Dixon's shoulder to view her caller. "Nicholas! I am so pleased to see you! Do, come in!"

"Aye, Lass, w'ull be a moment." Higgins bent to collect a rather large wooden crate at his feet, then, bracing it, squared himself carefully to pass through the doorway.

"Nicholas, what is that?" Margaret ducked out of his way, straining to see over his shoulder as she trailed behind him.

"Some'at for the kitchen, Miss," his cryptic words returned to her. "I'll follow yo', Miss Dixon."

Dixon sneezed her disapproval, but led the way- grumbling all the while that her kitchen had suddenly become a locale of interest for all manner of folk.

Nicholas carefully lowered his burden to the floor, then procured a short bar from somewhere within his coat. Bending, he began wordlessly to prise the top from the crate.

"Nicholas!" Margaret was laughing. "What is this mysterious thing you have brought?"

"'T'weren't for me to know, Miss," he smirked, straightening. He cast the wooden top aside and stepped away. "I was only asked if I'd bring it to yo'."

By this time, Margaret had become suspicious. "Indeed. Did the, er, sender have any other instructions for you?"

"Only that yo' was to unpack it yo'rself, Miss Marg'et." He cast a guilty glance in Dixon's direction.

"I see. In that case, I can do that later. You must join us; we were about to take our evening tea."

"Nay, Miss," he grinned. "Tho' I'll thank yo'. I gots to get 'ome."

Dixon had stood silently by, but as Higgins began to start out of the kitchen, she stopped him. "You may as well take it," she grumbled, extending a small parcel.

He took it, cautiously lifting the cloth wrapped about it. "A tart, Miss Dixon? I'll thank yo'!"

Margaret tilted a wondering smile to her old serving woman, but Dixon feigned that she had not seen it. "Good night, Nicholas!" she called after his retreating back. Her only answer was a wave of his free hand as he slipped back out the door to the outside.

Greedily she raced back to the kitchen. "What do you suppose it could be, Dixon?" She had a fair idea of who the sender might have been, but why would he be sending her such a large... her breath caught as she tugged away the shredded packing material.

"Dixon! Look!" Gingerly she withdrew an ivory tinted tea pot. Lacy roses trailed tastefully about its shape, while little golden accents tipped the edging.

Dixon drew near, her eyes wide. Reverently she received the pot, cradling it in her worn hands as though her mere breath might shatter it. Margaret was reaching inside again, and piece after lovely piece emerged from the tawny nest. "Why... it's an entire set!" Margaret breathed.

The next item her questing fingers found was of a very different composition. She paused, as though assuring herself that she had indeed found what she believed it to be. Hungrily, she dove for the item again and drew out a folded and sealed note. "Excuse me, Dixon!" she cried, and raced with it out of the kitchen.

Dixon rolled her eyes and heaved herself up from the floor. What on earth had possessed her to drop down like some common urchin? Never mind that Margaret had also done so! She began the methodical task of unpacking the remainder of the crate's contents alone.

It was no mystery to her where they had come from. Mr Thornton appeared to have decent taste, after all. Perhaps it was, in a respect, only right that he should try to replace the dear Mistress' old set. The question was whether her young miss would choose to accept it. Dixon hazarded a guess that she would, and began washing each item with care to put it away- at least, for now.

Margaret clattered up the stairs to her own room, her fingers cracking the seal on the note even as she climbed. Eagerly, she closed her door and dropped to the comfort of her bed as her eyes sought his firm, neat script.

Dear Margaret,

I hope you will forgive my presumption. I wished to set right the events of a few nights ago, if that is at all possible. You were most gracious not to cast blame where it was surely due, but I have cost you something that you must have held very dear. Please accept this humble offering as my apology.

I understand that you may hesitate to do so, or feel it improper. I beg that you would not. I hope it is to your taste, and that you will enjoy it for many years. I wish I could have had the joy of being present to view for myself what your impression was, but I feared that you might be made uncomfortable. I would not wish to offend or trouble you in any way.

Please give your father my assurances. I pray this does not cause him any disturbance of mind. I hope, Margaret, to see you and to speak with you soon.

My very warmest regards,
John

Margaret read and reread the note, searching for the words he had not dared to pen. There was not a single shred of doubt left that he still cared for her. If his tender adieu of the other evening had not been enough to reveal his heart to her, the pleasure shining in his face at their every encounter of late surely was.

She turned the paper over, as though hoping he had secreted some additional message for her eyes alone, but chided herself for being silly when she found nothing more. She discovered an unconscious smile warming her lips, which she had likely worn since she first suspected the origins of Nicholas' burden. He loved her! The most honourable, noble man of her acquaintance, the one she found she respected and admired above all others, still held her in his most tender sentiments.

She allowed the note to drift to her lap as she considered the implications of his gift. Surely he would know that he was giving her legitimate cause for expectations- and possibly even public embarrassment, should it become known. Even if she wished to refuse it, however, she could not think of a way to gracefully do so. It would surely hurt him, and that she was unwilling to do. He had already been wounded so deeply in his most vulnerable places, and some of that had been by her own hand.

Her fingers tapped the note thoughtfully. He would be at her door again soon; of that she was certain. Nothing would have brought her more joy than to allow her feelings to chart her course, to give him the answer he surely would be hoping to hear. How would his rigid features alter when he found his joy in her acceptance? How tender would be his voice, and how soft his touch? The very deepest parts of her ached to discover the man he kept hidden from the world.

Her father's words, however, still haunted her. She did not wish for him to feel obliged to her, merely because their relations had lately improved and he held her family secrets in trust. Marriage to her would only injure him professionally- and along with him, every soul dependent upon Marlborough Mills. What resentment could then take root, if she were to cost him everything he had worked for so long?

It was a rather preoccupied young woman who later joined Dixon in the kitchen. The rose spray set was properly admired and set in a place of honour among Dixon's shelves. Margaret, however, reflected that never would she be able to look upon them without thinking of the man who had given them, and that might, someday, cause her a great deal of pain.

~

He was watching for her. John helped his mother to their family's customary pew on Sunday morning, but it was a conspicuous moment before he took a seat himself. He leaned very slightly to his left, affording him a clearer view as the remaining parishioners filed through the doors to their seats.

"John!" hissed his mother from the side of her mouth. Mrs Thornton looked placidly forward, her gloved hands folded neatly across her lap, but her elbow twitched at her side.

He grimaced in mild disappointment. Once he turned around and took his seat, he would have no opportunity to meet her eyes to determine her feelings. An entire service struggling not to gaze in her direction, agonizing in suspense, before he could learn whether she had received his offering with pleasure! With an inward sigh, he took his seat beside his mother.

A moment later, his eye caught Mr Hale's familiar shape as the gentleman proceeded in his slow, reverent fashion to his own pew. Margaret was almost wholly concealed, walking on the far side of her father, and a tendril of worry curled round his heart. Was she so desirous of distancing herself that she would not pass directly by him? He had offended her with his presumption!

His fist clenched involuntarily in castigation. *Fool!* he thought to himself. It likely meant nothing at all, yet he could not contain his angst as the pair drew to a halt, approaching their seats.

At that moment, as she gathered her skirts, she turned to face her father... and he was directly in her line of vision. He gazed hungrily into her eyes, hoping for the faintest flicker.

"Thank you, Father," she was murmuring under her breath as Mr Hale assisted her into their pew. Her gaze, however, shifted over her father's shoulder. Her rosy lips drew into a sweet flash of greeting, but it was her eyes which captivated him. They were warm and eloquent, speaking from her heart and casting him the hope he craved.

She turned away again almost immediately, but she had given him the assurance he had been longing for. He released his breath, realizing only then that he had been holding it. He forced his attention back forward, but from his left he sensed the subtle lift of his mother's chin. He allowed himself a smile. Hannah Thornton had missed nothing.

The minister rambled on for far too long. Though he typically enjoyed this weekly time of quiet reflection and the opportunity to restore his spirits, on this day his very clothing seemed to stifle. He must speak to her!

His toes restlessly began to fidget within his shoes. Every muscle was strained with the effort of nonchalance, but so successful was he that even his mother could not have told. Valiantly he strove and won against the impulses which demanded that he spring from his seat the second the minister had dismissed the congregation. Forcing himself to behave the civil son, he assisted his mother and sister before planning to- very incidentally, of course- intersect his path with Margaret's.

The church door was drawing near! In only a moment more, he could catch her as she and her father stopped to visit with the few who would seek their company. He would ask to call upon them that afternoon, and those expressive eyes would give him the answer to quite a different question.

"Good day, Margaret!" His stomach pitted as he recognized Genevieve Hamilton's voice. From somewhere off to his right, the young woman had intercepted his target before he could.

Margaret turned up ahead of him. "Good morning, Genevieve," he saw her offer a welcoming smile. "How do you do today?"

He could scarcely keep from growling aloud when Miss Hamilton drew close to Margaret's side, monopolizing all of her attention and effectively isolating her. Her parents followed close after her, and though they did not stop to speak to either his own family or to Margaret, Hamilton acknowledged him with a terse dip of his head as he passed by. Clearly the gentleman still respected him, but had no intentions of renewing his interest in further relations.

Scowling just a little, he gave his arm to his mother and traced a wide path around the young ladies. He risked a brief glance at Margaret. Some sixth sense apparently caused her to blink in his direction, and he was sure he detected a flicker of remorse in her expression. She could not escape her eager companion, however, any more than he could loiter aimlessly about until they had finished their conversation.

There was Watson nearby. Perhaps, had he been less single-minded, he could have managed an intelligent discourse with one of his associates, but Fanny was already lengthening her strides in hopes of avoiding that very gentleman. Clenching his jaw, he acceded to her wishes to escape from her sudden admirer. The Thornton family, stately and everything proper, walked together back to Marlborough Mills.

~

M argaret's heart sank. All she could see of him now was the top of his hat and his broad, black shoulders as he disappeared up the street with his family. She had so hoped to speak with him! Of course she could not openly thank him for his thoughtfulness, but he was certainly perceptive enough to sense her gratitude. She would have given a great deal to know the full measure of what he might have expressed to her ears alone. Even in public, however, she had come to know his ways so well that a mere few seconds could have conveyed to her volumes of his thoughts and feelings.

To see his disagreeable mask back in place and his back turned once more made her wish she could retreat to the privacy of her own room to soak in self-pity. With all of her determination, she forced herself to attend Genevieve's words. That John Thornton was disappointed could not be just enough cause for her to forget her own manners! Indeed, there might yet come a day where she would be forced to disappoint him. She would have to become intimately acquainted with her feelings of regret.

"Margaret," Genevieve was imploring, "do walk with us this afternoon! Rupert and I were going to take in the Square, and we would so wish for your company."

"Oh, I do not know if I..." she searched out her father's face, trying to decide if she could neatly excuse herself. Walking might have been pleasant, but at the moment, time spent with the woman John ought rightly to marry was a bitter pill to her.

"Surely," Genevieve followed her gaze, "your father is quite well enough to do without you, is he not? He looks very well today!"

Margaret tamped down a sigh of resignation. "He is better, yes." She glanced quickly at the skies, searching for and finding the excuse she needed. "I fear, however, that it will rain rather heavily this afternoon, and I do not wish to leave him to return home alone."

"Oh, why I have just had the perfect idea. Let us walk you to your door!"

"Are you quite sure you wish to walk so far out of your way?" Margaret glanced upward uncertainly. "The weather looks rather unpromising for your return."

"Oh, we can hail a cab if need be," the other woman returned airily. "There are more Sunday cabs now, so we shall have no trouble securing one if the need arises."

"Of course, and you must stay to tea," Margaret smiled her acceptance. Genevieve had been kind to her, after all, and she had no right to avoid her friend simply to nurse her own bruised feelings. John would be only right to choose Miss Hamilton, and Margaret would not degrade her own dignity or destroy any hope of remaining friendship by spiteful behaviour.

Genevieve clapped giddily, pleased to have gained the point in effectively isolating Margaret from John Thornton for the remainder of the Sunday. "Rupert! Rupert, come! We are to see Margaret and her father home!"

The foursome set out, Rupert offering his arm to Margaret. Mr Hale gallantly escorted Genevieve, smiling gently all the while. Margaret accepted Rupert's arm with only the barest flicker of reluctance discernable. At the fore of her thoughts was that agonized gaze from John, months ago when he had seen her walking with Frederick at the station. She cringed, resting her fingers only very lightly on Rupert Hamilton's arm. Self-consciously she glanced about, glad now that he was not at hand to be made unhappy.

Chapter Twenty-Two

Fanny Thornton prepared to quit the house only half an hour after she had gained it. She had absolutely no desire to spend a dull afternoon reading with her mother, and even less to watch John mooning about the house; pacing, pretending to read his paper, pacing some more.... He was never more irritating than when he had nothing to do. He had never had any idea how to take his leisure, but he had been even worse of late.

Fanny sniffed to herself as she pulled her kid gloves back over her delicate white hands. There was a certain cure for John's boredom and restlessness- if he would only work up the courage to speak to Genevieve Hamilton! The other girl quite plainly wanted him, and her family obviously desired the match as well. What more was he waiting for? Certainly not Margaret Hale, as her mother believed! No, she knew her brother too well for that. Miss Hamilton it certainly was who had caught his eye.

He is a coward! she thought smugly to herself. *The mighty John Thornton, the Union's revered adversary and the most dominant manufacturer in all of Milton, quaking in his boots over a woman!* She would have laughed out loud, had she not been fearful that her mother would hear and discover her intentions to escape the house.

Perhaps there was more she herself could do to smooth the way for that hopeless couple- as well as for herself! She could see, if her brother could not, the many advantages to maintaining genial relations with that family. Her mother had expressly forbidden her to seek out either Genevieve or Rupert Hamilton, but she had said nothing about taking a leisurely stroll on a Sunday afternoon, had she? Walking was good for the health, after all. Surely there could be no objections!

It seemed, however, that the fates were against her. She had scarcely set foot out of her door when a remarkable downpour washed over Marlborough Street. Her cloak soaked after only a few seconds, she darted back into the house, glaring at the heavens for their failure to cooperate with her plans.

Angrily she jerked the gloves from her fingertips. Tomorrow, she decided. She would walk out tomorrow. As she began to peel her cloak from her clinging gown, a novel idea struck her. Perhaps she was in the wrong to be seeking out Genevieve. Perhaps she would fall more naturally into her friend's path- and avoid her mother's ire- by instead calling on Emmeline Draper.

A self-satisfied grin formed over her milky features. Tomorrow.

~

John had indeed been pacing the drawing room once more. His mother managed to disguise her own irritation- sensing, perhaps, that it would only agitate him further. Heaven bless his wise, patient mother and her poor abused carpets!

He had ruled out the possibility of calling on the Hales that evening. It just seemed awkward, particularly after assuming she had quite likely been monopolized by Genevieve Hamilton for much of her afternoon. The other woman's ulterior motives just after service that morning had been rather obvious, at least to him. How could he have ever- even briefly- thought her possibly a woman of Margaret's caliber?

He vacillated all afternoon, trying to decide what he ought to do. There was no choice but to speak to Mr Hale, and promptly, too. Mr Hale may have previously been oblivious to his interest, but his sudden intimacy with Margaret had been rather plain. He pondered for a moment about the tea set, and wondered if Mr Hale were even yet aware of its existence. If he were, the man would be doubly concerned about his intentions.

His own private desire was to announce himself at their door early in the day, speak privately with both of them, and to at last secure his future happiness. His spirits took ecstatic flights of fancy as he imagined her final surrender. Would she nestle in his arms, resting her soft cheeks against his chest and allowing him to bury his face in her hair? He tingled with joy and wonder at the prospect.

What breathtaking beauty was man's to behold in the form of woman! As one who had never indulged such natural inclinations, he still held the touch of a woman- *his* woman, if he could be so bold- in breathless awe. The comfort of her sweet companionship could be rivaled only by her delicious softness and- dare he imagine it?- her welcoming embrace.

John Thornton found himself, for the first time in his life, truly allowing himself to contemplate the profound mystery of man's strength and woman's grace. How such opposites perfectly joined and complemented one another was a marvel to him, and likely always would be. Happy was the man bestowed with the whole of a woman's heart and affections! Margaret- *his* Margaret... no greater joy had he ever known than when he ventured to imagine that possessive description before her name.

His buoyant hopes sank again when he reflected upon the very proper confession he would have to make to her father. He had no longer the assurance of relative financial security. He would be asking her to face uncertainty and very probable hardship with him. What sensible father would grant his blessing to such a union?

He narrowed his eyes as he paced. Margaret was well acquainted with the rise and fall of a man's circumstances, was she not? Would she truly object to his present lack of security? Ah, but while her father was no longer as respectably off as he had once been, neither was he likely to sink any lower. John chewed his lip in frustration. There was no telling what his own future would be.

He wrestled for the remainder of the evening and well into the night. As he lay back upon his pillow, just before restless slumber claimed him, he at last decided upon the perfect guide for his steps. Had he not always learnt that self-denial and adherence to duty reaped the greatest rewards? *Yes*, he groaned silently. If so, where was his duty in this case?

Margaret's reputation was in no danger, of that he felt rather safe. Had she been compromised in the slightest, he would have presented himself at her doorstep at midnight in a pouring rain to make his proper addresses. Mr Hale might be troubled by his recent familiarity with Margaret, but perhaps the gentleman's mind might be eased if he did not press matters for a few days.... Perhaps if he could instead spend that time searching out options he had not yet explored....

Aha! He could have cursed himself for having been so blind before. He knew the perfect man to approach! Perhaps there was hope after all. This was the last thought which slipped through his mind before he blissfully imagined kissing Margaret good night and reclined his head with a serene smile upon his lips.

~

"Mrs Draper, how pleased I am that you could call," Margaret greeted her morning guest. "Please, do be seated!"

"Good morning, Miss Hale," the other woman inclined her head generously as she entered the house. "I trust you are well?"

"Very well, indeed, Mrs Draper." Margaret flashed a quick look to Dixon as the maid withdrew, and Dixon sniffed in understanding. She would return shortly with tea for their guest, and fortunately Martha had finally returned to help her.

"Well, Miss Hale, how did you find your task of penning letters?" Emmeline Draper poised herself daintily upon the furniture, as though she were afraid of soiling her walking suit. Her eyes flicked about the familiar room once more, perhaps assuring herself that she had indeed assessed the house properly upon her first visit.

Margaret forced a cheerful smile. "Rather enjoyable, I assure you." She retrieved a thick folder and presented it to the other woman. "I hope Mr Draper is able to secure the support he requires."

Emmeline's golden brow lifted serenely. "I am certain he will. He has the endorsement of Dr Bronson Douglas, you know, which is certain to carry much influence."

Margaret's brow furrowed in mute confusion.

"Why, surely, you have heard of him, Miss Hale!" Emmeline ejaculated. "He was formerly a student and partner to William Farr himself!"

"I am familiar with Mr Farr's name," Margaret confessed. "He has done much to reveal the causes of disease, if I am not mistaken, but...." Her voice trailed off reluctantly.

"*Well*, Miss Hale, Dr Douglas is without his equal, I assure you, and he has great plans for our new Milton hospital," the other woman pronounced firmly.

"I think you mistake me," Margaret reacted in surprise. "I have indeed heard of Dr Douglas, but..." her voice dropped hesitantly, "was he not disgraced?"

"Disgraced?" Emmeline frowned. "You must be speaking of that little tiff last year, after the cholera outbreak. Why, t'was nothing, Miss Hale, but a spiteful attack! Dr Snow has always had it out for him, you know," she informed her confidentially.

"Oh," Margaret leaned back in her seat uncomfortably. "I... I am glad you told me as much. I would not wish to hold unfair prejudices against an innocent man, and a truly good doctor."

"Naturally," Emmeline favoured her with a sticky smile as Dixon arrived with the tea tray. She turned her eyes toward it with interest. "Oh! Why, I declare, Miss Hale, what an *ex*quisite pattern!"

Margaret flushed briefly, but it was not certain whether her guest had perceived her slight shock. She recovered admirably. "Thank you, Mrs Draper," she managed smoothly.

Emmeline could scarcely disguise her admiration as Dixon served her out of the pristine new china. She lifted the cup and saucer daintily, raising that golden brow again. The perfectly elegant setting seemed rather too lavish for the modest surroundings of the little Crampton house. Rather than commenting on that observation, however, she attempted to conceal her rather indelicate interest. "Roses," she managed carefully at last. "Most lovely, Miss Hale."

Margaret swallowed nervously. "My mother was fond of them," she offered lamely.

"Naturally," the other woman agreed, then swiftly changed the subject once more. "Now, we were speaking of Dr Douglas. Pray, Miss Hale, what had you heard of the man? It will not do for false reports to circulate, you know."

"I would circulate no such ill reports without good foundation," Margaret objected. "However, I had read in the London papers that his theories and remedies were all proven wrong!"

"Wrong! What can you mean, my dear?" Mrs Draper leaned forward with a patronizing look of concern on her face which Margaret did not quite fancy.

"Why, his old-fashioned belief in miasmas has been thoroughly ridiculed by more modern doctors, and new discoveries are finding that the purgatives and bleedings that he still espouses only serve to weaken the patient."

Emmeline Draper waved her hand with a bemused, dismissive air. "Rubbish, Miss Hale! Dr Douglas has treated so many with success! Good fresh air and healthful exercise do wonders for the constitution, do they not? And you must know, Miss Hale, that they also foster a more even temperament, which Dr Douglas says nearly always guarantees protection against cholera."

Margaret's eyes widened and her mouth verily gaped in awe at the woman's willful ignorance. "M-Mrs Draper," she stammered, "Have you at all read any of Dr Snow's reports on contagions in water?"

Emmeline fairly bristled. "My husband has, Miss Hale," she returned somewhat frostily. "Of course one cannot refute such evidence. Dr Douglas has proposed incorporating *all* of the modern treatments in the hospital, naturally, as well as the more traditional remedies."

Margaret let out a somewhat relieved breath. "I am glad to hear it, Mrs Draper. So many of the mill workers I have seen need *real* medicine. I am most grateful for your husband's efforts to bring such an opportunity to Milton."

Emmeline frowned. "I am sorry, Miss Hale, but you appear to have misunderstood. We cannot possibly open this hospital to all manner of rabble! Why, all of this new medicine costs a great deal, you know, to say nothing of the new facility my husband has designed! Who is to pay for all of it, Miss Hale, but the patients?"

Margaret swallowed hard. "Do you mean that the poorer residents must still do without?"

"Well," Emmeline sniffed, "I do not see why we should bring *more* contagion into our new hospital. Why, we would be no better than the hospitals in London, who bring in all manner of folk simply to die there, while people who can afford all of these new medicines must wait for the doctors to visit their homes! Better, I say, for the reverse to be the case. The working class will not be the poorer for it, as they shall be no worse off than now, but for people like us, Miss Hale, we shall have much to look forward to."

Margaret blanched. "Mrs Draper, by far the greatest need in the city is the poorer families, who cannot afford such luxuries!"

Emmeline shrugged lightly as she rose to her feet. "If they work hard enough and save their money, perhaps one day they can. Besides, Dr Douglas will still offer his advice and guidance where there is a true need. The newer remedies are rather dear, of course, but the tried and true methods, I always say, are the most reliable anyway."

Margaret felt sick. She watched with uneasy eyes as Mrs Draper prepared to take her leave. A hospital for only the wealthy! A presiding doctor who espoused outdated medical dogma! Where was the good in that? Her stomach churned nauseatingly as she realized that John Thornton's prediction had come true. She felt sorry that she had had anything whatever to do with it.

"I am certain my husband is most grateful for all of your assistance to our cause. May we count on you in the future, Miss Hale? Surely, some of your connections in London would prove most valuable."

Margaret's hand hovered unconsciously near her stomach. "I... I do not think I will be able to lend any further aid," she replied with the very greatest discomfort. She allowed her statement to hang there, resisting the temptation to use her father's fragile health as an excuse. Had she desired it, she would have made a way- but she simply could have nothing else to do with this endeavour.

Emmeline Draper coolly lifted a brow and sniffed down her nose. "More is the pity. Well, I shall bid you a very good-day, Miss Hale!"

Margaret, reeling and faint from her disgust, saw her guest out of the door, then leaned against it. Her face she covered in her hands. What would John say when he learnt of her humiliation? Her breathing slowed only a little as she assured herself that he would comfort rather than chide her.

It was Nicholas' family, and all of the others she had met, who took her concern next. It was the memory of her dear friend Bessie! She had been so hopeful on their account, that her efforts, small though they were, might help plant the seeds of something far greater- something which would reach down through the generations to speak of the progress Milton was making. It seemed to her now that she had only been an instrument of the elite in their pride and condescension.

All at once, her hands dropped from her face and she blinked her eyes free of their prickling mist. A new determination glinted from them as she lifted her chin, defiant now. Others might do as they pleased, but Margaret Hale need wait for no one to turn from insult to kindness.

Quickly she retrieved her purse, counting out the remaining coins which made up her monthly spending allotment. Smiling, she clenched them in her fist. There was a little girl of her acquaintance who might go on to make anything of herself, but just now, that little girl could use a new frock for school.

Chapter Twenty-Three

"Thornton! About time, old chap!" James Watson beamed jovially and pumped John's hand as he showed him into his study. "I have been meaning to call on you."

"Then my visit is most fortuitous. I regret that I missed last Friday's Master's dinner, but it could not be helped."

Watson grunted good-naturedly. "We heard you had been seen earlier that evening walking with that Higgins fellow. Hamper suspected you of spying on your hands- said some Union trouble was starting up again at your mill."

"One disgruntled former worker hardly qualifies as trouble," Thornton chuckled lightly. "And I certainly am not engaging in the sort of espionage Hamper suspects."

"Do tell! What other cause might you have to spend an entire evening with a Union leader?"

"It was not all spent with him," Thornton smiled, a distant light in his eye causing Watson some suspicion. "But more to the point, Higgins is a better chap than I had known. I have learned a deal from him."

Watson laughed heartily, shaking his head. "Don't let him charm you, Thornton. You'll never be able to look Hamper in the eye when that rascal turns on you- a bleeding fool, that's what Hamper will call you."

Thornton sighed. "He may call me what he wishes. I did not come to speak to you about Higgins, Watson."

"Aye," Watson stroked his chin thoughtfully. "You've heard about that rail speculation and you finally want a piece of it. Am I right?"

"I had heard of it, but no, thank you. You know where I stand, Watson."

Watson shrugged. "Your loss, man. What was it you wanted to speak to me about?"

Thornton took a tight, nervous breath and released it slowly. *Courage, man!* It galled his pride to have to come to Watson, who only a year ago had been by far his inferior in consequence and status. Watson was forever dreaming up financial schemes and wheedling others into investing with him. He was no charlatan, but he knew how to use other men's money to his own advantage during the time it was in his hands. The practice left a bitter taste in John's mouth, but if Watson was willing to use his resources to breathe life back into Marlborough Mills, perhaps it was worth setting aside his own vanity for a time. After all, he consoled himself, Margaret was the prize.

He tapped his fingers upon his knee and at last blurted out what he had come to say. "I came to ask about a loan, Watson."

Watson gazed back, silent and shrewd. It was a full minute before he responded. "How much, Thornton?"

"Well," he replied with a wry twist to his mouth, "I suppose that depends on you, Watson. I *need* one hundred fifty pounds to see the mill safely into next summer. However, if you were in the mood to make a little greater profit, I would borrow as much as five hundred, paying off my loan at the bank and one of my private investors."

Watson pursed his lips. "At what interest?"

"I could pay you four percent. That is a tidy profit."

"Tut, tut, Thornton." Watson tapped his desk with a pen. "I made a greater margin than that in a single month earlier this year."

"That was sheer chance," Thornton reminded him. "I offer a steady supplement to your income without fear of default or loss."

Watson sighed reluctantly. "I am sorry, Thornton, but I cannot commit my resources where the yield is not greater. Your offer would be attractive had I not already embarked on this most recent venture. It is a sure profit! Are you certain you have not fifty pounds to invest with me? You would recoup it and many times more in less than a month, you have my word. Why, you would not need to beg a loan of anyone!"

Thornton shook his head adamantly. "Even were I inclined to agree with you, I cannot in good conscience invest funds which are not rightfully mine. While I yet owe the bank and while I hold private money in my trust, spare capital is not mine to spend."

"It is not spending, my friend!" Watson cried. "It is no different than using the funds to buy a new loom which may break! Your creditors expect a profit, that is all. With this speculation, you would be able to repay them all the more readily. Egad, it is irresponsible not to put your assets to good use!"

"And what if your scheme should not pay out?" Thornton countered irritably. "Honest men are ruined by a rogue!"

"But it will, Thornton! It cannot fail, I assure you."

"I cannot see it as you do. I will not risk that which belongs to others, nor chance the livelihoods of my men on such a scheme."

Watson sighed and crossed his arms with finality. "I am sorry to hear it, Thornton. I wish I could be of more help."

Thornton grimaced for a fraction of a second, then his legendary self-control snapped firmly back into place. "So am I. I must thank you for your time, Watson."

He began to rise when Watson spoke again. "Hamilton was here yesterday."

Thornton froze, then shifted his weight back into the chair. Of what particular interest was that information? "Oh," he commented neutrally.

Watson studied him. "*He* bought into the rail speculation. Three hundred pounds."

Thornton cringed inwardly, but his face was a mask. "I must wish him good fortune, then."

Watson pursed his lips, then fumbled in his waistcoat for his pipe and began to fill it. "That daughter of his is a fine woman, Thornton." He tapped the tobacco to his liking without looking up.

"I do not deny that point," he replied cautiously.

Watson at last put his pipe to his lips and lit it, puffing repeatedly around the stem. If his intention was to cause his guest some unease, he had miscalculated the man. Thornton stared back impassively. Watson took a great final puff and lowered his pipe to blow an expressive wisp of smoke.

"Word is," he continued, "that Hamilton intended to give her to you but you refused. I did not believe the rumour, of course. I have never known you to act the fool, Thornton."

Thornton's jaw went slack in momentary horror. "How dare you!" he cried. "To speak such things, slandering an innocent young lady-"

"Calm yourself, Thornton!" Watson was chuckling. "I am not your adversary. I only felt you ought to know what is being said, that is all."

"By whom?" he questioned tersely. "Not by my lips were such things spoken!"

"Oh, come, Thornton, you know that nothing so juicy stays quiet for long." Watson leaned back and blew himself a rather inexpert smoke ring. "It was Hamper, was it not?"

"He had heard a few things, yes. Hamilton has spoken nothing that I have heard, but I expect that son of his has been running his mouth." Watson shook his head, lowering his pipe. "If that lad were any son of mine..."

Thornton growled, drumming his fingers. "Hamper must have found it all most amusing."

"So did Slickson and Anderson," Watson grunted. "Hamper says... well, Thornton, you must understand that I am only repeating-"

"*What* did Hamper say?" Thornton snapped testily.

Watson hesitated, dropping his eyes and tapping the contents from his pipe. For all of his posturing with that infernal prop, the man was only putting up a front. In truth, he possessed very little of the boldness which he tried to affect. "That... er... well, that is to say that... I suppose he suspects that you might have a... a reason for rejecting such a fine prize... a rather *compelling* reason...."

Thornton's eyes had squinted quizzically as he strained to make sense of Watson's jumbled excuses. "A reason... I do not understand you."

Watson's face scrunched for a brief second in the agony of his embarrassment, but then he plunged recklessly forward. "Margaret Hale." He watched the other's face bleed of all colour, confirming his suspicions. "I am sorry, my friend, but someone had to tell you. Hamper went as far as to openly suggest *carte blanche*... only to Slickson and myself, of course."

The blood rushed back Thornton's face, and he spat in a fury, "Miss Hale is a *lady!* To even suggest such a notion is the basest, vilest slander!"

"Of course, Thornton! Believe me, I do not think anyone present actually gave credit to the notion. You know Hamper, how he talks! The man is crude."

"He dares risk a lady's honour for his own amusement? I shall have words-"

"Stay, Thornton!" Watson jumped to his feet in pursuit of his guest, who had lurched from his chair and was already halfway to the door. "You will do your Miss Hale no good by calling out Hamper. If you will only sit! I may be able to offer you some assistance."

Thornton forced himself to pause, dropping the hand which had already reached out to take his hat. He stood, panting in rage, as his mind stumbled to make sense of Watson's words. After a moment, he slowly turned and resumed his seat.

Watson sighed in relief. "Thank you, Thornton. I always said you were a good chap."

"What do you have to say?" Thornton demanded.

Watson fumbled once more with his pipe, now beginning to grow cold. "I was thinking we could perhaps help one another, Thornton. Your sister..." Watson released a sentimental breath. "I fancy Miss Thornton- she's a right fine woman, you know- but she has eyes only for that Rupert Hamilton."

Thornton stilled, taking long, slow breaths in an attempt to think rationally. "What do you hope to gain from me? I will not force my sister to marry where it is convenient for me, Watson."

"No!" the other man fairly yelped. "I would not have it so! I beg your pardon, Thornton, that was not what I meant at all. I only hoped you might speak kindly of me to her, and perhaps... Thornton, I do not believe that Rupert Hamilton is a young man to be trusted. Call me a jealous man if you will, but.... I was only hoping that Miss Thornton might be made to see past his charms. He is young and dashing, I am afraid, whereas I am not."

Thornton sighed, swallowing the ire with which he longed to lash out at someone. It suited his own purposes as well to distract Fanny from Rupert Hamilton. "I will consider it, Watson. Perhaps you might call on Fanny yourself, allow her to see a little more of you. She has always been fond of gifts," he suggested slyly.

"Thank you, Thornton! And in return, I shall quietly defend your Miss Hale's honour."

"I did not confess-" he began to protest.

"Oh, come Thornton, I have seen you watching her. You look like a dog parched for water- if you will pardon my indelicacy."

"I will not. I will not tolerate anyone speaking of Miss Hale in such vulgar terms."

Watson shrugged in half-apology. "Well, let me only say that I understand your urgency to see to the mill's financial standing. I do wish I could interest you in the speculation, Thornton. Only consider! I must know within only a few more days."

"I have given my answer." Thornton rose determinedly from his chair. "Thank you for your time, Watson."

Chapter Twenty-Four

"Good afternoon, Mrs Thornton!"

Hannah Thornton offered her accustomed stately nod as she entered the dress maker's shop. "Good afternoon, Mrs Gentry."

Mrs Gentry spoke no more to her customer. It always delighted her when the dowager mistress of Marlborough Mills patronized her little shop. Hannah Thornton's business lent distinction and the lady's loyalty as a customer was a high compliment which she did not take lightly. She knew, however, that it was not her own sales abilities which brought the Thorntons' regular custom. Gentry's happened to be the only shop in town where one might find the latest and most fashionable dress goods to suit a young lady of Miss Thornton's taste, as well as an assortment of discounted selections to satisfy one of Mrs Thornton's economy.

Hannah browsed the front room of the shop only briefly, but naturally under the eager eye of Mrs Gentry. She gave but a cursory glance at the front rows of shelves. In her typical efficient manner, she soon directed her steps across the room. The farther one traveled from the front desk and the door, the lower the prices. From the far corner of the front room, Mrs Thornton would no doubt make her way toward the back room. There, rows and stacks of last season's styles, inexpensive materials, and smaller swatches offered the economically minded consumer a number of choices.

"Mrs Thornton, we have some new chiffon selections just in. Would you like to see the rose or the light blue for Miss Thornton?" Mrs Gentry offered hopefully over the counter.

Hannah could barely suppress a curl of her lip. Such a frivolous, impractical material, and for winter! Ladies' fashions had lost all semblance of rationality since she had been a girl. Light, fragile materials might do very well for those fine ladies of London, but a Milton girl ought to dress more sensibly! "No, thank you," she answered politely. "My daughter has quite enough gowns at present."

"Of course, Madam." Mrs Gentry silently scolded herself. She would have done better to have brought the lady's attention to the new bombazine, but it was too late now. Mrs Thornton had wandered to the back room, most probably in search of more fabrics for her charity sewing.

Unfortunately, it seemed she would not be making any extravagant purchases today. A moment later, Mrs Gentry's hopes had cause to soar again. The door jingled open to admit two of her very favourite customers.

"Mrs Draper, Miss Hamilton!" This time she came from behind her counter to greet the new arrivals. A typical visit by either one of these particular ladies tended to keep Mrs Gentry's household in gentle comforts for the week. "What can I do for you ladies today?"

"Oh, only browsing!" replied Mrs Draper airily.

"Let me know if I can show you anything," she smiled sweetly. She withdrew to a nonintrusive distance and awaited their pleasure. She kept her gaze averted, but, as often happened, she was soon privy to snatches of their conversation. The pair migrated about the front of the shop, admiring all of the newest fashions.

"Em, just look at this!" Genevieve exclaimed. "I always love wearing this colour." She fingered the very rose chiffon sample in which Mrs Gentry had, only moments ago, tried to interest Mrs Thornton.

"I thought you would have preferred something a little bolder," Mrs Draper replied archly. "Something to turn the head?"

"Oh! It is no use, Em. I have come to think it rather hopeless. He only has eyes for *you know who*."

Emmeline Draper laughed. "Margaret Hale! Oh, you cannot consider him wholly lost to the likes of *her*, can you?"

"Em!" Scandalized, Genevieve raised a hand in a plea for silence.

Emmeline tipped her feathered hat toward Mrs Gentry, who had turned away and seemed utterly preoccupied with folding her new samples. "Nothing to worry about, Gen," she smiled. They were far from the front door and counter now, having wandered over almost the entirety of the front shelves. In addition, the abundance of cloth filling the shop insulated the echo of any words.

She did lower her voice somewhat- just enough so that Mrs Gentry on the far side of the room might not overhear. Truly, secrets were safer in the dark corner of the dress shop than in her own home, where lived a number of servants with sharp ears.

"As I was saying," she whispered, "John Thornton is far too levelheaded to throw everything away over a mere *tendresse* for... well, I suppose she is handsome enough, but I simply don't see the appeal. There is positively nothing interesting about her, and so self-righteous! Why, you ought to hear how she goes on! Truly, I do not see how *any* gentleman, particularly a sensible man like John Thornton, would trouble himself."

"It is not *your* opinion which matters," Genevieve pouted. "And he just might do anything! He is rather tenacious- downright unmanageable, in fact!"

"Is that not what you have always liked best about him?" Emmeline teased. "He is rather the hard-headed, charismatic sort, is he not?"

A muffled sigh escaped the young lady. "Only think what a man like John Thornton could achieve if he had my father's resources to back him!"

"Mayor of Milton?" asked Mrs Draper innocently, pulling out another sample of fabric.

"Oh, darling, that might only be the beginning! Why, he is clever enough for Parliament! You just see if I am not right by and by. Only think how thrilling! Parliament! London! Think of the soirees, and the circles such a man might move in!!"

"I never thought he had any political ambitions. He is a manufacturer to the bone, dear."

"Oh, do not be silly. Of course he would leap at the chance! He only wants the opportunity, you know, and I would make certain that he had it!"

"Or perhaps," Emmeline suggested, slanting a coy look to her friend, "your father desires a son-in-law after a certain pattern, and of the available candidates, John Thornton is... shall I say the least repugnant?"

"Far from repugnant." Genevieve wrinkled her nose. "I declare; I do not know how ladies suffer marriage to such *old* gentlemen! You tell me it is not so dreadful, but would it not be more pleasant to find one's husband appealing?"

"Oh, one can always find other diversions, if that is what you refer to," was the blasé reply.

"*Em!*" Genevieve's hand flew to her mouth in horror. "You would not!"

"I confessed to nothing, darling," the other woman whispered neutrally as she sorted through some muslins. "I only suggested that others do. Gentlemen, for example, often marry where it is prudent and seek their amusements elsewhere."

"I do not think I would care for that," Genevieve retorted primly, forgetting to keep her tones hushed. "You might call me the jealous sort, but if I had John Thornton for my own, I would not share him!"

"Oh, but you would, darling," Emmeline assured her. "And really, where is the harm? If a man keeps his indiscretions quiet and does not trouble his wife with scandal, what is there to complain of? You would still have the social status as his wife, even if he did spend some of his time abroad. And one never knows- perhaps marriage will settle him somewhat, and he might get Margaret Hale from under his skin. Surely," she winked, "he must already be growing weary of her."

Genevieve crossed her arms, her face several shades of crimson. "He is too honourable for that, I think. And Margaret! No, she is as innocent as a dove! I really wish I could dislike her as you and Fanny do, but I cannot believe she would entertain such a proposition."

"Would she not? They've been saying that John Thornton is a regular visitor to the Hale's household- more so than ever lately. He has also been seen more than once returning with her from the Francis district- one can only imagine what goings-on might take place *there*."

"Oh, Em! Surely you cannot think...!" Genevieve gasped in revulsion.

"And there is the little matter of that tea service," Emmeline shrugged nonchalantly.

"Tea service? I do not understand."

"Oh! Surely it is nothing," she murmured, moving on to the next row of fabrics.

"*Em!*" her friend hissed, glancing over her shoulder to be sure that Mrs Gentry was still far out of earshot.

"Oh, very well. It is only that Mrs Hamper saw Mr Thornton purchasing an entire tea set, and she thought it odd enough to remark upon. He was selecting them himself, and rose patterns are not to old Mrs Thornton's taste, she claims- though, privately, I wonder if *anything* is to *her* taste."

"Oh, do go on with it!" her friend implored.

"*Well*, wouldn't you know, darling, I called on Margaret this morning to collect those letters she wrote for Randall, and she served me out of this perfectly delicious, brand new rosebud spray tea set!"

Genevieve's face had grown thoughtful. "I think... yes, now that you mention it, I do remember something different the last time I called upon her. Oh, Em, you do not think-"

Emmeline Draper confirmed her thoughts with a sage nod of her head. "Now, I ask you," she continued, "why would a gentleman purchase such a thing for a lady unless he meant to... enjoy them himself?"

"You are perfectly horrible!" Genevieve gasped.

"And perfectly right," she slanted a wicked grin at her friend over a swatch of wine-coloured satin. "Oh, do not be such a goose! Every man has his indiscretions! Think of your own brother, darling!"

Genevieve felt herself growing ill. "I would rather not."

"Oh, Rupert is quite charming! And you know, darling, he is not the sort a woman marries- too unpredictable, you see- but...."

"Please stop!" Genevieve begged.

Emmeline tilted her head, frowning at the other young woman. "You want what does not exist, darling. You may as well face it. A man does not reserve himself for only one woman, and John Thornton's eye is as apt to wander as any man's."

~

Three feet away and through a paper-thin wall, the hushed voices of the young ladies drifted to the ears of a properly horrified Hannah Thornton. Eavesdropping was shameful, of course- she ought to have declared her presence to the young ladies at the very first words of their conversation, but by the time she had realized what they spoke of, it had already been too late.

The best course would likely have been to distance herself from the door so that she might not overhear more, but it was impossible in this small rear chamber. Instead, the fiercely loyal mother was compelled to remain to hear the gossip propagating about her son. She lingered in astonishment and then stayed in utter incredulity.

Any allegiance she might have once tendered toward Miss Hamilton evaporated. *Manipulative, heartless girl!* she could have spat. And that Draper woman! A more shameless, brazen, graceless tart she had never had the misfortune to know! *And they say such things about my John!* The two trollops masquerading as ladies would not know an honourable man if he were to lay his whole heart at their feet- a thing, she assured herself, that her John would never do!

Her ire had caused her to single-mindedly focus on the infuriating conversation just around the door from her, but a soft noise finally caught her attention. It sounded like... like a young woman sobbing.

Having some premonition of what she might find, she peered around the tall stacks just behind her, into the rearmost set of shelves filled with the very cheapest fabrics. Seated on a step stool, her face hidden in her hands, was Margaret Hale.

She looked as though her strength had failed her and she had merely collapsed where she stood. It was likely fortunate that there had been a stool nearby, else she might have crumpled completely to the floor. At the sound of the creak in the floorboards before her, she raised her tear-streaked face to Mrs Thornton's.

Her pride still intact, she shot to her feet. "I-" she choked, struggling for something coherent to say. "*I-*" she whispered, then her features crumpled as her heartbreak overwhelmed her. Her hands covered her face once more and her body shook pitifully in her anguish.

Hannah drew a long breath, then another as she strove to calm her own rumpled sentiments. "Here," she whispered in reply, and gave the girl her own handkerchief.

Margaret received it hesitantly, glancing up at the older woman's face with her eyes full of questions. Hannah gave a grim nod, charging her to make use of the item for her dripping cheeks. Margaret silently complied, the tremours which still racked her frame gradually slowing.

"Now," Hannah whispered softly, "chin up, girl." She nodded in grave satisfaction as Margaret pulled her shattered feelings once more under regulation. Margaret blinked and nodded, summoning her courage.

Hannah Thornton took the arm of the woman her son loved and drew her out of the small aisle, just before the doorway to the front room. Margaret swallowed, visibly nervous, but at Hannah's encouragement she sucked in a deep breath of fresh air. Her eyelids fluttered as she sought serenity and poise once more. At last, she gave a firm nod. Whatever the matron's intentions were, Margaret was trusting herself to Hannah's direction.

Arm in arm, they strolled quietly through the dividing curtain to the front of the shop. Margaret unconsciously lifted her shoulders and chin, emulating her dignified escort. The hushed discussion was still underway, the participants blithely unaware that any of their acquaintance or social status might possibly choose to shop in any part of the store but the very front. As one, however, their eyes rounded and their lips remained parted in surprised little rosettes when they beheld the others.

"Mrs Draper, Miss Hamilton, how do you do today?" Hannah greeted them indifferently. "You remember Miss Hale, do you not?"

Genevieve gave a little rasping cough. "M-Margaret! Why, it is such a p-pleasure to find you here!"

"Indeed, Genevieve, the pleasure is mine." Margaret, having recovered her usual regal deportment, extended a polite greeting to each of the ladies. "I had tried calling on you on my way here this morning, but you were out. Mrs Draper," she smiled tightly, "It is good to see you again so soon. Do give Mr Draper my regards."

Emmeline, her features quite ashen, only nodded mutely.

"Well," Hannah beamed, causing Margaret to reflect that it may perhaps have been the first time she had witnessed such an expression on the woman's face. "It was lovely to see you both. Good-day, Mrs Draper, Miss Hamilton. Good-day Mrs Gentry!" she called cordially to the proprietress, who saw her go with some dismay.

"Miss Hale," she spoke clearly to Margaret as she began to steer her young charge toward the door, "I trust you still intended to take tea with me after our little shopping excursion today? I believe you said that your father was improving enough that you might spare the time?"

Margaret made her hesitant reply in the affirmative just as they reached the door, leaving two astonished and humbled young women in their wake.

Margaret's eyes were cast over her shoulder until she was certain that the door had closed behind them. "Mrs Thornton," she managed in a broken voice as they gained the street, "I beg you... you do not believe... that is, I-"

"Hush, girl," Hannah ordered from the side of her mouth, her eyes trained steadfastly forward. "I know my son. Come, we will not speak of this on the open street."

Margaret's breath escaped in a shuddering, painful rush. "Thank you, Mrs Thornton!"

Chapter Twenty-Five

I t had been some while since Margaret had partaken of Mrs Thornton's hospitality. On those few occasions, she had been impressed by the opulent, yet somehow austere decor which composed the family's drawing room. It was richly beautiful, but not welcoming. The room had seemed to her at the time to be of a piece with the severe, almost imperious family she had at first taken the Thorntons to be. Now, glancing around with the scales fallen from her eyes, she thought she understood.

Hannah Thornton was savagely proud and protective of her son, and that esteem for him had compelled her to present a home which reflected his status in Milton society. It was, however, a relatively new position in the memories of the old Milton families. Like many other self-made men, his rise to prominence had been nearly meteoric, and almost overnight Hannah had found herself mistress of one of the finest homes in Milton. She had rapidly secured furnishings and draperies she cared nothing about so that she might portray the proper image, impressing the right people to pave her son's way.

Naturally she was proud of her home, of the fine things her son's labour had purchased and the elegant taste which caused many to proclaim hers the most fashionable home in the district. Her heart and her light, however, were in the son who had been her helpmeet and comfort since her husband's death. The home appeared uninviting because Mrs Thornton welcomed into her deepest affections only the one who had always been there.

Margaret turned to her hostess as that lady took her own tea cup, her eyes now full of tender gratitude for the forbidding matron. "Thank you for having me, Mrs Thornton," she repeated humbly, uncertain the lady had heard the first time.

Hannah observed the young woman cynically as she stirred her tea. "You need have no fear of me, Miss Hale," she surmised at last. "I did not believe a word of what was said."

Margaret drew a deep breath of relief. "I was certain you would not have, but it eases my mind to hear it."

"Indeed. It seems, Miss Hale, that we are presented with a problem. Apparently my son's... 'gift'... is known about town."

"I know I ought not to have accepted it!" she whispered miserably. "He was so thoughtful, and I did not wish-"

"It is done," Mrs Thornton stated with finality. At Margaret's dejected expression, she softened. "It was his wish that you would accept, Miss Hale. He understood the risks as well as you or I, but he felt responsible and desired to do you a kindness. My son has never been one to shrink from his duties."

Margaret nodded, blinking rapidly. "I know, Mrs Thornton."

"Then you know that he will not do so now." Hannah took a long sip of her tea, not savouring what she had to say next. "Your reputation is compromised, Miss Hale."

Margaret looked up swiftly. "You do not think they would spread more rumours! After we exposed them today- and they saw us together! Surely they will be far too ashamed!"

"I do not think that Draper woman," Hannah retorted sourly, "knows the meaning of shame. However, it is not only they who are aware of the tea service. Mrs Hamper, and no doubt Mrs Slickson, must also be. I have never known either of them to exercise discretion with their tongues."

Margaret dropped her eyes sorrowfully to her tea. "'Death and life are in the power of the tongue!'[iii]" she quoted bitterly into her cup, more to herself than to Mrs Thornton.

Hannah's lips curled into a crafty smile. "'And they that love it shall eat the fruit thereof,'" she finished.

Margaret peered more carefully at her hostess. Hannah met her eyes with a flinty coolness, but that novel smile still played about her mouth. Margaret began, reluctantly, to smile herself. Of all the peculiar allies to discover at her side, none could have been more unexpected- or more potent- than Hannah Thornton.

She took another pensive swallow of her own tea, striving for rational thought. "I do not believe," she proposed at last, "that it can truly be so widely spoken of. Even if it were, can we not simply let the truth be known? Mr Thornton has been a regular pupil of my father's since we first arrived in Milton; everyone knows as much. Is it really so difficult to believe he might replace something which was broken?"

Hannah leveled a grim stare, arching a brow in silence. Margaret sighed. "I suppose you are right. What must we do?"

"You will have to marry my son, Miss Hale."

Margaret's face flushed. Her eyes leapt to her hostess in a mixture of joy and trepidation. "But the mill! He cannot marry me, Mrs Thornton!"

Hannah narrowed her eyes. "Are you saying you would refuse him... again?"

"No! I mean... Mrs Thornton, if I were to accept, I would only injure him! I cannot! Oh, please, do promise me you will not speak to him of this?"

"I am not in the habit," she replied carefully, "of keeping information from my son- particularly where his own reputation might be concerned."

Margaret's face pinched in some agony. "You heard as I did, Mrs Thornton," she whispered. "It is not he who would suffer. No one would think the less of him...."

"*I* would!" declared his mother vehemently. "I do not care to have my son's name slandered in any case."

"Mrs Thornton," she pleaded, "I beg you, do not bring this to his attention now! It would only trouble him the more, and it may all come to nothing, you know. I would not wish to obligate him... it may yet be that he will need... need more than I can offer, Mrs Thornton."

"If you think," Hannah returned coldly, "that I would allow him to ally himself with that Hamilton clan after what that strumpet said today...."

"Of course not!" Margaret soothed, her thoughts coming more clearly now. "Mrs Thornton, please forgive my candour, but am I wrong in thinking that the mill is facing rather substantial hardship?"

Hannah's eyes slitted suspiciously. "Why do you ask?"

Margaret bit her lip nervously, but forged on. "My father believes that J- that Mr Thornton is in great need of... of some other support... only because of the strike, of course!" she added quickly as she watched Mrs Thornton's face harden. "I did not mean to imply that Mr Thornton had in any way mismanaged-"

"Spare me your platitudes, Miss Hale," Hannah snorted impatiently. "Come now, out with it! I can speak as frankly as you."

Margaret drew a tight breath and swallowed, boldly now facing the affronted mother. "Mr Thornton needs a supporter of sorts, and times are hard now. There are likely very few such to be found."

Hannah's eyes flickered with savage ferocity, but then, as if in surrender, she lowered her gaze. "There are," was the terse reply. "You have come to take an interest in Milton matters after all, Miss Hale," she added drily.

Margaret relaxed somewhat, sensing that perhaps Mrs Thornton might be reasoned with. "Even in London, I think, many are more interested in the war and rail companies just now than in cotton. Surely, however, there must be other wealthy heiresses in the kingdom, and... why, certainly, Mr Thornton is a fine gentleman, and might find favour with-" her breath caught as her heart lurched agonizingly. She swallowed and somehow found the courage to utter her final words. "While Mr Thornton remains unmarried, perhaps there are yet other opportunities for him to- to-" she choked on a sudden knot in her throat.

"John will not marry for monetary advantage." Hannah cut her off before she could recover. "Nor would he wish to be dependent upon inherited monies, plundered from a wife's dowry! All of that matters little in any case. You know as well as I, Miss Hale, that he would have only you. I can see clearly that you wish the same, else you would not have suddenly taken such an interest in John's mill! Why, Miss Hale, would you now presume to judge for my son what is best?"

Margaret swept a hand before her eyes, wishing to tuck away her pain from Mrs Thornton's penetrating gaze. "I do not presume, Mrs Thornton," she rasped. "I only implore you- do not cause him to act hastily! I would not see him harmed; I am content to wait. If he should find it possible in the future to marry, and if he should still hold feelings for me-"

Hannah made a derisive noise. "I think you underestimate the depth of my son's feelings, Miss Hale, as well as his determination."

"He is also a man of duty, as you have said yourself," Margaret countered gently. "Many depend upon him, and he bears that weight with honour. I would not have him betray that responsibility simply to protect me. I have faced scandal before, Mrs Thornton," she finished softly.

Hannah stared thoughtfully at the young woman before her. "Miss Hale," she mused, "I did not approve of my son's attachment to you."

Margaret swallowed. "I know, Mrs Thornton. You think me ungrateful and unworthy."

Hannah shook her head slightly. "I no longer do so. You are headstrong and foolhardy, I think. Perhaps, though, you may be the only woman in all of the kingdom who might, just possibly, be worthy of a man like my son."

Margaret's heart skipped a beat. "I beg your pardon, Mrs Thornton?"

Mrs Thornton was still contemplating her in some wonder. "You have courage and dignity, Miss Hale; moreover, you are the most selfless young lady I have encountered in a long while. I must respect that, though you are heartily imprudent and unreasonable."

Margaret tilted her head in confusion. "I... thank you?"

Hannah sighed. "I will honour your wishes, Miss Hale, but only for now. I may choose to speak to my son if it is in his- or your- best interests. I did, after all, promise your mother that I would watch over you," she finished kindly.

Margaret stared in speechless amazement, then blinked away a sudden moisture from her eyes. "I appreciate that, Mrs Thornton. Thank you so much for your goodwill and your indulgence. I would not have been able to compose myself at all in the shop today, had it not been for your compassion."

Mrs Thornton's eyes twinkled sagely. "Do not underestimate yourself so. You have more strength than you know... Margaret."

The two women could not have told later how long they sate together, but both, at their parting, found their spirits lightened and their understanding improved. Hannah watched from her sitting room window as the petite, dark-clad figure made its way to the outer gates.

A heavy sigh left her. Mightily as she had striven to sustain and nurture her son, hoping to eliminate any desire he might have for a wife, she at last found herself replaced in his affections. She allowed the drapes to fall when Margaret's form disappeared behind the oaken gate.

She turned away, her fingers touching thoughtfully to her lips. It is often the case when confronted with the very event one has dreaded and railed against, that its final revelation takes on a far less bitter taste than had formerly been expected. She no longer feared losing her son to Margaret Hale. Rather, she thought she might welcome the one who could procure his happiness. She might even be proud of a daughter with sense and courage. Perhaps not all of her hope and joy were to be lost, after all.

She was suddenly seized with an irrational desire to once again set eyes on the flesh and blood woman, assuring herself that the genteel, humble young lady who had so recently graced her drawing room was not a phantom. Though her logical mind knew it to be futile, she snatched the drapes aside and peered hopefully toward the gates once more.

Margaret, of course, did not materialize. What she did see, and what lent her the purpose she required, was John. He had only just entered the gates, likely missing Miss Hale's departure by mere seconds, if at all. She studied his manner as he walked, and decided that his path had not crossed the young woman's. Her heart ached to see him, dejected and weary as he made his way toward the mill doors.

Hannah pressed her lips together in firm decision. She rang for her maid. "Jane," she commanded when the girl arrived, "please bring my jewelry box from my vanity to me."

~

Mr Thornton was of several minds after he departed from Watson's home. His strongest impulse and greatest desire was to rush immediately to Margaret's door and declare himself. At the same time, he longed to seek out those whispering about Margaret and crush them- with words, or even fists, if necessary. The other urge at war within him was to return to the bank, to see if there were some detail he had overlooked, some asset he might yet leverage to secure the funds he needed.

As his feelings battled for supremacy, his steps took him unerringly back to the mill. There, at least, he would be assured of doing some good while his thoughts churned within him. It would avail him nothing to pummel Hamper or Slickson- they would only laugh all the more loudly behind his back. There was little good he could do at the bank. He was certain that he had left no stone unturned there, and good Mr Smith would have done all he could.

He absolutely *must* call upon Margaret! All of his delay, allowing her the time and space he felt she needed, had to come to an end now. There was no other choice but to present himself to her and to beg for her hand once more. She and her father wholeheartedly deserved his assurances, his honour, and he was no less eager to give them.

He strode into the yard, his eyes on the ground as he walked. The blessed moment had come to obtain from his mother the betrothal ring that he had destined for the one who held his heart. An hour's time would see him at her door- and breathless and flustered would he be. His brow furrowed in thought.

Everything depended on this encounter. His entire future, the whole of his happiness- all hung precariously on her lovely lips as she uttered the words which would seal his fate. How often did a man twice dare to propose to the same woman? This time, it must be different. *He* must be different!

He glanced up at his surroundings at last. Here, amid the flurry and bustle of the shipping yard, his nerves calmed. He was always at his best when he was being useful and productive, and there was much to be done here. Perhaps, if he spent the last couple of hours of his work day in some worthy pursuit, he might feel justified in presenting himself at her door in the evening as a man who had not yet given up on his future.

With that resolve, he flung himself into his work. He first found Williams to apprise himself on all of the day's events, then ventured forth on his own. No detail of the factory escaped his sharp eyes that afternoon, and many a wary worker carefully dodged from the master's path. In spite of all of the superficial decisions and ideas which passed through his mind as he worked, there was only one matter weighing upon his heart.

Chapter Twenty-Six

It was no great surprise to Margaret that evening to discover that Mr Thornton had at last come to look for her. She had meant to avoid him this one final evening, hoping perhaps that Mrs Thornton had kept her word, and not revealed the things of which they had spoken. One day longer to collect her thoughts and put her feelings under regulation, that was all she had desired!

It was not to be. Though she had purposely been away from her own house the greater part of the day, there were few enough places for her to seek refuge. This evening as she sat in the Higgins' home with little Jenny upon her lap, her heart seized at the sound of his well-known tread outside as he knocked upon the door.

Higgins, too, appeared to know whom to expect. He rose to answer the door, glancing slyly toward Margaret as he went. "Master!" he cried cheerfully.

Thornton's eyes were only for her as he stepped into the little house. Higgins, fortunately, was of a quirky and humorous nature, and chose to find amusement rather than offense at either his besotted guest's unannounced arrival or his brusque greeting.

Margaret could not help the sheer happiness she found in his smile, nor the answering light in her eyes when she met his gaze. It was now her joy to be near him, as one finds delight in the company of one's very dearest and truest companion. Time spent apart, for those so blessed, only serves to sweeten the reunion. Such were Margaret's feelings as he reverently murmured her name in greeting.

She answered him warmly, but quickly chastened herself. Was she not trying to teach herself to live without this pleasure- at least for the present? She closed her eyes, firming her resolve. She must not give him any hope which she could not yet satisfy!

"I am sent by your father, Miss Hale," he was teasing lightly. "He feared you might have been carried off by vagabonds, or some other such calamity."

In spite of herself, she chuckled. Where was the grave, severe Master she had first known? Gone, he was, and with him the haughty, prideful Southern girl she had once been.

She wished to banter playfully, as he seemed to invite her to do, but she dared not. She merely smiled demurely and reclaimed her seat with Jenny. Disappointed, he gazed at her for a moment, as if unsure what to say next. Margaret stole a glance at his perplexed face as Jenny stumbled over the last page of their appointed reading for the evening.

"Master," clever Mr Higgins interjected, "ha' yo' heered aught o' Sacks?"

Thornton bit back a reluctant sigh and joined his employee in the opposite corner of the room. "Nothing since last week. Is there more?"

"Oh, aye," Higgins scraped his weathered chin in his hands, warming to his speech. Truly, it was a domestic matter, and not of the master's concern, but the wily old weaver sensed some tension between his two favourite guests and wished to divert them.

"Th' Union," Higgins went on, "they've shunned 'im."

"What, completely?" Thornton was surprised. The Union wielded considerable influence in Milton- not only in negotiating terms with the masters, but also over their own members. It was rare, however, that such harsh actions were invoked. "I was not aware that he had become so unpopular as all of that."

Higgins shrugged. "Folks' weary o' 'is frettin'," he postulated. "Tha's a'. No one wan's 'im makin' trouble jus' now, wi' winner an' a'."

Thornton grunted softly. Such logic he understood. In all of his years as master, never had the Union dared rouse trouble in the colder months, when men cared most about earning a meagre wage to feed their children. None wished to jeopardize their livings at such a time, no matter how greatly they desired a better wage or gentler conditions.

"Well," he sighed, "I suppose I must pity the poor fool, though I am not quite certain why. I certainly cannot help it if the man's habit of drink has cost him his place. I am sorry that he is such a burden to his family, though."

"Aye," Higgins agreed. "Tho', young Willy by 'imself's been bringin' 'ome 'most 'nough to keep them a' fed. 'E's a good lad, Master."

"I am glad to hear it. You have done well with him, Higgins. Williams has been observing you rather closely, as I expect you know, and even he is pleased."

Higgins winked and chortled happily. "Thank yo', Master." He cast his eyes to the other corner, where Jenny's laboured efforts had at last drawn to a close and she was sliding down from Margaret's lap. By mutual accord, both men moved in her direction.

Thornton offered his hand to help Margaret rise. She glanced up to him in surprise. Her better sense urged her to refuse his hand, for she feared that at his familiar touch, her resolve would crumble.

She lowered her eyes for half a second, deliberating, then with a deep breath she accepted his hand. It was clear that he intended once more to walk her home, and rudeness would avail her nothing. She would simply have to appeal to his reason.

Together they bade Higgins and his household a good evening and started for Margaret's home. As they walked side by side in the growing dusk, he glanced hesitantly at her downturned face. "Miss Hale- Margaret," he began uncertainly, "may I ask if something is troubling you?"

Those grey-green eyes, silvery now in the low light, flashed up to him briefly. She looked away again, biting her lip in agonizing silence. Her gaze found the ground once more as she blinked the hazy frustration from her vision.

He sighed and drew her to a halt, in the middle of the street though they were. "Margaret," he pleaded softly, "I had hoped that by now you would trust me enough to speak your mind. I believe, however, that I might already know the cause of your distress. It is I myself, is it not?"

She drew a shuddering breath before forcing herself to meet his eyes. Her reluctance shot a stab of fear and pain through his heart. "Margaret, I beg you," he slipped his free hand over the small one in the crook of his arm. "Please forgive my presumption! I had no notion to cause you such discomfort when I sent the china. I ought never to have done so! I was selfish, I-"

"John," her soft tones halted him. "It is not that."

His protests died in his throat. He simply gazed down, tenderly and fearfully. He silently wondered what he had done to cause her to withdraw once more, and was too terrified to truly wish to know the answer.

She set her mouth and turned back toward their path. He followed unhappily. "Margaret," he whispered, just loudly enough for her ears, "Perhaps you have heard the same rumours as I. I accept full responsibility. Please know that I will never forsake you. Surely, you must at least know that!"

She blinked, keeping her eyes forward. "I know, John. Oh, please," she glanced up at last, "let us not speak of this here!"

His jaw shifted in displeasure as he submitted to her wishes. Naturally, her suggestion was sound. There was nothing to be gained by further compromising her along their dusky way. What troubled his heart, what made his pulse drum uncertainly, was the way she seemed to close him off tonight. Had she grown ashamed of her feelings for him? It seemed the only plausible explanation!

It was with a tortured spirit that he held the door for her to her residence. He glanced about for Mr Hale- for he had, indeed, been sent to look for Margaret by her father after not finding her at her home.

Never would he learn precisely why Mr Hale did not come to greet him at his return that evening, as he had expected. Nor was there any excuse offered for Dixon or Martha, who were both certainly only awaiting Margaret's homecoming to serve the evening tea. Instead, the normally quiet house was shrouded in an unnatural stillness. His pulse quickened once more, his stomach balling nervously.

He helped her out of her walking cloak and followed her eloquent eyes as they flicked in the direction of the drawing room. His mind now singly focused on his purpose, he led her firmly in that direction. Pausing for only the barest of seconds to close the door behind her, he drew her to the centre of the room and breathlessly fell to his knees before her.

"John," she protested sorrowfully, "please don't!"

Hungrily he pressed the back of her hand to his mouth. "Margaret, my Margaret, I beg you, do not refuse me. Not again!"

"John," she sobbed, "I do not wish to hurt you!"

He fairly leapt to his feet, capturing her other hand. Tugging her willing form close- so deliciously close- he peered anxiously, longingly, into her beloved face. "Tell me, Margaret," he begged softly. "Tell me that you care, that I have not deceived myself."

"I..." she gazed up at him, wishing she could find the courage to ask him to wait. It had seemed such a simple thing only an hour ago! How could she bring herself to wound him once more? For she could see now that anything less than her complete and immediate acceptance would crush his heart.

"Oh, John, I..." she choked, her eyes closed. A stray tear leaked out. "I do," she whispered. She felt his hands tighten round hers, as though he were not fully sure he had heard her properly. She drew a haggard breath, clenching her eyes still. "I love you, John," she dared, in a hoarse breath.

She tried to pull her hand free from his to hide her face with it, but he anticipated her. She opened her eyes to find his fingers gently sliding over her cheeks, following the lines of her jaw. His thumbs traced her cheekbones, caressing her face with loving strokes.

Cupping her face in his work-hardened hands, he allowed his heart free rein for the first time in his life. Lowering his mouth near hers, he paused for only a breath, allowing her this one last chance to pull away. She did not.

His heart swelling in ecstasy, he eagerly drew her to himself. He scarcely even noticed the exact second his lips touched hers for the first time- he focused only on the sweet communion that he had longed for all his lonely years. The only thing that mattered was that she was his at last. She had confessed her heart! He poured all of his concentration into the single, overpowering desire to be one with her.

Margaret had no heart to deny him. Truly, she did not long preserve even the faintest shreds of her well-trained modest hesitancy. This first taste of the unfamiliar should have frightened her, but instead she thrilled in it. The strong, chiseled face she had long studied in annoyed fascination now bent down to her in glad surrender. She leaned into his arms and chest as first one hand, then the other slid over her shoulders and down to her waist to pull her ever closer.

He was so real, so warm and tender in this moment, she could do nothing but nestle further into his embrace. Even when his breath quickened and his caresses intensified with longing, she answered him in joyful concert. She would do anything to comfort and cheer him- nothing would she see him deprived of for the rest of her days. Anything, if it were in her power to give... or to withhold.

A chill washed through her. "John, please, we must not," she drew back, resting her fingers upon his lips.

Puzzled, he trapped her fingers and kissed them. "My love, what is troubling you tonight? Please tell me so that I may put it right."

"It is not you, John, nor anything you have done. Oh, I begged your mother not to speak to you!"

"My mother? What has she to do with this?"

Margaret cringed. If he had not spoken to his mother before, now he most certainly would demand her explanation. He would not rest until he knew all, and that revelation would only temper his resolve to marry her immediately.

"John," she sighed, shaking her head lowly and trying- unsuccessfully- to reclaim her hand. "I have nothing to offer you! You must not consider it, not just now. Please, I would not see you injured by-"

"Not consider it!" he cried. "Margaret, I have desired nothing but your love almost since we first met. I care nothing for wealth or status! Did you truly not believe me when I spoke before? What, I ask you, has changed beside your own feelings?"

"Nothing and everything," she murmured ruefully. "John, the mill- the workers! They depend on you, and it would be reckless of us to marry just now."

"How?" he demanded. "What have they to do with our affairs?"

"I know of your troubles," she whispered, dipping her crimson cheeks in shame.

He narrowed his eyes and gazed at her, his breast heaving in sharp outrage. "And you would not ally yourself with such a disgraceful circumstance, is that it?"

"No!" Her head shot up and her free hand grasped for his in reassurance. "John, I thought nothing of the kind! I only fear for you. I could not bear to cost you the opportunity to... to ensure the mill's future success."

He shook his head, baffled. "What can you mean? How could our marriage harm the mill?"

She clenched her eyes shut. "Surely, you must have considered...."

His jaw hardened, the firm muscles of his cheeks flickering in anger. "I had hoped you would have thought better of me than that, Margaret."

"It is because I think so highly of you that I would not deny you that opportunity, John," she returned painfully. "Only think if we married and you were unable to raise the support you needed to save the mill? In ten, twenty years, how much of the blame for it would you, even unknowingly, assign to me? I could not bear your bitterness, John!"

He listened silently, in aghast denial. At her final declaration, he was goaded into reply. "Margaret, how could you even begin to think such a thing? Do you think I would not choose you above the mill, a thousand times over? And has not the mill been under my own authority, during both plenty and hardship? How could any of that blame be yours to claim, even should it fail utterly?"

She swallowed, catching her breath. *Oh, how to explain!* "John, others are watching," she suggested softly. "Surely, if you were to appear to turn your back on other possible connections, if you married imprudently at such a time, your credit would be damaged in the district, and you may find it all the more difficult to-"

"Margaret," he cut her off, "you must know how deeply I appreciate your concern, but truly, none of it matters to me. It is you I love, and you I want by my side in the midst of these momentary difficulties- for such they are, Love."

"Are they?" she asked quietly. "What happens to the workers, John, if you lose the mill?"

He blinked, wordless for a moment. "I suppose," he answered at length, "another would take it up in time- after the banks have had their way with what remains of the collateral." He grimaced sourly, hating to be discussing such vulgar things with his elegant and gentle Margaret.

"Exactly, John. Such a transition may take months, and all of that time there would be no work, no pay. Some of those families would starve!"

"I cannot save the world, Margaret. What would you have of me?" he asked in exasperation.

"Only that you remain true to your duty, John." She tugged her hands from his at last and laid them across her skirts, gazing meekly up at him.

His face clouded. "You have, indeed, been speaking to my mother."

"In truth," Margaret's mouth- that heavenly treasure!- tipped very slightly at the corner, "it was her advice that we should marry immediately. I believe, after a fashion, that she has now come to see what I see."

He turned away and began to pace the drawing room, both hands raking through his hair in desperation. Margaret remained in the centre of the room, forlorn and motionless like some abandoned statue. He prowled restlessly back and forth, grasping for some argument he could make to persuade her. *Unreasonable, obstinate woman!* Could she not see that he *needed* her, and she him? Could she not see that the compassion which fixed her so immovably was the very quality he- and the mill whose interests she claimed to serve- most sorely lacked?

Seizing that thought, he spun on his heel. "You care so much for the workers, Margaret. Help me! Come work at my side, show me how I can do better!"

She shook her head gently, her eyes down again. "You do not need me, John. What you need, I cannot give you."

"That is untrue, and you know it! I have seen how they adore you, how your every suggestion would be met with acclaim and how you would intuitively see the needs that I have missed. I beg you, Margaret, please hear me!"

"John, my very presence would be a declaration to them that you cared more for your own felicity than for the food on their tables. They would turn on you, and on me, if the mill continues so."

"Now, that is an uncharitable remark!" he retorted. "What of your vaunted faith in all of humanity?"

"Have you not yourself tried to tell me that I am too trusting? Only today have I learnt that you were right!" She clenched her eyes shut and turned her face away, not wishing to bring up yet another subject which she found painful.

John, however, scarcely noticed her visible flinch. One thing only mattered to him. "You speak of trust. Do you trust me, Margaret?"

"Do you trust *me*, John?" she countered boldly.

He stared, incredulous. No other woman he had ever known- not even his own mother- would so confidently and fearlessly demand his respect. Then again, no other woman was Margaret. He could have wept in bitter frustration.

Instead, he closed his eyes and bit down hard on his upper lip, refraining from unleashing his grief and disappointment on her. Slowly he took a long breath, then another. At length, he answered her in broken tones, "You know I do, Margaret. I trust you with my life and my heart. I have no choice! For I have been yours from long ago."

The flinty heat in her eyes cooled, replaced by gentle affection. "Then please, John, I beg you would heed *my* words. I speak out of my concern..." she broke off when he closed the distance between them with a swift stride.

He pulled her suddenly close once more, one hand stroking her cheek and the other pinning her body near his own. "Say it, Margaret. I need to hear you say it!"

Her core quivered as she gazed up at him, panting in his need, and in pity she acquiesced. "... out of my love, then. I do love you, John! I do wish to marry you, but...."

"Oh, Margaret!" he cried, clasping her close. He could bear no more of her denials, and he silenced her in the best way he knew. Willingly she clung to him as he showed her, by the only means available to him, what she meant to him. Tremblingly he held her, daring to taste the pleasures of intimacy with the woman he cherished.

His heart raced ever faster when Margaret began truly to respond as fervently as he. She met each brush of his lips with tenderness of her own, and when, after a moment, he felt her curious fingers settle upon his face, he could not suppress a shudder of ecstasy. "Margaret," he whispered between kisses; her name a muffled mantra of sorts, serving to soothe his battered heart.

Only a moment later, gentle pressure from her fingers pushed him away. Robbed of her sweet lips, he began almost to sob in his deprivation. "Margaret, please!" He pressed her form scandalously close to his own, but his thoughts were only on the heart she refused to fully surrender.

Burying his face in her glorious hair- the hair he had so ached to touch- he choked out his plea. "How can you deny what you feel? Marry me, Margaret. Be my wife, build a future with me! Do you not long for the same?"

Margaret hid her face against his chest, fearing that if she looked on his broken expression, she would never hold true to her resolve. "I do, John. I am not refusing you; only asking that we wait."

"For how long?" he demanded. "Until distance comes between us, and your feelings have cooled? Until I have gone grey, and you have found some other?"

"If you are so fearful that I will cease to love you, John, you ought not to be asking me to marry." She pulled back to look at him once more, her fingers trailing distractingly along the lines of his cravat where she had been resting her cheek. "I will love you always, John Thornton," she vowed.

He shuddered in agonized relief. "Then what difference does it make when we wed?"

"Indeed. What difference does it make, John?" she allowed a glimmer of a smile, tinged with regret. "My heart is yours. I only ask that we not appear to act rashly, John- for *your* good, and that of the workers. I could not see harm befall you or them merely because I was impatient."

He shook his head slowly in combined frustration and awe. "What of your own reputation, Margaret? Perhaps you do not know the things which are being whispered about town."

She rested her head again on his chest, savouring this one small consolation. "I have heard. Surely, it is not the first time things have been rumoured about me."

"Which makes it all the more important that we confront the lies! Once may be overlooked in time, when your general conduct is shown to be above reproach. Twice- people will start to believe the rumours. I cannot allow you to be injured, Margaret. If we marry soon, all will be forgotten! It will be understood that we had been quietly courting- for I *was* attempting to court you, though clumsily so. If, however, the slander is allowed to propagate, with no marked and immediate response from us, it could follow us even after we are wed. It could be years before we might put it behind us!"

"Then," she swallowed an anguished lump in her throat, "we must make, as you say, some marked response. We ought not to see each other so often, John."

His face greyed. "What? You cannot be serious!"

She closed tear-filled eyes. "I am afraid so, John. It is the only way, I think."

He seized her shoulders, forcing her to look him in the eye. "Tell me to my face. You truly wish me not to come here any longer?"

She bit her lower lip as her eyes tried to slide away from his. "Perhaps that is too extreme- if you were to appear to drop my father's acquaintance, it would only make matters worse. I think, however, we ought not to be seen together in public for now."

"So I may have the honour of passing you in the hall for my lessons with your father, and the distinction of glimpsing your back in Sunday service, and that is all?" he asked bitterly.

She glanced uncomfortably at the window, noting that, fortunately, the drapes had been drawn for the night. "In the privacy of my own home... but you must not stay longer than you always have, John. I should think such a thing would be noticed, since others are now looking for it."

His tall, stately bearing had begun to wither. He stood now, his shoulders drooping, his face dejected. "Margaret, are you agreeing to a secret engagement? I have always thought such a thing shameful, but if you truly have such fears...."

"I am agreeing to marry you when circumstances are more favourable," she answered cautiously.

He pulled her close, nestling her under his chin with a wry and painful little laugh. "If any other woman were to say such a thing to me, I would assume her motives to be mercenary. Why does everything always come down to the vulgar and disgraceful pursuit of money?"

Margaret, secure for now with his strong arms around her, gave a tearful chuckle. "You have changed, John Thornton! You are no longer the fearsome captain of industry I first met."

"I am the same as I ever was, Margaret- though, perhaps I only allowed you to see those bits of my character I thought most under my control. You terrified me from the beginning, Margaret! I had never felt so small or insignificant in my life as when I looked into your eyes and did not care for my own reflection."

"That was my own pride you saw," she confessed. "I thought myself immune to such a feeling, but it proved my greatest vulnerability. It has cost me... oh! If I had accepted you when you first spoke, we would not now be concerned for what others might think. Mr Hamilton, the Drapers- none of it could have touched us! I could have stood by your side in your troubles, instead of having to step back."

"You cannot be blamed," he pressed a kiss to her hair. "I thoroughly shocked and offended you that day, I am sure of it. I hate to remember how badly I misunderstood you. To have your love and forgiveness now makes up for all the past. Margaret," he changed subjects abruptly, "tell me I may at least speak to your father. He deserves to know!"

She blinked, staring thoughtfully at the cravat she was fingering. "I think it hardly necessary just now, John. He knows your intentions, and none could have a higher opinion of your honour."

"I should like to preserve his opinion of me, if I may."

It was a moment before she answered. "I would prefer that you did not tonight, John. I can talk to him, if you think it important that he understand matters. I would rather that you had the honour of properly addressing him when we are prepared to consider our betrothal official."

He sighed and tightened his arms about her. "I was afraid you would feel that way. I do not like to come as the thief in the night, robbing a man of his daughter beneath his very nose. Is this all I am to have of you for now? A stolen kiss or two before I must again leave you for days on end?"

"You needn't steal anything," she assured him, lifting her chin to his with a new bravery.

This time, their embrace was long and precious, uninterrupted by more melancholy words before his departure. He ruthlessly pushed aside his sorrow for now- that would be unveiled and parsed over, alone in his own chamber... later. Just now, the love of his life was in his arms, and allowing him the liberties she would grant only to the man she intended to marry.

Chapter Twenty-Seven

Hannah's dark brow quirked over her square sewing glasses as she heard her son's step in the hall. His tread was measured and heavy, and if she listened very carefully she could discern a faint shuffling of his toes. Her pulse quickened apprehensively. None knew his ways so well, and before she ever saw his face, she knew his mood.

She began to set her needlework aside, her eyes never leaving the doorway. John had stopped in the outer hall, his profile silhouetted against the dim candlelight she permitted in that corridor. He stood as though reluctant, but at last he turned toward her.

Slowly, wordlessly, he trudged to her seat. Reaching into the pocket of his waistcoat, he withdrew his clenched fingers and deposited what he found there on her side table. The object dropped with a clear metallic ring, rocking once or twice before settling. Hannah's eyes fell upon the diamond band and she briefly closed them, blocking out temporarily the sight of her son's stricken visage.

Without a word, he turned to go. Summoning her motherly courage, Hannah rose and found her voice. "John, wait!"

He stilled, his face turned away from her. "You knew, did you not Mother?"

She froze, hesitant. Her hand, outstretched in mute entreaty, dropped.

He slowly turned round. "You knew what she would say?"

Hannah groaned. His agony was palpable, his disappointment sharp and bitter. She fought a sympathetic pang of her own. "Yes, dear John, I knew," she admitted.

"And yet," he looked her full in the face at last, "This afternoon I found that ring tucked safely in its box and placed upon my desk. Why?" His voice trembled in such pain that she reached a hand to him once more.

"I knew," she answered after some hesitation, "that she did not *wish* to refuse you. I knew that if she wounded you this time, it would hurt her as much... perhaps more."

"Yet you tacitly encouraged me to speak!"

"You were honour-bound to do so, John. I believed, and do still, that your assurances will bring her comfort in the months to come. I cannot help but wonder if her resolve might soften, once she has come to cherish hopes for a shared future with you."

"We both know Margaret better than that." His voice quavered but a little. "When once she fancies that she is in the right, that she is doing a service to another, she will not be swayed."

"You cannot say, after all, that you have not in the end won her loyalty," answered the sage Mrs Thornton.

His shoulders shook in something akin to a mournful laugh. "What good is that without her hand?"

"John," she crooned comfortingly, much as she had in the days of old. She reached for him, and he came to her as he always had. He eased her gently into her old chair- the only piece of furniture in the house which was not elegant and new- and then took his place at her feet. Just as when he had been a boy, she drew his head to her knee and rested cool fingers at his weary temples.

When she sensed a little of the tension ebbing from him, she ventured to question him. "She did not refuse you outright?"

"No, not utterly. Not as before."

Unseen by him, she closed her eyes in relief. "That is well. What hope did she offer?"

"A futile one, I fear. She wishes to see me achieve the impossible- oh, not out of vanity, but because she honestly believes it necessary for my ultimate good. How can she ask me to wait for something which may never come about?"

"Why should she not have faith in you?" queried his mother stoutly. "I have always done so."

"She ought to know that I care nothing for the mill by comparison!" he cried in anguish. "That even now, it is slipping through my fingers, and I wish only for her to hear my sorrows and encourage me in my distress!"

Mrs Thornton's hand upon her son's brow stilled. A wave of her old jealousy loomed. Why should this fine son of hers, whom she had loved and counseled with all of the wisdom and tenderness she possessed, wish to turn from her gentle mercies to a mere girl? A girl who had only very recently come to regard him with any esteem at all!

Where was Margaret Hale, her savage old self demanded, *when John was working long hours for a pittance in the draper's shop? Where was she when he swallowed his pride and used all of his hard-earned savings to pay off his father's creditors?*

She drew a trembling breath, scolding herself. Oughtn't she to have expected this? What man did not in the end betray the mother who bore him for another? *But my John,* that stubborn voice insisted, *John is different!*

She arched her spine, raising her chin proudly. Her teeth clenched, she bade that quarrelsome inner voice to depart. No loathsome spirit of jealousy should be found in her! A mother's sacrifices were never ceasing, and her delights ever multiplied with her sorrows. Her son's joys and hopes were now to be hers to treasure as well. She would lift up another, while she herself must diminish.

An unfamiliar mist grew over her eyes as she made to herself this bittersweet proclamation. Her hand trembled, then caressed her son's hair once more. No longer was this child of hers a mere boy, running to her with his hurts. He was a man- the man his father ought to have been, if she confessed it to herself- and he desired no more than what was natural and right.

Miss Hale was not so bad- certainly she had underestimated the lass. She could do far worse, she consoled herself, than to foster that girl as her future daughter. A young woman who could deny the stirrings of her own heart, stepping aside with the hope that the man she loved might prosper, was one who understood the sort of sacrifice that Hannah was only now coming to know.

At last she answered him, her voice uncertain and wavering. "Is it so certain," she ventured, "that the mill will fail?"

He lifted his head, his gentle blue eyes searching hers. "Not certain, no, but there is a high probability. I know not how to surmount my present difficulties. I have time yet, but I fear I only delay the inevitable."

"But you do have time! Why, there is no need to fret about what may happen in half a year. Many things could change in that time!"

"And many will not. What irreparable damage might be done to the business if I extend myself to the brink, hoping against hope that something might turn up?" He sighed. "It would be better to sell up right away, preserving what little I have left and leaving the mill to another. At least in that circumstance, operations may continue almost immediately and the hands are not left to starve."

"And," guessed his mother, "Miss Hale might find no further impediments to an engagement? Do you suppose she would accept you if you had no income?"

He gave a wry laugh. "I might say that would be the surest way to guarantee her acceptance. There would be no mill and no workers dependent upon my success or failure, and she might feel free to start over with me. She would not fear hardship of that nature."

Mrs Thornton was quiet a moment. "So... she did admit to her feelings?"

His face softened and his gaze grew distant. "She did." The warmth which briefly lit his eyes faded in only a moment. "If not for her misguided nobility, she would be mine even now, and that ring in its rightful place on her hand!"

Hannah's spirits rose and she found herself in the unfamiliar position of defending Margaret Hale to her son. "Do not judge her harshly!" she chided. "It cost her a deal to answer you as she did. She is right in asking for delay just now, but only for your interests. Her own, it is true, would be better served by accepting immediately, but she was more concerned for you, my son. Do not abrogate the honour she tries to do you by your rash words."

He gazed at her in wide-eyed astonishment. "Mother! Whence came these new sentiments?"

She stiffened slightly. "I may as well accept her," she reasoned. "She seems, after all, a sensible young lady."

A shadow of his cheerful, crooked smile played at his mouth. "You would not mind sharing a home with her?"

Her chin lifted yet higher. "Give me some time as well, son John."

He almost chuckled, but his eyes dimmed once more. "I have no choice, Mother. I fear you shall have more time, even, than you desire."

"Nay, John," she assured him confidently. "You will find a way. I have more faith than ever now that you will succeed."

He sighed. "I hope you are correct, Mother." He blinked a few times and rose to his feet.

She rose with him. "John, I should like to come to know her better. I think I will invite her to tea again in a day or two."

Stunned, he gaped down at her. "Mother! I thank you, but..." he pinched the bridge of his nose in frustration. At such a turn in his mother's regard, he wished to eagerly promote relations between the two women dearest to him, but Margaret's wishes would not permit it.

"Mother," he began again, more gently, "to protect her honour at present, our family must not be seen to take any particular interest in hers. Nothing more, nothing less than we have always done."

She peered over her glasses at him, the discouragement he hid behind his words shining clearly to her. "Then you may not visit her as readily as you have done of late?" Her brow clouded. "I am sorry, John," she told him sincerely.

He pressed his lips tightly together. "I may see her on Wednesday. I shall speak more to her then."

She nodded silently. He leaned near and embraced her tenderly, as he had not done in her recent memory. "I intend to go over my account books this evening, Mother. Do not wait up for me."

~

"Why, Fanny, dear! How good of you to call." Emmeline Draper proudly showed her guest to a seat and signaled for refreshments.

"I was pleased to find you at home today," Fanny replied, with only the barest hint of querulousness in her tones. She took the offered seat, and her quick gaze flitted about the room. It was impressively appointed, at no little expense, she was sure. This, certainly, was the kind of company she ought to be keeping!

"Ah, yes. Randall had me about the hospital's business yesterday," Emmeline answered importantly. "Tell me, dear Fanny," she glanced unconsciously toward the door, "how does your mother today?"

"Mother! Oh, I believe she is well enough. Why do you ask?"

"I see." Emmeline's eyes darted once more toward the door. "I might have expected her to accompany you, that is all. I wondered if she were unwell."

Fanny scoffed. "Mama is never ill. I may call on my own acquaintances without begging her leave, to be sure! I do not think I have called on you since your marriage, and I said to myself *that* was neglectful, but here I have come to visit at last!" She flicked at an unruly feather from her hat as she spoke.

Emmeline Draper relaxed a precious little. "You have not spoken to your mother at all today?" she asked cautiously.

Fanny sniffed. "Why, of course I have, do not be silly! She has shut herself up with all of the linens today. Goodness me, she has set the housemaids to bring down basketfuls of cloth such as I have never seen, and whole spools of marking thread! I cannot think what she might be doing, but she could not be called away."

Emmeline pursed her lips. "How very peculiar. Well, now, I suppose it is nothing to trouble yourself over. I expect that Mr Thornton's private affairs are not to be aired."

"My brother! John *has* no private affairs, I am convinced. Oh, mercy me, and that is what I came to ask of you!" She leaned forward in her seat, as though she were sharing a great secret. "I am *sure* that he intends to propose to our dear Genevieve within the fortnight!"

Emmeline's forehead creased. "I thought Mr Thornton *had* no private affairs. What makes you so certain?"

Fanny looked thunderstruck, caught in her own fabrication. "Well, to be sure, he has none *yet*. He is very quiet, you know, but Mama sent for that great diamond ring out of her jewelry box and gave it to him yesterday. My maid told me all about it later," she blithely informed her hostess. "Now, if you ask me, he is only waiting to have it sized, and of course to speak with Mr Hamilton."

Emmeline watched that stray feather fall from Fanny's tawdry hat and tried not to snicker. "I heard that Mr Hamilton left for London yesterday afternoon, on some urgent matter. He is expected to be there some days."

"How did you... why, of course, John had heard the same, naturally," Fanny assured her friend. "That is why he has not spoken yet, you know."

"Indeed. Well, my dear, you may be secure that *I* will keep these things to myself, but you really ought to tell dearest Gen. She has become rather despondent, waiting as she has with no address from Mr Thornton. Why, I should think after yesterday that she will barely stir from her room! It would encourage her to hear that not all hope is lost; do you not think?"

"Oh, dear me, that is what I had come to ask of you!" Fanny aired her face with just the perfect touch of distress mixed with self-importance. "You see, it would come so much better from you! After all, you are married now, and I think it would sound so much less indelicate if *you* were to bring it up, do not you?"

Emmeline cracked a sly smile. "Perhaps we could call together, is that what you suggest?"

"Oh, why, do you not think it would be far lovelier if you and I and Genevieve, and perhaps her brother- and John too, if I can get him- would it not be so nice for us all to have tea here in your splendid new home?"

Emmeline nodded in wide-eyed innocence. "That *does* sound lovely, Fanny. I shall see to the invitations."

"How wonderful! I *knew* you would wish to help me give our friend such glad tidings. Oh, goodness me, only look at the hour! I am afraid I must be going, Em."

The fluttering guest made her farewells and departed, leaving a highly bemused hostess standing in her elaborate foyer. Sighing and rolling her eyes, Emmeline Draper turned and walked to her husband's study. Randall was not there, of course- he would not return from his club for hours yet- but the study was not entirely empty. She entered and locked the door behind herself.

"Good gracious Emma, what sort of flighty goose was that? I could hear her honking from in here!"

"*That*," she informed her guest, "is the sister of a machine and the daughter of a she-dragon, who has never lifted a finger for the whole of her life. I do not see how she got out of her own front door, much less found my house all alone!"

Her companion smirked. "Fanny Thornton? What intrigue has her sneaking out of the house?"

"I suspect her ultimate goal is an engagement, but not necessarily between Mr Thornton and Genevieve. She really ought to leave the romantic scheming to her mother... no, perhaps not." She shuddered. "I hope I may never see *that* woman again!"

"Come, Emma, I did not come to talk about the Thorntons. I must be gone soon!"

She shook the vision of the scowling, disapproving matron from her memory. "Forgive me, Rupert. Perhaps you can help me think of other things."

Rupert Hamilton grinned in satisfaction. "I believe I can."

~

"Does it fit, Jenny?" Margaret tied the sash of the new frock behind the child's back and waited for her to turn. Fleetingly, she rubbed her burning eyes, dropping her hand quickly so the girl did not see.

Jenny stretched her arms forward experimentally, her face alight. "Thank yo', Miss Marg'et!" she beamed. "'Tis just like yo'rs!"

Margaret smiled. Indeed, the material in the child's new school frock was from Margaret's own personal dress bolt. She had lacked the courage to show her face again in Gentry's dress goods, but as sleep had fled from her the previous night, she had determined to make herself useful. She had finished the simple garment just before dawn, and it was now late afternoon.

"You look wonderful, Jenny!" she embraced the girl encouragingly. "I am quite sure you will be very clever in this new dress."

The child's eyes rounded and she nodded, assured that her beloved Miss Marg'et spoke the truth. This dress would only naturally make her smarter and able to study harder, because Miss Marg'et said so.

Margaret patted the girl's cheek. "Now, go take it off, and save it for school, do you understand?" She sat back on her heels as the girl scampered off, then as an afterthought, rose to her feet and dusted her skirts.

"Thank yo', Miss," Mary's small voice came from behind her.

She turned. "It is little enough, but if it lends her confidence for school, I am pleased to be of service. What of the other children, Mary, is there anything they need?"

Mary's cheeks pinked somewhat and she ducked her head.

Margaret flushed in sudden understanding. "Oh, Mary, do forgive me! I did not mean to imply that Nicholas was unable to..." she stopped herself, feeling that the apology would also sound like an insult. "I only wished to be fair to the other children, you know," she amended.

Mary hesitated. "The lads'll need shoes soon 'nough, but Da's sure, wi' me workin' now...."

"Working? At the mill? I had not heard of this."

Mary blushed pleasantly. "I start t'morrow, Miss, cookin' a' the Mill. Master Thornton told Da' this mornin', a' was ready."

Margaret was smiling, but her eyes drifted sadly to her hands. "That is good to hear, Mary," she whispered.

"Miss?"

Margaret steadied herself and met her young friend's questioning eyes. "Yes, Mary?"

Mary glanced about, ensuring herself that the children were not immediately at hand. "Is aught amiss? I know," it was Mary's turn to look regretful, "I know I'm not Bess, but...."

Margaret took the girl's hand with a reassuring smile. "No, but you do not need to be, Mary."

Mary's shy pleasure shone forth as her eyelashes batted. She cleared her throat and boldy asked her question. "'Tis only, Miss, that yo' and the Master... yo' look sad today, Miss."

Margaret's brow furrowed. "Perhaps a little, but it is nothing to worry about. You need not think poorly of Mr Thornton; he has done nothing wrong."

Mary's slim frame heaved a sigh of relief. "I'm ri' glad to 'ear, Miss! Da says yo'll make the Master 'appy."

Margaret chuckled softly at Mary's brazen innocence. "I am glad he thinks so, but there is no formal understanding between Mr Thornton and myself. Someday, I hope, but not yet."

Mary looked confused. "Yo're na' to be the Mistress? But me da', 'e said...."

Margaret shook her head gently. "Do not fret about it just now, Mary. Time shall resolve everything, I am sure." She watched the girl through fatigue-laced eyes, and even in her profound weariness she could detect the other's hesitation and distress. "Mary? Is there something else?"

Mary gasped uncertainly, glancing between Margaret and the floor. "Nay... 'tis naught, Miss."

"Mary," Margaret spoke kindly, but firmly. "What is troubling you?"

Mary shifted uncomfortably, looking anywhere but at Margaret, but she could not escape. Finally, she relented. "I were wond'rin', Miss... wha's it like?"

Margaret blinked questioningly, her head tilted. "What is what like, Mary?"

Mary's face bloomed her embarrassment, but she forged ahead. "I- I meant to... to talk to a man... but more than talkin', if yo' take my meanin', Miss."

"Oh," Margaret breathed. She stared, glassy-eyed, at some imaginary object on the far wall of the house. How was she to answer such a question? And yet, how could she refuse to at least attempt it? Mary had no other to turn to, and she was at a very trying age for a girl. Indeed, many of her age mates, other factory workers, were likely already wed.

"I hardly know, Mary," she replied at length. "I have always *spoken* to men; gentlemen and famers alike, more than most girls my age because they would call at the parsonage. I am perhaps a poor example. I little understood the difference between simple talk and more meaningful conversation between the sexes until I had made a rather notable blunder." She paused here to interject a rueful laugh. "It seems I have learned little since then! I continue to err, Mary."

Mary's abashed expression had evolved to one of awe. "Yo', makin' a mistake, Miss?"

"Yes, indeed! I have a host of regrets."

Mary pondered this for a moment. It seemed unfathomable to her that one of Margaret's education and poise might be fallible and human as any other. Such an admission, by one she so deeply admired, washed away some of her fears. Nearly trembling in her curiosity, she dared ask the one final question to which she longed to have an answer.

"I'm minded that Bess used to go on 'bout yo' at the big 'ouse, but yo' didn'a like the Master. Is… is 'e diff'rent, some'ow Miss? I mean," she cringed, chewing her lip uncomfortably, "yo' fancy 'im? 'Ow's to know 'e's betta' than 'nother?"

Margaret's expression softened. "I suppose one can never know for certain, but Mr Thornton has earned my respect. Yes, perhaps that is a good place to begin. I disliked him very strongly at first, you are right, but I slowly began to admire his qualities. He has been very kind, even at a time when I treated him shamefully. I expect it was that which convinced me that he was truly a better man than I had allowed him to be.

"Circumstances of late have brought us more frequently into one another's company, and we have at last become rather friendly. He…" she interrupted herself with a bashful smile and a soft laugh, "he is actually quite a charming man. He cares deeply for his family and… and for me." Her tones were hushed, and she shook her head in humble amazement.

Mary was grinning and hiding behind her hand in her embarrassment. The teasing sparkle in her eyes, as much as her next words, reminded Margaret very much of her dear sister. "'E's nice to look on, too," Mary snickered.

Margaret laughed aloud at this unexpected pronouncement from shy, invisible Mary. "Quite!" she agreed, and the two dissolved into helpless giggles.

Chapter Twenty-Eight

M argaret paced restlessly by the window of the drawing room, resisting the
urge to draw the drapes aside again. Her eyes drifted frequently to the
clock, each time finding the hands scarcely advanced since the last time
she had looked. She blew out a sharp breath, annoyed with herself for her
impatience.

She was aching to see him, but did not know how she would bear the
lingering disappointment in his eyes. How strenuously he would work upon
her to weaken her resolve! Yet, she must remain firm. She must not yield
to her heart's desire or the longing in his voice.

She blinked, drawing a deep breath. If only she felt certain that she
was doing right! His arguments had tormented her and cost her two nights'
slumber. Truly, what was the harm in surrendering now, in binding herself
to him in the sight of others? Could his business woes really be so serious?
Had she any right to demand such patience from him, placing- as he had
said- the interests of commerce before the needs of his heart?

Her breath became shallow and quick once more as she turned these
things over in her mind. Her entire being was tense now, and when the
knocker sounded she nearly leaped for fear and pleasure. Forcing herself to
still, she turned away from the window and tried to compose her features.
She could hear Dixon opening the door for him, and she clenched her fists
in a final effort at self-control.

Seconds later, he strode in, his eyes only for her. Margaret tried to hold
herself steady, but like an eager soldier breaking rank, her steps had
carried her halfway across the room before she was even aware that she
had moved.

His arms enclosed around her, and words were neither necessary, nor
even possible for several moments. One hand caressed her cheek and
tickled softly over her neck to cradle the back of her head, while the other

tenderly stroked between her shoulders. His lips, soft and oh! so expressive, grazed over hers, and she found herself smiling irrepressibly in his embrace.

Pulling back only slightly, he trailed the backs of his fingertips reverently down her cheek and pressed a kiss to her forehead. "Good afternoon, Love," he whispered.

"Do you intend to greet me like this on each of your visits?" she teased lightly.

"You object?" rumbled the deep voice she had come to adore.

"I ought to," she smiled, "but I am finding it rather difficult."

"Be generous with me, Margaret. After all, I shall have to make do with only one such visit per week, and even this must be short."

"John, I do not mean to-"

He shushed her gently, and by a most enjoyable means. "Margaret, I do not speak reprovingly. I will respect what you have asked of me, only do not deny me this one moment in your arms. I have thought of nothing else since last I saw you."

She rested her head against his chest, relishing his closeness. It would be so brief, but it was a taste, she hoped, of what she might daily look forward to. John's hand slid down her back, pressing her closer to the dark wool of his coat. Margaret's clamouring spirits found a moment of delicious peace, as though she had been some wayfaring stranger and at last had come to the comfort of her natural home.

"Is this how you meant to sway me?" she spoke thickly against his chest.

"Sway you, my love?"

She raised her head. "I expected you to object once more to waiting."

His eyes sparkled with something- was it mischief? "Why, naturally, my Margaret! You did not expect me not to try, did you?" He lifted his fingers and stroked down her face again, laughing softly as her cheeks dimpled in a deep smile.

"In truth, you may rest easy, Love. I may disagree with you, but I will honour your wishes. I can but admire your determination, and I know your motives to be true and pure. Indeed, if I were so readily able to convince you to abandon what was so important to you, I might come to respect you the less for it, and you might learn to resent me. No, I humbly submit to your request, my love."

Margaret studied him in astonishment. "Truly? I... I had not thought you would yield so easily!"

He drew her to his chest again, dropping his cheek to the top of her head. "I did not say it was easy! Please, let us speak no more of it now. Let me imagine for just a moment that I may hold you thus for hours yet."

They stood so entwined for long minutes, coming to learn the instinctive sense of one another which is so dear to lovers. Margaret closed her eyes in delirious wonder at the simple pleasure of his strong embrace. She drank in his scent for a precious second more, then lifted her face.

Understanding, he released her and stepped back. "I should go to your father," he murmured roughly.

"He is expecting you," she agreed. "I spoke with him, John... he understands everything."

His arms hung forlornly at his sides as his fingers twitched uncomfortably. "It seems wrong, utterly wrong, that I cannot speak to him as a man. You are certain this is what you wish?"

"I am certain," affirmed she, "that the subject will arise whether I desire it or not. You may be assured that my father wishes to bless an engagement as much as you would like to speak."

One side of his mouth tugged into that devastating smile, and Margaret's knees weakened just a little. "I doubt that."

He turned to leave her, but before he had gone two paces he was back, tugging her into his arms. "You will wait on me before I go?" he pleaded hopefully. "There are a few things I wished to say to you."

"Why not simply say them now?"

"I have already done so, but I think them of such import that I do not mind repeating them- as many times as you care to hear." He lowered his face to hers once more. He was several minutes tardy when at last he joined Mr Hale upstairs, but that well-bred and courtly old gentleman said nothing about it.

~

"Oh, John! I have been waiting for you. Fancy you coming home early today, too!" Fanny Thornton gushed down the hall, fluttering a note in her hand just as her brother was hanging his hat.

He turned with a raised brow. It had been years since the long-gone days of girlhood, when Fanny greeted him for felicity's sake at the end of his work day. Now, if she were pleased to see him, there was some outside reason.

"I return only briefly," he turned back to the rack, removing his coat. "I have work to do this evening."

Fanny paused. "Why come home at all, then? It is very early!"

"I am just returned from my lesson with Mr Hale. I thought to take some dinner back to the mill office." His tones were measured, but one who knew him well might have detected a distant twinkle in his eye, or a lingering softness in his voice.

She narrowed her eyes, slanting them up at the paternal figure who was her elder brother. The respect she had tendered back in her youthful days was fading quickly, replaced by the certain knowledge that her brother was not the paragon of wisdom and virtue her mother had always declared him to be.

"And how is *Margaret Hale* today?" she sneered- rather unwisely.

His eyes flared. "Fanny!"

"Oh, bother, John, everyone knows how she runs after you. How she has managed to lead you round by the nose, I shall never-"

She never got to finish her sentence. Her brother, seething in rage, twisted the note from her hand and stalked close, his face pressed near hers and his towering height bearing down upon her. Fanny flattened back against the wall with a small squeak, her eyes casting about for an escape.

"Fanny Thornton," he hissed, low and menacingly, "if I ever hear you speak another word against Margaret Hale, I shall cut off your spending money. Every penny of it! You shall have to work in the dress shop for your clothing, and if I do not throw you out of my house, you shall pay rent or work in the kitchen for your meals!"

Fanny cowered, unable to meet the savage determination sparking from his eyes. "John, don't hurt me! I shall tell Mother!"

He snarled in disgust, pushing away from her. "I have never laid a finger on you, Fanny, nor shall I ever. Had we still our father, however, he might have done well to have plied the rod when you were still a child. Your employment is all idle vanity, Fanny! You care nothing for anyone, and you stoop to your third-rate arts to get what you want. I have seen enough of how you manipulate Mother, and it is at an end now! What is this?"

He snatched up the note he had taken from her and scanned it quickly. A sarcastic chuckle rose from him. "Emmeline Draper? I suppose this was your idea, was it? You may forget it, Fanny. I shall not be taking tea with the Drapers, and nor shall you! Your behaviour has been a disgrace, Fanny, and I will not have you dragging our family name through the dirt. Unless Mother goes with you, you are confined to this house until further notice. Is that understood?"

She was blubbering pitifully by now. Whether John truly meant his threats mattered little- he had never before even spoken a word against her, and now, when she needed his cooperation most desperately, he had proven surprisingly intractable. "B-b-but J-j-john!" she gasped between sobs, then her speech lost coherency. She tried to say "I," but the word came out only as an inarticulate squeal. She doubled over in a helpless bundle of petticoats, heaving and hiccoughing against the floorboards.

He scowled, snaked his fingers through his hair, and stormed from the hall. He was ashamed that he had lost his temper, but it was above time that Fanny had someone set her down. He had best search out his mother to inform her of this most recent development.

~

My Dearest Margaret,

It is such a pleasure to be at home once more! Corfu was simply marvelous, and we did have such amusements there, but I have missed all of my friends here in London. Mama returns from Paris tomorrow, and I do so long to see her! Dear little Sholto has no memory of his Grandmama, but after tomorrow he shall see her every day.

Oh, Margaret, I do so wish for you to see my boy! Everyone here says he is the most beautiful child they have ever seen, but do you know, I think they would say so even if he were quite shocking to look at- some babies are, you know. It is your opinion I wish to hear, my dear Margaret! I have taught him to find your portrait when I say your name, so that he will know you at first sight. I am sure that you will positively swoon over him!

Maxwell has been out almost constantly since we returned. All of his friends at the club are anxious for him to call, and of course I have had a steady stream of visitors at home. I never knew I had so many friends! Many of them have asked about you. Oh, I do wish you would come to us, for I am sure I do not know how to explain where you and Uncle are living, or why he left Helstone. I cannot think what dreadful company you must have to keep there! There cannot be more than one or two respectable families, surely!

Margaret ceased her reading to laugh softly to herself. She had long since despaired of making Edith understand their move to Milton. It made no logical sense to anyone who did not fully comprehend her father's doubts or his sense of honour. Edith's assumption about what company Margaret kept, however, seemed to her now patently naïve... ignorant, even, as she herself had once been. She sighed, flipping unseeingly over the page.

Respectable company, indeed! For the first time in a year and a half, she had begun to feel herself among kindred souls. How quickly all had changed! The catalyst bringing about her late contentment, without a doubt, had been her new understanding of John. She smiled distantly. Not *Mr Thornton* anymore! Her eyes crinkling in her serene pleasure, she continued with Edith's letter.

So much has happened while we were away. Dear Sarah Jameson is engaged to a Navy officer, and Marissa Price was wed only last week to a friend of Henry's from the law offices. I know how glad you will be to hear that the Whites are all well, and they are planning their Christmas party again this year. You remember, that was where I met Maxwell! They asked me to be sure to invite you, and I told them I thought I might be able to work upon you to come. I am sure that Henry would be happy to escort you.

I suppose I must tell you something Henry said to me when he was here to dinner last evening. He received a letter from a colleague of his, some fellow by the name of Hamilton, who says that he recently made your acquaintance. He did not wish to alarm you, Margaret, but Henry implored me to put you on your guard about that man. I cannot think Henry would fabricate such a warning. He said only that the man was no gentleman and that a lady ought not to trust him. For myself, I cannot fathom any gentlemen living in such a wild, dirty place to begin with! But there, you write that there are one or two tradesmen of good character, and I suppose you must know what you are about.

I am afraid I must close now, for Sholto shall be wanting his Mama soon. Do write back and promise you will be with us at Christmas, Margaret! Bring Uncle too, for I know that a London break would do him much good. I remain affectionately yours,

Edith

Margaret finished the letter with a puzzled brow. Odd, wasn't it, that Henry Lennox, to whom she had not spoken since that disastrous day in Helstone, would suddenly beg Edith to send her a message? Odder still that his message should be a frantic caution- no doubt downplayed by Edith- about that Rupert Hamilton character.

Margaret shrugged, trying to pass it off. She had already judged the young Hamilton and found him to be a waste of her time, so she could not fathom what need she might have of Henry's warning. It was thoughtful of him to look out for her, despite their broken fellowship, but honestly, it seemed unnecessary.

She tapped her fingers on the letter as she scanned it once more, this time trying to gloss over the bit from Henry. How she did long to see Edith and her boy! She could think of more pleasant ways to pass her time than a large Christmas party, but to see her beloved aunt and cousin again would be truly wonderful.

Her mouth canted thoughtfully to the side. She could not leave her father, as she had told Dixon before, but now another tie bound her here. London was that much farther from John. She took a long breath, and making her decision, released it quickly.

She tugged a clean sheet of writing paper from her stack to begin her reply. Spring, perhaps, could see her visiting London. She smiled privately as she penned the opening script. Yes, spring might do, and by that time she might just invite along someone else to introduce to her family.

~

Days for John passed by in lumps of sevens. Once per week, he was able to feast his heart on the delicious repast of her sweet presence. One day out of seven, he would gather his precious love in his arms and she would whisper her affections in his ear. His soul nourished to fulfillment, that hour- perhaps hour and a half, if he were truthful- was the pinnacle of his week.

Always, and too soon, came the cruel moment when he had to let her go and once more resume his merciless fast. For the remainder of those blissful afternoons, his clothing carried faint wisps of her fragrance to his keen senses. But for that, it might all have been an exquisite dream, the kind which makes the reality of waking seem harsh and colorless by comparison.

On this, the fourth such week, he was nearly famished for her company. It had been a long, hard seven days in the desert. The mill was faring no better. Only half of his major accounts had paid in full this month, with the rest begging to delay or divide their bills. What choice had he but to allow it? A late or partial payment was better than nothing, but he still had his hands to pay and more cotton to purchase.

The domestic front was no better. His ultimatum to Fanny had created a tense, hostile atmosphere at home, and the longer her confinement lasted, the more restless both she and his mother became. The one good to come from it all was that Watson had begun to call on Fanny, and she had received him more graciously than he might have hoped. Perhaps she was so starved for outside company that she was willing to entertain almost anyone! Few enough of her "friends" had deigned to call on her. He had in the last few days begun to think on her with some pity. Perhaps a month was quite long enough for her.

The single bright spot to the remainder of his weeks had been that talk of Margaret had died down, or at least it had been kept from his ears. One glowering stare at Hamper and a few well-placed comments by his mother and- of all people- Watson, and Margaret Hale had quietly dropped from the public eye once more.

He had started to think he might dare to walk out with her again, but there was little sense in tempting fate. Margaret's concerns were well-founded, as he reluctantly admitted to himself, and he recognized as well as anyone that he had no business linking his name with any woman while his own affairs were so uncertain.

As he leaped up the worn steps to the Hale's residence, his thoughts turned more pleasantly. One short month may have wrought little change in Fanny, but in the case before him, it had been a great deal too long! One month since the day she had uttered those precious words of love, opening up a world of hope before him! One month, he realized with a sinking feeling, in which his circumstances had not improved. The time had been effectively wasted, but an idea which had taken seed had flourished during that month, and he thought now was the time to bring it forward.

Margaret greeted him in the dining room, looking fresh as one of the southern roses she loved so much. She had shown him some pressings of her mother's flowers, and it had inspired him. She came joyfully into his arms, but he held back. "Wait," said he, "I have something for you."

She dropped back from her tiptoes to her normal height with a canny smile. "What do you have, John?"

His face shining in boyish delight, he opened the front of his coat and gently tugged out a narrow green stem, prickled all round with blunted thorns and capped at the end with a moist cloth. "It is a cutting," he replied, handing it gently to her. "I had it sent up from a florist in Hampshire. It is supposed to be of the dark red variety, with the deep grooves on the leaves just as your mother's were."

She gasped in happy surprise, laughing. "John, how wonderful! Only, where shall I grow it? We have no garden space here!"

"I have thought of that," he chuckled. "I've a little spot near my front door which wants only for some good soil and a little tending. It is not large, but if it were planted all about with these wonderful roses of yours, it would make the entire house look more cheerful. I am told that if you start this here in your warm kitchen this winter, it will be ready to plant in the spring."

She cocked him a mock-serious gaze. "Is that all you planned for the spring?"

He grinned sheepishly. "I had hoped to bring more than one rose home with me. Margaret, I have something important to talk over with you."

Her playfulness vanished. She took his hand and led him to a seat, then fixed him with a level, intelligent expression. "What is it, John?"

He braced his forearms on his knees and leaned forward, looking at the floor. "I am thinking of selling my interest in the mill."

"What?" she sucked in her breath, stunned. "Whatever for?"

He leaned back and met her eyes. "I have been thinking of it since we first... well, since you...." He sighed, not wishing to sound as though he were casting the blame on her. "It doesn't matter. If I sell now to another who has the capital to carry it forward, my moral obligation to my men is fulfilled. The mill's future is secured, and I am left free to pursue other things."

"But John," she shook her head, not understanding, "the mill is so important to you! I know you, John, you would be lost without your work."

"Oh, I shall have work! I will doubtless have to seek it out, and it may be a far humbler position, but I have some contacts- good ones, many of whom would be only too glad to have me. I think it worth considering."

"Working under another? After you have worked so long to earn your position of authority, you would give it up and take a lower one? You have poured your life into building that mill, John, and I know how passionately you have striven for excellence and progress. Would you truly be happy in a situation you could not work to improve, if you had to follow orders you thought unjust or ill-advised?"

His brow lifted and that roguish smile dawned. "Do you really know me so well as all of that, Margaret? No, of course I would not like it, and I may well have more knowledge than any prospective employer, but what does it matter? I desire to support my family, and I hope one day that family may grow. I have dominated my field; I have risen to the top. Perhaps that is to be enough for me. Perhaps it is for me to let go of the control I have so long held, and yield it up in favour of a far greater treasure."

Margaret, her forehead creased in worry, silently laid her head over his shoulder. He wrapped his arm around her to pull her close and they merely sat in quiet reflection a few moments. "John," she murmured hesitantly, "I would not have you do all of this for me." She lifted her head to look him in the eye, her hand resting still on his shoulder. "It cannot be necessary, surely!"

"Margaret," he took her hand and kissed it. "It may be that I shall in the course of time have to do this anyway. If I can save myself a year of futile worry, and if I can preserve the business as a sound enterprise, why should I not think of it? I confess, had I not you to look forward to I may not have considered this so soon, but I am convinced that in the end, the result will be the same."

She dropped her head to his shoulder again, snuggling luxuriously against him when he caressed her hair. "I thought the mill property all belonged to Mr Bell, but you speak of selling. What is yours?"

"The property and the buildings are his- including the house, so we may need to find another place for those roses after all." He paused to offer her a playful wink, but at her compellingly arched brow, he continued more seriously.

"The equipment within, and the business itself, are mine. The equipment is heavily leveraged- I doubt I shall see any return of it at all- but the business is another matter. It has value in established clientele and suppliers, not to mention the lease of the mill property. Perhaps best of all, it boasts a full staff of trained employees, most of whom would stay on. Marlborough Mills has a steady reputation and the goodwill of the community. The value is all intangible, but it represents many years' worth of work, and a buyer would recognize the same. Should I try to hold out," he cautioned, "the business itself might collapse from under me, and have no value left to it whatsoever. No buyer would then take a chance on it."

"I see." She absently fingered the cravat at his throat, unknowingly triggering a contented, blissful expression to spread over his face. Ah, if she only knew how her gentle ministrations affected him! If she thought to frame up some argument to sway him from his course, the work of her fingers would sabotage her efforts. Had he the means, he would have consigned the mill away in that instant, all the sooner to start over elsewhere and make her his wife!

Before he could thoroughly melt to a puddle at her feet, she spoke again. "So what do you plan to do?"

He cleared his throat, hoping his voice did not crack. "Go on as before, for now. I believe it may be time, however, to start putting out word about the mill in the right circles. I do not expect to find a buyer right away, but the possibility of owning the business outright may be a more attractive option to someone than merely investing in my enterprise."

She took his face in her hands and steadily held his gaze. "John, you must do as you know is right, but are you certain? You will not feel regret, or... or shame? I would be sorry to see you burdened by such pain."

Taking advantage of the intimate posture in which she had placed them, he tipped forward to kiss her shapely lips. "Who has sent me my lot in life, for good or for evil? No, Love, I was not prideful in success; I shall not be ashamed in failure. I ask only that you speak to me the good, simple words of truth such as my mother did when I was young. Let me not despair of the wasted opportunities of my youth, but gladden my heart with your faith and loyalty. Stand at my side, and I shall be the most blessed of men."

"That I will do, John," she promised, and bent forward to seal her troth with a more tangible sign of her sincerity.

Chapter Twenty-Nine

"**M**iss Marg'et, Miss Marg'et!"

The panic-stricken voice of Mary carried to the back corner of the Hale's residence, where Margaret was looking over the household ledgers with Dixon. Martha had let the girl in, and the poor lass staggered to the kitchen with a flood of incoherent cries tumbling from her.

Margaret rose, alarmed at the wild pitch in soft-spoken Mary's tones. "Mary! Whatever is the matter?"

"'Tis the mill, Miss! An explosion!" the girl sobbed.

Margaret grasped the back of her chair for support. "An explosion! Where, Mary?"

"I dinna', Miss. The boiler, methinks. There's a part o' the wall gone!" Mary sagged against the door jamb, her light body heaving in her exertion and distress.

"The wall gone! Mary, is anyone hurt?"

Mary nodded, her breath coming in painful gasps. "The master, Miss."

"Lass!" Dixon cried in horror, for Margaret had crumpled to the floor at her feet. The stouthearted old maid bent her ponderous form to her girl, trying to drag her upright once more. Margaret, weak and helpless in her shock, was both numb and blind to the woman's assistance.

"John!" she rasped, her eyes unseeing before her. "Oh, dear God, not John!" Her throat stung and great torrents of moisture rushed to her eyes. She trembled uncontrollably, her heart convulsing. She had to know the worst, even if....

"Mary," she whispered hoarsely, "is he... oh, please tell me he is not dead!"

"I dinna', Miss, but 'e were bad 'urt. Me da' were there, but 'e's mindin' the workers."

"Then I must go!" Margaret darted to her feet, desperate hope making her insensible to Dixon's protests for her dignity or Mary's objections for her safety. John might even now be languishing near death, and if she could not see him once more- it was too dreadful to be thought of! Dixon's brusque calls for reason went unheeded as Margaret flew to her cloak and hat.

This far from the mill, the traffic on the street proceeded at its normal, stately pace. Nothing in the Crampton neighborhood seemed yet disturbed by the knowledge that the man she loved might be in mortal peril. She fumed in impotent agitation as various coaches and walkers crossed her path, detaining her in her great haste.

After several minutes of walking had cooled her first rush of impetuosity, she began to wonder if perhaps Mary had been mistaken. Surely all of the city would be in upheaval if such a dreadful thing had truly occurred. It could not be that the rest of the world could proceed in its mundane, well-ordered ways if her own world were on the verge of collapse!

Only a short distance further on, the cold fear crept round her throat once more. A team of fire horses were making the leisurely return to their stable, towing their unwieldy burden behind. All about them, however, was steadily growing chaos.

Margaret's path toward Marlborough Street took her along lanes and alleys frequented by the workers who lived nearby. As she looked about in breathless fear, she recognized many of the workers from Marlborough Mills. Many of them were covered in dust, and a few appeared to have sustained bumps and scrapes. It was not the hour for dinner, but the swelling press of humanity drove away from the mill in an overwhelming flood. Shouts and cries could be heard roundabout, and Margaret was constantly weaving to and fro to make her way forward.

Her anxious eyes sought a friendly face, craving news. At last, she spotted Jenny, a young spinner to whom Bess had once introduced her. "Jenny!" she cried, desperate to make her voice heard over the din. "Jenny, over here!"

The girl, her eyes staring and wild, at last turned in Margaret's direction. "Oh, Miss, i'n't it fearful?" she exclaimed once she had drawn near.

"What is, Jenny? What has happened?" she demanded- not very gently.

"Th' boiler, Miss! Why, th' 'ole wall is down!"

"Yes, yes, I heard as much," she shook her head impatiently. "How could such a thing have occurred? I thought the boiler at Marlborough Mills was a new one that was not inclined to fail!"

Yes, in fact, now that she remembered, she was sure of it! Had not John boasted once to her father, in those hazy old days, of the safety improvements he had made at the mill? His boiler could not have exploded!

"I dinna', Miss. I were in the other buildin', but we a' 'eard the crash, we did!"

Margaret waved her hands in agitation. "Yes, yes, of course. Jenny, do you know if anyone was hurt?"

Jenny shrugged. "Me da' said there was a fella' killed, and some 'urt."

Margaret, driven almost to madness with fear, grasped the girl's shoulders and fairly shook her. "*Who*, Jenny? Who was killed? Is Mr Thornton safe?"

Jenny tried to back away, terrorized by this new side of the gentle Miss Hale. "I dinna' Miss! I 'eard 'e were carried to the 'ouse, but...." She broke off when Margaret released her and spun about, bursting with her need for real information.

Seldom did woman, encumbered with heeled walking boots and swathed in hoops and petticoats, walk as briskly as Margaret did to the mill. If one were to dare speak truth, she did not walk so much as fly, her feet scarcely touching the ground. How her aunt would have been appalled at her lack of decorum!

One thing only loomed before her. Her entire being simmered in turmoil as she made her way to the unknown, the question which dominated her path. Was she to find immeasurable joy and relief in the strong arms of the man who held her heart, or were the rest of her days to be blighted with the darkness of his absence? In minutes, she would have the answer. What she would give to hear his reassuring voice in her ear!

The implacable stone house soon grew before her hungry eyes. Silent and brooding it stood, yielding up no clues to the welfare of its master. She rushed up the steps- those familiar steps, where once before a fateful encounter had taken place. Without waiting to knock, and knowing that none within would be listening for her anyway, she grasped the heavy iron handle and yanked the door open herself.

She hurried to the dining room, breathless and flushed, but skittered to an uncertain halt when she reached the doorway. Hannah Thornton, looking pale and shaken, held court there with three or four men whose faces Margaret did not even bother to recognize. Her searching gaze was all for the mother, whose trembling demeanor shot new spears of dread through Margaret's heart.

"Miss Hale! It was very good of you to look in on us." Hannah broke off her conversation and strode gracefully to her with her hand extended. Margaret peered anxiously into the older woman's haggard face, looking for even a hint of what she yearned to know.

"I was hoping you might come," Hannah continued, her tones measured and even to the ears of a casual listener. Margaret, however, detected the wavering heartbreak in her voice. "My daughter is in the drawing room, and I know she will find your presence most comforting."

Margaret's head shook only very slightly in denial. Fanny Thornton! Fanny could go bury herself in a cotton bale for all Margaret cared in this moment! She opened her lips in protest, but before she could declare her purpose, Mrs Thornton was speaking again.

"I would go to her myself, but Dr Donaldson and Dr Lowe are examining my son, and I must remain at hand. I thank you for coming to visit her." Hannah's dark eyes locked with her own, and Margaret began to understand. This was no mere request from the matron of Marlborough Mills. It was a command, and refusal would not be tolerated.

Margaret nodded hesitantly, and found herself ushered off to the next room. Just before leaving her, though, Hannah took her hand and wrung it painfully. Margaret winced, but listened acutely to the woman's hissed assurances. "I will send you word of John as soon as I know more," Hannah promised, and then she disappeared.

~

The door closed, and Margaret found herself abandoned in the dreary room where once before she had awoken in an incoherent haze. Blinking, she glanced about. It was not difficult to find Fanny Thornton, for her voluminous morning dress dominated the massive piece of furniture upon which she rested. Small whimpers emanated from her, and a young maid stood by with a fan and a cool cloth for her eyes.

Margaret cleared her throat. "Miss Thornton?" she ventured.

Startled, Fanny sat up. Had it been her mother's voice, she likely would have maintained her restful repose, for surely her constitution could bear no more shocks today. It chanced that she would have to weather another disturbance, for she was rather certain that she recognized the speaker, and it was most unexpected.

"Miss Hale?" she blurted incredulously. "Why, whatever are you doing here?"

"I... I heard about the explosion," she mumbled, her distracted gaze out the window. She slowly strode near, her fingers catching each other in restless tugs, as was her wont when nervous. Fanny Thornton's company she did not relish, but it was not that which troubled her. Mrs Thornton's pinched face and close-lipped greeting had terrified her. John could not have perished immediately, as Jenny had said one man did, but she sensed that he was in grave danger. How was she to pass the time with inane and selfish Fanny, when all she longed to do was to rush to his side?

Fanny shooed her maid away, and the grateful girl took the nearest side door out of the room. Margaret swallowed. Without even the maid to distract Fanny, it would be up to her to provide the other's sole diversion. She was not equal to it!

"I cannot fathom that you would have come here!" Fanny was proclaiming. "Why, if Mother had permitted, I would have instantly taken myself far out of danger! Goodness knows what that awful Union will do next, but I can bear it no longer!"

Margaret's eyes narrowed. "The Union? What can you mean?"

"Why," Fanny sniffed, "did you not hear? Someone tampered with the safety valve on the boiler! You did not think it was an accident, did you?"

Margaret's head was shaking vaguely. "I do not know what to think! What else do you know? Oh, please, tell me everything!"

Fanny eyed her cynically. "John is alive, if that's what you are wondering," she pronounced sharply. "I do not think he was conscious when they carried him upstairs, but the doctors have been working over him for half an hour already."

Margaret's eyes closed and her body shook in relief and trepidation. Her breath, ragged and shallow, released finally in one slow exhale. "Thank you for telling me, Fanny," she murmured sincerely.

Fanny tilted her head. "I do not suppose he will be able to marry *anyone* now, Miss Hale. Why, the mill is quite crippled, and goodness knows where he will find the funds to repair it!" She snorted, an expression reminiscent of her mother. "I can think of *no one* who would have him now. He will have to close the mill and go to work under someone else!"

Margaret's brow furrowed and she looked at the other in some dismay. "I confess, Miss Thornton, that was the farthest thing from my thoughts."

"Oh! You may say so, Miss Hale, but what of me!" She raised a handkerchief to her face and sobbed prettily. "How am I to marry respectably if my brother is a failure? Why, how shall I even be able to buy my gowns to attract a fine gentleman?"

Margaret squinted quizzically, stunned to indignant anger. "Can you even think such things now, with your brother lying wounded and perhaps dying upstairs? Miss Thornton, I am ashamed of you!"

Fanny's mouth fell open in horror. Her own mother scarcely addressed her so harshly, and now this penniless preacher's daughter presumed to lecture her- *her!*- and in her own house! "Margaret Hale!" she screeched. "How dare you speak to me so! I have a right to such concerns! We women must look to our own needs, after all, and we have no better means to do so than by marrying well! Do you think I do not know what you have been after all of this time, chasing after John as you have done? What makes you so righteous and perfect, Miss Hale, that you now scold me like a child?"

"You are behaving as a child, Fanny," Margaret returned coldly. The other gaped in speechless consternation as she continued. "Is that all you think of- the relentless pursuit of a rich husband? Tell me, *Miss Thornton*, do you truly esteem any man, or is he simply a bank account and a fine home?"

"What would it matter if I esteemed him?" Fanny struck out petulantly. "As long as he is not repugnant, I may be content. I do better than yourself, *Margaret*! You put on your airs to distract all of the men, and then cast them off! Oh, yes, indeed, my mother told me how you turned down John after you nearly threw yourself at him! Then there was that strange man you were walking out with not long later. Who was he, your lover? Where is he now, I ask you! And what of Rupert Hamilton, how have you tried to corrupt him?"

"Ah," Margaret breathed, a flicker insight sparking upon her. She did not even intend to defend herself- it was useless, and she would not sully her own dignity so. She might, however, be of some material good to this wayward and self-deceived girl. "So *that* is what you are about! Miss Thornton," her tone had altered rather remarkably to one of gentle imploring, "you must not look to Mr Hamilton. Truly, I beg of you, set your eyes elsewhere, for I have good reason to believe him a disreputable young man."

"How would you know, Miss Hale?" Fanny shrilled. "Have you already been in a compromising position with him?"

Margaret's eyes blinked wide and her brows rose sharply. "Miss Thornton!" she cried in abhorrence. "I will not even address such a charge!"

"Of course not," Fanny taunted. "He would never marry you, you know. You are wasting your time trying to ensnare him... but you already know that, do you not, Miss Hale? Is that why you have turned again to John?"

Margaret could bear no more. She lurched to her feet, her hands clenched into fists at her sides. "I shall say this only once more, Fanny Thornton! I have absolutely no interest in Rupert Hamilton, and you would do well to heed my warning! As for John, I do not think a better man exists in the whole of the kingdom, and it is clear that we have both been blind to that fact. I am grateful that I finally saw the truth, and I beseech you to do the same!"

Fanny gasped in outrage, but before she could utter her sulky retort, Margaret stepped away with a hasty swirl of her skirts. Comforting Miss Thornton had been a deal to ask of her, but to tolerate such profane, ignorant discourse while she longed only for John was simply too much! She quickly glanced to the right and left, knowing only that she could not go back out the way she had come. Furiously, she stormed to the door through which the maid had fled, Fanny's cries fading quickly behind her.

Chapter Thirty

She found herself in an empty corridor and froze. This was a large house, and she had no idea where she was. Muffled voices drifted through one door ahead of her, and she guessed it led to the other end of the dining room. Peering up and down, she tried to remember the dinner party from half a year ago, but her wanderings over the house even then had been sparse.

Across the hall from the one she suspected to be the dining room, another door offered her the quiet refuge she sought. It hung closed, but not fully latched, as though the last occupant had been preoccupied or hurried upon departure. Curiously, she pushed it open, and discovered that she had found John's private study.

Blinking sentimentally, she hesitated only a moment, then slowly tiptoed forward. She felt a check in her spirit- she was, after all, invading his private spaces, but had he not ardently invited her to share in his home and in everything he held dear? Might he object to her presence? A comforting conviction soothed over her heart. No, he certainly would not object.

Reverently she explored the perimeter of the room, her fingers touching lightly over the rows of books on his shelves. Most were of engineering and textiles, but she slowed when she found a whole section devoted to his beloved classics. She bit her lip to still its quivering as her gaze swept affectionately over the titles. All were in perfect order, of course. A trembling smile warmed her face. John's library exuded his precise sense of efficiency and structure, but his personal tastes were still evident in the arrangements.

She turned to take in the rest of the room. His mother's touch was little felt here, in this shrine to his work and thoughts. The furniture was large and strong, but simple, and even with its master absent, the room reflected his general good cheer and contemplative nature. She looked carefully about, trying to imagine John himself seated at the desk, his blue eyes sparkling and his lips curved with humour as though her interruption had been a pleasant one. She began blinking rapidly.

At the rear of the study were shelves of order books and ledgers, all neatly arrayed for quick access from the seat at his desk. Evidently, he brought a deal of his work home with him in the evening hours. Another little smile quivered on her lips, finding something in him to admire even in so minor a thing. Wandering near, she allowed her fingers to trail over the burnished wood of his perfectly ordered desk, and that was when her eyes fell upon the ring box.

Her breath catching, she took the seat at his desk. With trembling hands, she reached toward it, then stopped herself. Her eyes began to blur and her throat choked with emotion. As her hands withdrew once more, she glanced down at a paper before her, bearing her name at the head. She drew the paper close to study it.

It was his plain, understated letterhead; the same on which he had written his only other letter to her, as well as that one bitterly regretted note to the police inspector. It looked as though he had made a beginning at writing her once more, but had suffered from indecision or other pressures on his time. Perhaps it had even been merely a cathartic exercise, one intended to relieve his anguished feelings. All that he had written were the greeting and a scrawled closing, but this time, the wording was so intimate, so revealing of his heart, that her breast began to heave as she read his tender words to her over and over.

To my dearest Margaret,

Yours forevermore,
John

Tears started tumbling down her cheeks, and biting her lip once more, she reached in determination for the ring box which he had apparently intended for her. It opened with a creaking sound, revealing a small, bright diamond ring. It was flawless and delicate, and though it may not have been of wondrous value- as diamonds went- it had the look of a ring blessed by many years of wedded harmony. Clearly it was some treasured heirloom... and he had tried to give it to her.

She felt unworthy to touch it. How many times had she refused it? Leaving the box open so that her tormented spirits might still look upon it, she pushed it away from herself. Oh, her beloved John! She draped her head upon her arms and gave herself over to her tears. What was she to do if his injuries proved too much for him? How could she be expected to go on without him?

An agonized cry wracked her and she began to weep and sorrow as she had not done even for her mother. That had been different; her father and Fred had depended upon her, and that knowledge alone had given her strength. Here, she was all alone, and none could know the depth of her fears or the bitterness of her regrets! How long she stayed thus, she could not have told, but at length a cool hand at her shoulder bade her lift her head.

"Margaret," Hannah Thornton called softly.

She started, at first embarrassed to be found in this room and in such an attitude, but there was no hint of reproof in Hannah's pale, drawn face.

"How is he?" she begged tremulously.

Hannah blinked and gave a miniscule nod. "He is resting. He sustained a blow to the head, but he has awakened a few times and spoken to us, so it does not appear to be serious. The concern is that he has several broken ribs, and the doctors were fearful that a lung might have been punctured. It does not appear now that that has been the case, but they caution that he must not be moved. We still do not know the full extent of his injuries. The next several hours will tell us if there is something more than we presently know."

Margaret viciously swiped a tear from her cheek. "Mrs Thornton, I know it is not proper, but...."

Hannah pressed her lips in understanding. "You may see him. He asked for you earlier. Your father has arrived, and is already sitting with him. I told him I would send for you."

Margaret could find no words, but she clasped Mrs Thornton's hands in grateful effusion. The older woman stiffened, but managed to offer a grim smile. "This way, Miss Hale," she intoned, with all of the dignity and grace one might be able to expect of her under the circumstances.

~

Margaret found her father, his face grey and lined, posting watchful vigil over the man he held as a son. Mr Hale glanced up quickly at her arrival, sighing in relief. "There you are, my child. Come, sit with me."

Her steps bent obediently toward him, but her gaze dwelt steadily on John's rising chest. It moved still, but only fractionally, and Margaret could easily imagine the pain that such breath must cost him. His face was bruised, and gave evidence of having been hastily cleaned of blood. There was a bandage wrapped over his forehead, with a bulk of wadding just behind his ear where he had apparently been stricken by some object. How fortunate that the blow had not been more serious!

"Please excuse me." Hannah Thornton interrupted her survey of John's injuries. "If you will sit with John now, I must see to some other matters. I imagine I will have time enough to remain at his bedside."

Margaret's eyes snapped back to that good lady, and though her father might not have detected it, Margaret did not miss the weariness or the sacrifice in her voice. Had the Hales not been present, no force lesser than the hand of the Almighty could have torn her from her son's side at this hour. She looked to Margaret, and a deep understanding passed between them. Hannah was consigning the light of her life, for now, into her hands.

Margaret felt the full weight of such an honour. Her eyes clouded once more, and before Hannah closed the door behind her, Margaret grasped the worn hands tightly in both of hers. "Thank you!" she whispered meaningfully. Hannah blinked, nodded curtly, and retired.

"Sit, Margaret," her father gently insisted. She took a seat near him and resumed her careful inventory of John's condition. His body was covered with a blanket, but he appeared to have had his shirt cut off, for his shoulders were bare. She ought to have been petrified by embarrassment, but she felt only overwhelming concern.

"Father," she pleaded softly, "is he... will he...?"

Mr Hale opened his mouth to answer, but a low groan from John interrupted him. At the quiet sound of Margaret's voice, he had roused to wakefulness, if only for a moment.

"John!" she cried, and rose to lean over him.

His response was a pained grimace- the best he could do for a smile- and his lips mouthed her name.

"Shh, do not try to talk," she soothed. "Father and I are here."

"...Mmmm..." he cringed in agony and ceased the attempt to speak her name.

"John, I am here," she reassured him again. Her fingers stroked over the blood-thickened hair at his brow and he let his eyes fall closed. Tearfully, she pressed a tender kiss to his streaked forehead. Slowly, with a measured effort, his hand lifted to her. She clasped it eagerly, careful not to jostle his arm overmuch and thereby unsettle him.

Assured of her presence and comforted by her firm grip, he lapsed once more into arduous slumber. Margaret glanced helplessly to her father, for she was now constrained to stand at his side if she wished to continue holding his hand. Mr Hale, once a young lover himself, smiled indulgently and slid both of their chairs nearer the bed. Margaret took her seat gingerly, poising herself at the edge of her chair lest she wrench his arm and cause him more pain.

"Father," she whispered- more softly than before, "how badly is he injured? Surely you have seen such cases, back in Helstone when you visited the parishioners! What is to be done?"

Mr Hale's kindly face drooped in worry. "I do not know, my child. They have bound his ribs- a dreadful process!- but we cannot know what internal injuries he may have. The doctor has given him laudanum to help him rest, for even breathing must be quite painful to him. I expect that is the best man and his medicine can do for now."

Margaret's head dipped low, and a tear shimmered at the tip of her nose. Her shoulders shook with the effort of containing her tremours. She must remain stout and true, for John's sake! She would not disturb him with her grief for all of the world, nor would she wish to burden her father by baring her sorrows before him.

Valiant though her efforts were, Mr Hale's faded eyes had seen too much loss and trouble through the years for him to fail to recognize his daughter's distress. He placed a soothing hand upon her shoulder. "My child," he counseled gently, "fret not, for are not a man's days numbered, and is not even the hair of his head precious? Come, my dear, let us bow our heads together."

Margaret sniffled pitifully and, after a moment, nodded in resigned agreement. It was what she ought to have done before, but to her shame, her fear had overcome her. Humbled, and not a little comforted by her father's quiet wisdom, she joined him in petitioning the One who held the breath of life in His hand.

~

The following morning discovered Margaret, stiff and weary, roused early and prowling about her drawing room. She was anxious for news of John, and his blessed mother had promised to send word of how he had passed the night. This first night would tell all, or so the doctors claimed. If he had rested quietly, and not begun to cough blood or shown some other dreadful symptom, he had a good chance.

The news she sought was soon delivered faithfully, and by a welcome face. How or why Hannah Thornton had ensnared this particular messenger, Margaret could not tell, but she was relieved beyond words. Nicholas Higgins trod wearily through the door, looking as though he had neither slept nor eaten since the previous day.

"Nicholas!" Margaret heedlessly embraced him, so relieved was she that he was well. "Do, please sit down. Martha! Ask Dixon to send in something for Mr Higgins!"

Nicholas waved. "Nay, Lass, yo' dinna' need to fret 'bout me."

"Nonsense, Nicholas! You must keep up your strength. I am sure you have had much to occupy you."

He sighed, nodding. "Aye, then, do as yo' will. I'm near to clemmin' if yo' mu'n know."

"Nicholas," she settled intently before him. "What news do you have?"

He took in her tormented posture, her piercing gaze, and gave a reassuring nod. "Master's no worse, Lass."

Margaret's eye closed and she shuddered in profound relief. "Oh, thank God!" she cried. "Nicholas, what else?"

He shrugged. "'E's wakened, but na' for long. Th'ould Dragon says 'e's taken some broth...."

"Nicholas!" Margaret was shocked into sudden laughter. "You cannot call Mrs Thornton that!"

A wily grin tugged at the old weaver's face. "Nay, Miss, I just wanted to liven yo' a bit. Take 'eart, 'tis na' the first, nor the last time I've seed the like. Master'll be on 'is feet soon 'nough, Lass, don' yo' doubt it."

Margaret sighed, the bitter coil of dread loosening its hold on her heart. "Thank you, Nicholas. What happened yesterday? Did you see anything? Miss Thornton said someone had tampered with a valve!"

Nicholas' face set into grim lines. "Aye, Lass, I saw't a'."

Margaret leaned close, eager to hear all, but Martha came at that moment with a tray for him. Forgetting his manners or the house in which he sat- for only a moment, mind you- he tore ravenously into the biscuit and cold meat set before him. Blinking and looking to Margaret with abashment, he quickly composed himself. He made to apologize, but Margaret absolved him with a light smile and a wave of her hand.

Nicholas swallowed his bite of cold meat and cleared his throat. "'D'yo' mind Sacks?"

Margaret squinted thoughtfully. "Yes, I think so. I remember you speaking to John about him. He was causing some trouble with the Union, as I recall."

Nicholas nodded as he gulped down another mouthful of biscuit. He wiped his mouth hastily and set the tray aside so that he could speak without interruption. "'E'd a lad- a good lad- named Willy. Master 'ad me schoolin' the lad 'round the mill. Yest'rday we looked in on the boiler because Master 'ad a thought 'bout a new 'conomizer-"

"A... a what, Nicholas?" Margaret's brow wrinkled in confusion.

"A..." he gestured vaguely with his hands, his own face puckered in an attempt to explain. "Nay, Lass," he at last gave up in defeat. "I canna' 'splain, but it makes the boiler more 'fficient."

"Oh." She leaned back, perplexed. There was a deal about the mill she did not understand, but John seemed to hold all of those technical details in his clever mind. Once more awed at the marvel of it all, she merely shook her head and asked him to continue.

He sighed again, the weariness settling more deeply over his features as he relived the harrowing experience. "We three were walkin' to the boiler- there were others, mind, not so close- but we were jus' comin' to' the boiler 'ouse when Willy shouted out for 'is da'. Sacks were just steppin' away when Willy ran up. I dinna' see more, because then Master grabbed me and threw me on the ground."

Higgins stroked his chin, his eyes closed, while Margaret tilted her head at an utter loss. "I still do not understand, Nicholas. Young Willy's father was there? I thought he was no longer employed at the mill."

"Aye, Lass, 'e wasn'a. Snuck in, 'e did. 'T'was 'e 'o tweaked the valve, and 'is lad saw it." He shook his head sorrowfully. "Poor devils."

Margaret's eyes widened in alarm. "Was it Mr Sacks who was killed? I heard a man had been."

Higgins gritted his teeth in remorse. "Aye. 'E and 'is lad. 'Is poor wife!"

Margaret leaned back against her chair, stunned. "Oh, Nicholas, I am so sorry! You thought a great deal of the boy, did you not?"

Nicholas had been rubbing his hands roughly over his eyes, and whether it was from mourning or lack of sleep, Margaret could not be sure. "Aye," he mumbled brokenly. He harrumphed a little, ashamed at his weakness before a lady, and addressed himself once more to his tray.

"'T'were the master's idea," he remarked after a few bites. "The lad workin' wi' me."

Margaret smiled comfortingly. "You said that before."

"'T'isn't fair, Miss," he muttered. "When I think on my poor Bess, hoo' suffered, and now that good lad...." His voice choked, as though even his throat rebelled against further utterances of his griefs.

He poked at the remainder of the biscuit, crumbled now over the plate, before continuing. "Master saved my life, Miss. I didn'a see what 'e did- the boiler plate wen' ri' o'er our 'eads. I'd've ne'er got down. When the blast were o'er, Master were on top o' me. Kept me safe, 'e did, but some o' the wall came down on 'im."

"And the others? Were others hurt as well?"

"Master were the 'ardest 'it," Nicholas assured her. "Some others was 'urt- some broken arms and bruises, but a' in a', Lass, 'tis a wonder 't'were no worse."

"What of the steam? I have heard of boiler explosions causing tremendous burns, and even starting fires! How did everyone escape?"

Nicholas began to smile for the first time in several minutes. "The boiler 'ouse were brick, Miss, an' set back from the main buildin'. Master 'ad it fitted wi' steel beams and a tile roof some years back, so no wood in that room. No fire, Miss. The steam, t'was ev'r'where, but we were far 'nough back, the burns weren't so bad. Master fared worse, but most o' the steam went t'other way."

Margaret set her chin upon her hand, thinking over the layout of the mill yard. She was only vaguely sure of where the boiler house must have been located- that had never been a part of her tours on her brief visits there. Still, there was only one area which remained hazy to her, and it was near the back of the main building which housed the massive looms. "Nicholas," she asked slowly, "what of the rest of the mill?"

He shook his head, fixing her with a hollow expression. "'Alf o' it's gone, Miss." He rubbed weary hands over his face once more. "I still say t'were a right mir'cle we weren't a' killed, but the mill, Miss...."

Margaret groaned, sinking back in her chair. "What is to be done!" she exclaimed, more to herself than to Nicholas.

His head still wagging, Higgins stood. "I dinna', Miss." He sighed wearily. "I'll thank yo', Lass, for the biscuit. I mu'n look in on some o' the 'ands."

Margaret saw him to the door. "Come again as soon as you can, Nicholas," she urged. "How are Mary and the children?"

"Well y'nough, Miss. I'll stop by soon," he promised, and went away.

Margaret stood alone in the doorway of her comfortable, secure house, and wondered about all of those families left without a livelihood. What could she do? Helpless, and unable to consult the one who would likely have a sound answer for her, she resorted to resting her head against the door frame and counting the tears as they dripped to the floor.

Chapter Thirty-One

No rebuilding efforts were to be initiated at Marlborough Mills. Without the active, brilliant mind of the master to lend inspiration, and lacking the proper finances, there was none to begin the labour.

The paper was full of the hideous details of the explosion for several days. Mr Bell, as the landlord, had naturally received word immediately- though it was Margaret who had taken up her pen, rather than Mrs Thornton. It had been the very least she could do, for she was not able to sit daily at John's bedside as his mother had been forced to. The older woman's impressive vitality was more a testimony to her fierce devotion than her already remarkable physical endurance. She had scarcely left her son's chamber even to sleep.

Somehow, each day, Hannah had contrived a way to send word to Margaret of John's progress. The steam burns along his back and shoulders- of which Margaret had not even been aware on her first visit- had rapidly blistered. The doctors had feared infection, but whether they were less deep than originally thought, or whether Mr Hale's constant prayers had availed much, they began to heal without incident.

The real concern, one week after the original accident, was that he was still unable to breathe without excruciating pain. It had been decided, after the initial assessment, that administering more laudanum would only diminish his breathing and allow fluid to cluster. The pain he would have borne up under well enough, but since at least three ribs had been crushed under the wall and no longer performed their proper function, his lungs could scarcely draw enough air to fill them. Pneumonia became a genuine worry, as was the possibility that further movement of his broken ribs could end up causing new internal injuries. Haggard and strained were the faces of all who kept sentry over his recovery, from near or far.

Higgins beat a regular trail between the Thornton's household and the Hale residence. When he was not acting as messenger between the parted lovers, he occupied himself with Union business. He it was who was sought after for wages from the Union's store of emergency funds. In the immediate aftermath of the explosion, all of the workers' ire was focused upon the deceased Jonas Sacks and, unfortunately, what remained of his family. Higgins, however, was too experienced to believe that sentiments would remain as they were, and he looked to the coming tide of ill will with a growing disquiet.

It was a tense and dreary Christmas for many in Milton. On Christmas Day, Margaret and her father chose to ignore the embargo on visiting the grey house on Marlborough Street to bring some warm company and a precious measure of good cheer to its occupants. Mrs Thornton looked to have aged ten years, but she greeted them both with genuine gratitude. She was even generous enough to allow Margaret to sit with John, unchaperoned, for a brief interlude- so long as she kept the door open.

Her chest panging in sympathetic agony, Margaret padded softly to the bedside. "Merry Christmas, John," she whispered, wondering if he were awake.

His eyes, closed only against the constant ache rather than in sleep, snapped open.

"Does it pain you to speak?" she asked quickly, hoping to divert him before he made the effort. "Pray do not trouble yourself. I only wished to sit with you."

He managed a shadow of his former brilliant smile and reached for her hand. She took it and was immediately surprised by the strength of his grip. He held her hand as if he might never let her go, and indeed, he would fain have retained his grip indefinitely if he had not in that same moment also flexed his stomach muscles, resulting in another torturous spasm.

The hiss of air through his teeth caused Margaret to jump in alarm. "Forgive me, John, I did not mean to!"

He shook his head- very fractionally, it must be noted- and whispered "No. Not you." His pain-hardened features softened as he lovingly took in every detail of her hair, her gown, and her well-remembered face. "Kiss me," he demanded hoarsely.

Repressing an amused chuckle at his bluntness, she leaned over him and complied. "Better?" she asked in a hushed voice.

His mouth twitched in pleasure. "More," he insisted, almost inaudibly.

Margaret may have had her faults, but it could not be said that she was ungenerous. Lavishly she bestowed the favour he sought, wondering how long it would be before she could do so again. It might be many weeks yet before the doctors would suffer him to move about, and even longer before his full strength were recovered.

Eventually he permitted her to take the seat next to him, still clasping her hand. "Margaret," he wheezed, "the mill? Mother will not tell me."

"Because you ought not to be talking!" she surveyed him sternly.

"Have to breathe anyway," he smirked wryly from his pillow. "Tell me, Margaret."

Her expression became pained and she shook her head. "The boiler, house and all, are destroyed, John. Many of the bricks tore into the main building, and a good section of it came down- some right away, and some later. Several of the looms are destroyed as well, I understand."

"The workers are safe?"

"Aside from Mr Sacks and his son," she replied sorrowfully. "But I suppose you knew about that."

He nodded grimly, for indeed he had refused to rest until his mother had at least assured him that no others had been killed.

"It truly is miraculous, as Nicholas has said. I saw the buildings, John, and I do not know how there was not more loss of life. The mill, though...."

Another hiss escaped him as his face cringed. "All lost."

She lowered her eyes and nodded, swallowing. "Yes, John," she whispered. "I am afraid so."

He was silent for a long while, his thumb kneading over the back of her hand as his mind wandered in thought. "I must write Bell," he groaned.

"I have already done so. He wished to come, but he had rather a serious cough, and his own doctor insisted that he delay some while. I know he wishes to look over the damage and talk to you about the repairs, but surely that can wait until you are both stronger," she finished with simplistic hopefulness.

John, however, was shaking his head. "Have to give up my lease," he breathed. "It will take years to pay back the damages."

Margaret paled at his bald-faced presentation of the truth, but it was no more than she and her father had feared when they sat in the evenings around their hearth fire. So frequently had the subject arisen between them that together they had pondered an idea- a wild, unthinkable plan, but one which seemed too perfect to ignore.

"John," she began hesitantly, "where will you go? You told me before that the house is part of the lease. Will you not need to remove?"

His eyes closed and his brows lifted in silent confirmation. "Poor Mother!" he murmured softly.

She tightened her grip on his hand, the sudden intensity of her posture causing him to peer curiously at her. "John," she trembled, almost smiled, but bit her lip to contain her growing excitement. "Come live with Father and me!"

His eyes dilated incredulously and he tried to sit up until a sharp pain stilled him. "*What?*"

The light in Margaret's face was intoxicating. "We have talked it all over, John! There is my mother's chamber, I think your mother would find it comfortable enough. It is certainly not what she is used to, but it cannot need to be a permanent arrangement, of course. There is little enough extra space, but there is a modest little area, your mother could at least have Jane with her, and-"

"And where do *I* sleep, Margaret?"

Her cheeks burned at the suggestive flicker of his quiet smile. "I thought... that is, we decided-"

He gasped, and through a monumental effort, slowly raised from his pillow.

"John, you mustn't!" she protested.

His face contorted with pain, but after a hellish battle, he at last was propped up on his elbows. He offered her a sideways grin of reassurance. "Easier to breathe anyway," he winked. "So, you were saying, my love?"

She was still regarding him with a mixture of embarrassment and uncertainty. To give herself a moment to recover, she stood to rearrange the pillows behind him.

"Thank you," he sighed. Cautiously he relaxed back upon them and was pleased to discover how much easier it truly was to breathe from this position. His mother- bless her- had scarcely permitted him to shift his posture, so great was her fear of a lung injury. Pneumonia, he thought fleetingly, would be equally dreadful, and he instantly resolved to make some changes to her carefully prescribed convalescent plan.

All of this while, his probing gaze never left Margaret. "Now, back to what you were saying... if I count correctly, that only leaves your father's chamber and yours. I hope your father will forgive me, but I do not think I would be comfortable sharing his quarters."

The vivid colour flashed again to her cheeks, but she forced herself to stammer out a reply. "I thought... perhaps if we married right away... when you are strong enough, you understand...."

"Strong enough!" he choked back what surely would have been a most painful laugh. "Call the mininster! I am strong as a horse!"

"John," she chuckled at his determination, "you cannot be moved yet."

"Step back, Love." He grimaced and pushed himself upright once more. Gritting his teeth and screwing his eyes tightly closed, he began to roll his feet to the floor.

"John, what are you doing? Oh, do, please stop! You may harm yourself further!"

He stopped, panting and cringing from the pain. "I cannot marry you flat on my back!"

She tilted her head and crossed her arms. "You also cannot get out of bed attired as you probably are. I ought not be here as it is!"

He glanced down and coloured. Though he was covered head to toe in bedclothes, it was still highly unsuitable apparel before a lady- an *unmarried* lady. Looking back up, he graced her with a provocative grin. "If you do not like these, I can go without."

Margaret's hands flew over her mouth, her eyes as round as the tea saucers he had bought her. "*John Thornton!*" she cried. She choked and sputtered, her pale face dusted with becoming little blossoms of mortification.

John was as shocked at himself as she. "I am sorry, Margaret," he rasped, carefully easing himself back to a resting posture. "I do not know what came over me."

Margaret was still coughing and fighting for composure. "What has that doctor given you?" she scolded.

An impertinent grin still lingered on his face. "Hope," he winked. She was shaking her head and had begun to shriek with helpless laughter, finally appreciating the humour of his flippant comment. They had had precious little to laugh over of late!

He took a moment to catch his breath and to allow Margaret to settle herself. "Can you really mean it, Margaret? You would marry me now, when I have nothing left?"

The serious tone he had turned to at the end deserved a kindred response. Daintily clearing her throat, she sobered. "Yes," she took his hand and squeezed it in affirmation. "I would, John. Nothing else matters now- I only want to be with you."

He relaxed at last, dropping his head back upon his raised pillows with what looked to be a permanent ray of sunshine lighting his features. Lifting her hand, he tenderly kissed it and rested it gingerly above his broken chest.

"Margaret," he interrupted his happy silence after a moment, "it is not a very large house. We shall not have to share quarters with my sister, shall we?"

She blanched. "Oh, dear, I had quite forgotten!"

She started to apologize for her unforgivable omission, but his eyes crinkled with amusement. "Fear not," he consoled her. "Watson made her an offer a couple of days ago, and she found it an agreeable alternative to remaining here."

"Oh." She blinked and began to smile in relief. She naturally would have found *some* way to live with Fanny Thornton, but... gracious, what a comfort that it would be unnecessary!

He was toying with her fingers, tracing the length of each one meditatively and studying the minute details of her hand. His thoughts he did not voice, but beneath the obvious delight shining in his eyes, there were traces of worry.

Margaret was not wholly ignorant of his concerns. It was asking a deal of him to suggest that he take up abode in another man's house- and a modestly proportioned dwelling at that. Despite his avid interest in a quick marriage, she knew him well enough to expect objections, once he had recovered from the first flush of his enthusiasm. It only made practical sense to her- after all, it would be some time before John might recover his strength, and if he had a substantial debt to Mr Bell to repay... but his pride would surely suffer.

Well, they would simply have to discuss that further when the time was ripe. She smiled as he began drawing invisible circles around the base of her ring finger. If she had to guess, it would not be long before the final decision would be before him.

As if reading her thoughts, he lifted his eyes to hers. "Would you ask your father to come in? It is past time I spoke to him."

~

Nicholas Higgins' fears about public sentiment proved prophetic. Only a few days after Christmas, a number of Union members and leaders once again commandeered Mr Hale's lecture hour at the Lyceum Hall. It was a noisome and fractious crowd which gathered there, but the prevailing feeling seemed to be general frustration rather than directed anger. Higgins lingered uneasily to the side, carefully observing individual faces.

A few of the younger, less wise attendees railed loudly against Jonas Sacks- as though that miserable old devil could be made to recompense them for their losses. Higgins chewed his lip nervously. It was well that he and another kind-hearted neighbour had taken in Sacks' widow and remaining three children, for he feared the lone woman and her babes would no longer be safe on their own. One foolish young buck went so far as to cast blame on poor Mildred Sacks for throwing her husband out, for surely that act had exacerbated the man's boiling resentment against his employer. Higgins only shook his head.

At last, Miles and some of the other shop leaders took control of the discussion. Though the disaster at Marlborough Mills immediately affected only those employed there, the Union was hemorrhaging dues to support them. This caused strife enough, for the strike pay was intended to be precisely that- monies set aside to keep workers along the picket lines and out of the factories during lean times. Enough persons of influence had been affected, however, that a motion to provide two weeks' pay during this emergency had carried the day. A number of the other mill employees had found this move highly irregular, however, and meant to make their voices heard.

Meanwhile, men from Hamper's, Slickson's, and several of the smaller mills feared they might lose their jobs to some of Thornton's displaced workers. While they themselves confessed to no disparities within their ranks, all knew that most of the masters would be only too glad to snap up some of what they thought to be Thornton's best. Thornton's more modern mill and somewhat better pay had always afforded him a choice among the most skilled weavers, and now those craftsmen had nowhere else to go.

In the end, nothing at all was resolved upon, for what was there to do? The meeting devolved into a shouting match, with Slickson's men accusing Thornton's men of conspiring to rob them of their employment, and Thornton's men taking offense to the men at Hamper's, who had gone back to work after the strike under the agreement that they would not contribute to the strike fund which was even now feeding their families during this emergency.

Higgins had in the past proven himself as hot-headed and eloquently persuasive as any, but he had chosen a neutral position in this war. There was no clear solution, and no attainable objective he could rally behind. In time, the flux of unemployed mill workers would be absorbed into other factories, but it would be a painful metamorphosis for all of them. Many might find themselves taking positions of far lesser pay in a job they knew little about, for the textile mills were loath to hire on in the winter.

Additionally... he sighed. He could never again bring himself to speak a word which might be perceived to go against Thornton. Though no one was directly casting blame at the master of the destroyed mill, it would only be a matter of time before public frustration led to irrational accusations. Thornton was not at fault, and he was not at all bad, as masters went. As a matter of fact, had they been allowed to continue their working relationship, he thought he could have truly come to admire the dynamic young master.

The most humbling knowledge was that the man's selflessness and quick thinking had saved his life, or at the very least spared him the crippling and excruciating injuries that he himself now battled. Lastly, there was Miss Hale, who had been so kind to his family. How it would break her tender heart if he were to turn against her betrothed! No, he could not bring himself to engage in this particular Union conflict. The best he could hope to do was to remain a cool head among many who were not.

The meeting began slowly breaking up, with one or two factions yet swearing to loiter until something had been settled. Higgins let his arms drop wearily to his sides. There was little else for it but to collect poor Mr Hale, who sat dutifully outside the lecture hall, and to escort the gentleman home. He was still frail, and likely never would be strong again, but he seemed to find comfort in his established routine and the hope of making himself useful.

"Ah, there you are, Nicholas," the old gentleman smiled faintly in relief. "I do hope your meeting was productive."

"Now' but yo' could tell," he shook his head. "'Tis a bad business, sir."

Mr Hale rose to his feet and donned his top hat. "It is, indeed. I have not yet heard from my good friend Mr Bell, but I do hope he may think of some way to repair the mill!"

Nicholas shrugged as they began walking. "'Twill cost more'n t'will gain, sir," he retorted glumly.

"That cannot be true! Surely it is well worth the effort, for if it is a sound endeavour to build a mill, it cannot be less fruitful to repair one."

"Aye, sir, but nowt now," Higgins frowned, shoving his hands in his pockets. "Mills' a' 'ard 'nough set. In a few years, may'ap. I dinna' what's to be done 'til then."

Mr Hale, his soft heart aching for all of the misfortunes about him, lapsed into remorseful silence. They walked gently, in deference to the older man's more tender health, but as they came to a particular turn, he spoke up again. "We may as well walk to your home, Nicholas. I am sure Margaret is with the children this afternoon, and I confess, it would cheer my heart to see them as well."

Nicholas nodded. "I 'spect she is."

Margaret was, indeed, at the Higgins' home. There was much to care for there, and she had formed a fast friendship with Mildred Sacks- a soft-spoken woman with a backbone of iron. Margaret liked her immensely, and pitied her for the dreadful way many treated her on behalf of her late husband. Her younger children- the oldest just barely old enough for factory work- had fallen into league easily enough with the orphaned Boucher children. The strain, quite naturally, came rather from the families' limited resources than any lack of goodwill.

Little Jenny always accosted Margaret as soon as she had walked in the door, demanding rather bluntly that Margaret tell her all of the details of Mr Thornton's recovery. The little girl quite fancied him, and though she denied it when her brother teased her, she had shed many a tear for the nice man with the wonderful voice who had taken an interest in her.

On this day, as her father arrived with Higgins, Margaret had been just preparing to start out again. "Oh!" she exclaimed, "Father, Mrs Thornton sent me a note asking me to call at four-o'clock. I was planning to go now, before I return home. Did you wish to come?" She eyed him dubiously, thinking that he had already exerted himself enough for one day. He and John took such great comfort in one another's company, however, that she hated denying his wishes.

Mr Hale stood a little bewildered, pondering her offer. He was already quite breathless from this latest walk, despite his improving strength, and knew enough to think that another long cold walk of several miles would not do him good.

"We could take a cab," she suggested hesitantly.

"No... no, my dear," he sighed. "We ought to spare the expense. I shall rest here briefly, and then see you at home."

"I'll walk wi' yo', sir," Nicholas offered smartly. "But set and rest a bit."

"Thank you, Nicholas," he smiled weakly. "Perhaps I could take your place at reading to the children, Margaret."

She moved to accommodate him, but before taking her hat and coat to depart, she drew Nicholas aside. "What word?" she whispered.

Nicholas Higgins frowned and decided it was betraying no duty or loyalty to share with her all of the news of the Union meeting. She was not, after all, the wife of the master of Marlborough Mills, as she might have been. She was merely his friend, Miss Hale, and her concerns were as genuine as his own. That she would turn about and repeat everything he told her to John Thornton, he had no doubt, but since his former nemesis was no longer an employer, it mattered little. Reluctantly he shared with her all that had been said, and all that he feared for the coming weeks.

She closed her eyes in real sorrow before resting a hand on his arm. "Thank you, Nicholas. I must go to John now before it grows any later, but I plan to return tomorrow."

"Aye, Lass. Give the master my r'gards."

Margaret smiled sadly. "He is not the master now, Nicholas."

He laughed wryly. "Long's 'e's breath, Miss, Thornton'll be a master. 'E'll ne'er be otherwise."

Chapter Thirty-Two

M argaret walked slowly, not out of a lack of desire to see John, but out of curiosity at the faces she encountered. The streets were beginning to show some of the same early signs of tension which had led up to the strikes, so many months ago. Sensitive now to the things which she had been blind to before, Margaret made it a point to sample the climate on the streets whenever she left the house.

She was well-recognized now, where she had not been before. Word of her enduring friendship with Nicholas Higgins had endeared her to many of the working class, and for some while she had been used to friendly greetings along her way. Lately, however, the countenances she met were increasingly turned inward with dread.

Hannah Thornton met her at the door, and if it were possible, her face too, was more drawn than it had been. Margaret greeted her warmly as she removed her cloak. "I received your note. Has something happened?"

Hannah's eyes shifted to the maid who had entered behind her. "That will be all for now, Jane."

Margaret's stomach tingled with foreboding. She waited for the door to close and looked expectantly back to John's mother. Mrs Thornton blew out a weary breath, and before Margaret's troubled eyes the woman transformed from the proud matron of majestic grandeur to the diminished widow who knew not where she would lay her head in a month's time.

"Come," she offered graciously. "Let us sit a moment, and then you may tell me." As Hannah had once extended comfort and strength to her, Margaret now found herself able to return the gesture. She took the woman's arm and together they strode to the dining room, Hannah's favourite room of the house. Margaret helped her to a seat.

Hannah took a moment to collect herself, then looked her future daughter full in the face. "John has finally had word from Mr Bell."

Margaret straightened. This hardly sounded like the dreadful news she had prepared herself for! "What does he write?"

"You might say it is better news than any had dared to hope. It seems that Mr Bell had years ago taken out an insurance policy covering the structures here. John never knew about it, but apparently Mr Bell thought to protect his own interests. Industrial accidents are not at all uncommon, you must know, and though the policy cost him a great deal, he felt it a better strategy than to go without."

Margaret's expression had grown brighter with every word Hannah spoke. "Why, that is wonderful news! The mill may be rebuilt after all! However..." her face clouded, "the destruction was an act of sabotage, not an accident. Will the policy be honoured?"

"Well, it seems that was a part of the reason Mr Bell had delayed his response. The policy protects *him*, as a landlord, not John. Mr Bell's interests are in the structures, and as they were destroyed while under lease, and Mr Bell retained the services of a skilled attorney, the underwriters were obliged at last to authorize payment for the damages to be issued."

Margaret's eyes narrowed. "You say only that the structures are covered. I take that to mean that the looms and the boiler will not be replaced?"

Hannah nodded tiredly. "And the combers. That wing was damaged, too."

Margaret's dropped her gaze in long thought. "How are they to be replaced? Are they very costly?"

Hannah snorted. "Costly, and collateral. The bank will have their repayment before John can even think of purchasing more. However," her voice turned more serious, "it will not come to that."

"What do you mean?"

Hannah shifted uncomfortably. "The underwriters of Mr Bell's policy have made an unusual stipulation. The mill is to be let to another."

Hannah had never before been privy to the passionate indignation which had marked one of two of John's more memorable encounters with Margaret. Now, however, she witnessed a breathtaking transformation. Gold flecks flashed in her green eyes, rage blossomed over her cheeks, her fine nostrils dilated, and it seemed almost that she grew in stature. If Mrs Thornton had ever doubted Miss Hale's fire and grit, she did so no longer.

Margaret's slender fist crashed down on Hannah's dining table. "*Why?*" she demanded. "Do they blame John for all of this? Do they not know he is the most capable master in the city, the one who knows this mill the best? Do they not understand what he had already achieved here?"

"I doubt they care," the mother smirked drily. "Only that someone must be held to account, and that someone can be no other than the master."

"But it makes no sense! What could another do that John cannot?"

"You and I both know this, girl, but those men in their suits in London know only their bottom line. They will not honour the policy unless Mr Bell seeks another tenant. Once he does so, they will issue payment for the repairs under that individual's name."

Margaret's lips were pressed into a determined scowl. "And it will be even longer before the mill can work again! What does John plan to do?"

"What can he do? He must give up the lease, as he intended to do in the first place. I think he is relieved at least to hear that a start can be made at restoring the mill so that it may all the sooner become operational under the authority of another. My son is not vain or selfish," she asserted with a twinge of her old pride.

"No, he is not," Margaret agreed stoutly. "It is a hard blow, though! Is he taking all of this well?"

Hannah's lined mouth softened. "One who knew him less would think so. I doubt *you* would be fooled, so I shall not even try to pretend it."

The pair of women joined together in commiserating silence for a time. Neither the pretense of taking refreshments nor the effort of hollow platitudes were necessary, for they had at last come to acknowledge the commonalities they shared. Both would give over every remnant of their own gratification had it only brought him the least ‾ measure of contentment. For a man who gloried in his work and the glad satisfaction of leaving the world improved by his energies, to have the opportunities created by his youthful ambition snatched from him seemed too harsh a fate.

After a long spell, Hannah spoke again. "There is more, and I cannot say if aught will come of it. Mr Hamilton sent over a note, asking if he might call on John in the morning."

At this, Margaret's lips puckered in suspicion. "What does John think?"

"You may ask him yourself," the older woman sighed. "He is in his study."

Margaret's jaw dropped, aghast. "His study! I thought he had been remanded to his bed for the duration of his recovery!"

Hannah gave a low grunt. "He has not remained in his bed since Christmas Day! Dr Donaldson was most vexed when he found John had cut the binding from his ribs and has been wandering about on his feet. He *does* seem to be improving more rapidly, and his breathing sounds less laboured, but do not tell him that I admitted as much."

"Oh, indeed I shall not!" Margaret declared. She rose and began to sweep away in her exasperated grace, but some sudden impulse caused her to return. Placing her hands timorously on Hannah's shoulders, she leaned down to touch a quick, impetuous kiss on the older woman's cheek before hurrying off to see John.

Stupefied, Hannah watched her go. "Well!" she huffed to herself. "If I haven't gone and fallen under her spell! I said I never should, but she's bewitched me for all of that. She's a match for my John, and that's a deal for me to say!"

~

"John Thornton!"

The crisp, irritated inflection in the beloved voice jerked his spine to attention even as he was trying to ease himself into a more relaxed position. He reflexively dropped the ledgers he was studying, which alteration to his carefully balanced posture- however minute- triggered another jolt through his torso and left him breathless. An excruciating snapping sensation in the next instant drew an agonized groan from his lips, and it was two or three full seconds before he could brace himself to turn around.

Margaret had already crossed the room to him, contrition drastically softening her manner. "Oh, John, I did not mean to surprise you!"

He growled, barely in control of his pain, and not above extracting a full apology. "You most assuredly did, Madam! I shall demand restitution, you know, and if I remember correctly, you are already once in my debt. I should think that nothing less than your most convincing grovel will do."

She crossed her arms and leveled a cynical stare at him. "I am not good at groveling. What are you doing up and about, sir?"

"Not so hasty, *Miss Hale*. Let us return to the severe pain you have just caused me! If you cannot grovel, I shall have to think of another form of remuneration."

"While you thus employ yourself, I will ask again. I thought you were to be resting, yet I find you attempting to work!"

"You would not have found me so, had I any knowledge you were expected," he winked rakishly. "I would have packed myself off to my room with an ice bag on my head and a mournful expression upon my face. Surely you would have taken great pity on me and bestowed your very tenderest mercies."

"It is too late, John, for you have lost my sympathy."

"Oh!" he mimicked stabbing himself through the heart- very gently, of course. "You are a cruel woman, Margaret! You must try to comfort me in exchange for your harsh words."

She glared at him, but the amusement dancing in her eyes soon overcame her annoyance, and she gave way to her mirth. She bowed her head, kneading her brow in defeat. "What am I to do with you!" she laughed.

The victor grinned mercilessly. "Come here and greet me properly, of course."

"I hardly think what you have in mind is 'proper'."

"No harm in finding out for sure," he maintained, still smiling cunningly. "Ah!" he cringed as she came near and started to hesitantly reach for him. "Not there, Love," he groaned between clenched teeth.

Margaret's hands hovered uncertainly near his shoulders, but he flinched again. "Oh, your burns!" she winced in sympathy. She drew back helplessly. "It is no good! You are wounded everywhere!"

"Not quite," he smiled and gingerly reached for her. At last he dared to extend his arms just enough to rest his fingertips at her hips- such a pity that a more civilized posture would cause him even greater pain- and carefully kissed her forehead. He lingered a long while, catching his breath and reassuring himself that she really was there, loving him for all her scolding words, and that she really had promised him her future.

"What brings you to me today, Love?" he murmured into her hairline.

"Your mother sent for me. She told me about Mr Bell's insurance policy."

A slow whiff of his exhaled breath stirred through her hair, causing the back of her neck to prickle. He pulled back somewhat, his smile still rigidly in place, but there was a tightness around his eyes. "Yes, it is good news, is it not?"

"John, you need not feign happiness with me. I am sorry that you were cut so."

He would have offered a careless shrug, had it not been so painful. "It changes nothing for me, save that I must only repay Bell for the premium on his policy rather than the damages to his buildings. I had difficulties enough before all of this! I would never be able to replace the equipment."

"Do you think that Mr Hamilton intends to make you an offer of some kind?"

"Naturally. If it is anything like the last 'offer' he made me, it will not even be worth my while to listen." He slitted his eyes, his jaw tense, but Margaret's warm hand soon slid over his face.

"John," she whispered gently. Instantly he was all hers again. What he would have given to be able to crush her to him, to have her hold fast to him in his trials! His fingers crept more intimately along the curve of her hips, and very slowly he slanted his face down to hers. Sweetly, tenderly, she allowed him to seek his comfort. She curled her arms round his head, twisting her fingers deeply into his hair. For this moment, at least, there was only her.

"Aye, my Margaret," he breathed into her neck. "I've no idea how I ever survived without your kisses!" He trailed dusty caresses over the top ridges of her ear for emphasis.

Margaret shivered deliciously, arching up as high as she could reach so he did not have to bend so far to her. "You were a good deal harder to manage," she teased, gasping as he nibbled down her throat. "I think I have at long last discovered the secret means of controlling the indominatable John Thornton."

"You have possessed that secret for many months, Love. It is a pity you have only recently begun to employ it!" His lips traced a sweeping arch from her ear and over her delicate brows, imprinting his senses with the feel of her. How he had missed her! All at once, he raised himself away from her face. "Margaret, does it trouble you that I wish so much to hold you as we are?"

"Trouble me?" her muffled voice spoke against his jaw. "Why should it?"

"It is not the way of good society," he confessed.

An amused warmth lit her eyes. "I have long since given over the thought of you ever behaving with propriety."

"You do not feel I take advantage of you?" he inquired, his tone becoming more serious.

She shook her head gently. "No, John. I am not afraid to touch you, as some might say I ought to be. Growing up in London, it was sometimes days on end before one would feel an affectionate touch. It was sorely wanted at times! I would share this with you every day, and if by holding you for a time, I can bring you some little comfort, then I am glad."

Relieved, he lowered his face once more into the hollow of her neck-dash the pain in his chest, it was worth it all to explore the lavish bounty of her tenderness. He took his time about returning to her lips, but once there he lingered for a divine respite from all of his other cares. Reason, however, dictated that he must in the end stop. She was not yet his wife, and cost him what it may, he would not disgrace her.

"I expect," he pressed a last retreating kiss to the tip of her nose as his mind turned purposely to duller matters, "that you have spoken lately to Higgins?"

She nodded, nibbling her upper lip in apprehension.

"And what does he say about the most recent Union meeting?"

She glanced up in surprise. "How did you know there was a meeting? It only happened today!"

"They have to have some place to assemble, and most of the guest lecturers at the Lyceum Hall are rather territorial about their time. They took over your father's lecture hour again, did they not?"

She gave a little huff. "Indeed. Of course you would have expected that!" She sighed and told him all that Nicholas had conveyed to her.

He shook his head, his eyes misting over in thought. "Would that I had a way to reopen the mill in my own right! Troubled or no, it would provide everyone with some income during the winter. I fear for what may happen if Hamilton takes over the mill, as I believe he wishes to do."

"Why?" she tilted her head, puzzled.

"Hamilton himself cares nothing for the business, beyond his profit margin. Not that I condemn that- we are all businessmen at the end of the day- but he will take small interest in the proper restoration of the equipment. He will invest as little as he can to become operational in the short term, but he has not the inspiration for growth.

"And then there is that son of his! He wishes for Rupert to gain experience in trade, and no doubt plans to install him as master. I expect he will confirm all of this when he comes to talk to me tomorrow."

"You think he will ask you to work alongside Rupert for a time? Why, John, it could be just the thing! You would need to seek employment regardless, and here you could ensure that everything is done properly! None know the mill and the workers like you do."

He scowled. "I should quarrel with him within the first month. I would do better to go to Hamper! He wishes to set his own son up in a mill over in Leeds and has already approached me to work with him. At least in that case, I think I should endure six months before incurring a complete and utter breach of our working relationship."

"Well, we can do little good by speculating now. Perhaps you ought to hear Mr Hamilton out tomorrow before you decide there is no future in it."

The light returned to his eyes and he pecked a firm kiss to her forehead. "Wisdom from my future wife! Which reminds me...." Carefully he eased away from her and made his arduous, methodical way to his desk. "I have something for you."

He gathered a few papers from his desk and fanned them triumphantly before her face. "I spoke with the minister today. He will begin reading the banns on Sunday."

"My, you did not waste any time!" she laughed.

"On the contrary, the entire process seems to me sluggish and ridiculously protracted. Upon my word, Margaret, we would already be wed if I felt I could have endured the train ride to Gretna Green. Are you certain," his tone changed, "that you will not mind a simple- very simple- and economical wedding? You deserve so much better!"

"Absolutely," she assured him. "It has always seemed to me vain and silly to make such a fuss."

He grinned crookedly. "Thank heavens you and Fanny are not cut from the same cloth! You ought to hear the lamentations from her room when I tell her what we can afford to spend on her wedding. Watson has promised to buy her an entire trousseau after they are wed, which did comfort her somewhat."

Margaret shook her head in wonder. "I am glad she accepted him! He seems respectable enough. I might have feared she would reject him in hopes that Rupert Hamilton might be brought up to scratch."

"He has dropped from the face of the planet of late, to which I cannot say I am sorry. She was rather distraught to begin with, but I think my mother gave her a set down. She is annoyed with me and wants out of the house, so Watson is looking rather attractive to her just now."

Margaret could not help a little shiver. Decent enough fellow though he might be, she could not fathom giving herself to a blustering simpleton like James Watson just to secure a home. How blessed she was to admire, respect, and... and yes, passionately love the man whose name she would take!

Chapter Thirty-Three

"Thornton, it is good to see you on your feet again." Stuart Hamilton took the offered seat in John's private study. He bore less the air of the friendly colleague on this visit, and more the attitude of the masterly financier. Without preamble, he placed his case at his feet and began drawing papers from it.

"Thank you, sir. What can I do for you?" Thornton eased carefully back into his seat, resting his elbows on the arms of his chair and lacing his fingers together. Clearly Hamilton was working under the assumption that he had already obtained his objective, and only John's final signature was wanting. Thornton's jaw tightened. He might have no bargaining power, but Hamilton would not find him the soft mark he expected.

"Well, Thornton, I should think it all rather obvious." Hamilton spread before himself a proposal, but did not press it toward the other just yet. "You are quite ruined- a shame, my good man- but perhaps I may be of assistance."

Thornton's brow lifted. "You have been in correspondence with Bell, I presume?"

Hamilton's surprise was barely concealed. He cleared his throat. "Why, yes, of course. I have been associated with him from long ago, as you recall."

"Quite. So, what is your proposal?"

"Five years, Thornton. Give me five years of your time to get the mill operational and profitable again, under Rupert. He will require your assistance, for you know all of the contacts and technical information he will need. In exchange for signing the contract with me, I will repay your bank loan, but only the bank loan; not your private investors. You yourself will draw a modest stipend for your living expenses. That is the best I can do."

"And after the five years?"

Hamilton's eye twinkled. "That depends on you, Thornton. You may go your own way, of course. If, on the other hand, you find you prefer to stay, we may work out another agreement at that time."

"Under your son? Forgive me, sir, but no thank you. I do not think it prudent to so closely ally myself with a character so dissimilar to my own. I think we should not get on."

"No one is saying that Rupert must stay on indefinitely. He only wants some experience in business, Thornton. I intended," he shifted in his chair somewhat, "to eventually put the business in Genevieve's name."

Thornton sighed. So, Hamilton was about that again! "Perhaps I should be frank, sir. I have been engaged to another for some weeks already. The banns will be read in a matter of days. So, you see, it is impossible for me to take any interest in what you suggest."

Hamilton's eyes hardened. "Ah, yes. The lovely Miss Hale. Tell me, Thornton, how did you intend to provide for her? She and her father are nearly destitute as it is, are they not? Your stipend will not be *that* much, and you have other debts to repay."

"I do not care to discuss my personal affairs, sir," Thornton's voice was flinty and unyielding. "I insist that you refrain from further insinuations regarding your daughter, for I cannot satisfy you."

Hamilton tilted back in his chair, studying his adversary. "Did you know, Thornton, that I have a good friend in London- Charles Davis, one of the chief editors of the Times?"

"I did not."

"Good fellow, Charles. He keeps me appraised of any items I might find interesting- unofficially, of course, before the headlines break."

"And what, may I ask, is this interesting piece of news you seem to have gathered?"

Hamilton's face warmed shrewdly. "That is not for me to say yet, Thornton. I only suggest that you continue to keep your understanding with Miss Hale quiet. You may soon be glad that you did so."

"Let me be perfectly clear, Hamilton. I do not know the nature of this shocking news you claim, but I shall not be dissuaded from wedding Miss Hale at my earliest opportunity. I cannot understand why you display such zeal for engaging your daughter to a man who does not care for her."

"And I cannot fathom why you will not be persuaded to it, Thornton! Egad, man, think what you and I could accomplish! You stand to gain controlling interest again in the mill, with all of the resources you could desire at your fingertips and a charming wife in the bargain! What have you to lose? Why, there is not a mill owner in the city who would not have fallen over himself for such a chance!"

"Then go to another and be done with it!" Thornton fairly snarled, clutching his side when a sharp pain stabbed him.

"Did you know, Thornton," Hamilton's demeanor abruptly shifted to a more conversational tone, "that Marlborough Mills sits almost exactly in the centre of Milton?"

He stared. "I was aware of that. Why bring it up?"

Hamilton tapped his forefingers together thoughtfully. "How long, Thornton, do you expect it will be before the current design of the mill is obsolete?"

"That depends on advancing technology. Twenty years, possibly, before a substantial remodel is necessary."

"Hmm. And where does most of your cotton come from, Thornton?"

"You know very well where it comes from. American suppliers ship through Liverpool."

"Very interesting what's starting to happen over there. They're finally starting to catch up to us about the slavery laws. Why, they even have a new political party formed just this year around that platform."

Thornton grimaced. "And as yet they are scarcely a ripple upon the waves."

"So far, yes," Hamilton agreed. "But what happens to the cotton trade, Thornton, when tensions rise sufficiently over there? It's bound to happen, sooner or later. Heaven only knows how it will all shake out, but at the very least we are talking about a substantial hike in your raw cotton prices, if not a drastic shortage."

Thornton fell silent, his mind beginning to make the leaps of conjecture which formed Hamilton's reasoning. "You think," he responded slowly, "to make the most of the profit here for the next few years, then when the cotton market turns and the property loses value, you would purchase the property from Bell- or his heir, possibly by that time- for a mere song and tear down the mill. I suppose you intend to then build some manner of commercial centre on the site?"

Hamilton's mouth turned upward in satisfaction. "And you continue to wonder why I want you in my family, Thornton? You are a man of vision. You can foresee these eventualities, and together we can plan a far more profitable future than could ever be achieved in cotton alone."

"I will not marry your daughter simply to oblige your business stratagems, Hamilton! I find it repugnant... blasphemous, even," he winced inwardly as he found himself nearly repeating Margaret's first rejection of his proposal. "Even had I not sworn myself to another- one to whom I am thoroughly devoted- I would never have yielded to your obvious desire to control me through marriage. Why you cannot settle for a simple business arrangement, I do not know, but you have come to the wrong man!"

Hamilton's expression tightened, his voice now hard. "I take it, then, that in your studies of the Classics with that old parson, you have not yet stumbled upon Machiavelli. Keep your bit of muslin if you must, but if you reject my offer, you will regret it."

Thornton shot to his feet, nearly roaring in rage and pain. "Get out! Get out of my house this instant!"

Hamilton allowed a sly glint in his eyes as he rose. "I will wait for two weeks, Thornton. If you have not changed your mind, I will proceed without you. I'll require you to vacate the premises as soon as the lease transfers to my name. Good day."

Hamilton departed and the infuriated former master fumed and seethed about his study for fully ten minutes. He panted and gasped in his physical weakness, but his temper was high, his passion unabated. He stood at his study window and clenched his fists in the air, biting back the ferocious howl of wrath which would only make him choke in agony and alarm his mother.

His mother! Margaret had promised to come sit with her this morning, knowing how anxious she had been for his negotiations! Impatiently he stumbled from the room, longing only to hear the gentle reassurances of his two ladies; to feel their simple unwavering support and unshakable faith in him, no matter the circumstances.

"John!" Margaret rose first, apprehension written plainly across her features. "John, what has happened?"

Carefully he pulled her under his chin, not even caring that his mother was at hand. It felt so good to have her close, to know that she would look into his hopelessness and find something to believe in! Margaret leaned her head reassuringly into his embrace, but cautiously bent her body away from his wounded torso.

"Mother," he beckoned with his other hand. Her brow furrowed suspiciously, his mother came as well and her cool fingers took his fevered grip.

"John, tell us!" Margaret implored. "It must be truly dreadful; I have scarcely seen your face so white!"

At last, he found his voice, unsteady as it was. "It is as I expected. Mr Hamilton wishes me to work for him under contract for five years. And he wishes for me to marry into his family."

The reactions were, quite naturally, outrage mixed with confusion. "But why, John?" his mother demanded. "What matters it to Mr Hamilton what you do? You would be under contract to work, what more does he want?"

He released a taut breath, his eyes trained over his mother's head and out the window, on what remained of the factory roof. "Control. That is what he wants. I think I finally understand."

He pressed them both back, blinking and swallowing the last of his ire. Shakily, he made his way to the sofa where they anxiously joined him. "Mr Hamilton means to set himself up as quite the tycoon, and somehow, I am in his way. He sees me as competition, even now! I do not understand it. He will either have my cooperation, or he will see me ruined."

"And how does he mean to do that?" his mother scoffed. "You refused the offer, naturally! You may go to anyone else!"

"Mother," he spoke lowly, as though he himself had only just realized the truth. "Hamilton has invested in half of the mills in town already, as well as a score of other shops and firms. Hamper alone owes him nearly three hundred pounds."

Both of the women paled, their expressions united in horror. "Oh, John! Does that mean...." Margaret's hand covered her mouth before daring to finish her thought.

He nodded grimly. "He will make certain that I have no work in Milton. There is a fine network binding all of the partnerships in town, and none will wish to cripple his own business on my account. I am not *that* highly sought after," he gave his mother a sardonic half smirk.

Hannah gulped down her consternation and caught her future daughter's eye. She lifted her chin in defiance. "Then we go to Leeds, or Manchester. You still have your name, John! We need not be dependent upon Mr Hamilton, or his little empire."

He tried to smile. "You are right, Mother. Margaret, my love, you would not be troubled overmuch to go? Do you think your father would not wish to relocate?"

She wrapped her hand securely over his forearm. "I will go with you, John, and I am certain that Father will not object. You are his favourite pupil, after all." She accompanied her remark with that gentle warmth which never failed to make his heart skip.

There, right before his mother, he leaned forward and captured her
honeyed lips in a light, intimate caress. "Then to Leeds or Manchester we
go. I will begin writing some letters." He rose and left them staring after
him as he hobbled slowly back to his study.

Margaret shuddered in a deep sigh as the door closed. "Can he really
do it?" she asked hesitantly. "Has he the contacts there to find the sort of
position he seeks?"

Hannah's lips pressed together. "Perhaps. His name is well-known, and
he is respected in all quarters of the industry. Whether anyone will wish to
take him on is something else entirely. He developed something of a
reputation after breaking that strike. While other masters applauded him
to his face, behind his back they behave rather differently. Simply bringing
him on as an overseer might trigger unrest in the local Unions, and most
masters are anxious to avoid that sort of trouble if they can."

"But there are none who work better with the Union now!" Margaret
objected. "He has proven that he will not be dictated to, but has also been
most generous in his subsequent dealings. I would have thought that his
presence would avert strikes rather than stimulate them."

Hannah clicked her tongue and shook her head. "The leaders *here*
know that about him. Time will tell what others believe, Lass. Let John
worry about it for now. If I am not mistaken, we have a wedding to plan, so
let us to it."

Chapter Thirty-Four

On the second morning after Thornton's meeting with Hamilton, he crept his slow, laborious way down the stairs to break his fast. He would never reveal to his mother just how excruciating every movement was, but oh! Had he a pistol, he would have cheerfully shot the first man who designed stairs in a house. By the time he reached the bottom some minutes later, he was panting and his face was white with cold sweat. Thank heavens Dr Donaldson proclaimed him to be mending "despite your best efforts at killing yourself," as the doctor's pithy remark had reassured him. He did not think he could bear many more weeks of this!

Clamping down on his upper lip, he took his seat and sighed his thanks as Cook's assistant brought him his tea and paper. His face pinched. He was going to have to thin out the household staff, for what little ready money he had left was dwindling rapidly. He ought to have cut back sooner, but he had not wished to leave his long-time staff so unexpectedly without employment, nor overburden the remaining help at a time when there were two weddings to plan- modest though they would be.

Raising his tea to his lips, his mind wandered pleasantly to weddings and teacups and mornings spent lingering over breakfast. Presently he mused to himself that in three more weeks- the date he and Margaret had tentatively set for their wedding- he might not be in such dire physical shape. A silent grin tugged at his mouth even as he attempted to drink his tea without spilling. A groom had good need to be strong and fit, after all!

What might his delicious bride desire of him? He fairly tingled in his burning curiosity. Would she wish for him to keep her warm through the nights? Did she wear her hair loose or plaited when she slept? And what in thunder did a woman *wear* to bed with her husband? *Husband!* No more glorious title could he ever aspire to, except... except possibly.... He sighed serenely. If he had any say in the matter, there would be children one day- dozens of them! *Perhaps Margaret might object to that figure*, he chuckled privately.

"Well, now, has someone slipped a little extra sugar in your tea this morning?"

He started to clear his throat, but caught himself just in time. "Good morning, Mother. How are you this morning?" He moved to rise to his feet, but she put out a hand to stay him.

"Not as cheerful as you, I daresay. Is there some good news in your paper, or are you merely daydreaming?"

"Mother! I am a sober man of one and thirty! I, daydream? I think you mistake me for some young sod with little but romance on his mind."

"My mistake," she deadpanned, reaching for her own saucer. "In that case, perhaps you will be so good as to read me this delightful article in today's paper."

His expression cleared sedately as he craned his neck to look over the rim of his cup. Hannah smirked, amused that this boy of hers, who might easily have been mired by worry and cares, was able to sit at table and fantasize about his bride. Troubles or no, she was satisfied... no, that would not do. She was delighted beyond all that she would ever confess that Margaret Hale was a young woman of worth, and that the girl was at long last as devoted to John as he had always been to her.

The harsh clatter of John's cup on the saucer brought her eyes sharply to his face. "John? What is it?"

He had lifted the paper with both hands, his face dark with astonishment as he continued to read. She watched his eyes flying over the print as his expression grew more and more grave.

"John!"

He lowered the paper and looked up. "The Drapers- you remember them?"

"That fellow from Scarborough and his wretched wife. Yes, of course I remember them! What is it?"

Dazed, he let the paper fall to the table. "They have fled the country, and are suspected to have taken with them nearly four thousand pounds of contributions donated to build that 'hospital'!"

"What, fled? How could they do that? Surely it is impossible, even for *that* woman!" she sneered. "I thought all of those monies had to be kept in a special sort of account set aside for the proper purpose."

He shook his head vaguely as he continued reading. "The account appears to have been a fraud. They are still investigating, but they have not yet found who helped them set it up, or where all the money has gone." He kept reading. "There are a number of quite influential people righteously offended over this! It appears Draper obtained solicitations from some of the wealthiest donors from all over the country."

His eyes kept scrolling as he murmured the highlights from the article. "So far the investigators have very few leads back to the Drapers. One is that sham of a doctor, Douglas, who seems to have also disappeared, and...." His face suddenly bled of all colour and his fingers went lax.

"John! What does it say?" Mrs Thornton was nearly writhing in suspense at his abrupt pallor.

His lips mumbled as his eyes stared, unseeingly, at the page. "... 'And one Miss Margaret Hale of Milton, who penned and signed most of the letters of solicitation.'"

Hannah's own cup crashed to the saucer, spilling nearly all of its contents. Her eyes began to glitter fiercely. "The swine!" she spat. "Vulgar, slanderous fiends! How dare they discredit that girl!"

Shaking, he clambered up from his chair, nearly tripping in his awkward haste. "I must go, Mother!"

"John, you are not fit to walk so far! You must call for some horses and take your carriage, at the least!"

"I haven't time, Mother!" he cried over his shoulder, and not bothering to remind her that he had already sold his carriage. "They may already be at her door!"

~

Margaret peered nervously into the sitting room from the outer hall. "Dixon," she whispered quietly, "what do they want?"

Dixon, her eyes wide, shrugged helplessly. "You don't think it's about Master Fred, do you Miss?" she hissed back. "I thought Mr Thornton settled that."

"So had I! No, it cannot be that. It has been too long ago!" She frowned, looking back to the men loitering in her drawing room. "I suppose there is nothing else for it."

She drew herself up to her full height, unconsciously adopting the regal air which had first captured John Thornton's admiration and Hannah Thornton's contempt. "Gentlemen," she inclined her head graciously as she entered the room. "May I help you?"

The foremost man stood, and Margaret fought a visible twitch of her lashes when she recognized him. "Good morning, Miss Hale. You may remember me, Joseph Mason from investigations."

She dipped her head politely. "I do, Mr Mason."

He harrumphed a little, squaring his jacket. He had been frustrated by this woman before, and by heaven, he was going to have some straight answers this time! "This is Mr Davenport, one of the local magistrates, and Mr Crawley, from our London bureau."

"London!" she exclaimed. "Good heavens, has something happened to my cousin or my aunt?"

The three men glanced at one another. "Not to our knowledge, Miss," answered Mr Davenport. "We had some frank questions to ask you regarding your involvement in a fraudulent bank account set up under the name of Milton Charitable Trust."

Margaret stared back at him blankly, then her gaze searched the faces of the other two. "Gentlemen, I have no idea what you can mean."

Mr Crawley came forward. "Miss Hale, will you please be so good as to verify whether or not this is your hand?" He drew out a folded sheet of writing paper and opened it before her.

Margaret took the paper and her fingers began to tremble. She blinked. "Yes," she verified softly. "This is my writing."

Mason's chest swelled in a long, sweet breath of victory. "That letter," he pointed, "was one among dozens sent to wealthy donors throughout the kingdom. Were you aware of this?"

She swallowed shakily. "Yes," she answered in a still softer voice.

"Then I will ask you again, Miss Hale. What do you know about the trust account?"

Margaret opened her mouth to deny any knowledge, but the sound of a door slamming behind her caused her to jump and turn round.

"She knows nothing, Mason," John Thornton strode heavily into the room, masking his weakness almost completely to all eyes but Margaret's.

Mason's jaw hardened. "Mr Thornton, sir. I did not know you were well enough recovered to be about."

"I am," he retorted flatly. "Mason, may I have a word?"

The young inspector flinched somewhat, but stood his ground. He may have owed John Thornton his start in the bureau, but this case was simply too large, and too many important people wanted answers. Moreover, there was something queer about the way Thornton seemed to turn up whenever Miss Hale was in question. Mason straightened. "I'm afraid I cannot do that, sir. Mr Davenport is the magistrate assigned to the case, as we all feared you were not strong enough."

"Thornton," Davenport greeted.

Thornton glared from one man to the other. His incensed demeanour might have caused Mason, and perhaps even Crawley to quail somewhat, but allied with another magistrate, they stared boldly back. "I see," he at last responded, trying to keep his tone neutral. "Well, then, let us have it. What questions do you have, Mason?"

"Miss Hale has acknowledged this to be her writing, sir. I am afraid that is more than enough for an inquest. We would like her to answer what she knows about the account."

Margaret looked helplessly to John, revealing far more than she intended in that one desperate glance. He cut his gaze away, but not before Mason's suspicions were confirmed.

John's glare froze on Mason. If they were going to perform the inquest anyway, they had no right to force her to answer such a question now. Perhaps, though, her utter ignorance would be apparent to them, and if they were in a generous mood at all, they might even now leave her be. It was worth a chance. "Miss Hale," John asked evenly, his eyes still on Mason, "what do you know about the account?"

She gasped. "Nothing! I do not even know what has happened! Please, will someone tell me?"

John's eyes flickered. "The lady knows nothing. She was defrauded of her time and energies just as others were of their money. I am afraid you gentlemen will need to look elsewhere for your answers."

"Not so hasty, Thornton!" Davenport objected. "This is *my* case, after all, and not yours." He glanced at the two inspectors. "Gentlemen, I have heard enough to determine that an inquest is necessary. Perhaps, Miss Hale, you were an innocent in this business after all, but we will let the facts be heard. Thornton," he paused to level a significant stare at the other magistrate, "we will handle this. You look like you ought to be in bed, old friend."

Mason allowed a satisfied little smile for the barest half of a second. "We will notify you when you need to be present, Miss." The three men took their leave, and Dixon shooed them out the door with profound relief.

John's mask of invulnerability dissolved. His face white as a sheet, he shakily sought Margaret's strength, staggering a step or two nearer to her. "John!" she swept under the crook of his arm and wrapped her supporting hand low about his waist. "What were you thinking, coming so far! You did not walk, did you?"

He groaned and carefully eased himself to the sofa. "I did."

"John Thornton, I have never known you to be foolish, but this! Have you lost your mind?"

"Long ago," he winked half-heartedly as he slowly draped his tall frame against the back of the furniture. He took several long breaths, as deeply as he dared, trying to regain control of his pain. At length, "I am sorry they came to you. Are you well?"

"I am confused! Do you know what all of this is about?"

Wordlessly he tugged the folded newspaper from the inner pocket of his coat and handed it to her. She scanned it quickly, her face growing more pale even than his. "I cannot believe this! Have they really gone, and all of the money raised for the hospital is missing?"

"It would appear so."

"Oh dear!" she covered her mouth with her hand. "John, this is dreadful! All of those donors thought their money was going to a good cause, and the people of Milton are the losers!"

"And anyone associated with the Drapers," he scowled.

"John, what do they think I know? I only wrote those letters as a favour, because I thought I could be of help! Oh, I wish I would have heeded your advice in the first place!"

"You did nothing wrong, Margaret," he soothed. "Your motives were untainted. The investigators will see that, in time. I only fear for what trouble and mortification this will cost you! Your name is in every paper from here to Hampshire, you may be assured."

Margaret's cheeks flushed from her deathly pallor to vivid humiliation. "Oh, John!" She buried her face against his shoulder. "I am so ashamed! How could I have been so blind?"

"Come, love," he whispered into her hair. "You were no more blind than the rest of us. You in your compassion longed to do something which no one else could be troubled to do, that is all. Do not blame yourself, my Margaret. I cannot bear to see you hang your head in shame!"

She pressed her face against the wool of his coat collar, still sniffling. "My reputation is lost! How am I to look the people of this town in the eye? Oh!" She straightened as the most horrifying thought struck her. "John, you cannot afford to have your name linked with mine just now! If the banns are read, and you are known to be betrothed to me, what will that do to your chances for another position? Your own honour will be called into question!"

"It may already be too late for that." He stroked her hair, lovingly wrapping one of the rich dark curls over his finger. "I did you no favours by coming here today. I impulsively wished to protect you, but I only made you look the more suspicious."

"I do not understand. Do you have some animosity with Mr Davenport?"

"No, not at all. He is an honest chap, but he did not look kindly on my interference. One magistrate does not meddle with another's cases unless consulted; it is the unwritten law. Additionally," his cheek flinched and he looked down to her with a pained expression, "Mason is curious now. He is a good fellow, but when I called off his investigation into Leonards' death, he was less than content."

"But Fred had nothing to do with Leonards' death!"

"Yes, and he also was forced to admit as much, but he knew that something you said was off. I think he sensed that I was protecting you from further investigation. He will not be so easily drawn away this time, and now he may call my own motives into question."

She raised her head, looking steadily into his eyes. "What will that do to you?"

"In the end? Nothing at all, for you are innocent, Margaret, and there is no way to cast blame on you. Until then..." his jaw worked thoughtfully. "Things will be very uncomfortable for both of us.

"A case so large has surely attracted a good deal of notice. The inspectors are motivated to find all the answers they can, as quickly as possible, and they have your signature on connected documents. It will most certainly mean questions, and your good name might suffer. We ought to consider hiring an attorney, just to protect you. You don't happen to know of someone you trust from your connections in London, do you?"

Margaret's face grew hot. "I do," she whispered. "Henry Lennox, my cousin's brother-in-law."

John studied her in that intense way which only he could. His perceptive gaze lingered on her flushed countenance, the downcast eyes, and he smiled gently. "Do I need to be jealous of this Mr Lennox?"

"No!" she yelped. "That is... Henry is a friend. I think... once perhaps... certainly once, he thought to be more, but... no, John."

His eyes lit in sheer pleasure, and he worked his fingers more deeply into her upswept hair. He leaned close to her. "That is comforting," he murmured against her lips. "I am in no condition to fight the man just now."

She gave a little strangled laugh into his cheek, but it vanished into a worried sob. "John, what are we to do? We cannot marry now- I will not have you wrapped up in all of this!"

"And I refuse to abandon you, so we have quite the predicament, Love!"

"How long will all of this legal bother take? It cannot take more than a few weeks, surely."

He frowned. "That all depends on how quickly they find other witnesses. Once they have, I doubt not that the inspectors will find their information more useful than yours, and you will be left in peace."

"But there is still my name in the papers!" she reminded him. "Oh, what must my aunt be thinking? It is all so humiliating!"

"Anyone who knows you will immediately know the truth, Margaret. I do not care for anyone else's opinion."

She trembled, hot tears filling her eyes. "But we *must* care! It will affect how we are received everywhere we go!"

"The name in the paper," he whispered in her ear, "was Margaret *Hale*. Margaret *Thornton* is the woman with whom I intend to spend my life... and may I simply note how satisfying it was to say that just now?"

She cupped his cheek, smiling tremulously. "It is not that simple, dearest John. We have to start over in a new city, and there I will not have the benefit of my previous good reputation. All that will follow me is my maiden name and its connection to this scandal, for that much always comes out."

"You will not persuade me to delay our marriage, Margaret. This will all blow over in good time. Let us write to your attorney friend and find what advice he has. Would you prefer that I wrote?"

She shook her head. "No. I should do it. I owe him at least an explanation before... well, before he hears about you."

His face softened in understanding. "I would ask to include a note of my own with your letter. Hamilton made some mention of this to me two days ago, before I knew what to expect. I would like to know where his source is getting his information. Perhaps that will help your Mr Lennox. Will you write your letter now?"

She nodded, her mouth set into a determined line. "Good," he twined another curl around his worshipful fingers, reveling in her softness even now.

He kissed her once more, deeply and sweetly, sharing with her all of the courage and solace which she constantly infused into his own heart. Margaret clasped him tightly, wishing they were somewhere- *anywhere* else, with their nuptials behind them so she could truly lose herself in his embrace. Had they not been hindered by his infirmities, it is possible that his honour as a gentleman would have been forfeit. Never had she responded to him with such heartfelt abandon, but alas, he knew his duty, and it was not to take advantage of her in her distress.

With nearly heroic exertion, he pressed her away. His voice shook somewhat as he began to excuse himself. "I will explain what we know to your father while you write your letter."

Chapter Thirty-Five

Mason and the other men lost no time about their few remaining leads in Milton. Five hours later saw Mason returning to the Hale residence, alone. This time, to his satisfaction, there was no great guard dog snarling at anyone who came near. He found his quarry isolated and vulnerable, with only a suspicious and sullen maid to watch the door.

"Miss Hale," Mason began, his tones respectful but firm. "We have a witness who claims you sought out an introduction to Mr Draper and did, in that very house, converse at length about this enterprise."

She swallowed, remembering John's careful coaching on how she might best respond. "That is true," she answered simply.

"Oh, so you admit that you were there?" he allowed a faint note of brittleness in his voice. "Forgive me for my surprise, Miss Hale."

She stared silently back, her dilated pupils the only symptom of her disturbance.

He sighed in exasperation and continued. "I would ask you to confirm the details, Miss Hale. Who introduced you to Mr and Mrs Draper?"

"My fr-," she stopped herself. She could no longer claim that relationship. "Miss Genevieve Hamilton introduced me to Mrs Draper, and Mr Rupert Hamilton introduced me to Mr Draper, at a house party given by Mr and Mrs Hamilton."

"That matches what I was told. Mr Hamilton was adamant that it was *your* fixed desire to be introduced to Mr Draper. You pursued the acquaintance and inquired directly and of your own accord into this 'charity'. Is that true?"

Her breath quivered in her throat before she responded. "It is."

"And your interest in this enterprise, Miss Hale? What was to be your payment?"

Her nostrils flared in delicate outrage. "I was promised no payment, sir! I wished to volunteer my services for the founding of the new hospital! I believed, and still do, that Milton has desperate need of one."

He crossed his arms. "I beg your pardon, Miss Hale, but such altruistic notions are rare. I have learned never to take them at face value in situations such as this."

Her lids lowered and she regarded him coolly. "That is unfortunate, Mr Mason. I find that looking for the very best in people tends to inspire them to rise to my expectations."

"Naturally," he drawled, his voice dripping with irony. "I, on the other hand, find that when I look for complete honesty, I rarely stumble upon it. It really is quite a shame."

Margaret's stomach rolled nervously, but she spoke no reply. Mason held her gaze until she at last blinked and lowered her eyes, blushing. How unfair of him to use her well-trained feminine modesty to intimidate her! She gritted her teeth in frustration and looked boldly back once more.

"Miss Hale," he spoke softly, tempting her to trust in him. "I am inclined to believe what you say, but your manner is not at all constant. I think it is time we got to the bottom of something. Why did you lie to me once before, and why is John Thornton protecting you? I think I know the answer to the latter, but I would have it in your own words."

She drew breath and squared her shoulders. "The past has no bearing here, sir."

"On the contrary! It has a great deal of bearing, Miss Hale. You are asking me to exonerate you based upon your word alone- a testimony I have found unreliable."

"My presence or lack thereof in that prior case was irrelevant, sir." She lifted her chin with not a little measure of haughty grace. "Is it so difficult to believe a lady would prefer to keep her affairs private? There was nothing you could gain by coming to me."

He chortled derisively. "In that case, Miss Hale, I return to my other question. Why is John Thornton so eager to shield you that he walked three miles in the cold in his condition, only to challenge another magistrate? I have known Mr Thornton a long time, and he is a dogged administrator of the law. Strict to the letter, Thornton is, except where you are concerned. Have you a more personal relationship with him, Miss Hale?"

She met his eyes in silence, her teeth shut tightly against any response which might slip by her vigilantly sealed lips. He studied her manner for a moment. He had not risen to the rank of inspector without a powerful sense of intuition, and this woman's body language triggered every faculty he possessed.

"You know, Miss Hale," he uncrossed his arms and leaned them conversationally upon his knees, "I have the greatest respect for Thornton. It was his recommendation which secured my position. Without his word, I would likely still be patrolling the neighborhoods. So, you see, I owe him my gratitude."

Margaret inclined her head lightly in acknow-ledgement of the compliment to her John. Mason observed her for a moment, then continued.

"Thornton has a solid reputation. His word is gold in this town, Miss Hale. He is known everywhere as impartial and unwavering, even to his own detriment." He paused and his gaze bored into her. "I would hate to think of him throwing that reputation away."

"He has not done so," she countered neutrally. "What has Mr Thornton done to cast suspicion upon himself?"

Mason looked down at his hands, rubbing them thoughtfully together. "Nothing, so far as I know. You must understand, however, that for a magistrate to insist- twice- that the investigation of a certain person is not warranted... well, you can see why it gives me pause. I would not be the only one, either, if our entire history here were known."

Margaret threw her head back in contempt. "You are threatening me?"

"I need information, Miss Hale, and one way or another, I must learn all that you know. You are protecting someone or something, and Thornton is protecting you. I cannot simply take your word that it has nothing to do with this fraud until I know the whole truth. I will investigate every detail I can find about you, your family, and your connection to Thornton if you do not come out with it."

"My affairs are my own, Mr Mason!" she lashed out hotly, forgetting for the moment John's stern admonition against losing her temper. "I have done nothing untoward, and Mr Thornton is a friend of our family who has only attempted to protect my honour from further defamation of this sort!"

Mason sighed and rose. "I will look in again tomorrow, Miss Hale. I do hope you have something useful to tell me by then. It would trouble me in the extreme if I had to investigate the man who has been a mentor to me."

Margaret took a cleansing breath, willing her ruffled sensibilities back to order. "I cannot imagine you will find that necessary, sir."

Mason slid back into his coat at the door, then, taking his hat, turned back to her. "One thing more, Miss Hale. Clearly you do have some manner of relationship with the Drapers, as well as Mr Thornton. I would beg you to consider that in the absence of actual facts, people will assume the worst."

She arched her posture with the last burst of her indignation before her feelings of shame overcame her. "Good day, Mr Mason."

~

Thornton was faring no better on this afternoon. He had limped his painful way home, too hot and anxious to endure a bumping carriage ride. He cursed himself a thousand times over for the fool he had made of himself in Margaret's drawing room. After that spectacle, it would be a wonder if Mason did not uncover every detail of Margaret's past- including her brother! He swore bitterly under his breath.

Poor Frederick Hale had not thwarted the long, dispassionate arm of the navy for so long, only to be carelessly betrayed by some rash lover of his younger sister! He shook his head, mercilessly cutting down on his own lip with his teeth. On the surface, the case of a mutineer seemed rather plain.

Knowing the Hale family and their sense of compassionate loyalty as he did, however, he could well justify the fellow's reckless endangerment of his own life. He almost laughed, despite himself, imagining a bolder, masculine version of Margaret. He might like to meet such a man! Someday, perhaps, when all of this was over and Margaret was his wife.... He scowled at the ground.

The best defence of Margaret and her lost brother that he could conjure was to delay the investigation. He had absolutely no doubt that in time, Margaret would be exculpated of any blame in the matter of the fraudulent charity, but what was revealed before that time was a matter of great concern. It might be a few days yet before they would have word back from Margaret's attorney friend, and that was assuming her former admirer was willing to help.

Aside from going to Mason himself and confessing his engagement to Margaret, he was not sure of another way to stall the investigation- and he was not even certain that such a profession would improve matters. It could be that he would only damage his own creditability, as Margaret had feared.

The only other option to tickle his thoughts was mortifying... unthinkable! The solitary outside party who might be made to speak the truth of Margaret's affiliation with the Drapers was... his face crumpled in revulsion. Genevieve Hamilton.

He rejected the thought immediately. That was his last resort.

~

"Papa, what were all of those inspectors doing here before?" Genevieve Hamilton had been forbidden to stir from her rooms today, for no reason at all that she could discern. She had at last obtained an audience with her father, and she was simply crawling with curiosity over the matter.

Her father rose from his office chair and stood to look out of the window. "Nothing to concern yourself with, my dear. How did your piano studies go today?"

"Papa! I beg you, please tell me! Has Rupert done something amiss?"

The elder Hamilton scoffed. "Probably, but he was not the subject of the inspectors' questions. They came asking about some friends of yours."

"Friends of mine? Papa, surely not! I have no friends who could cause any such disturbance!"

"No?" he turned round, his fingers smugly hooked into his waistcoat. "Not Emmeline Draper or Margaret Hale?"

She tilted her head, stunned. "Why, no, Father! My, but they cannot stand one another! I do feel badly on that account," she exhaled wistfully.

After that humiliating conversation in the dress shop, she had been too ashamed to seek out either of them again- in fact, she had scarcely left the house for weeks, citing a nonexistent cough. She had been riddled with guilt, knowing that she owed Margaret an apology, but she had lacked the courage to offer it. Her sense of jealousy had been far stronger than her conviction, and she had been powerless to act even on that, with Mrs Thornton a witness to her disgrace. Surely *he* despised her now! And then there had been that awful accident at the mill, leaving him broken and ruined! No, it had been best for her to quietly disappear for a time.

"Oh, you needn't feel badly for Miss Hale," her father was laughing. "Nor Emmeline Draper! They are quite comfortable enough, I daresay."

"Papa, please tell me what you mean!"

Still chuckling to himself, he tossed her the newspaper and she caught it rather awkwardly. "The Drapers are doubtless on their way back to Italy with a tidy fortune. As for Margaret Hale, we shall soon see what she is made of."

Genevieve read in staggering disbelief; how her oldest school friend and her new husband had fleeced the residents of the city and any number of wealthy donors, and how Margaret Hale was implicated in the whole sordid business. Grief and remorse shattered her. "Oh, Papa! I cannot believe it!" she cried brokenly.

"Fascinating, is it not?" he queried.

"I cannot credit any of it! I thought I knew Emmeline!"

He chortled. "We may think we know a good number of people. I always thought there was a callousness about that woman. She has done rather curiously, I must say."

Something intriguing in his tone caught her attention. "You knew of this?"

"Me? I had some hints before it broke. That is the extent of my involvement. It was rather timely information, particularly as regards Miss Hale."

Genevieve shook her head vigorously. "Margaret would have had nothing to do with all of this, I can vouch for that!"

"Can you?" His bushy eyebrows jumped challengingly. She shrank somewhat. "In any case, it matters little whether she was actually involved or not. It buys me the time I need, and for that I am thankful."

"Time for what, Papa?"

"Time to get Thornton's head straight! Unless I miss my guess, the 'virtuous and upright' Margaret Hale will leave him holding his hat. Those thoroughbred maids are peculiar like that," he shrugged, smiling. "Do you still fancy Thornton, my girl?"

Genevieve blanched in apprehension. "Papa, what have you done?"

"Offered him an opportunity, that is all. I think he will find it appealing, once the besotted fog clears from his thinking. Ho, my girl, you should see your face! You need not fear for Margaret Hale; she will be well looked-after, but Thornton is mine. He will come round, you will see, and greatly to his own advantage I daresay."

"I did not want to be forced upon him!" she began to whimper. "Papa, can you not understand?"

"Bah, no one is forcing him to do anything! Ten days, that is my guess. A fortnight at the outside. He will want to speak to you alone, I should think, so take care to look well. The poor man will be wanting some feminine comfort." Hamilton turned back to the window.

Genevieve Hamilton, sensing the interview was over, rose numbly and made her way to her own room. What power had her father over the willful and magnetic John Thornton? She could not imagine the man caving to her father's demands simply because Margaret Hale's honour had been impugned in the paper. What more was there to all of this?

Perhaps, she mused, her father believed Margaret had something to hide, and that she would rather flee the public eye than withstand scrutiny. She had family elsewhere; might she not leave Milton for good to live quietly with them? Might she betray and hurt John Thornton in the process? A spark of possessive conceit flickered in her bosom. How dare the woman! Could Thornton really return to her, if Margaret Hale were to abandon him as her father expected?

She took a seat at her vanity and wiped her indignant tears. Blinking into her mirror, she realized that her fit of pique had done her appearance no good at all. Her brown eyes glinting in resolve, she lifted her chin and reached for her cosmetics jar. Whatever did happen, she would be at her best... just in case.

~

"Henry!" Margaret hurried to the drawing room, her cheeks becomingly rosy, when Dixon announced to her that she had a caller. "I did not expect you so soon!"

Henry Lennox rose stiffly, his expression tight. "Good afternoon, Miss Hale."

Margaret slowed her approach, the hand she had outstretched in greeting lowering in sorrow. The formality of his address grieved her. "I- I am glad you have come," she finished softly.

He pressed his lips together. "I saw the papers yesterday. I thought you might need some advice."

"Oh. Did you not receive my letter, then?"

His hand, still holding his legal case, twitched involuntarily. "I did. Just as I was leaving it arrived. I read it on my journey."

"I see." She lowered her gaze. She had wondered how Henry would take the news of her engagement to John. Apparently, not very well.

Henry frowned, shifted his grip on his legal case, and looked anywhere but at her. "Your cousin sends her condolences on this unfortunate circumstance."

Margaret's eyes snapped back up. "That is good of her! I was worried how it was all received."

"Your aunt, I fear, has taken it somewhat worse."

"Oh, dear," she groaned. "I am so very sorry to have vexed my aunt! Surely this will cause her some difficulties among her friends." Margaret's expression was so heartbroken, her familiar voice so gentle and sincere, that Henry's own manner softened in sympathy.

"Come, Miss Hale, we shall find a way to clear it all up. Perhaps if you start at the beginning."

Margaret offered her old friend a seat and some refreshments and slowly went over the details of her acquaintance with the Drapers. He listened attentively, jotting down a few notes as she spoke. "And this inspector," he clarified as he wrote, "what reason has he to doubt your word? I cannot imagine him pressing a lady so!"

Margaret hesitated. "When Frederick was here, just as he was boarding the train to come see you in London, someone who knew him saw him and attacked him. The man died later, and I had been recognized at the station with Frederick, so they came to ask me some questions. I was afraid to lead them back to Frederick...."

Henry narrowed his eyes. "You lied? Margaret, I am surprised at you," he blurted, slipping back to their old informal ways.

"I am heartily ashamed of it still, but I was so afraid for Frederick I did not know what to do!"

"What happened after that?"

"The doctors found that Leonards had died of some long-time ailment which had nothing to do with Frederick. The... the magistrate on the case called off the investigation."

Henry's frame stilled. "Would that be Thornton?"

She swallowed hard and nodded.

He pinned her with an exacting stare, allowing her to squirm under his unflinching gaze for a long minute. "Margaret, I will ask you this only once. Do you owe this Thornton anything? Are you a willing party to this engagement? So help me, Margaret, if that man holds anything over you...."

"Oh, no, Henry!" Scandalized, she almost laughed in astonishment at his assumptions. "I care very deeply for Mr Thornton. I... I know how it must appear to you. I would not have wished to... to cause you any pain, but that is the truth."

He stared back at her for another moment, as if trying to determine whether she were in earnest. Just then, the front knocker sounded. Both were relieved enough to interrupt their tense conversation to receive the caller, though Margaret feared and expected Mason once more.

It was John who soon walked round the corner. He stopped in surprise upon seeing another man standing so closely to his beloved Margaret. Lost for words, and still somewhat faint from his long walk, he merely glared back in wary silence.

"John!" Sensing all the more the awkwardness of the situation, Margaret rushed to his side- though not without a backward glance at her other caller. "John, you ought not have come!" she chided protectively.

He turned his raised brow on her. "Would you prefer to be alone with your guest?"

She shot him an annoyed glance. "Henry Lennox," she spoke crisply, with a firmness meant to chasten his flash of jealousy, "this is my fiancé, John Thornton."

The two men squared off across the room, taking opposite seats and observing one another guardedly. Margaret sighed in exasperation. What more confirmation did either of them need of her loyalties? She chose a seat nearer to John than to Henry, and noted some of the tension leaving his features.

They spent an uncomfortable half hour discussing the particulars of the Draper case, but slowly she watched the two men lower their defences. She was proud of them both, by the time they had done, and of the keen intellects and legal understanding each possessed. What a relief that they both wished to come to her aid!

"Well, Miss Hale," Henry, who had returned to formality when John had appeared, gathered his papers to depart. "I cannot stop an inquest at this point, but I can insist that I be present to defend you. I have already drafted a letter to Mr Mason, asking him to defer some days so that I may gather information. Davenport I intend to visit right now, to have that same conversation. I might recommend that you do not speak to the inspectors alone any further." He leveled an accusing glance at John, as though blaming him for not taking up constant residency in her drawing room during this crisis.

"Also," he continued with a measure of forced cheer, "I hear things at the club. Nothing of substance, usually, but I will keep a sharp ear about me. Many of us have our suspicions about that account the Drapers drew the money from, but of course we have no evidence. It is likely that it will come to nothing, but it cannot hurt to look into it."

"Lennox," John came forward, extending his hand. "I thank you for your efforts. I understand this is an unlikely situation in which to find yourself, but Margaret trusts in you. I am grateful to you, sir."

Henry checked himself, then hesitantly took John's hand. His voice was gruff and uncertain when he replied. "Take care of Miss Hale, sir." He departed quickly, without looking over his shoulder as the door closed behind him.

Margaret scowled at him rather convincingly. "You needn't have glared quite so menacingly, John."

He turned to her, somewhat shame-faced. "Was I truly such an ogre?"

"I thought I was looking at your mother for a moment!"

"That was harsh, Margaret," he pouted, a boyish gleam in his eye. "Come now, I am sure this Henry Lennox is a decent enough fellow. Forgive me, Love, but we primitives have to make our presence felt from time to time. I suppose I was a *little* unfriendly at first."

She lifted her chin scornfully. "A little! We are fortunate he did not leave immediately!"

He tugged her close, startling a little laugh from her. "Indeed. And I suppose I cannot blame the man for losing his heart to you. I hope for his sake he will recover without medical intervention. For myself, I fear it is a terminal condition, and I shall need daily treatments for the rest of my life."

Chapter Thirty-Six

The atmosphere in Milton became steadily more strained. Nicholas Higgins had begun reporting regularly to Thornton, justifying the exchange of information by stating flatly that he was looking out for "Miss Marg'et's int'rests". Indeed, there appeared good cause for concern.

Margaret could not leave the house without feeling herself the focal point of public disdain. Working class families who had been friendly with her before now refused to meet her eyes. Middle class men and women would openly sneer at her, and more than once she heard loudly voiced comments behind her back. After two heartrending forays into town, Margaret tearfully vowed that she would not stir abroad again until the paper had vindicated her.

The very next day, however, she could not remain home to pace her own house alone, and so she set off once more for the Higgins' residence. She disliked being seen walking to Marlborough Mills just now. Though John dismissed her concerns as paltry, she could not bear the thought that her own public excoriation might extend to him. It was bad enough for Higgins that he had been seen with her! He was close-lipped about it, but she knew that he had hotly assailed at least one group of workers whispering about her. What they had been saying, she could only imagine, but she felt badly that he had become involved at all.

Mason had not come again, to her relief. Apparently Henry's legal missive had done its work, for she received a note from Mr Davenport stating only that they were gathering evidence and would inform her of the date of the inquest. Margaret's fears, however, only continued to grow.

She was not fool enough to think that Mason had abandoned his line of questioning. Were she in his place, she would scarcely have done less! Her answers looked incriminating, and there was no denying it. So worried was she that she had even prevailed upon John not to visit her for a few days, and even to delay the reading of the banns.

He had accepted her mandate with as little grace as might be expected, but what was he to do against her determination? He had troubles enough of his own, for he was beginning to receive replies to his employment inquiries. None were encouraging. He had known he would need to be patient, but he had hoped for a little more favour from the other industrialists within his circles.

Thus, it was with the most profound humility that he stood to one side and watched Watson, his future brother-in-law, draw acclaim and widespread ovation as his rail speculation bore fruit. Overnight, Watson's investors had nearly tripled their original outlay, and Watson himself was declared a financial wizard. Chagrined though he was, Thornton looked ahead now with some measure of hope. Perhaps after their good fortune, those who could not be prevailed upon to lend a farthing might be more openhanded with their purses and their plans to expand their businesses.

It was not to be. The hospital fraud, the loss of Marlborough Mills, and the stagnant economy in general had touched more than one chord within the city. Those with money clutched it all the more tightly, while those without grew louder and more desperate. The Weaver's Union was on the verge of an unprecedented January strike over Hamper's and Slickson's slipshod hiring of his former workers, and the unceremonious layoffs of others. It was unlikely that they would be able to agree even on the strike, however, as there was so much infighting that nothing was ever settled upon.

Ten days after the headlines about the hospital fraud first broke, he collapsed wearily into his old desk in the mill. He had not been up to his office since the day of the explosion. Achingly he massaged his sore ribs. He was mending, though not nearly fast enough for his taste.

He squinted his eyes, casting them over the silent machinery down below. Everything was at a standstill, yet the world was marching on without him. He had never in his life felt so impotent, so shackled by his circumstances. As a youth struggling to cast off his father's shadow, he had a clear adversary. The blight upon his prospects, the pall cast over his mother, had galvanized his resolve into something tremendous and productive. Anger had evolved into ambition, and that driving compulsion had powered him for sixteen years.

Now... he released a long breath. He felt old. No, not quite old. Not young, either. He still itched to work, to make, to do with his hands! He longed to continue striving against the careless life of ease he had forever disdained. The complacency of middle age loomed before him though, and the allure of domestic comfort was a siren call to his maturing manhood. His highest purpose, if he were completely frank, was a quiet family life with Margaret by his side, his mother delighting in her grandchildren, and many years to reap the rewards of his early labours. He pressed his fingers into his eyes. If only there were something left of all he had wrought!

Even his reputation had failed him. No one was looking for what he had to offer, and even if they were, they would think twice before taking him on. His hiring of the Irish workers all of those months ago caused unease among masters and workers alike, none of whom would savour any immediate struggles of the kind.

He would never confess as much to Margaret, but he also sensed that some of her fears were justified. Their relationship had not gone completely unnoticed, despite her dashed precautions. What doubt had been cast upon his character he could not say, but the bright hope of readily finding some other suitable employment had already met an untimely demise.

Not for the first time, he began to wonder what his options with Hamilton truly were. If he signed the blasted employment contract and married Margaret anyway, what could the man do to him? He might remain with the mill- *his* mill- but he would see it suffer under the direction of a fool. The next five years of his life would be consigned to another, but at the end at least some of his debts would be satisfied. Had it not taken that much time and more the first time he tunneled from under the dark burden of debt?

He rose at last, surveying what was left of his domain with a final parting look. No matter the cost, he did not trust Hamilton, and could not commit himself to the contract. He and Margaret would simply have to continue in their patience, praying that in the end, all would be set right.

~

Margaret had a few letters from Henry, all assuring her that he was doing what he could from London and would be returning to Milton for the inquest. She could not understand why the date had not yet been set, as the inspectors had seemed so intent upon it to begin with. The papers still shouted forth their empty snippets of progress in the case, but more often than not, Margaret still found her name listed among the primary leads back to the Drapers.

Oh, how she ached for John during those days! She had come to crave his touch, to take her sustenance from his well-loved voice in her ears and her heart's revival from his secure arms wound tightly around her. How was it that one person, once so foreign and incomprehensible to her, had so completely possessed her inmost being?

This present forcible separation was costing her much rest. Her appetite was gone entirely, and her only waking thoughts were to find some way to resolve this whole despicable affair and get back to John's embrace where she belonged. Her father and Dixon both clucked over her with worried frowns, but Margaret brushed off their concerns without explanation.

She valiantly fought to be strong and patient, unshaken by the tides of fortune- much as she pictured John might have been as the newly christened head of his family- but inwardly, she was disconsolate. If this, she once thought mournfully, was even the slightest measure of the agony she had inflicted upon him at her first refusal, she was indeed the most wretched of women!

It was more than a week since she had last seen John. She lingered in her drawing room this morning, her eyes blurred with feeling, remembering the first time he had kissed her in here... and the last... and each tender touch in between. She bowed her head, her shoulders shaking.

A short while later, Dixon thumped into the room. "Miss," she interrupted kindly, "that inspector fellow is back."

Margaret sniffed, wiping her eyes and trying to compose herself. Henry had cautioned her against speaking with the inspector alone, but anything was better than this hopeless waiting! Perhaps Mason brought news. John thought him an honest enough man in general, did he not? She drew herself up. "Show him in, please, Dixon."

Mason entered with due courtesy. "Good morning, Miss Hale."

"Good morning, Inspector. Have you any new information on the case?" Her voice trembled with the faintest hint of eagerness, and she clenched her nails into her palms.

"Perhaps, Miss Hale. May I?" He gestured to a seat, and Margaret readily assented. This was going to be a serious conversation indeed! Tense with apprehension, she took a seat herself.

"I have been in touch with your attorney, Miss Hale. He has provided a number of character references, which certainly aid in your defence."

Her lids lowered in a tightly controlled approximation of a nod. "He has kept me informed, sir."

"Yes." Mason drew a written statement from a leather portfolio he carried. "I have reviewed the information your attorney sent us with Mr Davenport and Mr Crawley. They feel as I do, Miss Hale," he paused to ensure her full attention. "We feel that against the weight of this case, these general statements- excellent as they are- are not sufficient to clear your character."

Margaret nearly sagged in disappointment, but caught herself. "I do not understand, Mr Mason. What capability or motive could I possibly have had to participate in such a scheme?"

"There is always a motive where that much money is concerned, Miss Hale! We feel that when combined with your previous reticence- I apologize, Miss Hale, but it was necessary to lay what I knew before my associates- we feel that there is enough cause to suspect that you may have long possessed more knowledge of the particulars than you claim."

"That is preposterous!" she cried. "My mother had only just passed away! What manner of corruption could I have possibly entertained?"

He cleared his throat. "Miss Hale, we all have superiors to whom we must answer. If we do not perform our duties faithfully, we betray the public's trust. I have to consider all options here."

She cooled, lifting her chin. "What more do you require then, Inspector? There must be some specific assurance you desire from me, or you would not have come here today."

His mouth twitched. "I need you to prove my suspicions unfounded."

Margaret gazed back in that open, quiet way of hers, forcing him to reveal more without speaking herself.

"Miss Hale," Mason continued, "as I mentioned, I grew suspicious that you were covering something several months ago, but I am willing to concede that it may indeed have been of a personal nature and wholly unconnected to all of this. In interviewing other witnesses, one in particular gave a statement which could either acquit or convict you. It depends on you."

Margaret's eyes narrowed, but she held her tongue. She was beginning to learn the power of silence, and she was determined that this experienced agent would not draw more from her than she willingly confessed.

"What is the true nature of your relationship with Mr Thornton?" Mason asked bluntly. "I would ask you to clarify that for me, Miss Hale."

She blinked, her lips parted, but she hesitated. What was his purpose in asking such a question?

"More to the point," he continued, accurately reading her indecision, "if you truly are innocent of wrongdoing, Miss Hale, Mr Thornton need not protect you as he has done. It looks to others as though you and he both know something dangerous. Now, I have a very credible witness with a clear testimony who is willing to swear that your connection to the fraud was truly blameless, as you claim, but only if you relinquish ties to Thornton."

She stared, incredulous. "Pardon me?" she scoffed. "Why, what could you hope to prove by such a request?"

"That your relationship with Thornton is also innocent. My witness had no hesitation in confirming that you had only recently become acquainted with the Drapers, but the discovery of a prior incident in your recent history cast doubts once again. We do not know," he raised his brows with the air of one giving instruction, "the full extent of this scandal. We know there had been much planning and there are certainly others involved.

"It looks bad to my superiors, Miss Hale. If I can prove that you and Thornton also are mere passing acquaintances and have no serious ties, I can satisfy their questions and I will be able to persuade my witness to swear to your innocence."

"I cannot believe this!" she cried, her shock and grief turning painfully in her stomach.

"It makes sense," Mason shrugged, but not without feeling. "I would hate to have to call Mr Thornton's honour into question just now. Traumatic event like a boiler sabotage... financial ruin... there are the more suspicious among my superiors who might make unwarranted accusations against him, Miss Hale," he finished softly.

With sudden clarity, Margaret's eyes flashed and her cheeks grew livid. "Your witness is Mr Hamilton, is he not?"

Mason paled, shrinking somewhat. "I am not at liberty to reveal that information."

"Yet *he* is at liberty to manipulate me!" she snapped, her bitter anguish goading her temper. "He is a coward, hiding behind his veil of anonymity and leaving a lady exposed to his derision!"

Mason straightened, adjusting his cravat nervously. "Mr Davenport also found the condition on the statement reasonable. We would not ask our witness to pledge in all confidence without allowing him to confirm that he had not overlooked some crucial detail."

"Mr Mason, you are being used!" she pronounced contemptuously. "Mr Hamilton is moving you about a chess board, and you have proven a most obliging pawn."

"Miss Hale, these accusations are out of line!" he objected. "I have a witness whose testimony is strong enough to clear your name, allowing us to avoid the inquest and publicly vindicate you! All we ask is that you demonstrate by a show of good faith that you are not involved in any sort of secrecy. Distance yourself from Mr Thornton, and they will credit your word as the truth!"

Margaret rose, her wrath causing her to compose herself with all stately grace rather than to fly into a fury. "Mr Mason, I believe you should go now."

He gesticulated his frustration with this stubborn woman and stood, frowning and shaking his head. His countenance at once turned to something more humane.

"Miss Hale, I am serious," he almost pleaded. "Davenport means to investigate Thornton if he cannot first clear you. He will find nothing- you and I both know it- but I would not see his good name destroyed! I have too high a regard for Thornton, and I suspect you do as well."

Margaret paused, her façade crumbling. "What must I do?" her voice quavered.

Mason looked her directly in the eye. "Leave town, Miss Hale, in a modest way. Find some ailing relative to visit- something plausible and not extravagant, lest it be wondered where you obtained the funds. Let this all quiet down, but for mercy's sake, do not be seen with Thornton! Do not even correspond with him if you can help it, for you may be assured that you are both being carefully watched."

Margaret's eyes flooded once more and her throat closed up. She could scarcely speak, but in her suffering she choked out, "We are to be married!"

Mason closed his eyes and drew a remorseful breath. "I am sorry, Miss Hale, though I suspected it to be the case. I will keep that much to myself, but the fact remains that at present, you can only harm him. Come back and marry the man later, if you must, but bide your time for now. I wish I could do more for you, Miss Hale."

He turned to go, replacing his hat at the door. Margaret had followed, despondent and trembling in disbelief. "Mr Mason," she stopped him before his hand touched the latch, "are you quite sure? Truly, this is the only way?"

His mouth quirked into a sympathetic frown. "I am sorry, Miss Hale, but I see no clearer path before you. You are being offered a painless solution, legally. I might suggest that it is in both of your best interests to see the papers printing your innocence and restoring your reputation, and the sooner the better."

He tipped his hat to the lady and closed the door behind himself. He stopped on the steps to the house, shaking a little himself, and feeling dirty, shoddy, and used. He was absolutely certain that the lady was correct in her assessment of Mr Hamilton, and his clear, honest devotion to his duty was now besmirched by another man's ambitions- whatever they were.

Where it would all lead, he could not say, but he had given Miss Hale the best advice he had to offer. He earnestly did hope that suspicion would fall away from both her and Mr Thornton, for he truly esteemed the man. And that woman! His brows jumped in an appreciative sigh as he made his methodical way down the steps of the house.

Rarely had he been required to interrogate women- it was unseemly, not at all fitting. Still, never had one held herself so remarkably well as Margaret Hale. She was cool passion, controlled fire, and he had never before seen the like. The lady might have indeed possessed her secrets, but if Thornton was privy to them, he was a lucky man.

Chapter Thirty-Seven

The following afternoon, John received a caller of his own. Hamilton was shown into John's study, where he found the other reverently looking over his bookshelves, and dividing the items he wished to keep from those which could be sold. The once perfectly ordered study was littered with packing crates and stacks of waste papers to be burned.

"Well, Thornton, I must say, you are being rather hasty," Hamilton chided as he entered.

John glanced up in surprise at the intrusion. "How did you get in here?" he snapped coldly.

"The lease passed into my name only this morning," Hamilton informed him nonchalantly. "Your house maid learned a moment ago that I am her new employer."

Thornton's lip curled, but he made no response as he turned back to his task.

"I say, where will you go?" Hamilton pressed. "Not many options for a man of your station at a low rent."

John remained silent, biting down on his own tongue for fear that he might disgrace himself by an ill-conceived retort.

"Oh, I see," Hamilton jeered. "You think to take employment with Hamper? Leeds is a nice place, they say."

"I think you know that is impossible," Thornton returned with an edge to his voice.

Hamilton crossed his arms. "Oh, come, now Thornton! What will you do, move in down the row from your workers? Rent a room from Watson and your sister? That would surely be a harmonious arrangement!"

John's tongue was bleeding by now. The truth was, he hadn't the faintest idea where he would go! Even the imperfect notion of temporarily sheltering in the Hale's household could not work, as he and Margaret had yet to share their vows. *Margaret...* how he had missed her these last days! Even a note would have been some comfort, but he had been denied even that.

Hamilton was growing impatient. "Thornton!" he thundered. "Turn round and speak with me like a man!"

Turning over the pair of books he held, John reluctantly dropped them into the nearest crate and faced the other.

"There, that's better. Let there be no enmity between us, Thornton. I see no reason why we cannot work out some reasonable solution. You have a mother, and for yet a while longer a sister to care for. I see no reason why we cannot strike a compromise. I need your experience, and you need a living."

"That is not the limit of your demands," Thornton bit out. "What is it to be next?"

Hamilton rolled his eyes and exhausted a histrionic sigh. "I am not your enemy, Thornton! I wish to partner with you!"

"I have not the right temperament for your sort of partnership, Hamilton."

Hamilton stalked closer, his face taking on a reddish hue. "This is still about that little tart of yours, isn't it? I told you I don't care what you do with her, so long as you do not marry her!"

"You would have me enter this disgraceful union with your daughter and shame the woman I love- a *gentleman's* daughter, Hamilton! I would never be able to look her in the eye. I would be justly unworthy to even speak to her!"

"You self-righteous prig!" the businessman hissed ominously. "You would throw over the good of hundreds and- dare I venture so far- the future of this town's economic growth! Marlborough Mills is a key, both now and in the decades to come!"

"Then why are you so determined to have me?" Thornton spat. "What other master could not run this mill for you just as effectively? You will forgive my lingering cynicism on this point, for I have yet the sense that you know something which I do not."

"What if I do?" Hamilton folded his arms once more. "It will do you little good unless you choose to work with me."

Thornton clenched his fists, his ire building to a head, but abruptly turned back to his books. "No, Hamilton," he repeated firmly.

"That Hale woman," Hamilton suggested to his back. "Quite a shame how the Drapers set her up to distract the inspectors. Rather unfair, do you not think?"

Thornton only flipped over another book to examine the title and dropped it in a crate. He was not even certain whether the book had landed with the items he wished to keep or had decided to sell.

"I was talking to that young inspector- Mason, I think his name was. Did you know he has had dealings with your Miss Hale before? Something about her being rather uncooperative with a previous investigation of his? Oh! That is right, you did know, for you were the magistrate involved."

Thornton turned around, his eyes narrowed menacingly. Hamilton smiled, satisfied to have regained the other's attention.

"You were a fool to interfere, Thornton," Hamilton murmured quietly. "Now, you both look questionable."

Thornton shot out an accusing finger, his face white. "I was under the impression, Hamilton, that the findings of ongoing investigations are confidential!"

"They are, and then again they are not. It all depends on how badly the inspectors need information, and, you see, Davenport and I go back a long way. They thought my testimony regarding Miss Hale's acquaintance with the Drapers rather valuable, but upon hearing Mr Mason's history with the lady, I became hesitant to swear to what I knew."

"How dare-"

"I have just come from Davenport's office," Hamilton cut him off. "I was relieved to discover that the inspectors have been able to clarify some of their prior concerns. It made me quite comfortable enough to testify to her innocence. After all, she could not have known any secret details before meeting the Drapers, now could she?"

Thornton's expression became deathly livid, his rage only scarcely contained. "*You would threaten a woman, sir?*" he stormed.

"Threaten!" Hamilton scoffed. "I *helped* her! Her name will be cleared by tomorrow, so long as she has the sense to act prudently."

His eyes wide and staring in outrage, Thornton pushed past the older man and fairly ran for the door.

"I wouldn't do that, Thornton!" Hamilton called after him. "I can always express second thoughts about my statement!"

Thornton turned, his entire body quivering with unspent rage.

Hamilton nodded. "Aye, Thornton, and I will do it too, if you go near her! The lady is most sensible, and I think must have some very good reason for not welcoming further investigation."

"You- you *despot!*" Thornton bellowed. Name calling was beneath him, but the fire of his Teutonic ancestors roiled and simmered in his veins and his vision glazed over in something very close to abject hatred. Had he his full strength, he would verily have thrashed the older man against the bookshelves and systematically fed him the pages of that cursed contract!

Hamilton's boldness flagged as he began to recognize the very real physical danger he was in. He had meant only to pressure Thornton into compliance, not incite the hostility of a sleeping giant. The towering wrath of the imposing, powerful man who was closing in on him actually caused him to fall back a step, his hands held up in unconscious entreaty.

"Now, just a minute, Thornton!" Hamilton's voice cracked slightly. "It was not I who persuaded Miss Hale to involve herself in that ridiculous campaign! The lady did quite enough on her own! Her reputation is safe for now, but you know as well as I that she cannot afford to lose what security she has found. Take my advice; leave her be!"

Thornton ceased his threatening advance, his fists clenched and his chest heaving. One thing Hamilton had said, which he could not have possibly known before, struck a bitter string of guilt in his heart. *He* had encouraged Margaret to investigate on her own, despite his misgivings, and his folly had cost her dearly!

Hamilton saw only a slight banking of the fire in Thornton's eyes, but could not discern the cause. Sucking in a great draught of air, he recovered his composure. "I give you until tomorrow at noon, Thornton. Be at my door ready to sign the contract and speak to my daughter. If you do not do so, tomorrow evening's papers will read quite differently about your Miss Hale."

He self-consciously dusted off his shoulders, shrugging from his conscience the monstrous demands he had just made of the man, and swiftly left the house.

John's tall figure crumpled. His ire was replaced quickly with insurmountable grief. What had Hamilton forced Margaret to do? What would be the outcome if he ran to her now to learn the truth? He covered his face in his hands and gave way to heaving, gasping sobs of fear.

If only he could gather her in his arms, to know that she was safe and to ask her what she would have of him! Even now, if he knew she were well protected, he could have boldly defied all that Hamilton would do. He would run with her to Scotland, marry her that very evening beneath the anvil, and settle in some quiet corner of the world- far from newspapers and business rivals and labour unions and cotton. To the devil with all of them!

"John?" His mother's soothing voice soaked through his cares and roused him from his anguish. He slowly raised his eyes to hers, his face streaming with hot tears.

Hannah was pale, her dark eyes hollow in sympathetic misery. "Son John," she urged, "tell me what is your trouble!"

His chest shuddered as he heaved for a refreshing breath. "Hamilton has threatened Margaret!" he rasped.

Hannah's jaw set grimly. "She is strong, John. She would not have you waver in your determined course."

"But what is that, Mother? I know not which path to choose. All before me seems equally out of the question! I cannot endanger her, and yet I cannot align myself with that miscreant! I see no other option!"

"*John,*" Hannah's voice took on a sudden brittleness. "Where is my brave son, who made a way when there was none? There are always other options!"

Jarred from his self-pity by his mother's sternness, he stared blankly at her for a moment. His head shook vaguely. "I know not what it might be."

"You will find a way, John," his mother faithfully maintained.

"Would that I could see her! I must know what she is thinking, what I can do!"

"You would not change whatever she has determined, John. If you dare not go to her now, then do as you can. Have faith in her, my son, and do not yield to dishonour, no matter the temptation."

His breath was coming slower now, his thinking beginning to clear. His mother's simple truths resonated in his heart and some of the belligerent tautness left his muscles. "Mother," said he, very softly, "It seems that no matter my struggles, you have always possessed the knack for turning my mind back to the heart of the affair."

"There are very few things which truly matter, John. Guide your steps by what is right and noble, and do not allow yourself to become distracted by other grievances."

As she was speaking, an inspired light began to flicker in his eyes. "Hamilton expected me at his door tomorrow morning," he mused, almost under his breath.

"Then," she furnished him with a sage, if not devious smile, "you had best not disappoint him, John."

~

"Margaret, do you still stare out of the window? Come to the nursery to see my boy!" Edith Lennox pleaded.

Margaret turned languorously, her energies sapped from her utter lack of rest. "I thought he was sleeping," she answered indifferently.

"That was two hours ago! Do come now, for he is *so* charming when he first wakes. Not all babies are, Nurse tells us, but our dear little fellow is as sweet as can be! Oh, now Margaret, you must not let all of this worry overtake you. Come and have a little merriment with us, it is bound to cheer you!"

Margaret's gaze found the window once more. "How is my aunt this afternoon?"

"Oh! You know Mama. She is tolerably well, but she does suffer so in shock. Do believe me Margaret, I am so glad that you determined at last to come to us yesterday! It was just like you, you know, to arrive without first sending word by the post."

"I made up my mind rather spontaneously," Margaret offered, her eyes following a carriage rattling past the window.

"Yes, well next time you must at least allow Mama to send Hodges to travel with you! Do you really go all about Milton by yourself, Margaret? It truly is perfectly shocking!"

"I have always been quite safe, Edith." She closed her eyes. Perhaps she had not *always* walked the streets in safety, but she had always found a stalwart protector when she had needed him. A single tear leaked between her lashes.

Edith was not the most profound young woman, but she was not insensitive to her cousin's moods. They had, after all, shared their girlhoods together in this house. Even well over a year of separation, marriage, and motherhood had not diminished the sisterly affection they shared. She stepped near, resting her hand lightly on Margaret's shoulder.

"Darling, what is it? Do you still fear for that scandal? Why, there is nothing to worry about! Henry told the captain only this morning that he felt sure some great news was about to break. You will see, it will all be forgotten soon!"

Margaret shook her head mutely, and the movement caused little trails of moisture to tumble down both cheeks.

Edith pouted, discouraged, but did not give up. "Is it this Mr Thornton that you miss?"

Margaret made no response but a deepening of the sorrow inscribed across her features.

"Oh, darling!" Edith forcibly turned her cousin around and pulled her into a sisterly embrace. "I do know how you feel. Sometimes when the captain was out on exercises I would not see him for days on end. How glad I always was when he would come home!"

A little whimper broke free in Margaret's throat. Edith's attempt at empathy was thoughtful, but the inconveniences of a comfortably married young wife seemed nothing to the uncertainties darkening her own way. She might never know the joy of seeing John come home to her!

She did not doubt his constancy, but in his absence her old feelings of unworthiness had flourished, dwarfing all of the nascent assurances of his attachment. Why, even her own aunt had distanced herself when Margaret had entered this house- a home in which she thought to find refuge! What right had she to expect John to face public censure for her- a woman who had caused him so much trouble?

"Margaret," Edith drew out her own lace handkerchief and dabbed her cousin's face. "You must not cry so, for it does fearful things to your complexion!"

Margaret could not help the choking little laugh which came forth, but it was swiftly followed by more tears. Leave it to Edith to make some silly comment like that! She sniffled and ducked her head, making it impossible for Edith to continue her ministrations.

Edith bit her pretty pink lips in thought. Some swift inspiration- she knew not whence it came- lent her new direction. "Margaret," she began hesitantly, "will you tell me about this Mr Thornton? Henry says he is a formidable-looking fellow, and a number of years older than you. Was he really a tradesman?"

"Manufacturer," Margaret corrected, her eyes turning back to the window as she swiped at a final tear.

"Well! To be sure, I never saw much difference. Oh, Margaret, you must tell me all, for I am simply dying to know what caused you to engage yourself to such a man! I never could have imagined it!"

Margaret quieted herself. Haltingly, she began to describe her history with John- how at first she had tried to despise him, but found that he had earned her respect despite her best efforts to the contrary. She could not bring herself to relate any of the particulars of the riot or his first proposal- it was too fearful and yet too wonderful to put into words! She did force herself to share the incident involving Frederick, since her shame could no longer be hidden in that case. She laughed poignantly over that uncomfortable encounter in the graveyard, and every squabble, every improvement in their understanding since that day.

As she spoke, her downtrodden spirits found some relief in reflecting back on the tender man who had won her heart. Her anguish began to wither somewhat. Come what may, the John Thornton she knew would not relinquish her without a battle! She need only be patient. He would fight, his determination and ingenuity would carry him forward, and in time she could return to him.

When that might be, she could not say. The challenges set before them both were real, but grace was the master of every injustice. Somehow, she knew not how, there would eventually come restoration. It simply had to be!

"Oh, my, Margaret," Edith was blushing as Margaret finished her narrative. "You quite make me jealous! I thought myself quite over head and ears for the captain, but I see that I am nothing next to you! I had supposed you might forget him now that you are in London, for poor Henry would like to marry you, you know, but I think you are hopelessly lost."

She sighed theatrically and her light fingers flicked about the disturbed lace at Margaret's collar.

"Well," Edith brightened again and clasped Margaret's hand. "That's enough of all of that. Come, Sholto will be not nearly so enchanting once he grows hungry, so you must come see him now!"

Chapter Thirty-Eight

"**M**iss Hamilton, please." John gave his hat to the butler as he stepped into the elegantly appointed home.

"She is in the drawing room, Mr Thornton," the man informed him, "but Mr Hamilton desired to speak with you immediately upon your arrival."

"I am afraid my business is with *Miss* Hamilton first," John insisted with a winsome smile. "I believe it is the custom to first obtain a lady's permission before approaching her father."

This seemed to give the old butler pause. He had his instructions, but he also knew his master's desire, and that was to see the couple in question come to an unimpeded arrangement. He straightened his shoulders. "This way, sir."

He followed to a sumptuously decorated room, and discovered the lady he sought. She was seated demurely by the window, the light glinting handsomely off her hair and illuminating her classical features. The door closed behind him, and he offered her his most charming smile. "Miss Hamilton. You are looking well today."

She rose, blushing most becomingly, and approached. "And you, Mr Thornton. I am glad to see you so well recovered. It has been too long since last we met."

"Indeed it has. I beg you would overlook that unforgivable lapse of time. I have been rather preoccupied."

"It is quite understandable, Mr Thornton," she looked away with fluttering lashes. "I believe you have been several times in my father's company."

"I have," he agreed. "Miss Hamilton, if I may be so blunt, I had something of rather great import to speak of with you."

Her eyes warmed. "By all means, Mr Thornton. Will you be seated?"

He bowed very slightly in acknowledgement. "Thank you, Miss Hamilton."

~

Thomas Bell grimaced sourly as he disembarked from the obnoxious, foul-smelling beast which comprised modern transportation. The convenience of quick travel was scarcely compensation for the abominable shrieking and smoking of the lumbering behemoth at the head of the train! Waving his handkerchief before his face, he wrinkled his nose in disgust at the belching stacks as he walked by. This was why he did not live in Milton. The entire city was like this!

He coughed violently as his exertions began anew. Walking always set him off this winter. For four and one half weeks he had been bed-ridden, unable to move past his own door without a crippling bout of coughing. The burning cinder now trickling into his already beleaguered lungs made up most of the breathable air in this god-forsaken place, and though he had scarcely arrived, he looked forward to his departure back to his beloved Oxford.

He hailed a cab and paid a handsome tip to a young lad who set his luggage aboard. "M-Marlborough M-Mills, please," he coughed out of the window.

Settling against the squabs, he tried to quell the rattling in his chest. It *was* good to be up and about again, but he would not have stirred even yet from his home had not the affair been an urgent one. Nothing less than securing the happiness and fortune of his beloved god-daughter could have brought him hither.

Presently the carriage rolled by the side entrance to his property. The gate stood open, unguarded and desolate. He could see even from the street the devastation to the buildings. Good heavens! Had he any notion it had been this bad, he would have forwarded Thornton some small defrayal; an instalment, as it were, on his coming good fortune. This was truly dreadful! Even if the repair work began immediately, it would be many weeks before the mill was operational again! And why had it not yet begun? He thought Hamilton was attending to that!

He sat back, berating himself and his changeable health. He ought to have done more sooner, but he had spent half of his days either doubled over gasping for breath, or drugged on morphine to ease his cough and allow him at least a brief spell of rest. Well, there was no time quite like the present to make an amend.

The carriage drew to a halt and the driver got down to help him out. Nodding his thanks, he mounted the steps and dropped the knocker on the heavy oaken door. It was opened a moment later by Mrs Thornton herself.

"Mr Bell!" She looked past him, searching perhaps to see if he had come alone. "Do come in. We had not expected you."

"You had not? Why, I wrote to Hamilton not three days ago! Oh, perhaps he wished to keep it a surprise. I am also a day or two earlier than I originally expected to be," he explained.

"Indeed," answered the slightly confused Hannah Thornton. "We have heard nothing from Mr Hamilton regarding your arrival. We knew only that your agent had seen to the transfer of the lease."

"Ah, yes, that was most regrettable," sighed Bell, but immediately his traitorous lungs seized and bent him over in a new fit of coughing.

Hannah started. She had heard that Mr Bell had been unwell, but she had assumed him to be exaggerating his complaint. It did not look to her now to be any sort of ruse- the man was truly ill. "You must come have something to drink," she ordered.

He allowed her to lead him to the drawing room and took a seat, still convulsing with every attempted breath. In a few moments, she had returned and pressed a glass of cool brandy into his hand.

"Thank you," he gasped. He drank, and soon found his throat soothed. As he began to recover somewhat, he took in his surroundings in surprise. "Why, Mrs Thornton, are you redecorating? What mean these crates of belongings?"

She gaped at him. The old fool was senile! "Mr Bell," she spoke slowly and firmly, "we must remove. The lease belongs to Mr Hamilton now."

"Well, yes, technically," he shrugged. "But that was only out of necessity, Mrs Thornton. A temporary measure, of course."

"Mr Bell, I do not see what is so temporary about it! He is taking over the mill and the entire property."

"Well, yes, in name. Thornton will go on working it, naturally. I thought that was all settled!"

"What is settled," Hannah's patience was leaving her rather quickly, "is that Mr Hamilton wished to engage John to a five-year contract and marriage to his daughter!"

Bell, who had just been taking another sip of his drink, sputtered in surprise. "I thought he was to marry my god-daughter! Why, that was the whole point!"

Hannah rolled her eyes and clamped her teeth together. "No, Mr Bell, that was not. It was John's wish, but Mr Hamilton desired otherwise."

"But Margaret wrote to me of the explosion! Oh, I confess, she did not come out directly and announce her engagement to Thornton, but... well, Mrs Thornton, I remember how they used to look at one another, and if she took it upon herself to apprise me of Thornton's affairs.... Well! You can see how I would have drawn that conclusion. Oh, I am dearly sorry if I have misread it all. Why, that changes everything!"

"Miss Hale and my son *do* wish to marry," she clarified. "Present circumstances, however, make it impossible."

His brow clouded. "Mrs Thornton, please, you make no sense. Either they intend to marry, or they do not! Do come to the point quickly, for I still have the head-ache from that dreadful train!"

She blew air through her clenched teeth. "John and Miss Hale had an understanding, but after the mill disaster and Miss Hale's unfortunate connection to that bank fraud-"

"Oh, rubbish!" interrupted the old gentleman. "That is easily dealt with, for Margaret would have had nothing to do with that! Besides, I have one or two ideas regarding that she will like very much, I think."

"Y-yes," she growled, annoyed at his disruption. "As I was saying, Mr Hamilton found the situation to his advantage. He offered a conditional witness statement in Miss Hale's behalf, provided that John renounce their engagement. He hoped to force John to a contract to work here for him and also wished to wed his own daughter to my son."

Bell lowered his glass, his face quite pale. "Mrs Thornton, are you certain?"

"Indeed I am! John was most vexed, to put it mildly."

Bell began blinking rapidly, his complexion changing colours. He cursed under his breath, entirely forgetting that he was in the presence of a lady. "I trusted him! How could he... oh! If I could lay hands on him..." he continued to mumble and sputter indictments against his associate as his thoughts jumbled together.

"Thornton would not have agreed to all of this!" he at last comfortably assured himself. "Why, he has proven his mettle before, am I not right? Hamilton may have wanted the property, but I made it clear... and Thornton to capitulate to such a demand! Mrs Thornton, what was the last thing they said to one another?"

She arched a brow, unable to follow the old codger's ramblings. "Mr Hamilton was here yesterday. They quarreled rather loudly, and he gave John until noon today to sign the contract and make an offer to Miss Hamilton, or he would denounce Miss Hale to the magistrate."

"Merciful heavens!" Bell breathed. He snatched the watch from his pocket and stared at it. "Mrs Thornton, where is he now?"

"I believe," she intoned heavily, "that he has gone to speak to Mr Hamilton. I do not know what he planned to say."

"By Jove," he wheezed. "I've not an instant to lose!"

~

The oversized door rumbled closed behind him, and Thornton stood dazed and breathless on the front steps of the massive home. It was done.

Margaret would be safe, but the cost.... Oh, the cost!

He clenched his eyes, his entire being recoiling in horror at what he had been required to do. How could he even look himself in the mirror? Slowly, leadenly, he made the heavy descent down to the street.

He watched only the wet cobblestones as he walked, his conscience too overwrought by disgrace to lift his countenance to the passersby on the street. He needed to stop first to see his mother, to reveal to her the depth to which her son had lowered himself, and then... and then to Margaret. He owed her an explanation. A pained gasp shuddered from him.

"Thornton! Thornton, by heaven, there you are!" quavered a failing voice.

He stopped and raised his head, finally noticing the hired cab bearing down upon him. A fine brown hat waved frantically from the window and a spidery grey head poked out just beside it. He squinted. "Mr Bell?"

The old man leaped athletically from the cab, but soon nearly toppled over in a fit of coughing. "Thor-" he hacked repeatedly, never managing to pronounce his full name.

Thornton rushed to his side. "Mr Bell! You should not be on the street, sir. You are very ill!"

Bell waved him off, sputtering impatiently. He held up a hand for a moment of patience, during which he exerted his whole effort to force his breathing to regulate. Shaking and white, he finally raised himself to a stooped but somewhat more upright posture. "Thornton!" he gasped. "Tell me you have not yet been to Hamilton's!"

"I have just come from there, sir," he answered thickly.

"Surely not!" the old man lamented. "I had not thought you would do so! Oh, if I had only come sooner!" Bell sagged in his weakness, his hand clutching his aching chest.

"Mr Bell," Thornton grasped the old man's upper arm. "You must mount the carriage again. I will see you back to the mill. Truly, sir, you seem very unwell."

"I am well enough at the present!" Bell snapped. "Tell me, Thornton, that you did not break my god-daughter's heart. You did not sign any contract, did you?"

John Thornton stared at the raving old academic, completely befuddled. "Break Margaret's heart? I should hope I have not! I am sorry to say that she will be most disappointed in me, though. What I asked of that poor girl-"

"But the contract!" Bell fairly pleaded. "If you spoke for that daughter of Hamilton's, I think that can be dealt with, but tell me you signed nothing!"

"Of course I did neither! I may be ruined beyond hope of recovery and have in the name of passion forsaken my dignity, but I have still some measure of my independence!"

Bell sagged against the carriage, grasping the door for support. "Thank heavens! By thunder, Thornton, had I known Hamilton would try to take you in, I should never have brought him in to all of this!"

"Mr Bell," Thornton insisted firmly, "you must return to your carriage. I fear your spirits are so agitated that you make no sense whatever."

Bell relented at last, but motioned very firmly for the younger man to accompany him. Thornton instructed the driver to return them to the mill. Once they had both settled inside, with the doors closed, Bell allowed his head to drop back against the padded seat. "Now, then, Thornton, we must first talk about the repairs to the mill. How much will the reconstruction cost, and how quickly can it be done? I think the work ought to recommence immediately, and I am sorry to find that it has not already begun!"

Thornton was kneading his brow in confusion. "Mr Bell, I have nothing further to do with Marlborough Mills. It is in Mr Hamilton's name. Even if you are put out with him now, you cannot rescind the contract!"

"I bleeding well can!" Bell raged unexpectedly, then stopped shortly as his body convulsed with more suppressed coughing.

"The terms are only temporary," Bell recovered after a moment. "My attorney spoke with the underwriters of the insurance policy and they were satisfied- as long as you were technically under the authority of another for the time being- but that agreement was to terminate as soon as the repairs were complete and you assumed proper ownership! I am afraid you will have to purchase your own policy after that, if you wish."

Thornton's head was starting to swim. "Assume ownership! Mr Bell, do forgive me sir, but I think you must lie down as soon as possible."

"Lie down! My boy, what the devil did Hamilton tell you?"

Thornton shook his head in bewilderment. "That he intended to put the business in his daughter's name, and that he would repay some of the debts the mill had incurred in exchange for a five-year agreement. He then hoped to purchase the property in the future for a pittance so that he might have his way with it."

"Bah! The scoundrel!" Bell spat. "That was all a sham, Thornton! Why, the only way he could have succeeded is if you had cooperated and he had you bound by a legal contract- and also persuaded you into wedding the wrong woman, thus blocking you from the deed! I suppose he thought to press the matter with you before I could make it up here to find him out. Thank heaven you are so thick-headed, Thornton! Now, of course, I may proceed as I originally planned."

"And what," Thornton asked wearily, his head spinning from Bell's ramblings, "might that be, sir?"

"Why, to give you and Margaret the mill as your wedding gift, of course! It would have become hers anyway at my death, for I have no other heirs, but when I realized there was something more serious between the two of you, I thought it all a fine idea.

"I foolishly thought to keep it a surprise, however, and as I had been corresponding with Hamilton, it seemed natural enough to engage his assistance until such time as I had recovered well enough to make the journey myself. He seemed quite willing to help, particularly when I told him that Margaret was my heir, and... why, what has come over you, Thornton? You look positively daft!"

Thornton had, indeed, changed complexion and expression so frequently during Bell's explanation that he now merely sat, a dreamy and perhaps somewhat fatuous look gracing his stern features. "Mr Bell," his voice shook with the tremours of lingering doubt, "can you be serious?"

"I most certainly am! I must tell you, Thornton, that girl has my heart. Just after my last visit to Milton, I made certain to change my will so that all of my monies and· properties will eventually pass to her. I charge you most solemnly to take proper care of her, or I shall defy the edicts of the Church and come back from the grave to haunt you!"

"Then," the single-minded suitor breathed, "I need not find another situation... we may marry right away! There remain no further impediments!" Seized with frenzied inspiration, he at once leapt to the window. "Driver! Please take us instead to Crampton!"

~

They found the homey little dwelling in Crampton more barren and melancholy than they had ever seen. Dixon's lined face looked puffy about the eyes, but she uttered nary a word about her own cares as she stepped aside for them to enter. It was Mr Hale's grey face and haggard, sunken cheeks which truly caused his visitors some alarm.

He had been sitting alone by the hearth fire, a letter in his hand which Thornton thought looked to be written in Margaret's elegant penmanship. He turned in surprise at their entry. "John?" He stood. "Thomas? I had not thought to see you!"

Bell was beginning to cough once more, and Thornton helped him unceremoniously to a seat. With a quick glance back at Dixon, he requested a drink for the old man. "Mr Hale, sir, I came to speak with Margaret," he explained as soon as he was able.

Mr Hale's face drooped. "I am afraid she has gone, John."

He blinked, stunned. "Gone!" He looked back to Bell for confirmation that he had heard correctly. "Surely she is only visiting the Higgins family," he consoled himself.

But Hale was shaking his head. "She left two days ago, John. She did not wish you to know. She feared that her presence might bring you to ruin, and so she has gone!"

The floor seemed suddenly unstable as he moved, disbelievingly, to Margaret's father. "I cannot believe she would go! Has she so lost faith that she would not tell me?"

"You must not think ill of her, John," the old man murmured. The creased stationery shook as Hale offered him the letter he had been clutching. "This arrived today from her."

John took the missive, which the father's anguished hands had crumpled somewhat, and read in disbelief. "She thought she was protecting me!" he cried in denial. "It should not be for her to bear!" He continued to read. "Her aunt would not see her? Margaret does not deserve... why would she take it in her head to go?" he demanded of the weary father.

"I could not persuade her to stay," Hale mumbled, paralysed by his own loss and utterly unable to empathise with John's outrage.

Bell, who had been watching the commotion in some wonder, at last scoffed in impatience. "Come, Richard, stop all of this fuss. Thornton, man, clear your head!"

John, indeed, had been so lost in his own self-loathing that he only gazed blindly at the letter. Did she really think he would be better off without her? She should not have taken such blame upon herself! He ought never to have been persuaded to stay away! Bell's words, however, broke through the haze clouding his thoughts and he looked back to the anxious father.

Hale lifted his face to his favourite pupil and steady friend. "John, my son... bring her back. Bring back my daughter!"

Chapter Thirty-Nine

Gilbert Hodges had been the butler in this Harley Street home for three and twenty years. He had opened the door for the pretty young Mrs Shaw when her much older husband had first brought her here, and he had ordered carriages when the new Mrs Lennox had celebrated her own marriage in this house. He had been one of only a handful of household staff left to keep up the place when the family had been away for over a year, and he had been the one to welcome them all back at their return.

A butler got to know the family he worked for. Mistress Shaw was proper and everything fashionable, and her people might be proud to claim her employment. The younger lady- the true heir to the home- was light-hearted and kind, and easily directed, while her husband the captain was content to allow the household to flow as it always had.

The enigma, and the one who had long intrigued Hodges the most, was the cousin. It had always cheered him when little Margaret would return in the fall after the summers in the country with her parents. She tended to be grave and steady, in contrast to her more frivolous cousin. Hodges had, on more than one occasion, discovered the young miss tucked away in the service staircase with a book, so that she might enjoy it without interruption.

He had struck up a kindly friendship with the little girl, and as he had with the younger mistress, had watched her grow into a graceful woman. Always she had retained something of that far-away quality; in the world, but not of it, as the saying went. That was not to say that she was oblivious to her surroundings. If he had been forced to describe it, he might have said that she cared little for people- their name or their place in society- but was deeply sensitive to persons. She was fascinating to watch.

On this particular late afternoon, he was passing by the library in the normal course of his duties when he discovered her in a most mournful posture. She was seated upon the floor, of all places, her head and arms prostrate over the cushions of the sofa. Under her hand, predictably, was a book, but he did not see the title- nor could he have understood the significance of Plato to her if he had.

He rapped slightly upon the door as he entered. "Miss Hale, forgive my interruption, but is there something I can do for you?"

She lifted her head, and he could clearly see the evidence of a long battle with tears streaked over her face. This alarmed him, for though Miss Hale's nature was not as boisterous as her cousin, neither had she been prone to fits of depression. She was always balanced and sensible, and to know that something had shaken her so troubled him greatly.

"Miss Hale! Shall I call Mrs Lennox to come to you?" he inquired kindly.

"No, thank you Hodges," she shook her head. He came near and offered his hand to help her rise, looking away as she sorted out her tangled skirts. "I am only weary, that is all," she explained at last.

"Of course, Miss," he bowed very slightly. "Would you like some tea, or perhaps some warm chocolate?" His eye twinkled cheerfully as he made the suggestion. It had always been her favourite treat as a child, and well did he remember it.

She returned a wistful smile. "No, thank you, Hodges. I am afraid that chocolate will not help today."

"Miss Hale," he frowned uncomfortably, glanced over his shoulder to see if anyone else was about, and recklessly decided to plunge forward. "Naturally it is no concern of mine, but this awkward business in the papers... I beg you would pay it no mind, Miss. I have heard no one in this house speak against you. I do not think anyone believes a word of it."

Her eyes lowered. "I know, Hodges. It will all come right in time, but... thank you."

His heart went out to the poor girl. What a year she had had of it! There was little an old butler could offer a young lady in the way of comfort, but clearly she had a heavy burden on her mind. "Shall I send one of the maids to you?" he offered hesitantly, unsure what that effort could hope to accomplish, but wishing to do something.

"No, thank you," she answered. She blinked, as if struck by inspiration, and her chin lifted in swift resolution. "I think I should like to take a walk."

"It is raining, Miss Hale!" he objected. "If it is fresh air you seek, would you not prefer an outing in the carriage?"

"No," she declared firmly. "I prefer to walk, and I would like some time alone, Hodges." She leveled an assertive gaze at him, ensuring that he understood her properly.

"As you wish, Miss Hale," he relented. Mrs Shaw would be most distressed, but it was not his place to prevent her going. It would certainly not be the first time in his experience that she had done so.

A short span of a dozen minutes saw her out of the door. Hodges peered unhappily out into the downpour, but possessed too much the dignity of his post to display any outward signs of disapproval. He certainly hoped the young lady knew what she was about!

Some twenty minutes later, the bell was rung, and Hodges answered to its summons himself. If it were the dripping young lady returned from her walk, it would not do for the rest of the household to see her thus! On the doorstep, however, he discovered not a shivering Miss Hale, but a rather large, coarse-looking fellow he had never seen before.

Slightly annoyed, he greeted the man stiffly. "Solicitations to the back door, please." He began to close the door, but the man's raised voice objected.

"I have come to see Miss Hale, please!"

Hodges paused and took a second look at the man. He was clearly a tradesman of some manner, and he spoke in that wild northern dialect, but his enunciation was clear enough. Perhaps an educated tradesman, then. "I am sorry, sir, but Miss Hale is not available at present," he replied with all hauteur.

The man's face expressed clearly that he had expected such a response. "I believe she will see me, even if she is not taking other callers. Will you please tell her that John Thornton wishes to see her?"

This name caused the butler to look at the man full in the face, examining him carefully. He had heard the name whispered among the servants as Miss Hale's intended, but none knew any specifics about the fellow. He could certainly see why! Miss Hale betrothed to a tradesman? The very notion was offensive! That such a delicate flower should be thrown away on one who could not appreciate her worth was unpardonable! Hodges straightened, aware that it was not he who had the right to oppose such a match, but feeling it his duty to protect the young lady where he may.

"I am sorry, sir, but that is impossible at present. The young lady is not available at all," he explained.

At this response, the caller's eyes took on a sudden clarity. "She has gone walking. Do you know when you expect her to return?"

Hodges frowned, surprised that the man seemed to anticipate the young lady's movements. Indeed, he must at least be well acquainted with her. "I do not, sir. In this weather, I should have looked for her to return already."

The man- Thornton- actually smiled despite the evident worry in his demeanour. "Not if I know Margaret," was the softly voiced reply. He looked over his shoulder to the street, clearly not feeling comfortable asking to wait for the lady within the house. "I shall call again in perhaps an hour," he decided, his entire bearing reluctant.

"If I may, sir...." Hodges stopped the man as he began to retreat down the steps.

Thornton stopped. "Yes?"

Hodges studied him for one final second, reading the disappointed hope in the man's eyes and finally matching it to the despondency he had lately witnessed from the young lady. "I may suggest, sir, that if you should so choose, there is a rather pleasant park three blocks to the south. You may find it an agreeable means of passing the time, if you can tolerate the rain."

The light of understanding flickered in the tall man's eyes. "I thank you, sir!" he answered eagerly. Hodges watched him stride away, his steps light and impatient. He closed the door, but determined to stand by himself to answer it once again. He wished to be assured of the young lady's pleasure with his own eyes when she came back on Thornton's arm.

~

Margaret had chosen an ornate little stone bench beneath a sprawling pine; one of the few varieties in this park whose branches still afforded some protection in the barren winter months. It was cold, she admitted, and miserable. Little wonder that not another soul had ventured out on a pleasure walk today! It was exactly as she would have wished.

The tears came again then, in this private place where she could be assured that no unsympathetic ear might be troubled. She could not depend upon Edith to allow her to explore her second thoughts or her ponderous cares, for Edith could not bear to look into sorrow without turning from it in discomfort. Margaret had learned in this past year to embrace it for what it did offer her- an opportunity to reflect upon her regrets, and how she might on another occasion do better.

Why, she chided herself, *was I persuaded to leave Milton?* Distanced now from the immediacy of all that she had feared, the looming giant of sure ruination and calamity seemed but a fuming toddler when compared to what she had done. She had betrayed John.

In her very efforts to shield him from herself and the swath of destruction which presently followed her, she had effectively lost faith in his ability to prevail, to beat back his circumstances and claim the victory. What greater disloyalty could she have exhibited? He had asked nothing more of her than her faith, and she had failed him! Tears mingled with the raindrops pattering over her skirts.

If Mr Hamilton had a shred of honour within him, and if Mason had meant his assurances, she should soon be exonerated of wrongdoing, but at what price? The trust that she and John had so slowly built with one another was now damaged. That was the worst of it! He might have been brought to understand the urgency with which she had left town, if she had only found the courage to tell him of it. She had known, however, that he never would have permitted her to make such a sacrifice. Had he known what she intended, he would have employed any means to stop her, including actions which would doubtless only expose him further.

She closed her eyes, squeezing out more tears and lowering the brim of her hat to shield her face. She could not bear even for the elements to witness her degradation! One thing only remained for her to do- she must make it right. Was it too soon to return to Milton? Would she only make matters worse? Was John even aware yet that she had gone? Poor John! What a shock it would be for him when he discovered her absence!

"Excuse me, Miss," a rich voice interrupted her reverie. "I was wondering if I might share your umbrella?"

Gasping in recognition, she had fairly leapt to her feet before she had quite recovered her powers of speech. "John!" she cried, tumbling into his arms. She burrowed her face into his wet coat as far as her hat would allow, wrapping her arms tightly about his neck. "Forgive me, John!" she sobbed into his chest.

John was grimacing in pain. "Ah, Love, not so tightly!" he groaned.

Startled, she jumped back. "Oh! I nearly forgot! Are you not much better?"

"My entire world is better now," he sighed, taking her gently into his arms again. "Please do not ever leave me again, my Margaret."

She shook her head vehemently against his coat sleeve. "Never again!" she agreed. "Oh, John, I am so sorry! I do not deserve...."

"Lift your head, love," he whispered to her ear. When she did so, he tenderly cupped her cheek in his hand. "Listen to me, Margaret. If either of us was undeserving, it was me. It was my own failings, not yours, which occasioned such trouble. It is for me to ask forgiveness!"

Margaret had tipped her head back to look him full in the face as he was speaking, but scarcely had he finished when she arched up to her toes and pulled him down to her.

For long minutes, the air all about them misted with the warmth of their shared breath, and the only sound to be heard was the soft, insulating patter of the rain in the trees. John held the woman he loved tightly within the sanctuary of his embrace, as if at any moment the world might intrude to snatch her from him once more. He worked his way up her jaw until his mouth hovered over her ear, and in a hoarse voice, murmured his plea. "Come home with me, Margaret."

She began to nod wordlessly, but then her eyes widened in realization. "The investigation! John, is it not too soon?"

He gave a short, rueful laugh. "It is all settled, but I fear you will think the less of me when you discover how."

She tilted her head curiously, and he released a long sigh. "Hamilton expected me this morning to sign his contract and to speak to his daughter. I arrived on schedule, which I think gave him reason to believe I had decided to cooperate. However," here, his face took on an aggrieved look, "I think I may have misled the lady to think I had come for quite a different reason than my true purpose."

"You did not deceive her, surely!"

"Not precisely," he cringed, not at all proud of himself. "I *was* rather cordial, hoping only to obtain her assistance. I am afraid I disappointed her in the extreme with what I had to say," he sighed again, "but I asked a very great thing of her, a thing which I ought never to have demanded of any young woman."

"John!" Margaret's stiffened in apprehension. "What is this dreadful thing?"

"I made her to defy her father, jeopardizing her own security, and, I am afraid, permanently disrupting any chance at harmony between father and daughter."

Margaret regarded him in some confusion. "I do not understand. What could you have asked of her?"

His mouth tugged wryly. "I asked her to provide Mason with two witness statements- one in your behalf, vouching for your innocence in the fraud- and one a charge against her father, exposing his attempts to intimidate and coerce you into doing as he wished. After she had signed the statements in duplicate, we had them taken directly to both Mason and Davenport... and then we went to inform her father of what she had done. He was... displeased." His face twisted into a pained grimace. "I lost my temper most fearfully, and may possibly have given him cause to send *me* before the magistrates, but only if he is not too ashamed to do so."

Margaret drew back in alarm. "John, you did not attack the man, did you?"

He cleared his throat. "I suppose you might say I was defending Miss Hamilton from her father's wrath. I think I might have broken one of his teeth, for I have a dreadful cut just here." He lifted his wounded appendage in a weak attempt at sympathy, but found very little.

"That is appalling!"

"Abominable, I know," he agreed seriously. "I have the manners of a barbarian. You really ought to keep better company, Margaret."

She scoffed impatiently. "I meant about having to protect his daughter from him! Poor Genevieve... what is she to do? Has she anywhere to go?"

"I think the young lady is even now on a train to visit some distant relative she claimed in Leicester."

Margaret was pale from the shock of it. "I still cannot believe she would go against her own father! How did you persuade her to it?"

He shrugged lightly. "She is not a bad sort, after all. I may have tugged a little on the lady's sympathies by sharing my own woeful tale of heartbreak and true love," he grinned widely and clasped his hand over his heart with exaggerated affectation. "She has more compassion than Fanny, I will say that for the lady."

"John!" Margaret cried, still suffering some in horror despite his jest. "Her father might very well cut her off entirely! Why, this could ruin all of her prospects!"

"She knew that, but in the end I think she believed she owed it to you. She felt badly about losing your friendship, Margaret. I think she has had few such genuine companions."

Margaret blinked and set her jaw in determination. "Then I- we- shall do all we can for her. I insist, John- though, at present, I do not know what that can be!"

Smiling, he tugged her back into his arms once more. "I thought you might feel that way. I think when I tell you the rest of what I have to say, you will be able to think of some ideas."

Puzzled, she frowned. "What can you mean by that?"

His smile grew wider. "Mr Bell came looking for the both of us this morning. Apparently, as soon as we wed, he intends to sign the deed to the mill property over to you. So, I was thinking, Margaret, would you object to obtaining a special license while we are here in Town? The sooner we marry," he intoned with all seriousness, "the sooner all of the hands can get back to work."

"What?" she laughed. "Do you mean that *we* would own the mill?"

"I can scarcely believe it myself, but it is true. The buildings are to be repaired, and Mr Bell also intends to set up a generous bank account in your name, with, as he says, the remaining balance to come to you at his death. Did you know he owns three whole blocks of commercial buildings in addition to the mill?"

"He cannot be serious!"

"I assure you, he is. You may, of course, choose not to marry me and simply wait for your inheritance. Perhaps you may in the end catch a finer husband by that method."

She slanted a grave expression up to him. "I think I shall take my chances on my first choice. I think I would find a fine gentleman rather dull by comparison."

"Indeed," he flashed his most distracting grin, blue eyes twinkling his pleasure. "Did you plan to put up that umbrella, or shall I keep you here and kiss you in the rain without it?"

~

Gilbert Hodges did, as it turned out, receive the assurance he hoped for of Miss Hale's satisfaction with her caller. When the couple he awaited returned to the house, they were sheltering intimately together under a single umbrella, laughing most indecorously, and both thoroughly drenched. His face twitching in discomfort, Hodges gestured for a maid to help Miss Hale with her cloak, but the gentleman had already assisted her by the time the girl arrived.

"Oh, Hodges!" Margaret came to him, breathless and- thank heavens-smiling. "Will you please ask if my cousin may join us? Mr Thornton and I wish to warm by the fire for a few moments."

"Captain and Mrs Lennox are already awaiting you in the drawing room, Miss," he informed her. "While you were out, Mr Henry Lennox called, and I believe he waits within as well."

The couple traded serious glances. "Thank you, Hodges," she replied distractedly.

Mr Thornton took her arm and looked down to her with such reassurance and comfort that Hodges felt himself to be intruding upon some private, wordless conversation. The young lady drew a breath, her courage bolstered, and he led her away.

And that, Hodges assured himself with some sorrow, *will be the end of Miss Hale living in this house!*

Chapter Forty

"Miss Hale, Mr Thornton," Henry Lennox stood and greeted them tightly as they arrived together.

"Henry!" Margaret broke away from Thornton's escort and came near. "Have you some news?"

He looked uncertainly to Thornton. "I do, Miss Hale. It will be all through the papers in the morning, but you may be relieved to hear of it a little sooner."

Margaret turned over her shoulder to glance at John. "It must be good news from the way you speak!"

"Indeed. You knew, of course, that I have been acquainted with Rupert Hamilton for some while."

Margaret froze, relieved to feel John's hand slipping reassuringly over her shoulder. "I did," she replied quietly.

"Well..." Henry, despite his discomfort at watching Margaret with her manufacturer, allowed something of a satisfied smirk. "It appears that he was also better acquainted with the Drapers than anyone had thought. It seems that he, and another connection of his in London- I shall not name him yet, as he also was someone I knew from the club- assisted them in setting up the fraudulent account. It is not yet known how much they gained by their assistance, but it appears to have been substantial."

"Rupert!" Margaret cried in horror. "I would not have thought him capable of *that*!"

"I had my suspicions from the beginning, as did others who knew him, but of course nothing could be proven until the Drapers were found."

"So they have been caught!" John exclaimed. "That is well. I was hoping that some justice might be served there. How was it done?"

"As to that, it was not so surprising. It seems that one of the more generous 'donors to the cause' was the wife of a rather prominent admiral. He took the offense personally. I am told his flag ship is quite fast," Henry laughed.

The gentlemen all found some common ease in expressing their mutual gratification with the way matters had settled. Soon, however, an awkward silence ensued, to be broken at last by Captain Lennox. "Margaret," he spoke, looking pointedly to Thornton, "I do not believe we have been introduced to your...."

Pride shining from her eyes, Margaret tipped up her chin. "Maxwell, Edith, this is my fiancé, John Thornton of Marlborough Mills."

~

The following days were intense and joyous ones for John. Each sunrise brought him measurably closer to all that he had dreamed and hoped, and during the course of each day, new delights pressed around him. As the final week of his bachelorhood drew to a satisfactory close, he could only look ahead with eager anticipation. The freedom of his lifelong independence he would gladly trade for a loving yoke about his neck and upon his hand.

His first instinct had been to pack Margaret on the very first northbound train they could find, but better sense prevailed. He lingered with her in London only long enough to call it a polite visit with her family, and to obtain a particular item he most desired. He had been quite serious in his light-hearted threats to Margaret about a special license. She may have evaded the reading of the banns, he would remind her, but there was no reason he should have to wait yet another month to bring her home with him!

The visit was not all anxious delay. It *was* a gracious home in which to pass the time. Margaret took it upon herself to show him her favourite childhood nooks in that house where she used to retire to read, and he came to appreciate them quite as much as she. It was a mercy, he reflected at one point, that his sore ribs were less of a distraction than they had been previously.

On his second afternoon in the house, when the young Mrs Lennox and her child had retired for a rest and the captain was out on some business call, John caught Margaret firmly by the hand and led her from the library. She stared mutely at him as she followed, wondering what he could be about, until he drew her very pointedly to the music room he had just discovered.

"I believe, my darling, it is time to settle a debt," he grinned.

She shrank, her face pinched unwillingly. "Oh, John, I do not think...."

"I shall turn the pages for you," he promised with a sultry little pout. "Come, Margaret, it is just me, and you *did* give you word."

"I never did!" she objected. "You only heard what you wished to hear, *Mr Thornton.*"

"And right now, *Miss Hale*, I wish to hear you play. Please?" he added, with that impossible grin of his.

Margaret groaned reluctantly and moved to the piano. She took a long while picking over the music, as Edith's favourite selections were a great deal too complicated for her. At last, with an unhappy frown she scarcely bothered to conceal, she sat down to the instrument.

John settled himself at her side, anticipating an afternoon of pure enjoyment. With her first hesitant notes, however, Margaret proved that she had not, in fact, been misleading anyone. She was quite out of practice. Her cheeks grew ever more red as she fumbled through the piece, and as soon as she had finished, she hurriedly covered her face in mortification. "Are you satisfied?" she begged through her fingers.

"Not at all, Love," he teased lightly. "You did not sing!"

"Oh, John, please! Do let it pass!"

"Slide over, Margaret. I shall take a turn, and you may sing for me." John proved no more practiced than Margaret- in fact, he was considerably less so- but he was confident enough to laugh at himself. He frequently clutched his aching ribs, but could not be diverted from their fun. *This*, he thought happily to himself, *is the joy that I shall find in life hereafter!*

An hour later, a properly astonished Edith Lennox followed the discordant racket from her music room and found them nearly doubled over with mirth. Standing in the open doorway, she gaped in awe at her sober-minded cousin and that stern-looking manufacturer fellow. They were both in utter hysterics, with tears streaming down their faces as they systematically butchered the works of the great composers.

"Margaret!" she cried in horror. "I just had that piano tuned! How can it possibly sound so dreadful?"

This sent them into a new wave of laughter, until Margaret, recovering, assured her that no fault could be assigned to the piano.

"Well!" she gasped. "I have never heard you carry on so, Margaret. Milton must be a savage place indeed!"

Margaret and John stole guilty glances at one another. "Only the manufacturers," Margaret answered with a perfectly straight face. It was some while before John could stop laughing again.

They stayed only two days more, though each day to John was as much torment as it was pleasure. He itched to be back in Milton, and moving ahead with all they had planned, but this time with Margaret among her family was precious to him. Henry Lennox, to his very great surprise, proved a most intelligent and agreeable fellow. His brother the captain was a less stimulating companion, and John had more than one occasion to marvel at Margaret's abiding devotion to a woman so given to trivialities as Edith Lennox. At least it gave him great hope that she might also come to care for his own sister.

Mrs Shaw had finally emerged from her self-imposed seclusion, claiming that she was suddenly feeling quite herself again and begging her niece to forgive her the uncomfortable ailment which had kept her to her bed. Margaret accepted the renewal of her aunt's affections with philosophy, if not genuine gratitude. Upon meeting the large, rough-looking tradesman from the North who was determined to carry off her niece, Mrs Shaw had found it necessary to again take very cautious care of her poor aching head. John saw very little of her through the remainder of his visit. He at first expected that circumstance might trouble Margaret, but later found that the avoidance of potential conflict had rather been a relief to her.

The very afternoon on which he at last obtained their marriage license, he whisked her to the train station to tearful good byes on the part of Edith, but a firm and purposeful farewell from Margaret. The former was quite heartbroken that John and Margaret did not intend a large ceremony for her to attend. Alas, as she had only recently discovered herself to be in an interesting condition, her husband the captain had prevailed upon her to delay their own visit to their Milton relations until a later date.

He handed Margaret into the rail car, grateful that it seemed likely they would enjoy the ride in privacy. It never occurred to him for a moment that he should not claim the comfortable place at her side, rather than the proper one opposite her. Her bright eyes smiled at him as he dropped his arm about her and pulled her head to his shoulder. "Are you warm enough, my love?" he murmured into her hair.

"I am now," she answered, nestling contentedly into his arm. "John, did you write to Father yesterday?"

"Mmhmm," was the inarticulate response.

"And he is expecting us? I feel badly that we have not returned sooner."

"Bell is with him. From his letter, it sounds as though they have scarcely left the library since Bell arrived. I imagine it is your Miss Dixon who misses you the most."

Margaret chuckled. "What of your mother?"

"You had her letter, did you not? I expect Fanny has kept her rather busy. Apparently my dear sister has decided that circumstances warrant a somewhat larger wedding than she had initially planned. Let us only hope she does not put it off to a later date! For Watson's sake, naturally," he added as an afterthought.

"Naturally," Margaret smiled mischievously. "And what were you thinking for us, John?"

"The minister is meeting us at the railway station, of course," he shrugged nonchalantly.

"I see," her grin widened. "And did you think to arrange a bouquet for me?"

"Indeed I did, but I think it may be a few months yet before it is in bloom. I think I shall send to Hampshire for a few more rose varieties. What do you think, Love?"

"I think you are going to have to be just a *little* more patient, John."

"Nonsense! I have a mill to run, after all. You mustn't delay, Margaret. Think of the mill!"

"Perhaps we could negotiate that," she arched one brow.

He leaned close in interest. "I am listening."

It might be noted that very little negotiating- or indeed verbal conversation of any kind- took place for quite some time.

~

It was not a happy town they returned to, but perhaps a hopeful one. Word had rapidly circulated that not only was Margaret Hale quite innocent in the recent scandal, but also that she was the means through which Marlborough Mills would soon be operational once more. This did much to secure the good opinion of the working class, and Margaret was stopped on the street whenever she ventured out.

The more well-to-do citizens as well began to seek her company, but for a somewhat more prosaic reason. In truth, they suffered from simple, morbid curiosity. Surely, they reasoned, a woman who could survive unscathed after public defamation, then emerge as an heiress betrothed to the most elusive bachelor in the city must be something interesting!

That Mr Hamilton, after being known to clash with her and seeing his son charged with the very crime which had slipped from her shoulders, had suddenly retired to his country home only added to the mystique. Thus, it was to her very great surprise that Margaret found herself to have gained a rather formidable stature in that town since she had left it. It would, in the end, prove rather useful.

"Margaret, my dear," Mr Bell eased his creaking old body into a chair next to her at breakfast one morning, "have you thought more about that hospital?"

She set down her cup and regarded him quizzically. "How should I have?"

"Well, the authorities seized what remained of those funds," he reasoned. "They were already earmarked for a set purpose. I think if someone were to come up with a workable plan for a *real* hospital, they might be persuaded to release them- at least, a small portion of them," he smiled sardonically as he found his fork.

Margaret had straightened in interest. "Do you really think...? But who could do such a thing?"

Bell's grey brows arched innocently. "Well, it ought to be someone of good repute, of course. I should think after that last debacle that it will be difficult to take up the project again. And too, it should be someone with some resources of their own they may pledge, as a sign of good faith."

"That is true," she mused. "I wonder if any such can be found!"

"My child, I speak of you!" coughed the old man.

Her eyes grew large. "Of me! Oh, no, I could not possibly! Why, where would I even begin?"

"Marlborough Mills is not my only property," he shrugged. "I've a warehouse over on Raleigh Street. The rent is in arrears, and the current tenant scarcely uses half of the warehouse as it is. My agent has already asked him to relocate. It occurs to me that you might remodel the building."

Her eyes kindled in wonder, but just as quickly her brow furrowed in disappointment. "I do not know how we should make the rent. Surely, it will be difficult enough to make a beginning as it is, and it will cost a great deal to go on from there! Perhaps one day...."

"Margaret," he interrupted brusquely, "you and Thornton can be both so insufferably diffident in some matters! Did you not remember that it is all to become yours eventually? What matters it whether I allow you to use it rent free? No, perhaps I shall simply sign it over now. Yes, that will do. I *did* tell you, did I not, that I received a sizeable payout after that rail speculation? Well! Where should an old bachelor like myself spend that much money?"

"Mr Bell," she objected, "I cannot even consider it! You have done too much already, and I should be dreadfully unqualified to take on such a task! I know nothing of the proper management of such an establishment."

"Come, my dear, surely you know of some competent doctor hereabouts. He will have to volunteer, of course- they always do- but you will be able to keep him in comforts for his trouble, I daresay."

This gave her pause. Slowly she acknowledged that she did, in fact, know of a worthy doctor who might be persuaded to take up the project.

"Well, then it is settled. You shall be the public figurehead, raising support and donating the use of your property, and you shall allow this doctor of yours to oversee the details. I hope, my dear, that he is an honest chap and not some quack like that Douglas fellow."

"Why, he is, but... Mr Bell, really, I do not know if I have the head for such an undertaking!"

"You will do, my dear. You are clever and sincere, and I think you currently enjoy something of a benevolent notoriety in this town. You may as well make use of it." Bell began to cough gently again and took up his tea.

Margaret was still looking somewhat thunderstruck at the idea. She gazed blankly at the table, her mind whirring with all manner of new prospects. At last she shook her head gently. "It is a wonderful idea, Mr Bell, but my time and energies shall be no longer my own. I would have to talk all of this over with John, and he has enough to occupy two or three of him with the rebuilding of the mill! I think he would prefer that I did not take this up just now."

Bell waved his cup. "If you want to do this thing, Margaret, Thornton will be the last to say you nay. It will be your mother-in-law who will give you the most trouble."

Margaret smiled. "She is not quite so fearsome as you think!"

Bell grunted. "So you say, but I shall continue to maintain a safe distance."

Margaret chuckled gently, but a moment later stilled when her father came into the dining room. His gnarled hands smoothed down the front of his best suit and he looked to his daughter with a tearful, radiant joy. Margaret drew a deep, final breath, and rose to take his arm.

"Are you ready, my dear?" he asked softly.

Margaret's own eyes filled with tears. She pressed her lips into a trembling smile and nodded. "Yes, Father."

Mr Hale raised quaking fingers to squeeze the hand wrapped over his elbow. "I have prayed for this day since you were born, Margaret," he choked. "First that it would never come, but then that it should be just as it is. John...." His voice failed him and he merely clasped her hand tightly as the tears fell.

"I know, Father," she whispered. She raised up to kiss him on the cheek, and slowly- very slowly- the glowing anguish in his eyes subsided, and he was her quiet, serene father once more.

"Well," he smiled bravely, patting her hand. "We must not be late."

Chapter Forty-One

John Thornton had never in his life found so much difficulty at patience. His fingers twitched anxiously at his side. He could sense his mother's dark eyes boring into him, but his own gaze never left the door- the portal through which his whole future would momentarily arrive.

He had not long to wait, which was well. A sliver of light appeared, then was filled with shadowy figures. The light soon vanished again, and there was only her. She came to him veiled in her innocence, but boldly did she hold up her head to meet his breathless adoration. Each heartbeat of his own brought her closer to her rightful place, and to that moment when he would deliver up to her everything he was or ever would be.

Through delicate lace, he sought her clear, honest eyes, and saw nothing else through the remainder of the short ceremony. Mr Hale gave her hand into his, and he clasped it solemnly as the words of the service began. Gladly, he pledged away all that was his own and bound himself to her, promising to cherish her to his last breath and to receive humbly what she swore unto him in return.

At the minister's blessing, and with one final, respectful glance toward her father, he at last drew the veil from her face. She was his! His ring sparkled upon her finger, a solid testament that she would now willingly share the name which he had so long borne alone. In awe, he paused for one last, loving look before tenderly taking her to himself.

The church was scarcely populated on this glorious day, which was as Margaret had wished it. It had seemed too sacred and holy a thing to sully it by obligatory invitations, and so only a handful of those dearest to them were in attendance. One such sat in excruciating solitude, on the right side of the church. Her daughter had abandoned her to sit with her own intended, and her son... her light, her cheer, her comforter... was no longer hers. Through blurred eyes, she blessed him as he gave himself to another, and silently commissioned that young woman to bear his heart in faithfulness.

For one wicked, piercing second, her own heart's voice had cried out to bring the proceedings to a halt, to return back to the way things had always been. It happened to be just then that John lifted his bride's veil, and the jealous mother was privy to all that he beheld. Shining back was the equal of his fervent love, a devotion as fierce as her own. Her son had indeed cast off her exclusive maternal embrace, but in return for her heartbreak, he had brought to her another to share in her affections. She had not lost love today, but gained more. Chastened once again, she bowed her head in silent gratitude.

When she lifted it, she found her new daughter's laughing, jubilant eyes searching for her, in defiance of the custom for bride and groom to look only forward. John, too, had turned round, and something in his face made her gasp in wonder. She had not witnessed such unbridled joy since he had been yet a child.

Perhaps it was her own wishes, perhaps some flash of insight, but for half a moment, she saw him again as he had been- before years of want and worry, before the bitter struggles of manhood. The face she looked into was simply her boy, though it seemed to her that she could almost envision his own youthful features blended with another's. She nearly laughed for astonishment imagining her little John- but a John with brilliant green eyes and freckles dusted over an upturned nose. Unashamed, she beamed proudly over the new couple as tears pooled in the corners of her eyes.

Margaret could never have fancied all that passed through Hannah Thornton's mind. She knew only that she had been welcomed. Content in that, she turned her face once more up to the man who was now her husband. In speechless delight, he impulsively kissed her again before the assembled witnesses, and then took her hand under his arm.

"Come, my love," he whispered, and together they made the long walk to the church doors- leaving behind them the safety of all that was known, and facing together all that lay ahead.

~

Hannah had insisted upon a wedding breakfast, though Margaret, and even John to a certain extent, had objected. "It seems wrong to put out so much just now, when so many others are presently going hungry!" Margaret had reasoned.

"Margaret," Hannah had patiently explained, "you are an heiress now, and all of Milton knows that you are to be the owner of the mill property. You must show yourself to be... receptive," she had finished uncomfortably.

As Margaret had still looked unconvinced, she suggested further, "This is a hasty wedding, which means all the more that it must be done properly! You must not look as though you are marrying in secret." Margaret had relented, but it was not until Mr Bell and John had heard of her misgivings that a happy solution to her concerns had been found.

Thus, when the wedding party had returned to Marlborough Mills, it was for several hours of festivities. Many of John's business associates came to wish the couple well. Mr and Mrs Smith offered their congratulations, Watson proudly dandled his own fiancée- with her stunning engagement ring- on his arm, and nearly every mill from the city was represented.

There was even a lovely gift and a personal note to Margaret from Genevieve Hamilton, which touched her very much. Showing it privately to John, she informed him very firmly of her intention to keep up the acquaintance. Poor Genevieve's adored brother was now imprisoned, and her parents hiding in disgrace. She would certainly need a friend.

After the proper breakfast guests had departed, the wedding party joined in processional once more. Mr Bell and John walked on either side of Margaret and met a growing crowd of former Marlborough Mills employees at the site of the boiler explosion. At the fore, quite as they expected, stood Nicholas Higgins, and on his arm- much to their surprise- was Mildred Sacks. Margaret thought she had never seen such a pleased twinkle in Higgins' eyes, but whether it was from the day's event or the company he kept, she could not be sure. When the new Mr and Mrs Thornton were first sighted, a cheer rose from those gathered.

Mr Bell, admirably holding back his rasping cough, made a short speech in which he conferred the mill property to the new couple and gave to them the deed. Margaret had begged not to speak, so John humbly accepted Mr Bell's gift on her behalf, then turned to address his men.

"I have not the gift of eloquent speech making. I expect, however, that you came here today not to hear platitudes, but to know the future of Marlborough Mills. I have already sent orders for four new combers and three new looms, and we can expect deliveries to begin within four weeks. A new boiler is to arrive within the fortnight as well. I have high hopes that before that time, we will have completed the repairs on the buildings.

"You may also be interested to know that the rebuilding process has garnered us some little notice within the industry. I have on my desk four large new contract offers from established textile merchants throughout the kingdom. These will help to immediately ensure orders to get the mill working again!" He paused as shouts of general approval arose from his audience.

"Unfortunately, little more can be done until the rebuilding is complete. However," here he turned to offer his new wife a wink, "Mrs Thornton asked only one thing for a wedding gift, and I was glad to bring it about for her.

"Starting today, and continuing until the mill re-opens, every man, woman, and child previously on the payroll may come to the new kitchen for a hearty meal each day. Mr Higgins shall administrate the kitchen. It is not charity, lest any should feel grieved in his pride. Such is a noble sentiment, but consider this rather my effort- poor as it is- to enable those who would choose to return to Marlborough Mills as soon as the repairs are complete to do so, rather than leaving Milton to seek employment elsewhere. It would honour me very greatly if you should decide to place your confidence in this mill for your future livelihoods."

He looked once more to his pretty young wife, whose kind smile and earnest generosity were already well known to many in the crowd. The knowledge that John Thornton had chosen such a woman as his wife, and that his marriage to her had not only restored the viability of the mill, but also had softened the toughest mill master in the city, brought perhaps more good cheer than his generous offer of support during hardship.

He glanced again over the hopeful expressions assembled before him. One meal per day was scarcely enough to keep them alive for that time, and well he knew it. He had already budgeted and disbursed two weeks' additional pay to each worker. Other masters had berated him publically for it, but he firmly believed that the sudden loss of employment constituted a breach of contract between himself and his men. As he was now able to make some amends, he had determined to do so. He bitterly regretted that he could not do more, but Higgins had assured him that the Union had pledged a little more support of their own, once they had been assured that Marlborough Mills would reopen. It was, Higgins had persuaded them at last, to everyone's benefit.

Wishing to draw his little speech to a close and to steal Margaret away for good, he tugged her gently to his side. Jeers and good-natured heckling rose from the crowd, but though his face grew hot, he chose to ignore it. "My wife and I are humbled by your well-wishes. Today, I consider myself the most blessed of all men."

One taunting voice- suspiciously like Higgins'- called out, "Prove it, Master!" The cry was taken up, and within seconds the assembled throng was clamouring the same.

Red to the tips of his ears, Thornton peered uncertainly to Margaret. She was blushing and laughing merrily, her arm crooked intimately through his. The hoots from the audience had grown intense, and she offered him a teasing little lift of her brows.

That settled it. He spun her into his arms for a quick but decidedly scandalous kiss, and Margaret's willing reciprocation instantly fixed her as "a fair lass" among the rough weaver crowd. He released her and cast a suspicious eye about, hoping he had not caused any loss of respect for his wife among those gathered. Laughter at his own expense, he could handle, but at Margaret's was not to be borne! All he noted were cheers of approval, and a number came to clap him on the back in congratulations.

His grin as brilliant as the one pair of eyes which held his attention, he waved them away in embarrassment. Let them go to the kitchen! He had better things to do.

~

It was not the wish of the new couple to embark upon an extravagant wedding tour. Indeed, Margaret had felt it quite unnecessary to go anywhere at all, feeling that John's guidance would be needed during the rebuilding of the mill. John, however, would not hear of spending their first days together amid the distractions of his work, nor even in the company of others dear to them. The bricklayers would be the better part of a fortnight at their labour, and the new looms and combers would not arrive for long after that.

His argument had prevailed, and as soon as they could get away from their well-wishers, he fairly carried her off to the train station. To the coast they were bound, and he cared not how long it took to get there, so long as he was alone with his *wife*. He curled his arm possessively about her, exulting in the knowledge that she was now *his*. She nestled her head against his shoulder, and together they watched as the fading winter sun cast its receding warmth over the sky. This day had seen everything change, and it was now retiring in peace.

He secured a quiet little inn by the shore, and was not disappointed to find that they had arrived well past the evening meal. Neither were in the least bit hungry, nor did the couple wish to call attention to their status as newlyweds. They were shown to a private, airy suite of rooms, and very soon they were left completely alone. John sighed in relief and began to shed his restraining coat and cravat.

Margaret turned bashfully away, and made a great show of gazing out of the window at the sparkle of the moon over the waves. Logically, she knew that all was as it should be, but now that she had come to it, those long-held habits of maidenhood cried out in doubt. She was alone, behind closed doors, with a man! A bed stood not ten feet from her, and not one of their faithful chaperones were within thirty miles. This was no momentary circumstance- she was to stay here with him! What had she been thinking to agree to all of this? Her stomach fluttered and her pulse quickened when she heard his step behind her.

He said not a word, merely siding his arms about her waist and pressing his face into her hair. He seemed to sense that she needed a moment, and was, in fact, suffering from his own battle with nerves. They stood together some while, her arms wound over his, their bodies swaying imperceptibly together to the rhythm of the waves breaking over the nearby shore.

At last he whispered in her ear. "Are you well, Love?"

The calm that she had only just achieved vanished in an instant as her neck prickled with the thrill of his breath over her skin. Not trusting herself to speak, she simply nodded.

He closed his eyes, nuzzling her cheek. "I wanted to tell you how beautiful you looked today, my Margaret. You always are, but today you were an angel, my love. I have a special fondness for this gown."

Margaret glanced down in confusion. It was only a walking dress; in fact, Hannah and Fanny had despaired of her when she had refused to have a special wedding gown made. This was one of her favourites, but it was not new at all, as she had felt such an expense in poor taste. It was not even the fine white gown she had worn to the dinner party, because that one had been suitable only for evening wear. This one had simply been a practical choice for a bride intending to board a train straightaway. "Why do you like this one so well?" she wondered.

"Do you not remember that evening in your kitchen?" He turned her around in his embrace, then lifted her hands in his own so that she stood poised before him like a dancer prepared to twirl. "This was what you wore, and seldom have I had an opportunity to admire it since. How I wanted to take you in my arms and kiss you that night!" he declared with feeling. "From that day, I began to hope for more than I had ever dared before."

Margaret laughed at the memory. "I as well! I was glad to be on friendly terms with you at last."

His brow furrowed in mock hurt. "Only friendly?"

A saucy light glinted in her eyes. "That is all I shall admit to, sir."

"I will have to draw out a confession, I see." He raised her left hand to his lips and, just as he had on that first evening, placed a soft kiss on her fingers. Another gentle kiss followed on the little diamond she now wore, and still more trailed up the back of her hand, while his fingers beneath began seductively unhooking the many buttons of her tight sleeve.

Margaret shivered. The quiet of this place, the sensuous touch of his lips on her flesh, the dim light of the room beyond him, all served to sharpen and focus her awareness. Her vision filled with his powerful shoulders, shrouded only in his thin white shirt, and his shining dark head bent low before her. He lifted his face, a playful smile teasing his mouth. "Do you surrender?" he asked softly.

Smiling, she shook her head, and thought he looked like he had rather hoped for such a response. He flipped the sensitive inner part of her wrist up to his mouth, and she trembled anew when the fresh stubble from his chin and upper lip tickled her skin. Slowly, deliciously, he worked his sweet torment over the tender place where her pulse beat the strongest. His fingers cradled the back of her arm, pressing her loosened sleeve ever more out of his path, and he seemed fascinated with the way her flesh dimpled at his touch.

He continued tantalizing her, the warmth of his breath swirling over her exposed skin in little eddies with the cool permeating through the window. Margaret's eyes had fallen almost closed, but the exquisite sensations he created trembled over her whole arm and brought to life every vulnerable, responsive longing through her body. At one moment she gasped and opened her eyes in disbelief. Could he still only be kissing her wrist? Tingling thrills raced over her, awakening secret yearnings from deep within. Her entire being was alive and intent on that single point of his attentions.

His mouth caressed to the limits of her sleeve, nearly to her elbow; though in truth, she felt his presence long before his lips touched that delicate place. Once he had at long last claimed the length and breadth of her bare flesh, he drew closer and commenced a similar assault just below her ear. It was not the first time he had ever done so, but never before had she sensed the coiled desire slipping from his control, nor felt so clearly the promise of intimate pleasures to be discovered.

She shivered anew when he daringly explored the line of her collar, the immutable boundary which had always before defined the extremity of what he could see and touch. There was no stricture of morality or propriety to hold him back now. He waited only for her to answer his growing thirst for her sweetness.

"Margaret," he breathed in her ear, "my Margaret, how I love you!"

She turned her face into his and captured his gaze. She looked up into those eyes she trusted so well; the eyes of the man who had opened to her the very deepest recesses of his heart. She brought her hand to his cheek. "And I love you, my John."

He lowered his forehead to touch it to hers. Never before had she called him her own! Her arms came up around his neck, as they had on that first, fateful day of the riots and on so many memorable occasions since. Gently he slid his fingertips over the backs of her loving arms, still in awe that she had willingly taken him to her heart.

Margaret sensed clearly that he was waiting for some sign from her. Drawing back only slightly, she met his eyes and deliberately pulled the combs from her hair. It tumbled down in thick waves as she tugged free the coils.

John's breath left him. Here was the vision which had so long mesmerized him in his dreams! His devout fingers hesitated; then, gathering courage, stroked through the rippling currents flowing from her glorious crown. Her hair was spun satin, and his fingers- calloused and strong from years working a far humbler material- caught and snagged the priceless strands as he touched her. He began to quiver. She was so soft, so lush and exquisite! What right had he, a rough man from birth, to partake of such gentle, innocent wonder?

His throat constricted and he drew back his hand. "Margaret!" he whispered in the darkness, his words trembling in genuine fear. "I do not dare... I am but a coarse, simple man! I cannot bear if you should shrink from me."

"John," she called to him warmly, sliding her hands up his chest and pulling close to him once more. "You are the one I love, and you alone will I hold."

He captured her hands and kissed them by turn. "I am not worthy, Love!"

"Nor am I," she breathed, standing upon her toes and brushing a gentle kiss to his lips. "But we have been so favoured, nonetheless."

He pressed her close to him, his doubts subsiding under her faithful caress. More daringly this time, he combed his fingers backward through her hair and drew courage from the obvious pleasure she took in his attentions. She leaned into his hands, slightly parted lips breathing his name.

"Margaret," he touched light kisses over her face, his pulse hammering in longing and exhilaration. "Will you come to me? Let me hold you, and make you my own," he pleaded.

Her lips, etched so softly against his cheek, drew into a smile. "I am yours, John, forevermore."

Epilogue

John Thornton awoke at exactly five-thirty in the morning, just as he had every single day for nineteen years. He lay awake for a moment, rubbing his eyes. While it was true that he still naturally roused at the same time, it was no longer the case that he would instantly spring to his feet. His bed had, in recent times, become a far more appealing place to linger.

The faint jostling of his body caused Margaret to stir beside him. She rolled toward him, mumbling in her sleep with a shock of dark hair tousled over her forehead. He smiled, and settled into the pillow to gaze at her in contentment. Perhaps it would do no harm to stay a while longer. It was always enjoyable to wake his wife.

She was still not accustomed to the early rhythm of his days, but it must not have troubled her overmuch. She had refused to even use the bed in her own room until their daughter had been born. Now, the room which had been originally meant to be the mistress' quarters was neatly converted into a nursery.

His eyes raised speculatively to the door between the two rooms. Little Maria had for a few months now ceased to need her mother quite so often, and was not likely to wake for some while yet. Still... it would not do to disturb her. Children needed their rest, of course. He would have to be very quiet.

Leaning over Margaret, his fingers brushed the thick locks of hair from her face. He began dusting light kisses over her brow. So gently did he touch her that her forehead only twitched as though some stray hair tickled her. His smile grew. This was a game he played with himself, always trying to determine how long he could get by with teasing her before she awoke. His prior record was ten minutes, but Margaret was quick to point out that had been hardly fair, as she had been heavy with child at the time and quite exhausted.

He tilted his head to survey her lovely form, concealed as it was under the coverlet. Only last night she had given him the divine news that he was to be a father again! He wondered how long it would take this time before he could see with his own eyes the life of his child taking shape within her.

The remembrance of the prior evening's joy caused his smiling lips to bump her cheek in some impatience. Margaret started and her eyes flashed open. Her round pupils contracted almost immediately and set off the dazzling green of her irises in the pale light from the window. He kissed her again, laughing softly at the blank look on her face when she first awoke. "Good morning, Love."

She blinked, then scowled at him and flipped the counterpane over her head. "It is still the middle of the night!" came her muffled retort.

"I thought you used to live in the country. Poultry crowing, and all of that?"

"I *left* the country," she grumbled good-naturedly, but still she refused to come from under the covers.

"The steam engine starts up in half an hour," he reminded her.

"Then let me sleep another half-hour!" was the cross rejoinder.

John fell silent. Perhaps it was unfair of him to wake her for his own purposes when she had just cause to be fatigued. A little sorry that he had disturbed her, he began to slink out of the bed. In another instant, however, a pair of warm arms had wrapped around him to restrain him from going.

"I was going to leave you alone," he smiled, turning back to pull her closer.

Margaret's only answer was a sleepy moan, as she closed her eyes and buried her face in his chest. He decided he could content himself with simply holding her, and occasionally stroking his fingers through the dark, lustrous hair which she kept loose at his request. He closed his own eyes and allowed himself to be at peace. Very soon, Margaret's breathing was soft and even once more.

It was another full hour before he rose completely, although it would be misleading to suggest the entire hour had been spent in slumber. It was a most self-satisfied grin looking out from his mirror when he finally made his morning preparations. Some things were worth the delay!

Indeed, he reflected as he gave his cravat a final tug, he almost never kept his precise schedule any longer. It had been something of a poorly kept secret about the mill for nearly two years that if one wanted to see the master, they would do best to first seek the mistress. For his own part, he had at last found both the means and the incentive to promote more supervisors within the mill-one of whom, naturally, was Higgins- freeing himself up to greater flexibility. What work he could bring home, he always did. Rather than the isolation of his lonely mill office, his working hours were now often punctuated with welcome- though not always helpful- interruptions.

A soft giggling sound caused him to turn. Margaret had entered, with a bubbly, bright-eyed Maria snuggled to her hip. She was tickling their daughter as she walked, and the child's round cheeks were pink with glee. Laughing, he took her and tossed her high in the air, eliciting a squeal of delight. Margaret always cringed when he did so, but he insisted solemnly that it was his fatherly duty to properly frolic with his daughter.

Thus played out his mornings of late. Margaret and Maria would breakfast later, but before he went downstairs, they would spend a precious few moments together in privacy. He cuddled his little girl close, kissing the downy softness of her dark curls. She looked to have her mother's rich hair, but the sparkling dark eyes were all his. Every other feature and expression, even his mother avowed, was somehow a perfect blend of them both.

"Did you know, my pet," he whispered into her dimpled cheeks, "that you are to have a little brother next summer? What shall we call him?"

Margaret was shaking her head and rolling her eyes. "You are so certain, are you?"

He looked up, feigning hurt. "Naturally! We could not possibly have another daughter so enchanting, so a son it must be. What do you think, Little One?" he turned his attention back to the child and resumed the lilting croon he often used to tease her. "I think we should call him Thomas, after your mama's godfather."

Margaret stepped closer, blinking now. She rested a tender hand over his. "That would be a fine idea, John. I do miss him so!"

He wrapped his free arm about her. "I know, Love," he soothed. "I think your father also would be pleased."

She nodded wordlessly, a few tears threatening to spill. How glad she was that she still had her father, at least! His health was yet fragile, but he soldiered on for the sake of his daughter and her growing family. Mr Hale had been visiting his old friend Bell in Oxford when the latter had contracted that last, fatal round of pneumonia. His lungs had not been strong for years, and he had succumbed while Margaret was still recovering from Maria's birth.

Mr Hale had returned to Milton and quietly taken up abode in his son and daughter's home. A spare room had been converted to a private study for him, and he still saw one or two pupils each week. His evenings he often spent in spirited debate with his son-in-law, or simply admiring the warmth of the fire in the company of his granddaughter. He seemed content, and for that, Margaret was profoundly grateful.

Maria had begun to squirm restlessly, so John set her down to crawl about their feet. She was very close to walking, he noted proudly, and each day she tested her limits a little more. He tugged Margaret under his chin as they watched her some while together. With regret, he at last acknowledged the clock. "I should go, Margaret," he murmured, but his manner did not correspond with his words. He held her even more tightly to his chest, nuzzling her cheek.

Margaret sighed. John would not be John without his work, but parting from him in the morning was her least favourite part of the day. She had found many ways to occupy her time, not the least of which was helping with the mill accounts, and had quickly discovered herself to be quite as busy as he.

A portion of her day was set aside for managing the household- a much larger task here than it had been for the little home in Crampton. She still left much of it to Hannah, citing, as she said, the growing demands of the hospital charity upon her time. John also, while not wishing to deny Margaret what was so important to her, desired his mother's help to lighten Margaret's burden as much as possible. In truth, she thought, her mother-in-law was only too glad to find herself very much needed.

"What do you have planned today, my love?" John wondered aloud, just as she had been pondering that very thing. "Are you going out at all?"

She pressed her lips, deliberating. "I should stop by the hospital. Dr Donaldson is talking about creating a separate wing for the children, and he asked me to come."

He curled his arms more snugly around her and whispered- demanded in her ear, "Go tomorrow. Spend the afternoon with me today, Margaret."

She turned to look at him curiously. "It is Friday! Do you not have work in your office, and then your Masters' dinner this evening?"

"Not on our anniversary. Today, I am all yours after I see to some matters at the mill."

She quirked a cynical brow. "Our anniversary is in February. I ought to know, for Maria was born in November."

He treated her to that mischievous grin which never failed to melt her. "Do you not remember what today is, then?"

Her face clouded as she thought for a moment, and then her eyes widened in contrition. "October the seventeenth! Oh, John, I am so sorry that I had forgotten! Are you well?"

He laughed freely. "You mistake me, Love! It is not a day for sorrow, but for rejoicing. Two years ago today, you found a poor lonely soul cursing his miserable fate, and extended to him hope. You have redeemed this day, my Margaret, and every day since has been more blessed than the last. I wish to commemorate it with you today."

Her lips quivering into a tender smile, she caressed his freshly-shaven cheeks. "You never mentioned this last year," she mused, fondly touching the deepening laugh lines crinkling near his eyes.

"You were not able to enjoy long walks at the time, as I recall. Do you not remember that Wednesday when we simply lingered in bed, reading to one another?"

Her face washed in wonder, she smiled and nodded. "I had no idea! You did not go...?"

He shook his head. "And I shall not do so today. Let us take a long walk today, Margaret. After we have chilled ourselves thoroughly, I shall have Dixon draw a hot bath for you in here, and then we shall spend the remainder of the day naked before the fire."

She sputtered in surprise. "*John!*"

"I was going to put out blankets, of course," he shrugged defensively. "Ever since you so callously insulted my bedclothes...."

"John!" she pleaded. "You are positively scandalous!"

"Only with you, my love," he assured her. "I think the rest of the world is still convinced that I have *some* dignity left."

"What will they think when they discover it all a sham?" she asked with mock seriousness.

"They will think that I am the luckiest man alive." Once more flashing her that magnetic grin, he tipped low. Softly at first, then with growing passion, he worked his persuasive abilities on her. When he parted from her several minutes later, it was only far enough that he might admire the darkening of her eyes and the breathless daze playing over her features. He lowered his mouth to hers again. "Come walk with me, Love" he whispered against her lips.

She began to nod in silent agreement, but as she did so, her eyes caught the sheets of rain pelting against the window. "John," she smiled, tilting her head in that direction.

"Ah, I have the solution to that," he winked. Releasing her, he walked to his dressing closet and returned with a long item wrapped in a red bow. "I thought you might like to have your own, rather than borrowing your father's all of the time."

"My own umbrella! Did you happen to purchase one for yourself?"

"My darling, what do you take me for? I would much prefer to share yours!"

"By which you mean that you have misplaced yours again?"

"I know precisely where it is. It is safely locked in my office at the mill, where it cannot interfere with my plans for the afternoon. I am afraid you have no choice but to come to my aid, Margaret."

"I suppose I can hardly refuse!" she laughed. "I should be grateful that you only asked for a walk- or have you any other dastardly schemes which I shall be forced to accept?"

"Well," he circled his arms about her again, a playfully reflective expression on his face. "I have given some thought to hiring a piano master... for Maria, of course."

Margaret pursed her lips, nodding agreeably. "That sounds reasonable. And when were you planning to tell me about the large section of paving stones you planned to have pulled up in the centre square of the yard?"

He froze, caught. "That was supposed to be a surprise, Margaret. How...?"

"Nicholas, of course. He told Mildred, who told me."

"I'll fire him," John growled. "Him and that chatty wife of his!"

"And I will hire them back. So, John, which colors shall you be planting in the new rose garden?" She reached to poke his ribs, having discovered early in their marriage a secret that he had for years preserved even from his mother. John was intensely ticklish, and could not long bear such torment. She was exquisitely talented at wringing information from him.

"Foul!" he cried, clamping his upper arm down upon her wicked fingers and writhing away from her reach. "As to colours, madam, you shall have to be patient. Spring is months away, after all. As you have long made a habit of keeping me in suspense, I shall do the same!"

"That is hardly gentlemanly, sir!" she turned away in a mock pout.

"That is what you get when you marry a cotton manufacturer, my love," he returned seriously. "I could have warned you, but I decided not to."

A smile flicked on her face, but she remained resolutely turned, her arms crossed. She waited patiently, and she was not disappointed. The little dimple on her cheek puckered into his view as he stepped closer to her.

His arms slid around her from behind. "*Red*," he whispered in her ear. "Every single one of them. Deep, crimson red, for your mother's roses, and your ruby lips. A single shade of deepest red for the one love who holds my heart and for the vivid colour she brought to my life. Even on the greyest of days, I always feel your warmth, my Margaret. No other colour would do."

"Those Helstone roses," Margaret turned, smiling sweetly, "tend to have rather sharp thorns."

"I have been pricked a time or two!" he laughed. "But for their softness and beauty, for the fragrance they give and the delight they bring, I can tolerate thorns."

"Then I can do no less than to tolerate a little rain," she answered, rolling up on her toes to kiss him lightly. "It is good for the flowers, after all."

"And rather convenient for me! I shall be forever grateful for one particular rainstorm."

John Thornton, one of the wealthiest and most powerful men in the city, never made it to his office that day. Instead, he with his wife wandered aimlessly in the downpour, having no particular object in mind but to mark a date which had changed his life more than once. A few passersby were heard to comment later that Master Thornton seemed not at all the same man, and that he never bothered to look in any direction save at his laughing young bride.

Fine

About the Author

Nicole Clarkston is the pen name of a very bashful writer who will not allow any of her family or friends to read what she writes. She grew up in Idaho on horseback, and if she could have figured out how to read a book at the same time, she would have. She initially pursued a degree in foreign languages and education, and then lost patience with it, switched her major, and changed schools. She now resides in Oregon with her husband of 15 years, 3 homeschooled kids, and a very worthless degree in Poultry Science (don't ask).

Nicole discovered Jane Austen rather by guilt in her early thirties- how does any book worm really live that long without a little P&P? She has never looked back. A year or so later, during a major house renovation project (undertaken when her husband unsuspectingly left town for a few days) she discovered Elizabeth Gaskell and fell completely in love. Nicole's books are her pitiful homage to two authors who have so deeply inspired her. Northern Rain is her third published work.

Notes

i.   Plato, and Harold North Fowler. "Crito." Euthyphro, Apology, Crito, Phaedo, Phaedrus. Cambridge, MA: Harvard UP, 1990. Print.

ii. English, E. Schuyler. "James 6:34." Holy Bible, Containing the Old and New Testaments, Authorized King James Version; with Notes Especially Adapted for Young Christians. New York: Oxford U, 1948. N. pag. Print.

iii. English, E. Schuyler. "Proverbs 18:21." Holy Bible, Containing the Old and New Testaments, Authorized King James Version; with Notes Especially Adapted for Young Christians. New York: Oxford U, 1948. N. pag. Print.

Made in the USA
Middletown, DE
23 May 2021